THE
SPEED
OF
SOUND

THE SPEED OF SOUND

ERIC BERNT

THOMAS & MERCER

Text copyright © 2018 by Eric Bernt
All rights reserved.

No part of this book may be reproduced, or stored in a retrieval system, or transmitted in any form or by any means, electronic, mechanical, photocopying, recording, or otherwise, without express written permission of the publisher.

Published by Thomas & Mercer, Seattle

www.apub.com

Amazon, the Amazon logo, and Thomas & Mercer are trademarks of Amazon.com, Inc., or its affiliates.

ISBN-13: 9781503950153 (hardcover)
ISBN-10: 1503950158 (hardcover)
ISBN-13: 9781503949317 (paperback)
ISBN-10: 1503949311 (paperback)

Cover design by Damon Freeman

Printed in the United States of America

First edition

For my mother and father, Connie and Benno Bernt.

It seems that for success in science and art, a dash of autism is essential. For success, the necessary ingredient may be an ability to turn away from the everyday world, from the simply practical, an ability to rethink a subject with originality so as to create in new untrodden ways.

—*Hans Asperger, 1944*

Richard Woodbridge III coined the phrase "acoustic archeology" in the August, 1969, issue of *Proceedings of the I.E.E.E.*, the engineering journal.

"We speak, and the sound waves vibrate the molecules in the air, bounce off the walls, and vibrate the molecules some more . . . ," [sound expert] St. Croix said. "It wouldn't be hard these days to reconstruct a conversation you thought you were having privately."

—*"Audio Archaeology; Eavesdropping On History,"*
The New York Times Magazine, *December 3, 2000*

Echo. Echo. Echo. Echo. Echo. Echo. Echo. Echo. Echo. Echo. Echo.
Echo. Echo. Echo. Echo. Echo. Echo. Echo. Echo. Echo. Echo. Echo.
Echo. Echo. Echo. Echo. Echo. Echo. Echo. Echo. Echo. Echo. Echo.
Echo. Echo. Echo. Echo. Echo. Echo. Echo. Echo. Echo. Echo. Echo.
Echo. Echo. Echo. Echo. Echo. Echo. Echo. Echo. Echo. Echo. Echo.
Echo. Echo. Echo. Echo. Echo. Echo. Echo. Echo. Echo. Echo. Echo.
Echo. Echo. Echo. Echo. Echo. Echo. Echo. Echo. Echo. Echo. Echo.
Echo. Echo. Echo. Echo. Echo. Echo. Echo. Echo. Echo. Echo. Echo.
Echo. Echo. Echo. Echo. Echo. Echo. Echo. Echo. Echo. Echo. Echo.
Echo. Echo. Echo. Echo. Echo. Echo. Echo. Echo. Echo. Echo. Echo.
Echo. Echo. Echo. Echo. Echo. Echo. Echo. Echo. Echo. Echo. Echo.
Echo. Echo. Echo. Echo. Echo. Echo. Echo. Echo. Echo. Echo. Echo.
Echo. Echo. Echo. Echo. Echo. Echo. Echo. Echo. Echo. Echo. Echo.
Echo. Echo. Echo. Echo. Echo. Echo. Echo. Echo. Echo. Echo. Echo.
Echo. Echo. Echo. Echo. Echo. Echo. Echo. Echo. Echo. Echo. Echo.
Echo. Echo. Echo. Echo. Echo. Echo. Echo. Echo. Echo. Echo. Echo.
Echo. Echo. Echo. Echo. Echo. Echo. Echo. Echo. Echo. Echo. Echo.
Echo. Echo. Echo. Echo. Echo. Echo. Echo. Echo. Echo. Echo. Echo.
Echo. Echo. Echo. Echo. Echo. Echo. Echo. Echo. Echo. Echo. Echo.
Echo. Echo. Echo. Echo. Echo. Echo. Echo. Echo. Echo. Echo. Echo.
Echo. Echo. Echo. Echo. Echo. Echo. Echo. Echo. Echo. Echo. Echo.
Echo. Echo. Echo. Echo. Echo. Echo. Echo. Echo. Echo. Echo. Echo.
Echo. Echo. Echo. Echo. Echo. Echo. Echo. Echo. Echo. Echo. Echo.

Echo. Echo. Echo. Echo. Echo. Echo. Echo. Echo. Echo. Echo. Echo.
Echo. Echo. Echo. Echo. Echo. Echo. Echo. Echo. Echo. Echo. Echo.
Echo. Echo. Echo. Echo. Echo. Echo. Echo. Echo. Echo. Echo. Echo.
Echo. Echo. Echo. Echo. Echo. Echo. Echo. Echo. Echo. Echo. Echo.
Echo. Echo. Echo. Echo. Echo. Echo. Echo. Echo. Echo. Echo. Echo.
Echo. Echo. Echo. Echo. Echo. Echo. Echo. Echo. Echo. Echo. Echo.
Echo. Echo. Echo. Echo. Echo. Echo. Echo. Echo. Echo. Echo.
Echo. Echo. Echo. Echo.

CHAPTER 1

Harmony House, Woodbury, New Jersey, May 19, 4:09 p.m.

Dr. Marcus Fenton, the senior and most respected doctor on the grounds of the government-funded facility, studied the applicant closely. Skylar Drummond. The young lady's résumé was impeccable, but that was only the beginning of what he knew about her. Humble background in Richmond, Virginia. Parents divorced when she was young. Raised by her father, who was a professor, but not much of one, at some forgettable state school. She played lacrosse well enough to get a full ride to the University of Virginia. Started all four years, and did even better in the classroom, which was why she didn't have to pay a dime to attend Harvard Medical School.

"You have a lot of other options. Duke. UPMC. Why Harmony House?"

"I believe your patients could change the world."

"That's quite a statement."

"I'm quoting you."

Of course, she was. He appreciated the flattery. Fenton's expression then turned serious. "Would you mind if I ask about your brother?"

She stiffened almost imperceptibly in her chair. "Not at all."

He admired her bravery. Her drive to help others because of the one she couldn't. And whatever else had brought her into the cold metal chair across from him. "Could he have changed the world?"

"Theoretically, yes. But it was a long way from Christopher's ideas to meaningful translation in the real world." A hint of sadness crept across her face. There was a long, uncomfortable pause, but she continued to hold his gaze.

"What was his area of interest?"

"Quantum physics."

"Specifically?"

She paused for just a slight moment because she knew how ridiculous it sounded. "Black-hole travel. Christopher was convinced he was on the verge of revolutionizing the travel industry by being able to bend time and space."

The old man didn't bat an eye, both out of deference to her deceased brother and in testament to some of the seemingly preposterous theories Fenton had encountered over decades of research with patients at the highest-functioning end of the autism spectrum. Because some of their far-out thinking turned out to have validity, which was exactly why Harmony House had been brought into existence. It was Dr. Fenton's genius to recognize the potential lurking within his patients long before anyone else did. Special thinking in special people. The kind of research no one in the cognitive mainstream would pursue, which every so often turned out to have meaning—of a magnitude even the most acclaimed scientists in the world could only dream of.

Few people knew that some of the most startling scientific advances in the last twenty years had come from people who couldn't wipe themselves.

"It's quite possible Christopher was merely ahead of his time."

"If you had seen the crayon drawings he insisted were technical-design documents, you would appreciate how generous a statement that is."

"That's the battle—to translate from their realm into ours." He paused, reflecting on just how many of these battles he had fought over the years. Most had been losing campaigns, but he was the rarity who had more than a few notations in the *win* column.

Fenton, and all that he had accomplished, was why Skylar had picked this facility when she could have picked from any number of more obviously prestigious and lucrative positions. She genuinely believed in Fenton and his work, and that a patient here just might change the world. That one of their radical ideas just might actually translate.

Little did she know how many already had.

After making one final notation, which Skylar could not see, Dr. Fenton closed her file. This was it. The moment of truth. He watched as she took a long, deep breath, like someone who had practiced it. *Inhale through the nose. Exhale through the mouth. Slowly, deliberately. Control the breathing; control the mind.*

He stood slowly, relishing the moment. Dr. Marcus Fenton was confident in his decision. He extended his hand across the modern desk. "Congratulations. You got the job."

CHAPTER 2

Eddie's Room, Harmony House, May 19, 4:13 p.m.

Eddie sat quietly on the bed in his room, which was exactly the same size as all the other patient rooms in Harmony House. Twelve feet by eighteen feet, or, as Edward Maxwell Parks preferred to think of it, 3×2^2 by 2×3^2. There was a symmetry to the dimensions that made Eddie feel comfortable, and feeling comfortable was important to him. Because he couldn't think if he wasn't comfortable. And if he couldn't think, panic could set in. And if panic set in, well, that was not something Eddie liked to think about. But that didn't stop him from occasionally dwelling on the matter, so he utilized a technique he had developed as a child to stop himself abruptly when thinking such things. And that was to SLAP himself as hard as he could.

The slap left his cheek bright red, except for the areas covered in scar tissue—a number of small, haphazardly crisscrossing scars pockmarking his right cheek. There were no scars on his left cheek because Eddie was right-handed. When he self-mutilated, the right side bore the brunt. The scars were reminders of just how bad his outbursts could get.

Eddie glanced in the mirror, inspecting his cheek. No blood. That was good. He checked his watch to record the exact time of the slap in a binder labeled *#101* sitting next to him. It was his third slap of the day, which put today's count over his daily average of 2.7. Eddie was certain that Dr. Fenton would have something to say about this at their next therapy session, because Eddie was supposed to be slapping himself less, not more, but at least there hadn't been any picture frames or kitchen utensils involved. Those were among the items that drew blood and left scars. Hearing footsteps down the hall, he quickly put down the binder.

Eddie's room was unique in Harmony House in that it was the only patient room with acoustic tiles affixed to the walls and ceiling. He had been so excruciatingly sensitive to sound, upon arrival at the facility, that the staff couldn't imagine how he'd survived in the outside world for as long as he had. Heightened sensitivities were nothing new among patients on the autism spectrum, but Eddie brought the matter to an entirely new level. Even the slightest noise could send him wailing. His agonal screams had been so unsettling to the other patients when Eddie first arrived that they almost caused an uprising of sorts. And no matter how valuable this particular patient and his gifts might be, he wasn't worth more than the entire lot.

At least, not yet.

The acoustic tiles in Eddie's room were not like those affixed around the interior of most recording studios. They were fabricated to Eddie's exact specifications, at an initial cost of $91 per tile. There were 335 tiles in the room. With labor, the project ended up costing American taxpayers close to $35,000. Eddie brought the cost down slightly by developing his own epoxy-based resin to affix the tiles, but the money factor had nothing to do with it. Eddie didn't grasp the concepts of commerce or currency. Money had never played a part in his life. His concern was that the installers had intended to use glue with an unacceptably low adhesion factor. The wrong glue could have ruined the acoustics of the room and, therefore, Eddie's life. And Dr. Fenton wasn't about to allow that.

The tiles weren't much to look at. In fact, they were downright ugly, but only because Eddie had given absolutely no consideration to their appearance. (The aesthetics would later be improved by the engineers tasked with fabricating them for commercial use. Total revenue to date had exceeded $17 million, making the initial outlay of $35,000 look like quite a prudent investment.) He cared about only one thing, and that was how the tiles made the space sound.

The result was amazing. The very air in this room seemed to be quieter than anywhere else in the entire facility. And, in fact, it was. Measurably. Dr. Fenton had demonstrated it on numerous occasions for high-profile visitors. Any sound anywhere else in the facility seemed magnified in comparison. Like the FOOTSTEPS of the young woman walking briskly down the hall, away from Dr. Fenton's office, which could be heard through the crack beneath his door.

Eddie stopped moving as he listened intently. He even stopped blinking. The footsteps ECHOED lightly but clearly. The strange thing was that Eddie didn't recognize these particular footsteps. He could identify everyone who worked at Harmony House—the doctors, nurses, cooks, janitors, security guards, deliverymen, repairmen, and even the regular visitors of certain patients, none of whom ever came to see him—by the sounds of their footsteps. He also knew most of their names, where they were from, and other odd tidbits he picked up from the snippets of conversation he'd hear from inside his room.

But he'd spoken directly with very few of them. Eddie didn't feel comfortable around most people, but particularly not around strangers. They made him nervous, because he never knew what they would do next. Eddie didn't like surprises. To make matters worse, most strangers stared at him like he was some kind of oddity, reminding him just how different he was from most people. And how alone. In all his twenty-seven years, Eddie had never had a real friend. He often wondered what that would feel like, but knew that he would probably never have a friend, so he contented himself with listening to the comings and goings of others, learning as much as he could about each of them.

The one person he knew nothing about was the muscular man Eddie sometimes saw sitting in a beige Chevrolet Impala in the parking lot. The man clearly worked at Harmony House, because he was there almost every day, but Eddie had no idea what he did. He had asked Dr. Fenton about this mystery man on several occasions, but each time Dr. Fenton insisted that the man was none of Eddie's concern.

Whoever the stranger in the hallway was, she'd been in Dr. Fenton's office for one hour and thirteen minutes, which was an unusually long visit. The old doctor rarely met with anyone for more than thirty minutes, much less an hour. Eddie made a note of it in a binder labeled #37, where he kept a log of every meeting Dr. Fenton had had in the last six months. Logs of the doctor's meetings from prior to six months ago were contained in binders labeled #1 through #36. Each contained approximately six months' worth of meetings. The first date in binder #1 was April 14, 2001, the day Eddie had arrived at Harmony House at age eleven. The nursing staff referred to Eddie's binders, at least #1 through #37, as "The Old Man's Minutes." They called #101 "The Book of Slaps," but never to Eddie's face. They were all too fond of him—and of their jobs.

Other numbered binders, such as #121 through #125, contained logs of temperature readings; the ones beginning with #131 listed what kinds of food had been served in the cafeteria, and whether or not they were prepared to Eddie's liking. The #150 series listed the number of people who'd walked past his door during certain hours. The clear winner was always 5:00 p.m.–6:00 p.m., because that was when the daytime staff left.

The binders were all carefully arranged in numerical order along five evenly spaced wooden shelves. Eddie didn't mind if any of the staff used his logs for reference, as long as they returned the binders to their original locations. He was surprised at how few of the doctors and nurses ever utilized his data. There was so much to be gleaned from it.

One day, he would show them.

He continued listening to the unfamiliar footsteps, tilting his head slightly to one side and then the other. He guessed this stranger was about twenty-five, the average age of medical residents when they started working at Harmony House. Most were slightly younger than Eddie, which sometimes made him think that he should be their doctor and not the other way around. The fact was just another on the long list of things Eddie wished he understood, but doubted he ever would. Like all other things, he kept a list of these bits of unattainable knowledge. It was Eddie's Book of Questions and was housed in binder #1000. He had chosen that number when he'd calculated that if he lived an incredibly long time, he might need all numbers through 999 for his other areas of interest, but one thousand seemed safe enough. And it was such a nice number, being ten cubed and all.

Her footsteps moved briskly along the cold linoleum floor. Not like she was in a hurry, but more like she was excited. Happy. Like she couldn't wait to tell somebody something. Eddie knew that feeling. Had it his whole life. This feeling like he was on the verge of something so special, so great, so amazing that he would be happy forever and ever. At least, that's how he had tried to describe it. But to hear Eddie talk about his emotions left most people with the sense that he had no idea what he was talking about. Like he was just guessing. Or parroting. Which couldn't have been further from the truth. Eddie, like most with Asperger profiles, experienced a complete range of feelings, but had considerable difficulty identifying or discussing them. He didn't know how to show his emotions—at least, not like those in the neurological mainstream. The "normals," as many thought of themselves. The sixty-seven out of sixty-eight people, on average, who were off the spectrum, and who defined the standard practices for interpersonal communication, which often didn't leave room for those who struggled to express what they were feeling. If only there were an emotional Google Translate app for those living with autism. Perhaps one day someone would invent such an app—someone on the high-functioning end of the spectrum, diagnosed with Asperger's syndrome. One of the group that Hans Asperger first labeled in 1944 as "little professors."

But until that day, Eddie would have to memorize the appropriate responses to specific situations. He spent hundreds of hours practicing in front of the mirror, making a sad face when told something sad, a concerned face when told something worthy of concern, when, in fact, he felt nothing at all. So, as Eddie sat on his Batman sheets in room 237, listening to the world around him, he made a mental note that, should he ever encounter this woman stranger, he would ask her to describe what she was feeling so that he would be able to repeat it one day and sound like he knew what he was talking about.

CHAPTER 3

Parking Lot, Harmony House, May 19, 4:16 p.m.

Skylar exited the facility, moving briskly across the lot to the visitor's space where her 2009 Honda Accord with Virginia plates was parked. As Skylar got into the driver's seat, she had no idea that a pair of high-powered binoculars was trained on her. The person looking at her had a steady hand. After sixteen years of surveilling people, he should. Michael Barnes was adept at all the requisite skills involved. Wiretapping. Records retrieval. Breaking and entering. He would have made an excellent criminal if he hadn't gone to work for the government.

His hands were massive and weathered. Well-used instruments of strength and lethal destruction that were also capable of surprising precision. Barnes watched Skylar closely as she called somebody from inside her parked Honda. He glanced at the laptop sitting in the passenger's seat next to him to see the number she was dialing: 212 area code, New York City. The number belonged to Jacob Hendrix. Her boyfriend.

In the three months Barnes had been keeping tabs on her, which coincided with Dr. Fenton's decision to consider her a serious candidate for a Harmony House position, Barnes had learned significantly more about her relationship with Hendrix than anyone outside the two of them had a right to know. Among the surveillance expert's key takeaways was how rarely Skylar let her guard down. She deftly managed to keep her lover at a safe emotional distance. Barnes chalked it up to her ambition. She was married to her career. Anyone involved with her would never be more than a mistress. In his generation, this was something only men did. Now, of course, it was a whole different deal. Which fascinated Barnes. In fact, he'd privately started to think of Skylar as the most beautiful man he'd ever met.

When Skylar had moved into Jacob's apartment two weeks ago, Barnes had wired the apartment within hours, but he still hadn't found the opportunity to install the transmitter that would allow him to listen to the apartment remotely. For the moment, he would have to be in immediate proximity to the building, which was just fine with Barnes. He preferred to familiarize himself with a location in person before retreating to his sanctuary in the bowels of Harmony House, if time and circumstances allowed. And in this case, they did.

Jacob answered his mobile phone; Barnes listened through his laptop. "How'd it go?" the young professor asked expectantly. The reception on his cell phone was sketchy, which always seemed to be the case whenever he was on the NYU campus. It made Barnes wonder if the government might be running something out of one of NYU's departments. Most every major university had at least one covert operation stationed on its campus. Some had over a dozen. Institutions of higher learning made perfect covers, and operations could run for years without ever drawing attention to themselves. Except from someone like Michael Barnes.

The reception on NYU's campus was as bad as the immediate areas around federal buildings, and those were bad because the government liked it that way. They'd have kept us miles away if they could, but even the government had to live with certain constraints.

At least, that's what they wanted us to believe.

"I guess some things aren't meant to be." Skylar exhaled with feigned and exaggerated disappointment.

Listening from inside his vehicle, Barnes couldn't help but smile. The girl did have a way. No wonder the old man was so smitten with her. Barnes sharpened the focus of his binoculars onto the back of her dirty-blonde head ninety-seven feet away. He could hear her breathing.

"I'm sorry. I know how badly you wanted this." Jacob's voice was compassionate. "You still in Woodbury?"

"Yeah." Her voice wavered ever so slightly. She was having trouble containing her excitement. "I guess I'm going to have to get used to it . . ."

He paused. The man was no dummy. "You're messing with me, aren't you?"

She held it for as long as she could. "I did it! I got the job!"

"Congratulations! You deserve it." He paused, genuinely thrilled. "Hurry up and get back to the city so we can go out and celebrate."

"I have no intention of going out the entire weekend."

Barnes watched her turn left out of the parking lot, not through the windows, but on his laptop. A transmitter affixed to her right rear wheel well tracked her location. It was a redundant system in the unlikely event that the GPS transmitter in her phone went down. The wheel-well transmitter was also more accurate. The phone could only pinpoint her location to within five yards, while the other was accurate to within five inches. Barnes would concede that it was overkill, but also saw nothing wrong with that.

Before starting his engine to follow her into Manhattan, Barnes sent the recording of the phone conversation to Fenton. Nothing in the conversation would concern him. Shrinks were given greater latitude than most others he typically surveilled, which was part of the reason Michael Barnes had enjoyed his employment at Harmony House for the last fourteen years. It seemed more forgiving.

Until he was asked to kill someone.

CHAPTER 4

Tisch School of the Arts, New York University, May 19, 4:17 p.m.

Jacob Hendrix clicked off his cell phone inside his small, cramped office. At thirty-six, he was the youngest tenured professor in NYU's Tisch School of the Arts. He'd been offered similar positions at Northwestern, UCLA, Stanford, and Duke even before he'd gotten his doctorate from Harvard. It seemed inevitable that one day, these institutions would have to create a formal draft for these hotshot young professors, just like the ones used by professional sports. Maybe CNBC or PBS would cover it.

NYU was lucky to have Jacob. He was published. He was produced. He was awarded. And to top it all off, the guy wasn't just good-looking. He was cool. The rarest achievement for an academic.

The sounds of the city were present even through the double-paned glass in the office's two windows, which were sealed shut. New building, new materials, new technologies, all designed to mute the city around them, but achieving only nominal effect. A beast the size of New York City can never be fully silenced, but it can be quelled, or so thought the big-name architect from the prestigious firm who'd successfully pitched the campus-expansion committee and built this edifice of higher learning, only to be humbled as all others had been before him.

The student sitting across from Jacob was Barry Handelman, a nineteen-year-old burdened by coming from too much money. A billion-dollar-hedge-fund baby. Matisse in the living room, Monet in the dining room. But it wasn't his fault. Barry wanted to be a filmmaker, and that was his fault. Jacob apologized for interrupting their meeting by taking Skylar's call.

Barry shook his head. "No problem." His haircut cost more than most college students spent on food in a month.

Jacob looked over his young charge. "You were saying?"

"When I saw everyone else's films, it was pretty obvious how shitty mine was."

"You're right. It honestly wasn't great."

Barry nodded, appreciating Jacob's honesty, even if he had probably expected something a little less than both barrels between the eyes. "So you think I should quit?"

God, rich kids. "Let me ask you something. Are you here because you want to be, or just to piss off your father?"

"Because I want to be." And he obviously meant it, too.

"The two most important kinds of work I've done fall into two categories: the best shit, and the worst shit. The best shit gets you jobs like the one I have and people to say nice things about you, and might even make you famous, but it doesn't help you grow. Not as a person. Not as an artist. Not as anything. But the worst shit does. The stuff that you bust your ass on and truly suffer for that turns out to be absolute crap. Because it's how you respond—whether you can handle the criticism, and what you learn from it—that will determine whether you have a future communicating something or if you should just quit and see how much money you can make."

Barry smiled just a little. "I could make a lot, you know?" Jacob was certain his student was thinking of a number with nine zeroes.

"I do." Jacob stared into his charge's eyes. "But that would be easy, wouldn't it?"

Barry stared back defiantly. "I'm not a big fan of easy."

"Prove it." The mentor didn't blink. Neither did his protégé. Barry stood, accepting the challenge.

CHAPTER 5

Jacob Hendrix's Apartment, Greenwich Village, New York City,
May 19, 9:33 p.m.

It was several hours later when the police siren screamed past Jacob's building on Bleecker Street, but up on the third floor, neither of them appeared to notice. Both he and Skylar were too busy catching their breath. He was lying naked on the couch, chest heaving. She was sprawled on the floor, somewhere in the vicinity of her clothes, which were strewn around the room.

Veuve Clicquot was Skylar and Jacob's celebration drink. It was what they had downed when Jacob accepted his offer from NYU, as well as when Skylar graduated first in her class from Harvard. And it was what they were drinking now as Skylar finally got around to asking, "So how was your day?"

"Not quite as good as yours." He smiled in the disarming way she'd loved from the first time she met him.

"Your day isn't over yet." She threw back the remainder of her glass and poured herself another.

"Good thing I bought a second bottle."

Sounds of the city poured in through their cracked-open window. Another siren immediately followed the first, this one heading south on MacDougal Street. It was accompanied by tires screeching.

((•))

Outside, those close enough to the police vehicle speeding through traffic could smell the tire rubber burning. These included a stooped elderly man slowly making his way down the sidewalk, an Albanian mother carrying a screaming child over her shoulder, and a muscled man sitting quietly in a Chevy Impala, listening to a conversation that was being automatically transcribed on the laptop sitting next to him.

Michael Barnes barely gave the screeching NYPD vehicle a second glance. He had been a cop once, a long time ago, but that was another lifetime. The job he was now so well compensated for was to ensure the sanctity of America's most important, and least known, scientific-research facility. At least, that was how it was referred to in the federal budget every year. *Scientific-Research Facility.* Outside the Senate Select Committee on Intelligence and the current occupier of the Oval Office, no one in the government was aware of Harmony House and its importance. That was how it had been for twenty-five years. And that was how it was to remain for another twenty-five, if Barnes had anything to do with it.

He ignored the cacophony around him. The screaming baby. The teenage couple arguing. And the dueling television sets blaring over each other. Mets seventh inning versus *I Love Lucy* dubbed in Spanish. Barnes filtered out the white noise, listening only to one source.

He had placed seven different wireless microphones throughout Jacob Hendrix's apartment. One of the adjectives used in every report ever written about Barnes was *thorough*, and for good reason. He had no life. No outside interests. No serious relationships. And that was the way he liked it. To be this good at what he did, it couldn't be any other way. And he really was this good.

Barnes heard the sound of another cork being popped. Yes, indeed, it was going to be a very long night. For some, much longer than others.

CHAPTER 6

The Rittenhouse Hotel, Philadelphia, Pennsylvania,
May 20, 12:01 a.m.

The US congressman from New York's Seventeenth District preferred to use his American Express Platinum card whenever he prepared lines of cocaine, for the same reason he used a hundred-dollar bill instead of a twenty to snort it. Because it impressed the young ladies he paid handsomely to consume the drugs with him. Most didn't seem to care that he was the most powerful representative from what its residents considered the greatest state in the Union. And even fewer seemed to care that many in Democratic politics considered him a good bet to be their next presidential candidate. Perhaps it was because the little whores didn't believe him. But then again, how could they possibly fathom what kind of money and power he had backing him? And not just his family's, either.

The escort service did include on their roster a number of better-educated, more articulate young ladies, but Henry Townsend figured if he wanted to debate, he could always argue with his wife when he got back home. That was what he was getting away from. Her, the kids, his staff, the press, all of it, for just a few hours. A mini-vacation. A layover in Valhalla. Where time stopped. And he could enjoy the view from the penthouse suite of whatever hotel in whatever city he happened to be in while he created nice long lines of cocaine for himself and whatever her name happened to be.

Tonight, it was the Rittenhouse Hotel in Philadelphia, and her name was Allison. At least, that's what she claimed it was. Allison had brought the drugs with her, because they were included in the $5,000 fee the congressman had already wired her employer. This outfit was the most exclusive, most reliable, and most discreet entity of its kind in the world. New clients were thoroughly vetted before being taken on. In fact, if it hadn't been for the personal guarantee of Henry's father, Terence Townsend, a longtime customer, the service would not have taken on Henry as a client.

The New York congressman never did much of the cocaine himself. It was mostly for the girls. He liked them all cranked up. He knew to be careful with his own intake, because too much would impede his performance. But a line or two would get him going like nothing else could. The rest was for her. Allison. Or whatever her real name was. He didn't care. She liked to party, and that was exactly what she was here for. She leaned over the mirror on the bed, did two of the lines, then threw her hair back.

Henry admired her beautiful young face, as well as the magnificent curves beneath her Victoria's Secret lingerie, which looked brand new.

Henry chopped up another dozen lines of the white powder. Two for him, ten for her. Somewhere around number eight, she'd taken a break to service him. He was rough with her from the start, just like he planned on being the rest of the night. He tore off her brand-new lingerie and took her from behind. His hands were around her throat. Not quite choking her, but on the verge of it. Letting her know he could at any second. Because that's what he really enjoyed. Letting them know.

"Allison" slowly leaned downward toward the mirror on the bed to finish her last two lines, which should have been enough to last awhile.

All Henry could think was that the young lady multitasked with ease. He pulled her up by the back of her hair, shuddering with anticipation. Oh, did he have plans. The things he was going to do to this young lady.

Because the congressman was behind her, he couldn't see her face when it happened. Her stunning young eyes bugged out, more in shock than in pain, because she couldn't breathe. Her skin suddenly turned pale. Her hands clenched the sheets as she went into cardiac arrest due to what would later be determined a congenitally thin lining of her left artery. For the moment, all she knew was that she needed to scream, and couldn't.

She arched, and clenched, and then went completely limp. At first, he thought the girl just might have passed out, which would have been disappointing, but not devastating. It had happened before. But when he rolled her on her back, her skin was blue. It was clear she wasn't breathing. And that he was now in a full-on crisis. "This is not happening!"

It had been over two decades since he'd taken any kind of CPR class, but he did his best to remember the basics. He tilted her head back, opened her airway, gave three strong breaths into her lungs, then placed both hands on her chest and gave three firm compressions. Nothing happened. He repeated the sequence. Still nothing. "Come on, breathe, you stupid little bitch!" He continued the compressions, pausing only to fill her lungs with air. His rage now turned to desperation. "Please, dear God, breathe!"

Over the next several minutes, his pleas grew increasingly pathetic. But there was nothing he could do. The girl was dead. Finally pausing to catch his breath, he looked around the room to assess the damage. Cocaine was sprinkled all over the bed. Ripped lingerie and empty champagne bottles were strewn about the floor.

If it wasn't for the dead girl, the scene would be inviting. But there she was, cold and motionless. Ruining everything.

21

Henry quickly paced around the room, figuring out what he should do. There would be no getting out of this cleanly. The suite was registered in his name. The hotel had lots of security cameras, which undoubtedly had captured him coming and going. He had no access to a vehicle, even if he could magically transport the body outside the hotel. And he was much too high to seriously consider driving, anyway. The thought of being pulled over while transporting a dead hooker was so ghoulish it was almost funny.

Henry was going to need help, and knew exactly who he would turn to. The group who'd been in the shadows his entire political career, helping him whenever and however necessary. Like his derelict record in college that had somehow been sanitized. And his many other indiscretions that had never reached the light of day. Most importantly, he had won every election he had ever entered, by doing exactly as he was told. Not only did these people have the ability to rewrite the past, they could determine the future as well.

Henry had never once deviated from their instructions or guidance, because while certain aspects of his character left much to be desired, his survival instincts were superb. He knew better than to disobey them, whoever they were.

He took out a second phone, a device they had given him with explicit instructions: use only in case of emergency. Well, this certainly qualified. Henry pressed the "1" button, speed-dialing the only number he was ever to call from this device.

"Yes?"

"I need your help." Henry's voice quivered slightly. He knew he sounded high.

"Is the matter urgent?"

"I wouldn't have called otherwise."

The phone's GPS transmitter let the man on the other end know that Henry was calling from inside a hotel in Philadelphia. "What is your room number?"

"It's 3902." Henry decided to ignore how unsettling it was that they already knew what hotel he was in. He convinced himself this was a good thing.

"Two friends will be there within ninety minutes. Do not leave your room. Do not communicate with anyone else. When they are outside your door, I will text you."

The two men were seven minutes early. The time was 2:28 a.m. Eastern Daylight Time when the text message arrived on Henry's phone: knock knock.

Henry peered through the peephole at the two expressionless men. They wore nylon sweat suits and baseball caps. Phillies and Mets. Henry had never seen either man before, and knew he would never see either one again. He opened the door and stepped back as they entered. Both men put on surgical gloves. There would be no trace they were ever here. They locked the door behind them and moved quickly from room to room to assess the situation.

It was bad.

Henry followed carefully behind them. "Please tell me you guys can get me out of this."

Mets fan turned to him and spoke evenly and clearly. "You must do exactly as we say."

"Just tell me what to do."

Phillies fan pointed to the beige carpet next to the bed where the dead girl was sprawled. "Stand here."

Henry did so. It seemed a little strange, but he was not about to question a damn thing.

"Face her."

Henry turned toward the body, even as his instincts told him something was wrong.

Unfortunately, he was right.

The two men moved swiftly and in perfect unison. Mets fan stepped behind Henry, grabbing him from behind. Phillies fan grabbed his right arm, placing a handgun into Henry's hand and forcing his fingers around the handle. The man's grip was incredibly strong. There wasn't anything Henry could do to stop Phillies fan from forcing the gun barrel into Henry's mouth.

Having thoroughly rehearsed the sequence, Mets fan knew to duck just as Phillies fan pulled the trigger. The back of the congressman's skull covered a good portion of the wall behind him as he dropped dead to the floor. The weapon remained in his hand. The residue on his fingers would clearly show that he had pulled the trigger. Any forensics expert in the world would conclude this was a suicide. The congressman had gotten away with too much for too long. Anyone who read the newspapers knew it. But his luck had finally run out.

Mets fan retrieved the encrypted phone from Henry's pocket, and the two assassins exited the room. The body would be discovered shortly after nine o'clock the next morning when he didn't show up for a breakfast with his chief of staff. A hotel security guard would tweet the news at 9:17 a.m. Within fifteen minutes, the guard would receive competing six-figure offers from three different news outlets for photographic evidence from the scene.

The Democratic Party was going to have to find another front runner for the upcoming presidential election. And the man who had ordered the death of Henry Townsend knew exactly who they were going to turn to.

CHAPTER 7

Harmony House, Woodbury, New Jersey, May 20, 5:30 a.m.

Eddie's eyes opened bright and early, as they did most mornings. This was his favorite time of day, these very first moments. Because the day would never be more quiet, more peaceful, or more beautiful than it was right now. He just lay there, head resting upon his Batman pillowcase, listening to the magnificent SILENCE. There wasn't another living soul moving anywhere in Harmony House. But Eddie knew that outside his window, it was a different story. He cracked open the window—no more than an inch, because an inch was all that was needed to let the glorious chorus come pouring in.

This morning it was a black-capped chickadee and a hermit thrush. Other mornings, it was a common tern and a green-winged teal. And if he was really lucky, a blue-winged warbler joined the ornithological chorus, but that was only on rare occasions. The chirps of each bird were distinct. And Eddie could mimic each just about perfectly. Puckering his lips, pulling his cheeks tightly against his teeth, and exhaling ever so slightly in quick bursts, he turned the duo into a trio.

Eddie could talk to the birds.

The three birds seemed to have a lot to say. CHIRP, CHIRP, WHISTLE, WHISTLE. CA-CAW, BRRRIP. It lasted for one minute.

Then two. But seemed more like days. By his count, thirty-seven different varieties of birds had made early morning music with him, and he hoped for more. Like a belted kingfisher or a swallow-tailed kite. He hoped that if there was a heaven, one day he would get to sing with a chorus of every kind of bird in existence. How truly glorious that would be.

The only thing Eddie could imagine sounding more beautiful was the sound of his mother's voice, which was the one voice he most wanted to hear, but was also the one he never could. She had died giving birth to him. One of the few kind aspects to Asperger's was that it kept Eddie from being burdened with the sense of guilt over her death that many in his situation might suffer. That kind of emotion just didn't compute. Not for most people diagnosed within the autism spectrum. All he knew was that he wanted to hear his mother.

Many of those who had known Michelle Parks during her short life had told Eddie that her voice was like nothing they had ever heard. That she sang like an angel. That on more than one occasion, she had brought people to tears. Eddie found this confusing, even when it was explained to him that they cried in a good way. He would nod, pretending to understand, while thinking it was not nice of his mother to have made people cry. The only times he cried were when he was hurt or confused, and neither felt very good. And since he was certain that his mother had been a nice person, he was equally confident that she would have never intentionally brought anyone to tears.

Many who'd known her believed that Eddie's mother had been on her way to a recording career when she met her untimely demise. Unfortunately, no one had ever bothered to properly record her voice before the tragic event occurred. Sure, there had once been the usual collection of home videos, but those didn't count for two reasons: the audio quality of the VHS tapes was so poor that it was almost impossible to hear her to begin with, and her parents had watched them so many times in the years following Michelle's death that the tapes had become unplayable. Which was why her parents had tossed out the recordings when they decided to sell their home. It was just too frustrating to hang on to them.

Eddie remained undeterred. For as long as he could remember, his only goal in life was to hear his mother's voice. He wanted to hear the angel. His angel. And he knew he could find a way to do it. That was what he'd told himself every day since his arrival at Harmony House.

One day, he would hear his mother sing.

Eddie supposed the reason she had never been properly recorded was because angels weren't supposed to be. Never mind that she was trailer trash from a small eastern-Pennsylvania town called Saylan Hills with a population of 811. Or that Eddie wasn't altogether sure what angels were, even though he had memorized numerous definitions from multiple sources. He did know that people nodded with approval whenever he made the statement that angels weren't supposed to be recorded, so he made sure to say it whenever talking about his mother. He liked it when people thought he knew what he was talking about. Because then they didn't look so strangely at him, and he wouldn't feel so uncomfortable.

Most of the time, however, they knew he didn't have a clue.

Eddie glanced over at the hard-shell camera case sitting on his simple wooden desk. At least, it looked like a camera case. But it was not. It was a device. A prototype. Which was the primary reason Eddie had been brought to Harmony House. The echo box. To date, the government had invested over $27,358,916 into its development, but still had nothing to show for it. Nothing tangible, anyway. All they had were Eddie's theories, theorems, algorithms, and mathematical equations, literally thousands of them, which filled over thirty of the binders stacked neatly along his wall. And none of the scientists at the government's disposal, including the nation's very best and brightest, had been able to make heads or tails of his work. In fact, many of them were now convinced that Eddie's Theorems, as they were known, were utter nonsense. A pipe dream.

The scientists were tired of seeing such a vast amount of research funds being directed to this nonsense when they had far better uses for the money. Feasible uses. Practical, even. *How dare they have to take a back seat to a deficient!* A showdown was brewing. High noon would be at the annual closed-door budget meeting, which was to occur in three days. The only question was whether one of these brainiacs was finally willing to stand up to a force of nature. They needed a dragon slayer.

What none of them could possibly know was that one would arise from the least likely of places.

CHAPTER 8

Jacob Hendrix's Apartment, Greenwich Village, New York City, May 20, 11:22 a.m.

Jacob and Skylar slept as long as they could. Neither was in any sort of a hurry. They hadn't gotten into bed until after three, and tumbled out of it sometime after four. They didn't fall asleep until close to five.

Skylar opened her eyes slowly. Her head hurt. Of course it did. It took her a moment to remember why, which made her smile. She stared at the man staring back at her. "How long have you been awake?"

"Only a couple minutes."

"How long have you been staring at me?"

"Only a couple minutes."

She never broke eye contact. "If I asked nicely, would you get me three Advil?"

He paused to make her think it was an imposition. "Look behind you."

She rolled over to see three Advil and a glass of water sitting on her nightstand. She gulped down the pills with the entire glass, then turned back to him. "Well, that was fun."

"It wasn't bad." She hit him with a pillow. "Tell me about your job again, so that this time, I'll remember."

She shook her aching head. "There's really not much I can tell."

"Because you haven't started work there yet, or because you're not supposed to?"

"Both."

He grinned slyly. "You know, the less you tell me, the more I want to know."

"That's true of everything, isn't it?"

"Touché."

She paused briefly, surprised that she actually did want to talk about her new job. "My boss is a legend. Dr. Marcus Fenton. Probably the most famous name in autism research since Hans Asperger."

"Asperger was a Nazi, wasn't he?"

"He acquiesced like every other Austrian during the war. It was the only way he could keep seeing patients."

"I thought Hitler was busy exterminating anyone who didn't have a perfect blond genetic disposition."

"He was. That's why what Asperger was doing was so amazing. Even in that climate, he was able to show the value of neurological outliers."

He marveled at her. "I can only hope that I convey half the passion talking about what I do as you do talking about your patients."

"Wait until I start working with them."

CHAPTER 9

Harmony House, Woodbury, New Jersey, May 20, 12:03 p.m.

Eddie carried binder #138 into the cafeteria as lunch was being served. He carefully tucked it under his right arm as he selected a plastic tray and waited in line with the rest of the Harmony House patients, at least those capable of selecting their own food. It was Saturday. Meat Loaf Day. Meat loaf and green beans and mashed potatoes and a chocolate-chip cookie, with a choice of seven beverages from a fountain dispenser. Eddie liked the menu on Meat Loaf Day, not particularly because of the main course, but because this was the one day of the week when he could be certain there would be no purple food among the offerings.

There were no grapes, no eggplants, no blackberries or plums to be found anywhere. There were no grape juices, no grape sodas, no desserts with any kind of purple decorations, as there sometimes were on holidays and patient birthdays. Purple was the color of bruises, and bruises hurt, so no food the color of bruises could possibly be good to eat. Eddie liked red foods and yellow foods and, really, most other colors of food except for purple. As a child, he used to think that if he ever got to be president, he would outlaw purple food, but dismissed the thought as he got older, because he assumed that no one with autism could ever become president. Unless, of course, you accepted a recently published theory in a New York magazine that two of the four most recent presidents were on the spectrum. Eddie contented himself with the notion that one day, he could convince whoever did become president that bruise-colored food was no good for anyone.

Eddie did the same thing every time he entered the cafeteria: tilted his head to one side, then the other. Then slowly rotated his head left, then right. He was confirming the familiarity of the many sounds he knew so well.

The room was the largest in Harmony House and, therefore, echoed the loudest. The CLANKING of silverware. The WHIRRING of mixers. The MURMURING of conversations. The SQUEAKING of rubber-soled shoes. The overhead fluorescent lighting created a slight, constant BUZZ that Eddie had complained about numerous times, to no avail. Even Eddie didn't get everything he asked for. At one point in 2008, Eddie became so frustrated that he attempted to go on a hunger strike, but only until he got hungry after skipping lunch. More than the actual hunger, the break in his routine was more than Eddie could bear. Fenton told him he needed to set a better example for the other patients. Eddie promised he would.

That explained the tissue paper sticking out of his ears. It had been years since he had entered the cafeteria without it. Standing in the food line, Eddie inhaled deeply through his nose, smelling his surroundings. He turned to the nearest cafeteria employee, whose name was Jerome Barris.

"The meat loaf smells like it's burned again."

"Not all of it." Jerome was Harlem born and bred, and every word he spoke was a reminder of it.

"How much is not burned?"

"Fifty-three point eight two percent." Jerome cracked a smile. He liked Eddie, and wanted to make sure Eddie knew it.

Eddie made a BUZZER sound. "Not true."

The cafeteria worker stared at Eddie from beneath the hairnet containing his closely cropped flattop. "How do you know it's not true?"

"There is no way to make such an accurate assessment with the limited measuring equipment you have at your disposal."

"Okay, fine. About half. That better?"

"Yes, that is better. It is a more reasonable approximation. I would like a piece from the about half that is not burned, please."

Jerome used a plastic spatula to inspect the various pieces of meat loaf before him. He selected the one that showed the least signs of char, and served it to Eddie. "I'll say one thing about you, man. You sure is polite. Your mama done raise you right."

Eddie blinked several times. "No, she didn't. She died when I was born."

Jerome froze. He felt bad, and it showed in his face. "Sorry, man."

"Why are you sorry?"

"About your mom."

"Did you know her?"

Jerome was drowning, and he knew it. So did his superior, Ida Peroni, who carried her 260 pounds on her five-foot-four-inch frame with the grace of a dancer. She approached quickly. "No, Eddie, Jerome did not know your mother. He was only trying to express his sorrow that you did not get to know her. Do you understand now?"

"Yes." He turned to Jerome and spoke mechanically. "Thank you, Jerome, for expressing your sorrow that I did not get to know my mother."

Jerome glanced at Ida to make sure it was okay to continue the conversation. "You're welcome."

"Did you know your mother?"

"Yes, I did. She was one pretty amazing lady."

"Did she die?"

Jerome nodded. "Seven years ago next month."

Eddie calculated the approximate number of days in his head: 2,525. "Do you miss her?"

Jerome nodded. "Every single day."

Eddie nodded, imitating Jerome. His nod was followed by a brief but awkward pause. "I'm going to hear my mother sing one day. Did you know that?"

Jerome hesitated, not sure what to say. Ida intervened. "Yes, he did, Eddie. Just as soon as you get your thingamajig to work."

"You mean my echo box."

"Yes, that is exactly what I meant. Now go enjoy your meal before it gets cold. I don't want to get no poor marks for temperature just because we stood here gabbing for too long." She motioned to the binder tucked under his arm.

"Don't worry, Ida. I will take into account the extra time spent on this conversation." Eddie moved on to a table where he sat alone, some thirty feet away. He placed the binder next to his tray and then methodically began removing the plates. Each plate was spaced evenly around the table.

Ida eyeballed Jerome as Eddie went through his mealtime ritual. She spoke quietly but intensely to her subordinate, never taking her eyes off Eddie. "How fucking stupid are you?"

"Won't happen again."

"You're goddamn right it won't. I should fire your ass right now."

Jerome turned to her, looking her straight in the eyes. "You know I need this job."

She studied his face long enough to make him squirm. Ida knew the man and wasn't about to fire him. "Then don't be such a numbskull. I know you were only trying to be friendly, but just keep your mouth shut, okay?"

Jerome nodded, looking around the room, anywhere but at her. A man dealing with what he was dealing with had no choice but to acquiesce.

She looked at him with compassion. "How's Marla doing?"

"Shitty. I don't know what's harder for her, the nausea or going bald."

"Nausea, women know how to deal with. It's in our childbearing genes. But going bald is a whole other thing. You telling her she looks beautiful?"

"Every night."

"Keep doing it." She put her hand on his shoulder and moved on, only to stop suddenly when she heard Eddie repeating their entire conversation. His imitation was monotone and his cadence mechanical, but his inflection was perfect.

"Won't happen again. You're goddamn right it won't. I should fire your ass right now. You know I need this job. Then don't be such a numbskull. I know you were only trying to be friendly, but just keep your mouth shut, okay? How's Marla doing? Shitty. I don't know what's harder for her, the nausea or going bald. Nausea, women know how to deal with. It's in our childbearing genes. But going bald is a whole other thing. You telling her she looks beautiful? Every night. Keep doing it."

Never looking up, he focused on his meal ratings without expression. His scale was one to five. Ida moved to him, checking to see that the tissue was still stuck in his ears. "No way."

Eddie still did not look up. "What are you saying 'no way' in reference to, Ida?"

"Even with cotton in your ears, you can still hear like that?"

"It's not cotton. It's tissue paper."

She stifled her smile. "Eddie, just because you can hear something does not mean you should repeat it."

Now he looked up. "What does it mean?"

She paused, trying to use just the right words. "I mean, when you hear something, you need to use your best judgment as to whether or not you should repeat it."

"What is my best judgment?"

"It's when you consider the feelings of other people before you just go and repeat what they say."

"I am not good at understanding the feelings of other people. I have considerable trouble with my own feelings."

"People don't like it when you eavesdrop on them, Eddie. You can understand that, can't you?"

"I didn't mean to eavesdrop. I just hear. Everything. I can't help it."

"You didn't have to say anything, though, did you?" She searched his face, studying his reaction, as he finally shook his head no. "So next time, just keep your mouth shut, and no one will be the wiser." She winked at him.

He attempted to wink back, then took a sip of his fruit punch and cringed. "Ick. Too watery." He rated the beverage a three. The meat loaf had already been scored a five, which upped the item's average for the year to 4.27, he calculated in his head. It also explained why he finished the entrée so quickly. But the chocolate-chip-cookie dessert was not up to par, and was only given a two. Eddie didn't eat anything rated less than a three, so he spit out the bite of cookie, carried his tray to the "Dirty Dishes Here" sign, and placed it on a conveyer belt beneath it. He counted steps as he returned to his room. It was 113 steps, which was a prime number, and he liked that.

CHAPTER 10

Russell Senate Office Building, Washington, DC, May 21, 9:32 p.m.

It had already been a fourteen-hour day. Most of Corbin Davis's staff looked exhausted, even his workaholic chief of staff, but the camera-ready senator from Indiana looked like he had just stepped out of the shower. He had used his good looks to marry into money, which served to finance two unsuccessful congressional bids, before he finally succeeded by outspending his opponent four to one. It was clear to all who worked for him that Corbin wouldn't slow down until he got the Big Job. And if he did get it, that would be very good for all of them, which was why his six key staffers worked so tirelessly day in and day out. Like tonight.

Empty sandwich wrappers and Styrofoam cups littered the coffee table in his office. The final item on the meeting's agenda was the following day's schedule, which always started with a breakfast when he was in DC.

The senator thought the name sounded familiar, but he couldn't remember exactly why. "Tomorrow's breakfast. Bob Stenson. American Heritage Foundation."

"They gave us fifty grand last week. Unsolicited."

"What did they ask for?"

"Breakfast."

"That's it?"

"I'm sure you'll find out more tomorrow."

"What do we know about them?"

"Not much," his chief of staff answered somewhat uncomfortably.

"Well, who are they?"

"We're not sure, exactly."

"Come on." The senator was certain he was being kidded.

"I'm serious." The chief of staff glanced to the youngest member of their team, a twentysomething genius whom they relied on for all their due diligence and data gathering.

The young staffer handed several spreadsheets to his bosses so that they could read the information along with him. "They're easily the most secretive group I've ever looked into. Other than a post office box and a phone number that goes straight to voicemail, there's no other information available about them."

The senator didn't believe it. "How is that possible?"

The twenty-five-year-old MIT grad shook his head. "I'm still trying to figure it out."

"What about the guy I'm meeting with, Stenson?"

The young staffer read the little he had gleaned. "Graduated UVA with honors, 1976, then went straight into the CIA. Had a promising career as a field agent until he was hired by the American Heritage Foundation in 1988, where he's worked ever since."

"That's it? You couldn't find anything for the last twenty-nine years?"

"That's it."

Corbin shook his head. "I thought you could find anything about anyone." He glanced to his chief of staff, who was going to hear about this later.

"I did, too, which is why I kept digging." The young staffer turned to his immediate superior, clearly preferring his boss to reveal his findings to the big boss.

The senator grew impatient. "Well?"

His chief of staff spoke methodically, as if he, too, was struggling to wrap his head around what he was about to say. "As best as we've been able to determine, and I've confirmed this with every resource at our disposal, the American Heritage Foundation has backed thirty-seven candidates over the last twenty years."

The senator interjected, "So?"

His chief of staff paused. "Every candidate they've ever supported has been elected."

Corbin Davis chortled, then realized his number one was serious. "Every one?"

"Every one. They're thirty-seven for thirty-seven." The room went quiet as the chief of staff handed the senator the list. There were governors, senators, congressmen, and every president for the last twenty years except one.

"This can't be right."

"That's what I thought," answered his chief of staff. "That's why our young friend hasn't slept in three days."

He motioned to the recent MIT grad, who yawned as he spoke. "I triple-checked every candidate. It shouldn't be possible. I especially don't know how they've kept such a low profile, but somehow they're managing to excise any retrievable data about them."

Senator Davis looked out the window at the lights of the nation's capital. "Tomorrow's starting to look like it's going to be a rather interesting day, after all."

CHAPTER 11

Harmony House, Woodbury, New Jersey, May 22, 5:30 a.m.

Eddie began his Monday the way he began every morning. With the birds. A red-throated loon and a horned grebe. He then showered for exactly two minutes and twenty-four seconds after the water reached the proper temperature of eighty-eight degrees Fahrenheit, which he measured with a digital thermometer. Two minutes and twenty-four seconds was an ideal time for a personal task, in Eddie's mind, because it was one hundred and forty-four seconds, which was twelve squared. It was also two to the fourth times three squared. This was all very reassuring, so two minutes and twenty-four seconds became the designated time for all his personal tasks. Shaving with his self-cleaning Braun electric razor was accomplished in this time. So was brushing his teeth with his Sonicare electric toothbrush, which had bristles that oscillated thirty thousand times per minute. Given that the average person manually brushed three hundred times per minute, Eddie figured the device saved him nearly three hours and fifty-seven minutes every day compared to doing it by hand. This was good, because brushing his teeth for nearly four hours twice a day wouldn't leave much time for anything else, and that would be bad.

Three times a week (Mondays, Wednesdays, and Fridays), the patient recreation room was converted into a lecture hall. Each of the seventy-six patients who called Harmony House home took turns presenting twenty-minute lectures on a subject of their choice to a dozen or so of their colleagues. This meant that each patient gave a lecture every six months. Of course, each patient always chose the same subject, because that's the way it is with autism. But to date, no one had ever complained about the repetitiveness of it, and it was a near certainty that no one ever would.

Today was Eddie's turn. He was dressed in his best approximation of a professor, including a houndstooth blazer and an untucked oxford shirt, while the ten other patients in the room wore sweatshirts from prestigious institutions. Harvard, Yale, MIT, Stanford, Cal Tech, and the others watched with great apparent interest as Eddie began to fill the large whiteboard with the same complex equations that appeared in his binders.

The sound of the dry-erase pen Eddie used to write his complicated algorithms was soothing to him. Not because it was pleasant. Far from it. But the SHRILL sound meant that he was teaching, or as close as he would ever come to actually teaching, and that made him feel good. Important. Even scholarly. At least, his approximation of those feelings. Some of his favorite people in the world had been teachers. While many of his proctors were downright overwhelmed by the challenge of handling a special-needs student with an IQ of 193, a special few understood that Eddie was unlike anyone they would ever teach again, and relished the opportunity. These were the ones Eddie hoped to emulate.

All but one of the people currently in the recreation room had already heard his lecture multiple times, but they didn't seem to mind, just as he didn't mind listening to their lectures when it was their turn to teach. The staff called it *academic therapy*. Another brainstorm of Dr. Marcus Fenton. Like kids playing house, only this was neurologically diverse people playing university.

Today, Eddie was the professor, and the other patients were his students. Two were adolescents. The oldest was in her sixties. The other seven were somewhere in between. Some appeared to be neurotypical, like anyone you'd expect to see attending a lecture on acoustics by the world's leading authority. Others, like the guy picking his nose with a disturbing vengeance, could never fool anyone for an instant in the outside world, former Mensa chapter president or not.

Among the other patients, specialties included string theory, cold fusion, biomolecular construction, silent propulsion systems, and machine learning. Among the staff supervising the proceedings was Gloria Pruitt, whom all the patients called Nurse Gloria. She had worked at Harmony House since 2007 and had a natural air of authority about her. She carried the wisdom that came from age and experience. Gloria stood steadfast by the door with her hands clasped behind her. She had already heard Eddie's lecture a great many times, but you never would have known it from her expression.

Also in attendance was the one person in the room who hadn't previously heard Eddie's talk. She was the new medical resident he had just been introduced to.

((•))

Earlier that morning, after a breakfast of Froot Loops (with the purple loops removed) and orange juice that both rated a four, Eddie had recognized her footsteps well before Dr. Fenton knocked on his door and asked if they could come in. Right away, he knew what he wanted to ask her, which he did before even seeing her. "What were you feeling last Friday afternoon when you left Dr. Fenton's office?"

The old man smiled as he opened the door. "Eddie, I would like to introduce you to our new medical resident, Dr. Skylar Drummond."

She knew not to try and shake his hand. Many people with Asperger's cannot stand physical contact, particularly with a stranger. Skylar raised her hand and waved very slightly. "Hi, Eddie."

He stared at her for a moment. His face was, of course, without expression. He didn't say a word.

Dr. Fenton grew concerned. "Eddie, are you all right?"

The patient stared at his new doctor without blinking. "You're pretty."

"Thank you."

Fenton glanced over at a framed photo of Eddie's mother and father sitting on his desk. The similarity between Michelle Parks and Skylar was unmistakable. And no coincidence.

Eddie kept staring at his new doctor. "People who are pretty get told that a lot. Do you get told that a lot, Dr. Drummond?"

"No, not really."

He made a BUZZER sound like the response on a game show when a contestant gives the wrong answer.

Fenton turned to Skylar. "Eddie is a walking polygraph. It's pointless to be less than truthful around him." He paused as if to say, *Yes, really.* "You'll get used to it."

She turned to Eddie, doing her best to conceal her amazement. "It's very nice to meet you."

No buzzer. She was speaking the truth. "Thank you," he replied mechanically. He liked the sound of her voice. It was soothing. Warm. He repeated his question, asking what she had been feeling the first time he heard her footsteps.

"Dr. Fenton had just hired me, and I was feeling happy."

"Did you feel like you were going to be happy for the rest of your life?" Eddie hoped her answer would be yes.

"Well, maybe not for the rest of my life, but I knew I was happy in that moment, and probably would be for the foreseeable future."

Eddie jotted down her exact words in one of his binders, then paused. "Exactly how long would you say the foreseeable future is?"

Edward Parks was just as Dr. Fenton had told her he would be. "Well, I expected it would last at least until the end of the day."

Eddie nodded, seeming satisfied with the answer. "Dr. Drummond, would you like to attend my lecture this morning?"

"Yes, I would, Eddie. But, please, call me Skylar."

"It starts at nine o'clock sharp, Skylar."

"Then I will be on time."

He looked at her without emotion. "I will, too."

As Skylar and Fenton walked away from Eddie's room, her expression was the same one that most people had after first meeting him. Dr. Fenton glanced at her. "That was a big deal, you know."

"What was?"

"For him to invite you to his lecture. It usually takes Eddie quite a while before he feels comfortable enough with someone new to share his work with them."

"Why did he want to know what I was feeling?"

"So he could say what you said the next time someone asks what he is feeling."

"But he never saw me."

"Doesn't matter. He heard you. Just like he can hear us now." They were over fifty feet away from Eddie's closed door.

She glanced behind them. "You're joking."

"When the opportunity presents itself, ask him to repeat this conversation. Eddie's sense of hearing is astonishing."

"Is there a connection to the Asperger's?"

He nodded. "Having one of their senses heightened is commonplace among patients on the spectrum. We believe those on the lower-functioning end simply can't communicate what they are experiencing, which compounds their feelings of being overwhelmed and frustrated. That's what makes Eddie so unique. He can tell us."

"Does he hear more than we do, or does he simply process the same things we hear better?"

"We're honestly not sure."

The answer surprised her. "Why not?" It was quickly becoming clear why she'd been required to sign a seventeen-page confidentiality agreement as part of her employment contract.

"He once had such a severe panic attack in an MRI that he broke the machine. He can't handle electrodes or anything else being attached to his body that would allow us to gather any meaningful data."

"I think I can help with that."

"I believe you can, too. I want your initial focus to be on Eddie. He's very close to a breakthrough."

"What kind of breakthrough?" She assumed he meant developmental.

"After you've heard his lecture, you'll understand."

Skylar's footsteps echoed as she and Fenton neared the end of the hall. "He can't possibly hear us now, can he?" she asked quietly.

From nearly one hundred feet behind them, Eddie poked his head out of his door. "After you've heard his lecture, you'll understand." Eddie's delivery sounded more like a male version of Siri, but it was still striking. Then he closed his door.

Skylar shook her head as she and Fenton turned a corner. "Amazing."

"You have no idea."

CHAPTER 12

Hay-Adams Hotel, Washington, DC, May 22, 8:30 a.m.

The Lafayette was a statement kind of DC restaurant. How often some-one dined there, and at which table, told the world exactly where that individual ranked in the political scheme of things. It was a never-ending game of musical chairs. Those who could afford the private dining room, however, bought a speed pass. Everyone got to see them enter the establishment, but was then denied the pleasure of watching them eat. Which meant, of course, that any real business conducted in the Lafayette was done back there.

The maître d' greeted the Honorable Senator Corbin Davis from Indiana as he entered the restaurant. "Welcome back, Senator."

"Thank you, Antonio."

The maître d' corrected him. "Alfonso."

"Alfonso, right."

"Your host is expecting you. Please follow me." He led the senator through the restaurant to the private room. Davis exchanged pleasant-ries with several other politicians and influence peddlers as they made their way back.

Davis's breakfast companion stood up from the table as he entered the private room. "Senator, it's a pleasure to meet you. Bob Stenson."

Davis gave Stenson a firm handshake. "Bob, the pleasure is all mine." He glanced at Alfonso, who excused himself.

Davis was attired exactly the way Stenson's research had told him he would be: navy-blue pinstripe suit, handmade; off-white dress shirt, lightly starched; Brooks Brothers tie, yellow; Tiffany cuff links, brushed platinum; Patek Philippe watch, vintage. Stenson intended to tell him the watch was a poor choice even if it had been a wedding gift from his father-in-law, but only in due time. "Please, have a seat." The two men sat at the table. "I ordered you a double cappuccino with nonfat milk. That is how you like your coffee, isn't it?"

"It is." Davis took a sip. "I gather you've done your homework on me."

Stenson stifled a smile. "You could say that." Only for the last fifteen years.

"Fifty thousand dollars is a hell of a contribution, Stenson. It's rather unusual to see that kind of money come in without any fanfare."

"We don't care for fanfare, or publicity of any kind."

The senator nodded as he studied the man across the table. "From what I could gather, while people have heard of the American Heritage Foundation, nobody knows much about you." Stenson stared back impassively across the table. "Except that every candidate you've backed in the last twenty years has won."

Stenson remained without expression. "We're rather selective."

"I suppose I should be flattered."

"That depends." Stenson took a sip of water.

"On what?"

"On whether you would like to be the next president of the United States." He looked directly at the perfectly tanned man across from him.

Davis knew this was not a joke. His next few words might very well be the most important he'd ever speak in his entire political career. "Very much."

Stenson took another sip of water. "We can make it happen."

Coming from anyone else, the statement would be ludicrous. But from these people, it was to be taken at face value. "Based on your track record, I don't doubt you."

"Would you like our support?" Stenson did not blink. He kept his gaze locked on his target.

"Why wouldn't I?"

"We're what people today refer to as old-school. We require complete trust. And absolute confidentiality."

"I've never betrayed a friend in my life."

"We would not be having breakfast if you had." He slid a manila folder across the table.

"What's this?"

"We need to know if we've missed anything."

Davis opened the folder to find a handful of items. Among them, records of a $175,000 payoff from a union representative in 2005; Davis's ongoing affair with a twenty-three-year-old staffer; and his 2013 drunk-driving arrest, which he'd managed to have expunged at considerable expense. Each offense was well documented with photographs, paperwork, and other damaging evidence.

They knew everything.

The senator's blood went cold. He was shaken. The documents he was looking at were not supposed to exist. "Where the hell did you get all this?"

"That's not important. What is important is that we know everything. We cannot protect you without full disclosure." Stenson sipped his water. "Is there anything we don't know?"

"I . . . I don't think so." Davis couldn't think at all. His mind was spinning. *How could they possibly know? How did they get any of this?*

My God, who are these people?

Stenson's expression remained completely unthreatening. "If something comes to you later, don't hesitate to contact us." He placed an encrypted phone on the table. It was the same model Henry Townsend had used to call Stenson the night he was murdered, only this one was brand new. "Keep this with you at all times. To reach us, all you have to do is press '1.' You are never to use this phone to contact anyone else under any circumstances."

Davis couldn't stop staring at the documents. "And you can make sure none of this can come back to bite me in the ass?"

"Yes."

"May I ask how?"

Stenson sipped his water. Clearly, the answer was no. "The phone will be our primary means of communicating with you. If we call you, we expect you to answer it."

"Doesn't seem too much to ask." He studied the phone, and then pocketed it as a waiter arrived to take their orders. Stenson ordered the oatmeal. Senator Davis ordered the eighteen-dollar eggs Florentine with a side of apple wood–smoked bacon, just like the American Heritage Foundation research said he would.

Stenson waited for the server to leave the room. "Senator, there is a small favor we'd like to ask."

Senator Davis had been waiting, since the moment he sat down, to find out just how much this little breakfast was going to cost him. "What can I do for you?"

"Tomorrow, at the annual budget meeting of the Senate Select Committee on Intelligence, one agenda item is of great importance to us."

CHAPTER 13

Recreation Room, Harmony House, May 22, 9:15 a.m.

Fifteen minutes had passed by the time Eddie finished writing his equations. Turning away from the whiteboard, he glanced around the room to the other patients. "Good morning." They all stared at him expectantly. Even the guy who was drooling. Eddie cleared his throat, took a deep breath, and then started. "Matter can be neither created nor destroyed, though it can be converted from one form into another."

His delivery was slow, methodical, and surprisingly dramatic. He seemed almost to physically transform himself, Skylar thought. Something inside him had turned on. He wasn't merely imitating. He was expressing himself. Which meant that he was capable of it. On her mental list of priorities, understanding the trigger mechanism had just risen to the top.

Eddie moved to a phonograph, which was as old as he was. He glanced confidently at his audience, then picked up the stylus and turned on the device. The vinyl record on the platter began to spin, gradually moving faster until finally reaching a constant speed of thirty-three and one-third revolutions per minute.

Eddie carefully placed the needle into the outermost groove of the record, which happened to be Wilhelm Kempff performing the

Schubert Impromptu D. 923, one of the finest Schubertians playing one of the finest pieces of music ever written for piano.

Eddie closed his eyes to relish the sensation as it washed over him. Everyone else looked on in envy, wishing they could hear even part of what he was so enjoying. He moved his finger up and down, then side to side. "The stylus vibrates vertically as well as horizontally, causing the transducer to produce varying voltage, which is amplified and fed into the speakers." He pointed to the speakers on either side of him. "The physical movements are converted into electrical energy, which is then converted into acoustic energy."

After a moment, he lifted the needle from the record, and the music stopped. "But when it's no longer audible, where does that energy go?" He looked around the room to the various members of the audience like a master showman. "Ha! Wrong question, right? We know it's here. Know it, know it, know it!" He looked in one corner, then another. He checked under a trash can, then peeked behind the whiteboard.

The room was SILENT. Or, at least, as silent as it could be given the constant din of the fluorescent lighting, heating vents, and other nuisances, which Eddie did his best to ignore.

He continued. "The question is, what form?"

Skylar looked on in amazement as he moved to the echo-box prototype, which was now connected to a somewhat bulky-looking laptop computer. At the press of a button, the sides of the echo box sprang open, revealing eight one-inch satellite microphones pointed around the room. Each one cost $20,000. When Eddie clicked a command on the laptop, the microsatellites came to life, performing a perfectly synchronized ballet as they acoustically mapped the room.

Their movements were mesmerizing. Programming them had been a nine-month project during which Eddie almost never left his room. Everyone on the staff had grown worried about him except for Dr. Fenton, who had assured them that he would never let any harm come to any of their patients, especially not Eddie.

The statement was a lie. Eddie would have had no trouble flagging it as such, had he ever heard it. Which was why Fenton had never said it in front of him.

Everyone in the recreation room sat perfectly still, staring at the echo box, except for Nurse Gloria, who moved slowly toward Eddie.

"The basis for sound-wave retrieval and reconstruction, which is called acoustic archeology, has existed since 1969. We just haven't had equipment sensitive enough to acoustically map an enclosed space or the algorithms necessary to re-create the original sound wave." He paused for emphasis. "Until now."

Several of his spectators turned toward the computer, realizing it did not bear any type of familiar brand name. That was because the machine wasn't commercially available. It was a portable supercomputer, one of the very few in the world. Clocking in at 17.2 PFLOPS (petaflops, or quadrillions of calculations per second), the machine could easily make the International Supercomputing Conference's biannual list of the five hundred fastest supercomputers in the world, if the government ever admitted this machine existed. There were fewer than a dozen laptops on the planet with this much unique computing power. The machine cost in excess of $3 million—which had utterly no meaning to Eddie, because he had never used money in his life. His father had never allowed him to buy anything as a child, and residents of Harmony House had no need for currency. They were never allowed to leave the facility, so no one on the staff had bothered to teach the patients about money and its purpose.

Gloria kept creeping toward him.

"While decaying infinitely, a sound wave retains a distinct signature, which can allow us to reconstruct its original form the same way a mastodon can be re-created from a partial bone fragment." Eddie had read about the recent proof of gravitational waves when two different Laser Interferometer Gravitational-Wave Observatory detectors, instruments two and a half miles long, simultaneously moved one-thousandth the diameter of a proton. That was an almost unimaginable level of sensitivity, which had led Einstein to believe that no one would ever be able to prove his 1916 theory. It only took a hundred years. By comparison, Eddie's scientific leap of faith was more of a small skip. He was truly certain the proof of his theory was at hand as he clicked "Reconstruct" on the laptop. The computer was SILENT for a moment, then produced a horrendous, shrill SCREECH.

Eddie cringed, quickly closing the laptop. He then exploded, screaming at the top of his lungs, *"As soon as I can figure out what the equations are!"*

He slapped himself hard across the face. Once. Twice. Then instinctively grabbed for any sharp object within reach to do some real damage. Nurse Gloria immediately moved to restrain him. His flailing arm punched her repeatedly in the face and pulled her hair, but she was not about to let go. She gritted her teeth as she held on tight. "Easy, Eddie. Take it easy." He was hyperventilating and on the verge of a seizure.

The other patients all reacted immediately. The shy woman in the front row wearing the Harvard sweatshirt began to whimper uncontrollably. The heavyset Dartmouth guy in the back fled the room, pulling his hair out. Stanford, Princeton, Northwestern, and all the others screamed or cried or babbled incoherently.

Nurse Gloria raised her voice loud enough to be heard over the cacophony without sounding too alarming. "That's all for today, everyone! Head on back to your rooms!"

More staff arrived quickly. So quickly, it was as if they had expected this to happen. Which, of course, they had. Each knew exactly what to do. They moved with precision. It was impressive. Skylar went toward Nurse Gloria, who continued holding Eddie tight, carefully pulling him down to the floor. Nurse Gloria turned to Skylar. "Do us all a favor.

Before you think of them as geniuses, think of them as children, because that's what they are."

"How did you see it coming?"

The veteran nurse shook her head at the young doctor. Even with all her schooling, she still could not see what was right in front of her face. "I didn't see anything, Doctor. It always happens at the exact same point every time he gives his lecture."

"Always?"

"Since the day he first walked through the door."

CHAPTER 14

Eddie's Childhood Home, Philadelphia, Pennsylvania,
April 9, 2001, 4:00 p.m.

Eddie was eleven years, two months, seven days, and eight hours old when the envelope containing the brochure arrived at his home. His father brought it in from the mailbox. "What the hell is Harmony House?" he muttered out loud, in an accent that was pure Philadelphia. Their town house was small but respectable, a perfectly fine place for a residential electrician to call home in South Philly.

"I don't know what Harmony House is," Eddie answered. He had no such accent.

His father, Victor Parks, rarely got such official-looking envelopes except ones he didn't want, like from the IRS or some stupid lawyer. "Shut up, Eddie. I wasn't talking to you."

"Who are you talking to? I'm the only other person here."

Victor stopped and stared at his son. "You know how I told you there are some times I just need you to be quiet?"

"Yes."

"This is one of 'em."

Eddie turned back to the computer he had disassembled, whose parts now covered the kitchen table along with a half-eaten cheesesteak.

Victor passed him without looking up from the large envelope. "You're going to be able to put all that back together, right?"

Eddie didn't answer.

Victor repeated the question a little louder. "Right?"

Eddie still didn't answer.

"Right, goddammit?"

"I thought this was one of those times you just need me to be quiet."

"Answer the question!" Victor yelled.

Eddie yelled in response, *"Yes, I am going to be able to put it back together."*

Shaking his head, Victor moved into the den, where he opened the brochure to Harmony House. Included in the packet was a letter addressed to Victor: *Dear Mr. Parks, Harmony House is a government facility uniquely qualified to help your son, Edward . . .*

The more Victor read, the more excited he became. Eddie could hear his father's breathing get faster with excitement, kind of like it did sometimes when he watched the Eagles playing football on television. Harmony House said it could take good care of people with special needs like Eddie, and even help him in ways nowhere else could.

Best of all, it wasn't going to cost Victor a dime.

When given a winning lottery ticket, most people don't wonder how they came to receive it. They're just lucky, they figure. The same was true of the parents who'd received brochures from Harmony House.

Five days later, Eddie packed his Teenage Mutant Ninja Turtles suitcase and got into the car with his father. "This is for the best," Victor told him on the drive from Philadelphia. "These are people who can help you a hell of a lot better than I can. It's not that I don't want to, believe me."

Eddie nodded, knowing with certainty that his father was not telling the truth. Eddie didn't understand why people sometimes told the truth and sometimes lied. He just knew that was the case. Dr. Fenton would later tell him that he was the best human lie detector ever tested.

Upon taking exit 24A off the 295 into Woodbury, Victor glanced at his son. "They will even help you with your experiments, which you know I never could." At least this statement was true. Why they would help Eddie was something else entirely.

Eddie looked out the window of his father's Volkswagen Bug as they rode up a long driveway. An eight-foot-high barbed-wire fence lined the perimeter, but most of it was hidden by lush greenery. Rolling lawns and beautiful gardens surrounded the facility. There was a single guard at the driveway gate who already knew Victor's and Eddie's names. They were expected. Victor was surprised by how poorly marked the place was, almost like they didn't want anyone knowing about it who didn't already know. That was, of course, exactly the idea.

"Do they have yellow Jell-O?" Eddie grinned mischievously. He could never mention his favorite food without cracking an awkward smile, which was the only kind he knew how to make. Purple Jell-O, or any other purple food, had the exact opposite effect on Eddie. But yellow Jell-O was the one food that was as fun to say as it was to eat. Eddie's question was also an invitation to play the one game he and his father could enjoy together. The Rhyming Game.

"I bet so, don't you know. But if they do not, uh, make another pot."

"Am I to believe that I can just leave?"

Victor struggled to rhyme his reply. "Uh, no, I don't think so. I doubt you can just go."

"So this is my jail where I will receive no bail?"

"Look, Eddie, you can't think of it like that."

Eddie raised his hands in triumph because Victor's response didn't rhyme. "The winner and still champion." He had memorized the response watching professional wrestling. Eddie liked games. He wished his father would have played more with him, but his father just didn't seem to like them, so Eddie settled for the Rhyming Game.

"Yellow Jell-O." Eddie's smile slowly faded as he stepped out of the car and onto the grounds of Harmony House for the very first time. He closed his eyes and stood completely still, slowly rotating his head from side to side. Victor knew enough not to get out of the car, or ask Eddie a question, until his son spoke first.

Eddie liked what he heard, which was next to nothing. No passing trains. No interstate rumble. Only leaves RUSTLING in the wind. A dog BARKING somewhere in the distance. It was a Rottweiler. An old one. Eddie recognized the sound from the dog his grandparents kept on their modest farm in Saylan Hills.

Eggplant was among the crops his grandparents grew, and Eddie never failed to mention how he felt about purple food every time he visited. They didn't seem to appreciate it much, which might explain why they had answered no when Victor had asked if Eddie could live with them, a few years back.

Eddie finally opened his eyes and turned to his father. "Okay."

"Okay what?"

"Okay, I can stay here."

Dr. Marcus Fenton approached them with an inviting smile. "Welcome to Harmony House, Edward. I'm Dr. Marcus Fenton."

Eddie stared at the ground. "I don't like being called Edward."

"What would you prefer that I call you?"

"Eddie."

"Well, Eddie, then that is what I will call you."

His tone disarmed Eddie, who not only smiled as best he could, but even glanced briefly at Fenton's eyes. They didn't make him feel uncomfortable the way most people's did. He made a mental note to ask why later.

"I would like to be the first to welcome you to your new home."

"Why would you like to be the first?"

"Because I have been looking forward to meeting you for quite a while now."

"How long is that?"

"Since Dr. Tuffli first wrote me about you, several months ago."

"What did he write about me?"

"That you were a truly extraordinary young man."

"Is that why you invited me to live here?"

"We invited you to live here because we think it is the very best place for you." Fenton never looked away from his newest patient. "Eddie, would you like a tour of your new home?"

Eddie nodded. "My dad can come, too."

Fenton showed them his office, the play yard, the cafeteria, the recreation room, the infirmary, and every other common room patients used in the facility. In each space, Eddie closed his eyes and stood completely still, slowly rotating his head from side to side. Victor grew increasingly impatient with each room, but Fenton acted like he had all the time in the world. He understood better than the boy's own father that Eddie needed time to process each space in his unique way.

When they finally arrived at patient room 237, which already had the name *Edward Parks* written in the name slot, Victor looked relieved. Only now did he truly believe the invitation was real. They walked into the cement-block room. After rotating his head from side to side, Eddie turned to Dr. Fenton. "There is no way I can live here."

Victor immediately blurted out nervously, "Shut up, Eddie."

"Why not?"

"Too hard. The surfaces. The surfaces are too hard."

"I understand." Fenton glanced around at the cinder-block walls, realizing he should have anticipated this.

Eddie quickly became upset. "Hard surfaces produce echoes. Can't you hear them?" He rotated his head, listening to the echoes that only he could hear. "It's making my head hurt."

Dr. Fenton attempted to allay Eddie's concerns. "No, Eddie, I can't hear any echoes," the doctor said.

"I would be too uncomfortable to live in this room."

Victor's blood pressure skyrocketed. "Eddie, goddammit—"

The doctor cut him off quickly. "Curtains might help."

Eddie thought for a moment. "Yes, I agree. Curtains might help."

"I'll have someone on the staff put some up right away."

"Really?" Victor could hardly believe his ears.

"Really. Eddie, do you have a preference of colors?"

"Red, yellow, blue, green, and orange. In that order, with red being first choice. But no purple. Definitely no purple."

"Red, yellow, blue, green, orange, and no purple. Got it."

"I won't have to eat purple food, will I?"

"No, Eddie. You won't have to eat any food you don't want to."

"I don't like purple food. I don't like plums, I don't like eggplant, I don't like purple berries, and I don't like purple grapes. Green ones are okay, but not purple ones. They look like bruises, and bruises hurt. Purple food reminds me of bruises."

"I promise that no one here will ever force you to eat any purple food." And it was the truth. The human lie detector confirmed it. The most senior doctor on the grounds of Harmony House then excused himself to find someone to put up the nonpurple curtains that would later become the inspiration for Eddie's acoustic tiles.

Victor Parks's last words to his son before leaving were, "Never forget I love you, and I always will." Eddie nodded, mechanically repeating the sentence. The intonation and emotional resonance were poor replicas of what he'd just heard.

Eddie could hear his father starting to cry as he turned and walked away on the cold linoleum tiles Eddie would soon become so familiar with. It was the last time he would ever see his father. Victor put his face in his hands all the way to his car.

((•))

The sight no longer surprised Michael Barnes, who was then only a part-time independent contractor for Harmony House. He watched emotionlessly as Victor Parks drove away from his one and only child. Barnes had already witnessed this scene a dozen times.

What did surprise him was that none of the parents had a clue what was really going on here. These kids were brought here to save the government money while protecting our national interests. It was more cost effective to house potential security threats like Eddie in facilities like Harmony House than it was to monitor them out in the real world, where they were so ill-equipped to survive, much less protect themselves.

The brain drain from Nazi Germany and the rest of Europe had been what gave the United States the bomb and killed any chance of the Aryan Dream. Well, that and the kidnapping of several high-ranking German rocket scientists who were forced to complete their work for the mongrels and not the Master Race. Robert Oppenheimer once said during the Manhattan Project that the greatest threat to national security was the secrets kept inside the brains of his employees when they went home at night.

If that was the case, Dr. Marcus Fenton had told Ronald Reagan one fateful Sunday afternoon in the Oval Office, the brains of the little professors were the greatest threat in the modern world. While most were too far gone to be useful to anyone, the needle in the haystack was out there somewhere, and the nation couldn't risk any other entity ever acquiring it. On that spring day in 1987, Reagan committed to a decade of funding in a matter of thirteen minutes.

CHAPTER 15

Eddie's Room, Harmony House, May 22, 11:47 a.m.

Eddie clutched the weathered brochure in his hands as he sat on his bed. His cheek was still red where he had slapped himself earlier in the recreation room. Listening to the footsteps approaching, he knew it was Skylar before she KNOCKED, which she did three times. She opened the door slowly and sat down next to him on his Batman sheets, which reminded her of the sheets her brother used to sleep on, except that Christopher's had featured rocket ships. Skylar didn't say a word for over a minute, something she had learned to do when her brother was very young. She would sit with him for hours, not saying anything. She was the only one in the world who just wanted to be with him. Eventually, he seemed to understand that, and he opened up to her. She could only hope the same would be true with Eddie.

It worked in surprisingly short order, because it made Eddie curious. Usually, the doctors who came into his room started talking right away, asking him all kinds of questions. Eddie didn't like this, particularly the ones whose voices were not very pleasant to listen to. But Skylar wasn't in this category. She was different. "Dr. Drummond, why are you just sitting there?"

She did not attempt to look at him. She simply stared at the floor, much like he was. Her hands were clasped in her lap. "I'm actually doing far more than just sitting here."

"What else are you doing?" He turned to look at her, which Skylar knew was a victory in and of itself. Eddie studied her from head to toe. As far as he could tell, she wasn't doing anything else, which was why he looked puzzled.

"For one thing, I am nonverbally communicating with you."

"What are you communicating nonverbally?"

"That I care about you and want you to know I'm here for you."

"How are you communicating that?"

"By not saying anything." She smiled ever so slightly, like when a cat owner first holds a ball of yarn just out of a new pet's reach.

Eddie looked confused. "I don't understand."

"I'm trying to reassure you without using words. Have you ever heard the expression, 'Actions speak louder than—'"

He interrupted her. "Does everyone who sits down next to me want to reassure me?"

"Most definitely not."

"Then how do I know what someone is communicating nonverbally when they sit down next to me?"

"That is something I'm going to teach you."

Eddie blinked several times, trying to process the information. "Dr. Drummond, why didn't you just use words to say that you wanted to reassure me? That would have been simpler."

"It also would have been less memorable. Tell me, how many people have told you that they wanted to reassure you?"

"I don't know the exact number, but I would have to say at least twenty-seven."

"I didn't want to be just the twenty-eighth person. I wanted to be different. To stand out from everyone else."

Eddie digested this for a moment. "So you wanted to reassure me, and you wanted me to know that you were different from everyone else."

"Yes."

"You are right. That is a lot more than just sitting next to me."

Skylar smiled again, enjoying the incredible silence in room 237. "It sure is quiet in here."

"I don't like noise." He stared out the windows, looking at the empty tree branches. There wasn't a bird in sight.

"Are you okay, Eddie?"

He continued looking out the window. He wasn't sure how to properly answer the question, so he didn't.

"I mean, about what happened earlier, during your lecture."

He nodded, now pretending to understand what she was asking. He showed no emotion as he tried to decide which of his memorized responses to give. "Yes, I'm fine." He scribbled something in his Book of Questions.

She mimicked his BUZZER sound, which immediately made him stop writing and look up with surprise.

"Why did you do that?"

"It's the sound you make when you don't think someone is telling the truth, isn't it?"

"Yes, but I'm not supposed to. Dr. Fenton said so."

She paused for effect. "I think it's okay."

He seemed genuinely surprised. "You do?"

"Each of us has some unique way of communicating that is part of who we are. Me, sometimes I just like to sit next to someone and not say a word. You, sometimes you buzz when you think someone isn't telling the truth."

Eddie nodded, glad that he had something in common with his new doctor. At least, she said he did. "Why did you think I wasn't telling the truth?"

"It's not that I thought you were being dishonest. What I think is that you gave me the answer you thought would make me stop asking you questions about what happened."

He finished making his notation in the notebook, and immediately felt uncomfortable.

Studying him closely, she decided she had pushed him far enough for an initial foray. "If you don't want to talk about it, Eddie, that's okay. But whenever you're ready to talk, I'm ready to listen. I like listening to you."

He watched her as she moved toward the door. "Skylar, you are different from everyone else." His voice was monotone. Without emotion. But then he smiled ever so briefly. It was more of a flicker, really, but, just for a moment, it was there. And it told Skylar everything she needed to know.

"So are you, Eddie." And with that, she left. If there was a breakthrough lurking somewhere within Eddie, she was now certain she would be able to bring it out of him.

CHAPTER 16

Russell Senate Building, Washington, DC, May 22, 3:53 p.m.

Dr. Fenton was reminded of Eddie's influence on him every time he went to Washington, DC, because the first thing he would notice walking the hallways of any government building was their echoes. They were louder than those in Harmony House, and this was for two reasons. One was sheer size. These corridors were practically canyons. The second reason was the hardness of the surfaces. The glistening floors were polished every night as if our democracy depended on it.

The old man still had a few fans left within the exclusive club of intelligence research, but most had left public service during previous administrations. Bush Sr. had been a fan because he was not about to mess with a Reagan legacy, and Clinton loved people he considered almost as smart as he was. George W. knew that Fenton still had his father's ear, so the doctor's position was secure during his terms, and Obama's wife, Michelle, had a cousin on the high-functioning end of the spectrum, so given the failures of the Affordable Care Act for families raising autistic children, continuing to fund Harmony House was the least he could do. But now was a different deal. The new president was too much of a wild card. Non-Defense budgets were being obliterated. Members of the Senate Select Committee on Intelligence had been instructed to take hard looks at every program, particularly fringe projects like Harmony House.

Waiting to be ushered in, Dr. Fenton sat on a black bench, the same bench he sat on every time he made this godforsaken trek. He even sat in exactly the same spot on the bench, because when you come down to it, every human being is a creature of habit, not just those with autism. And therein lay one of the good doctor's ultimate fascinations with the condition: people who had it weren't so different from the rest of the world. They were merely an extension of what all humans were, and were capable of. It was the same reason people had always been fascinated by spoon benders, mind readers, seers, and others with unusual abilities. The same potential lay within all of us.

Researchers, Fenton reflected, had spent years studying every aspect of the exceptionally gifted to learn what triggered universal potential, awakening it from something dormant to an active ability that could be revealed, heightened, honed, and put into useful practice. How did such gifts get unleashed? Answering this question was Fenton's mission. Ultimately, the key to releasing the genius in all humanity was the Holy Grail of Harmony House. Something about autism allowed some people to think in ways that others could not. While no one might want the limitations, every human being on the planet could benefit from the discovery of that genius mechanism.

Dr. Marcus Fenton was ushered into the mahogany-paneled room where the fifteen-member committee was already seated around a large conference table. Fenton made sure to glance at each of them before taking a seat. It was as if he was lining them up in his sights, should this not go as planned.

The committee was chaired by Senator Corbin Davis, who was twenty years younger than Fenton. Marcus had disliked him on the spot when they first met, eight years ago. How this pretty boy had maneuvered himself into chairing the committee was beyond Fenton, but at least he wasn't president. Not yet, anyway.

"I have a great deal of respect and admiration for you, Dr. Fenton," the Indiana senator lied. "The same can be said for most everyone in this room." He glanced around the committee, confirming his majority support. There were only three dissenters. His new benefactors at the American Heritage Foundation had asked him to give Fenton a pass on the budget cuts, and Corbin Davis had secured one, but not without much heated discussion. The camera-ready senator certainly wasn't about to fail this first little test of theirs. "While funds are increasingly tight these days, you can rest assured that our faith in your mission has not wavered. Your funding has been approved."

Fenton struggled to hide his surprise. This was the last thing he was expecting. The newest member of the committee, Denise Claybourne, a proud tree-hugging Democrat from Maine who also happened to be one of the committee's two females and one of the three dissenters, quickly chimed in. "Doctor, if you don't mind, I have a few questions." She flipped through some of the classified Harmony House research materials. "What, for example, is acoustic archeology?"

Fenton smiled. "Think back to some of the most sensitive conversations you've ever had. Now imagine that someone could walk into the space where you had one of those conversations, and use a device to re-create the exact dialogue from the degenerated, but still identifiable, waves of energy that were first created when you were having that private dialogue." He used the analogy of paleontologists re-creating an entire dinosaur from a fossilized bone fragment.

Claybourne's expression was a mixture of amazement and concern, just like that of every politician who first heard about the possibility. "I would say it's a good thing my divorce is final." It got a good laugh—nervous, but good. "Are you telling me that it's possible?"

"Not only is it possible, it's on the verge of becoming reality." The others around the room knew that this had been true for over a decade, but no one made comment. There were clearly bigger agendas at work, and if you didn't know who you were fighting, it was best not to fight.

Fenton continued. "A more academic variety of acoustic archeology has already been featured in several investigative television shows."

"What do you mean, 'more academic'?"

"If this room were being painted as we had this conversation, our words would be etched into the wet paint the same way music was originally recorded onto vinyl records. Once the paint dries, it's fairly easy to use lasers to measure the microscopic scratches in the paint, which could then be translated back into sound.

"It's useful if you want to hear what Michelangelo was saying as he painted the Sistine Chapel, or what Anasazi were saying to each other while decorating their caves, but its contemporary relevance is limited." Dr. Fenton leaned forward. "Senator, what would you like to hear?"

"Everything that happened on the fifth floor of the School Book Depository next to the grassy knoll on November 22, 1963."

The doctor smiled. "I would go to the Oval Office and listen to every word ever spoken for the last seventy-five years."

Senator Claybourne now realized the true potential of the science. "It would change law enforcement as we know it. And intelligence."

Fenton put it simply. "There would be no more secrets."

The Democratic senator's mind was racing. "Any lie ever told . . . any crime ever committed . . . my God."

"Exactly." Fenton's eyes were penetrating.

The chairman gritted his teeth like a prizefighter taking a dive. It was only now that it dawned on him why Bob Stenson and the American Heritage Foundation had asked him to approve funding for Harmony House: *They know something. They have to. Jesus Christ, what if the echo box finally works?*

Dr. Marcus Fenton smiled ever so slightly. "Now imagine another government got it first."

Denise Claybourne's voice was low and steady. "We can never let that happen."

Senator Davis took a moment to congratulate himself. "Thanks to this committee, it won't."

((•))

Watching the capital disappear from view as he rode an Amtrak Acela Express out of Union Station, Fenton had no idea how hollow and predetermined his victory was. He knew something seemed off about the whole thing, but after getting his entire operating budget approved, he was not about to start asking questions now.

He checked emails, including the daily security report from Michael Barnes, then went to the café car to see what kind of scotch they were serving. He settled for twelve-year-old Dewar's. It would have to do. Those around him had no idea they were in the presence of a legend whose reputation remained securely intact.

At least, for another year.

CHAPTER 17

Harmony House, Woodbury, New Jersey, May 22, 6:37 p.m.

Michael Barnes sat at his desk in his office, which was located in a secure area of the basement and looked like a smaller version of the Homeland Security critical-response center. The man had electronic snooping devices tapped into eighty different telephones and inside the residences of several dozen people who worked for the facility. Listening to them all, and ferreting out the rare but potentially important nuggets from the massive amounts of chaff, required vigilant organization, serious discipline, and considerable experience. He had all these qualities in spades, and he delegated the work to no one. He didn't trust anyone to do as thorough a job as he did. The only way he managed to sleep was to know with certainty that nothing had slipped through the cracks. Completing the job often required superhuman effort, and often resulted in the kind of punishing headaches he suffered from now.

He massaged his temples as he listened to transmissions originating in Manhattan, specifically from the newly installed antenna atop Jacob Hendrix's apartment building. Barnes popped two Excedrin, which he kept in a desk drawer next to a box of hollow points, then continued listening. The professor's residence was quiet. The only sounds came from the city surrounding it. This didn't surprise Barnes, because he had already heard an earlier phone conversation between Skylar and Jacob in which they'd decided to eat dinner at a neighborhood Chinese restaurant. Mostly, he was listening to the Manhattan ambience as a sound check.

He could, quite literally, hear a pin drop.

Barnes decided to move on to their email accounts. Skylar had three: a Gmail account, where she received personal email and which she used to log in to social media like Instagram and Snapchat; one for Harvard alumni; and the third was her new Harmony House account, which she hadn't used yet. Jacob also had three. His main account was at nyu.edu. He sent and received over sixty emails a day. His iCloud account was for personal use. He regularly communicated with his parents, as well as several friends from high school and college.

It was his third account, which was no longer active, that Barnes found the most interesting: ProfJaHe@yahoo.com. It hadn't been used in over six months. All mail sent and received by the account had been deleted. A quick search of Yahoo's backup servers revealed why. One of Jacob's students had begun pursuing a relationship with him when Skylar was still at Harvard. The student, Celine Markowitz, had come all the way to NYU from Redondo Beach, California. Her email address was CutieC2020@nyu.edu.

If the young lady was half as seductive in person as she was in her emails, it was no wonder the professor had succumbed to her charms. Barnes figured they probably only slept together a few times, because Jacob quickly cut it off. She apparently didn't take it well, and her pleadings grew increasingly desperate. Her last email threatened suicide. A quick check of the university-hospital records that same day revealed she was admitted for observation. She did not return to school the following semester. Like so many other gems he had in his possession, Barnes pocketed this one for safekeeping. If necessary, it could be used to keep Jacob Hendrix in line, or to get him out of the picture entirely.

If that didn't work, there were always more drastic measures Barnes was prepared to take.

CHAPTER 18

Shu Han Ju Chinese Restaurant, Greenwich Village, New York City,
May 22, 8:22 p.m.

Shu Han Ju was the kind of little-known Chinese restaurant that makes
New York the city it is. The eatery was small, the seating was cramped,
and the windows hadn't been cleaned in years. The cantankerous proprietor, who was in his sixties and bore a constant scowl, almost seemed
to have gone out of his way to make the place look dingy. The unkempt
plainness kept the tourists away, and that was just fine, because tourists
kept away the locals, and those were the patrons he wanted. Repeat
business. Like the handsome young university professor who was one
of his best customers.

Jacob Hendrix loved Chinese food, and this restaurant in particular,
which was only three blocks from his apartment. It was also surprisingly
reasonable. This confluence of factors explained why he'd eaten there
137 times over the last three years.

That, and Jacob didn't know how to cook.

Skylar could take it or leave it. Chinese food just didn't do it for
her. No shrimp fried rice or boiled dumplings or lemon chicken would

ever come close to well-chosen tuna sashimi or a great bone-in rib eye, but it made Jacob happy, so she was fine with eating here more than she cared to. Because she had to eat somewhere.

Skylar couldn't cook, either.

Both had brought work-related reading with them, but Jacob quickly grew bored with his student scripts and put them down. He watched her closely across the table as she read through a thick file on one of her patients and jotted down notes.

"Stop staring." She didn't look up.

"Stop working."

"You should have invited somebody else to dinner if it bothers you."

"Eat with somebody else if you don't want to be stared at."

She kept right on putting down her thoughts. "I thought you had reading?"

"I do." He savored the last bite of his crispy coconut shrimp.

She kept writing, so he kept staring. Until she finally put down her pen. "Okay, what?"

"I didn't say anything."

"You didn't have to. What?"

He paused, clearing his throat, trying to find just the right way to say what he had to say.

And then it hit her. The only time Jacob fumbled around like this was when he started thinking about the future. Their future. "On second thought, don't."

"God, you can be frustrating."

"You want to talk about the future, and I don't."

He hated that she always knew what was on his mind. "We have to talk about it sometime."

"Not right now, we don't."

"When?"

She closed her composition book and clasped her hands on top of it. "How about after I settle in to my new job? Would that be all right?"

His timing was admittedly terrible. "Fine. Whatever."

She studied him incredulously. "What's the sudden rush?"

"It isn't sudden, and you know it." He shook his head, mostly mad at himself. He returned to his reading as she returned to hers. They barely spoke the rest of the meal.

Skylar took a long, hot shower as soon as they got back to the apartment. Jacob turned again to his laptop, where he was on number nine of the twenty-two student scripts he had to get through. He glanced at Skylar's composition book, which she had plopped onto her pillow before getting in the shower. He looked over toward the bathroom. He turned back to the composition book and considered what he was about to do. Invading her privacy would be wrong. He expected her to respect his boundaries. He should respect hers. If she caught him, it would seriously damage or possibly even end their relationship.

Jacob glanced again toward the bathroom, then quickly opened the composition book. He read as fast as he could. The patient's name was Edward Parks. He had been diagnosed with Asperger's syndrome at the age of four. Jacob was moderately familiar with the disorder from their earlier conversations, but had never heard of acoustic archeology.

The more he read, the more his eyes widened with amazement. He actually mouthed the words *echo box* the first time he read them. This truly was astonishing stuff. No wonder she was so eager to learn more. He was, too.

That's when he realized the water had turned off. He quickly tossed Skylar's composition book onto her pillow and resumed reading a student's work just as she came dripping wet out of the shower. She stood next to the bed, staring at him. "I'm sorry about dinner."

"Me, too." He admired her body because he couldn't help himself, and because he knew she wanted him to.

"How much more reading do you have?"

He smiled slightly. "A ton." It would take him all night.

She walked around the bed. "Not anymore." She removed the laptop from his hands and climbed on top of him.

CHAPTER 19

Harmony House, Woodbury, New Jersey, May 22, 10:43 p.m.

The facility had a lights-out policy at nine thirty in the evening, and tonight was no exception. The lights in every patient's room had already been off for over an hour. The night air was cold and still. The only sounds were the leaves crunching beneath the feet of the perimeter guard on his rounds, and those could barely be heard. You could see the man had training simply by the way he moved. His gait was rhythmic and determined. An intruder would be unfortunate to come upon him or his associates. The night security staff consisted of four personnel: one outside, one inside, one at the driveway gate, and one at the front entrance, who checked in with the other three at exactly twenty-minute intervals. "Baker, do you copy?"

The outside man answered quietly through his headset. "Baker clear, over."

The front-desk guard tracked the locations of his two men on patrol with transmitters in their radios, which appeared on an electronic map of the facility. Surveillance cameras provided views of every inch of the grounds, both inside and out. "Copy that, Baker. Charlie, status?"

"Charlie's clear, over." He continued patrolling the hallways.

"Copy that, Charlie. Danger, do you copy?"

"Danger clear, over." He continued watching the driveway-gate monitors.

"Copy that, Danger. Able out." *Able, Baker, Charlie*, and *Danger* signified military, confirming the training evident in the gait of the outside man, Baker. Each was considerably overqualified for the job he now held. They had each taken the lives of no fewer than three people. One had killed eleven. These were men capable of becoming death machines, but only if the circumstances required it and they were ordered to do so.

Over the years, they had been required to make adjustments for Eddie. The boots initially provided to security personnel made a particular clicking sound on the linoleum floors, which disturbed Eddie's sleep, even after the installation of the acoustic panels in his room, so he developed a composite rubber for new soles that made the boots practically silent. It turned out this new composite also lasted three times as long as the previous one, so Eddie's composite soon became part of standard-issue US military footwear.

For someone who didn't understand the concept of money, he was certainly doing a nice job making the government quite a bit of it.

$$((\cdot))$$

It was exactly 10:47 p.m. when Eddie's eyes opened. He sucked in a deep breath as if he'd been punched in the stomach. Or hit by a lightning bolt. And maybe this time, he had been. Maybe, finally, this was it. The answer. The fix. The conclusion to his equations, Eddie's Theorems, which had eluded him for all these years. Could this really be it? *Could it?*

He raced to the light switch by the door, then over to his desk, where he grabbed the most recently filled book of equations and a number-two pencil. He had a cup full of them—twenty-four, to be exact, because the number was the product of two cubed times three, and Eddie liked that. Each pencil was properly sharpened and awaiting its turn.

The math was a blur, simply flying out of him at stunning speed. Lost in a torrent of thoughts, he went through one pencil quickly, maintaining its sharpness with an electric sharpener that was over ten years old. Having filled the remaining pages of the current notebook, he readily went through another. And two more pencils in the process.

Like a composer lost in his own world, the incomprehensible equations were pouring out of him so rapidly that his writing hand struggled to keep up with his brain. It was frenzied and spontaneous moments of revelation like this that had made him wonder, earlier in life, if he should learn to write with both hands simultaneously, thereby doubling his already tremendous output. But his left hand proved to be less adept at writing, and although he had two eyes, the two hemispheres of his brain refused to act independently of each other, forever condemning him to the one-handed pace of the rest of us.

Whatever he was hearing in his head, he was not hearing anything else. Nothing in his room or outside the windows. Nothing down the hall. It was as if his remarkable sense of hearing had shut down to focus all his considerable processing power on the singular task at hand. When a person experiences extreme cold, frostbite results from the body trying to survive by withdrawing blood circulation from the extremities to protect the critical organ, the heart. That same principle seemed to be at work as Eddie continued writing wildly. Two hours passed. Then three. He showed no signs of slowing down.

Eddie didn't notice that five thirty, his usual wake-up time, had already come and gone. So did dawn's first light. So did his would-be morning singing companions, a red-necked grebe and a northern gannet. The birds left the branches outside his window quickly, as if the light through the window of Eddie's room told them there would be no chorus today. He was visible at his desk, still writing away furiously.

Occasionally he would pause, looking up from his notebook, staring at the wall, not looking at anything in particular. Nothing tangible, anyway. What he was seeing was anybody's guess. His pencil would remain motionless. He wouldn't blink, and barely seemed to breathe. A human mannequin. Just as quickly as these frozen moments would start, they would stop again, and the graphite in Eddie's number-two pencil would resume its frenzied trail across page after page.

A short while later, Eddie put his pencil down and quickly turned on his laptop supercomputer, which he had dubbed the Hummer because of the DRONE the machine's cooling fan produced whenever it was left on for an extended period of time. Fast, it was. Quiet, it was not. Not by Eddie's standards, anyway. But right now, that didn't matter. All that mattered was that his calculations would prove correct, and that the Hummer would finally be able to interpret the inaudible recordings made by the echo-box microsatellites.

CHAPTER 20

Parking Lot, Harmony House, May 23, 7:02 a.m.

Skylar pulled into the lot and quickly walked up the stairs to her small office on the second floor. The desk was utilitarian, and was probably older than she was. A scuffed Formica top with a metal frame. The sliding drawers were a little rusty, but she didn't have much use for them, anyway. The only decoration she'd brought in so far was a photograph that sat on her desk. The five-by-seven walnut frame contained her favorite image of her and Jacob, taken while she was still at Harvard.

Along one of the walls were two dozen storage boxes containing materials related to Eddie. No other patient in the facility had more than three boxes of materials, but no other resident produced anywhere close to the volume of papers Eddie did. She had decided to start at the beginning, in the oldest box, with the first communication Dr. Fenton had received about Edward Parks. The single-page letter was from Eddie's child psychiatrist in Philadelphia, Dr. Gordon Tuffli. The doctor was part of Children's Hospital of Philadelphia, which, while respected within the medical community, had the misfortune of possessing the initials CHOP. How they ever got a single parent to take a child for treatment at CHOP left something to the imagination.

Tuffli stated that he had never once, in his twenty-seven years of practice, encountered a child like Eddie, who was eight at the time. Autism was diagnosed much less frequently in those days, and Asperger's had only recently been reintroduced into the lexicon. What little literature there was included nothing about how to properly deal with a special-education child whose IQ was within spitting distance of two hundred. The boy was doing calculus, but couldn't tie his shoes. He had completed a Rubik's Cube in less than two minutes the first time he saw one, but couldn't look another human being in the eye. Any type of physical contact instantly triggered a screaming rage, and the boy's only method for expressing frustration was to slap himself in the face, or worse. His father, Victor Parks, had claimed to Dr. Tuffli that Eddie once slapped himself so many times that he had to take the boy to the emergency room. The medical staff doubted the father's story until something in the ER triggered the reaction in the boy, and Victor was cleared of suspicion.

Little Eddie Parks was a genius savant; there was no doubt about it. The only question was what to do with him. Every teacher or aide who attempted to help him quickly realized how ill-equipped they were for the task. No one on the staff at CHOP had any idea, either. Dr. Tuffli wrote to Fenton hoping that he might know what to do with the boy.

Skylar could only imagine Fenton licking his chops as he read this letter.

Fenton had then commenced his typically thorough due diligence on the boy, retrieving every available medical record going back to Eddie's birth, which was an emergency C-section. It wasn't clear from the records exactly what went wrong during the delivery, but Michelle Parks lost a tremendous amount of blood and never recovered. Dr. Wolfgang Oelkers declared her dead when her son was forty-three minutes old. She never got to see her beautiful and unique baby boy. It took his father almost three days before he would hold his son.

What surprised Skylar most was the extent of Dr. Fenton's research into Eddie's past. Fenton left no stone unturned when it came to his examination of this wonder child. He corresponded with or interviewed every doctor, teacher, and therapist who had ever come in contact with the boy. But the research didn't stop there. Fenton examined every record he could find about the father: his employment, his health, his academic and credit files. Skylar didn't understand what these things had to do with a potential patient. It was clearly an invasion of privacy, but Fenton obviously had no trouble gathering the information, so somebody must have approved the release of the data.

It never occurred to Skylar that he might be as thorough with his hires as he was with his patients.

((•))

Breakfast in Harmony House was served at seven thirty, so Skylar went to look for Eddie there. Besides, she was in dire need of coffee. While a double-shot nonfat Starbucks latte might have been enough to get her through the drive to Woodbury, it certainly wasn't enough to keep her going through the morning. But when she arrived in the cafeteria, there was no sign of Eddie. That was strange, she thought. People with Asperger's never deviated from their routines.

Coffee in hand, she walked toward Eddie's room. Passing Fenton's office, she noticed a silhouette sitting in a chair next to Eddie's door. It was Nurse Gloria, who was reading the latest issue of *People* magazine. Skylar quickened her step. Hoping not to disturb Eddie, she whispered, "Is everything okay?"

Gloria whispered reassuringly, "Everything's fine."

"Why are you here?"

"To make sure it stays that way." She turned back to her magazine article about some reality-show contestant's recent weight loss after pregnancy. "Dr. Fenton hasn't told you about Eddie's sessions, has he?"

He hadn't. "I'm still getting up to speed." Skylar began to doubt whether starting at the beginning was the right way to study Eddie's history. She wondered if she should have started with the most recent reports and worked her way backward, so that she would be better prepared for something like this.

"He gets a certain kind of idea in his head, and wild elephants can't stop him from seeing it through. Sometimes it only lasts a few minutes, but sometimes hours, or even days. We used to try to force him to rest, or eat, or use the bathroom when it happened, but that only worked against us. He once snapped at a nurse trying to make him eat and smashed a plate over her head, knocking the poor thing unconscious. Another time he went catatonic on us for a week. So now, we just let him go until his engine runs out."

"How does it end?"

"Sometimes good. Sometimes not so good."

"Like yesterday?"

"Exactly like yesterday. Only worse."

Skylar glanced at the door, desperately curious to know what was going on behind it.

"You can go in if you want."

Skylar looked surprised. "You sure?"

"Knock first. If he doesn't want you to come in, he'll tell you. But more than likely, he won't respond at all, because the boy is just gone. Trust me."

Skylar approached the door to room 237 with caution. She looked down at her feet, surprised that Eddie wasn't already talking to her as he had done the other times she approached his door. She knocked ever so quietly, certain there would be a response.

But there was none.

"Told you." Nurse Gloria returned to her magazine.

Skylar spoke softly to the door. "Eddie, I would like to come in. Would that be all right?" Again, there was no answer, so she let herself in. She entered the room cautiously.

Sitting at his desk, Eddie had his back to her. He was typing on his laptop and didn't look up or acknowledge her in any way. His hands were moving so quickly around the computer's keyboard that they were a blur. She sat down on the bed next to him, watching him with wonder. "You sure can type fast."

He gave no response.

"Eddie, can you hear me?"

He nodded almost imperceptibly, but it was hard to tell if he was responding to her or to something else. His lips moved ever so slightly.

She leaned in closer, trying to hear what he was saying.

"Dr. Fenton!" He screamed the doctor's name so loudly it hurt Skylar's ears. She winced as he snapped the laptop closed. He picked it up, along with the echo box, and raced out the door.

Skylar went after him. Nurse Gloria followed close behind. "What the hell did you do to him?"

"Nothing. All I did was sit down next to him. You said I could go in."

"I didn't say to upset him; now did I?" They both followed him down the hallway, where he made a beeline toward Dr. Fenton's office.

"Dr. Fenton, I did it! Dr. Fenton!"

The first time Dr. Fenton's secretary, Stephen Millard, had experienced Eddie bursting into the foyer of Dr. Fenton's office was seven years ago. Stephen was, naturally, alarmed, and proceeded to physically block Eddie's path while tersely explaining that patients were not allowed to enter the office without an appointment. Eddie had started screaming the moment Stephen touched him. When Eddie started slapping himself, he dropped the echo box, which crashed to the floor. The resulting damage cost upward of $67,000 to repair.

From that point on, Stephen was instructed not to intervene when Eddie rushed into the foyer, like he did now. Stephen managed to remain pleasant and nonconfrontational. "Hello, Eddie."

"Dr. Fenton, I did it! Dr. Fenton!" Eddie didn't even acknowledge Stephen as he continued into Fenton's office, where the doctor was on the phone.

"I'll have to call you back." Fenton hung up the phone and acted pleased to see Eddie. "Well, this is certainly wonderful news."

"I know it's going to work! I know it!" He closed the door behind him because it would facilitate acoustic mapping. At least, it was supposed to. He placed the echo box on Fenton's coffee table and connected the laptop to it.

"My boy, I never had any doubt."

Eddie made his BUZZER sound without looking up as he continued typing instructions into his computer. "Not true. Definitely not."

Fenton smiled. "Well, almost never."

Eddie held his index finger above the "Return" key on the keyboard as he counted down like he'd heard mission-control officers on TV do before launching a space shuttle. "Five . . . four . . . three . . . two . . . one." He pressed the key, activating the device. The sides of the echo box sprang open, revealing the eight spherical microphones. The microsatellites began to move in coordinated fashion, mapping the room.

Dr. Fenton joined his prized patient as he watched the computer screen. A three-dimensional image of the physical space began to slowly appear on the screen. A progress bar appeared below the image. It read: *Six percent complete*, then, *seven*. This was good, thought Dr. Fenton. Very good. The first tangible progress in months. His eyes widened with expectation.

Eddie moved back and forth between watching the movement of the microsatellites and watching the image on the screen. "Come on, come on, come on, come on."

Nine percent complete. Ten percent. Their eyes were glued to the counter. *Eleven percent. Twelve.* But *thirteen* came slower. And *fourteen* slower than that.

"No . . . no . . . no . . ." Panic rose in Eddie's voice. The fuse was lit inside him. The dynamite in his head was about to go off.

Fenton moved right next to Eddie and spoke reassuringly. "Just give it some time, Eddie. It's working."

"No it's not!" He pointed to the counter, which remained stuck at fourteen. The rendering of the three-dimensional image had stopped.

The bloodcurdling scream then let out by Eddie shook Skylar to her bones. It sounded like a dying animal. The tone was guttural. Deep. And terrifying.

Stephen looked on smugly from his desk as Nurse Gloria and Skylar burst through the door to Fenton's office.

Fenton hovered over the echo box, using his body to shield it from Eddie's tantrum. The doctor was not about to risk any damage to the device, which was clearly his priority. Eddie spun around in circles, flailing wickedly at himself. These weren't just slaps. He was hitting himself as hard as he could. Punching. Gouging. Trying to draw blood. Even tear his own flesh.

It took both Skylar and Gloria to hold him down. They crashed atop him as he fell to the floor. The veteran nurse shouted instructions to the young doctor as her head and other body parts got in the way of Eddie hitting himself. "Grab his arm!"

"I'm trying!"

With the majority of her body weight lying on Eddie's chest, Gloria used her girth to still his left arm, and then helped Skylar hold his right.

Eddie finally stopped fighting and slowly caught his breath. The nurse climbed off him, noticing that Skylar's fists were turning white from clenching around his arm. "You can let go now. Once the fight leaves him, it don't come back."

Skylar released Eddie's arm. Just as Nurse Gloria had predicted, he remained calm. Skylar looked deeply into his helpless eyes and caressed his forehead, saying, "It's okay, Eddie. I'm here."

Nurse Gloria was just about ready to take issue, thinking, *What the hell do you mean, you're here? Who the hell are you?* But she decided to bite her tongue after watching Eddie's reaction. He was looking into the young doctor's eyes. Edward Parks didn't look anyone in the eyes, but here he was, looking into the eyes of this new princess doctor. What the hell did she know? What spell had she cast?

The veteran nurse did not know, but she was certainly going to find out, both out of personal curiosity and because she was secretly being paid handsomely to do so.

CHAPTER 21

Eddie's Room, Harmony House, May 23, 8:42 a.m.

As Skylar and Nurse Gloria escorted him back to his room, all Eddie kept repeating was, "I'm tired."

"We'll get you to bed." Skylar's voice continued to have its soothing effect on him. They saw his face relax.

"I'm tired."

Nurse Gloria tried her best to reassure him, too. "You let me know if you want something to help you sleep."

His face was once again tense. "I'm tired."

They helped him into his Scooby-Doo pajamas, then tucked him between his Batman sheets. Gloria pulled the blinds as Skylar sat next to him. "Would you like me to stay with you for a few minutes?"

He nodded. Gloria managed to hide her growing curiosity as she moved toward the door. "I'll have a special meal ready for you in case you get hungry."

"Thanks, Nurse Gloria." He kept his eyes on the ceiling as the nurse closed the door behind her.

"She's a very good nurse." Skylar meant it sincerely.

"Yes, she is."

"How long has she worked here?"

"Nine years, two months, twenty-nine days."

"But who's counting, right?"

"I am always counting."

"Yes, you are."

His eyelids grew heavy, slowly starting to close. "Nurse Gloria is nice, but I don't think she's as nice as you are, Skylar."

She smiled. "Wait until you get to know me better."

"Why should I wait?"

"When you get to know me better, I think you'll change your mind."

"I think you're wrong." And with that, his eyes closed, and Eddie drifted off to much-needed sleep. Skylar sat there for another minute, watching him curl into a fetal position. So peaceful. So innocent. So vulnerable.

He reminded Skylar of her little brother, Christopher. He had thrown a similar tantrum the day she told him she was leaving for college. Perhaps the memory wouldn't be quite so searing if he hadn't hanged himself three days later. While depression and other psychological issues were common among people with autism, it was rare for someone on the spectrum to commit suicide. Christopher was the outlier.

And Skylar would never forgive herself for it.

CHAPTER 22

Gloria Pruitt's House, Parsippany, New Jersey, May 23, 7:17 p.m.

The text message that Nurse Gloria sent that night was brief. Those were her instructions. The only times she sent such messages were after one of Eddie's "sessions," or anytime there was a development worth relating, particularly regarding the echo box. She was also supposed to send messages involving advancements made by any other patient in Harmony House, but Eddie was the primary subject of her clandestine employer's interest.

New EP session. No improvement. Box still no go. The only device Gloria sent such messages from was identical to the one now in the possession of the fine senator from the state of Indiana. Gloria's phone was updated annually, as the senator's would be. Each New Year's Day, she would awaken to find her current device had been removed from her duplex and a new one in its spot. It was a bit disconcerting the first time it happened. There was nothing else out of place, and absolutely no sign of any breaking or entering. Just the new phone. She had never given her clandestine employer a key to her residence. But they had access. And they wanted her to know they did. It was just a little reminder, not that she needed one. She was truly grateful for all they had done for her, including her current position, and intended to remain loyal to the end.

((•))

Gloria first met them when she was still working at Thomas Jefferson University Hospital, located within a stone's throw from the Liberty Bell in Philadelphia. This was just over twelve years and three months ago. She'd had a fine, if unspectacular, nursing career spanning nearly twenty years, notable only for its lack of complaints against her. There were absolutely none. Zero. Which almost seemed impossible, and, in fact, was. There were a number of performance-related issues in her thick employment folder. Some were justified, like when she misread the dosage for a cardiac patient and accidentally put him into a coma for seventeen days. But most were somebody else's fault. Gloria had proven herself ill adept at the political aspect of nursing, and often found herself the target of a colleague or superior seeking to lay the blame on somebody else. Basically, she was an innocent, and innocents often got chewed up and spat out.

Then, one day, all that changed.

That day began in a nondescript office building in Sandy Hook, New Jersey, where she and her then-seventeen-year-old son, Cornell, had been invited to a scholarship interview. They had applied for so many different scholarships that year neither could remember the specifics of this one. Gloria and Cornell only knew two things: it was sponsored by the Commonwealth Equal Opportunity Trust, whatever that was; and, more importantly, this was a full ride: tuition, room, and board. The whole enchilada. Money, money, money.

Cornell was certainly deserving of financial aid. He was a straight-A student with nearly perfect SATs who had been elected to represent New Jersey at Boys Nation, which Bill Clinton, among other political notables, had also attended while still in high school. Cornell's involvement in politics at the national level made his student-body presidency seem trivial by comparison, but like any good politician, he made his fellow students at Parsippany Hills High School feel they were all that mattered to him.

As early as the eighth grade, Cornell knew he wanted to study political science at Georgetown. The kid didn't lack for ambition. His mother dutifully explained how competitive it was to get into such a prestigious college. Her son answered matter-of-factly that he would just work harder than everyone else. She promised him that if he did indeed get accepted, she would somehow find a way to pay for it.

But certain promises are harder to keep than others. Cornell kept up his end of the bargain. The boy was a model citizen and one she was damn proud of. Any mother would be. Disappointing him would kill her. But affording an elite education as a single parent earning $68,000 a year seemed practically impossible. At that time, tuition at Georgetown was $36,140. Room and board were $11,478. There was no way she could make it work without help.

There was all kinds of scholarship money out there, but, for some reason, Cornell wasn't qualifying for any of it. Apparently, the majority of the money was intended for those who earned less than thirty thousand a year. Those who earned above sixty were just plain out of luck. It almost seemed like she was being penalized for doing just well enough. The middle class was getting squeezed out of leadership-caliber educations, and Cornell was due to be the next victim.

Then the scholarship invitation from the Commonwealth Equal Opportunity Trust arrived. This was his best and last chance to afford the education he'd been dreaming of since middle school. Cornell wore his only suit, and did all he could to look his very best at the interview.

Gloria wished her son luck and squeezed him tight as he was ushered into a room by two well-dressed women. Gloria sat quietly in the waiting room, intending to busy herself with the array of magazines she had brought, when a man sat down next to her.

It was Bob Stenson, but he did not introduce himself to her. Gloria would never learn his name. "Hello." His voice was pleasant and unassuming.

"Why, hello." Gloria tried to be as charming as she could be. For all she knew, this conversation might have some impact on their decision. Little did she know how absolutely right she was.

Stenson removed a cellular phone from the breast pocket of his suit coat and held it in front of him. "May I ask if you've ever sent a text message from one of these things?" After all, this was 2005. The first iPhone wouldn't come out until 2007.

She glanced at the phone, which looked like so many others. "Why, no, I haven't, but my son has many times. Today, in fact."

The man chuckled. "Of course he has." He then turned to face her more directly. "Ms. Pruitt, what if I told you there was a way you could guarantee your son will receive our scholarship?"

Gloria looked at him inquisitively, certain that he would not be suggesting anything sexual to a woman of her age and abundant figure. "What would I have to do?"

"Come work for us."

"Where would that be, exactly?"

"The physical location will vary from time to time, depending on which of our clients is in need of nursing care, but we would never ask you to commute more than a fifty-mile radius from your place of residence."

It made Gloria uncomfortable that these people knew where she lived. It also made her wonder what else they knew about her. "I hate to ask this, but why me?"

"We're what people consider old school. We require complete trust. And absolute confidentiality. While we will arrange your placements with our clients, you may not reveal your association with us—to them, or anyone else. Any breach of discretion on your part will result in immediate termination, both of your employment and Cornell's scholarship."

She looked Stenson directly in the eyes. "I would never betray your trust."

"We wouldn't be having this conversation if we thought you would." He handed her a plain manila folder that contained a copy of every performance-related issue from her employment records. "Before we have these items expunged, we need to know if there is anything else we should be aware of."

Flipping through the documents, her hands trembled. Gloria had trouble speaking. "These records are supposed to be confidential."

Stenson studied her without expression. Within seconds, he would know how well he'd selected.

She turned back to the items from her file. "You know, most of these weren't my fault."

"We do know." He said it like it should have been obvious.

While concerned, Gloria would later remember that she was also somewhat excited. "You can really have my record cleaned?"

He nodded without blinking. "As long as we know everything."

She flipped through the documents once more, then handed them back. "This is all of it." She would never learn that this man and his associates were the reason Cornell had not received any offers from the many scholarships he had applied for. Unbeknownst to Gloria, Cornell's applications had all been withdrawn. The rejection letters she'd received certainly seemed legitimate. And what reason could she have possibly had to think that someone was forging the documents, forcing her to desperately need the one and only scholarship still available to her son?

She nodded. "So while I will technically be working for other people, I will actually be working for you."

"In the strictest of confidence." He glanced around the offices, which would be broken down later that day. Within twenty-four hours, there would be no sign he or his associates were ever there. Commonwealth

Equal Opportunity Trust did not appear on the short-term lease, or on any other legal document or registry anywhere. For all intents and purposes, it did not exist.

"How will this work?"

He handed her the phone. He explained that their communication would primarily be via text. They would notify her when and where she was to fill a new placement. She would go through the application process like every other potential hire, only with the knowledge that she alone had a perfect record. Her placement would be guaranteed. Her first position would be in the home of retired New York governor Terence Townsend, who had recently suffered a traumatic brain injury. The elder Townsend was also the father of New York City congressman and tabloid favorite Henry Townsend.

At the conclusion of each shift, Gloria was to report the names of any visitors the retired governor received. If there were none, her text message was to read: NONE. All messages were to be kept as brief as possible. She was never to use the phone for any other purpose, even in a life-threatening emergency. She was not to let anyone know of the phone's existence, any message she ever transmitted on it, or the true nature of her son's scholarship. Any deviation from these instructions would result in the immediate termination of his scholarship and her employment.

Of course, the true repercussions would be far more serious, but those were not discussed. For the next three years, Gloria performed her duties in the Townsend residence exactly as instructed. In fact, she was utterly vigilant. But little of interest occurred during that time, leading Stenson to believe that Gloria's talents might be better utilized elsewhere. It wasn't long after that Bob Stenson learned of Harmony House, and the echo box in particular. With his help, she sailed through the application process, even with the overly zealous background check performed by Fenton's security team. The other job applicants had all failed the test. Since 2008, Gloria had been dutifully reporting on the progress, or lack thereof, of Edward Parks's echo box.

The longer Gloria was in their employ, the more Bob Stenson and his American Heritage Foundation associates were convinced the real value of this particular hire might not be in the pipe dream of the echo box, but in the fine young man Cornell Pruitt was turning out to be. After Georgetown, they paid for him to attend Yale Law School. Then facilitated his hiring at the New York District Attorney's Office. They were now certain he was capable of becoming someone of political import. A senator in the making, for sure. Possibly even more.

All they needed to decide was what they wanted him to be.

CHAPTER 23

American Heritage Foundation, Alexandria, Virginia,
May 23, 7:18 p.m.

Gloria's text message arrived at the American Heritage Foundation within seconds via one of its many sophisticated satellite antennae well hidden atop its roof. There wasn't another private-sector company in the world with any of this technology. Even the FBI didn't have some of this stuff. By the time they did acquire it, the AHF would most certainly have already installed the next generation of systems, if not the one after that.

The building itself was another story. The structure was a drab, two-story cinder-block box in an office park on the outskirts of Alexandria, Virginia, whose other tenants included a web-design firm, a fledgling toy manufacturer, and a financial-consulting group. None of them would ever suspect one of the most influential political entities in the world was housed next door. Which was precisely the idea.

The notion of the American Heritage Foundation had been born shortly after the Kennedy assassination and cemented during Watergate. American politics was out of control. The system had run amok. The Great American Experiment of democracy was on the verge of collapsing under its own weight, and somebody had to do something.

Even if it meant undermining the entire system.

That was when seven like-minded midlevel officers from several of the government's intelligence agencies decided the only way to effectively play the game was off the field. Completely. No official ties. No official funding. No official anything.

While the Church and Pike Committees were busy conducting their official investigations into the CIA and the other intelligence agencies in 1975, these men quietly left their government positions and opened the doors to the American Heritage Foundation. Their seed money was entirely private and under no one else's scrutiny. The funds were received on a handshake for future consideration.

Each of their wealthy patrons would go on to state that this investment was the single smartest thing they had ever done with their money. They all grew even more rich as strategically selected policies and rulings were granted in their favor, courtesy of the American Heritage Foundation's influence and reach. Even then, there were few politicians, judges, or intelligence or law-enforcement personnel they couldn't get to.

The financial resources of the Foundation grew impressively. After thirty-six years of remarkable growth, the Foundation's endowment hovered around the $5.2 billion mark. That was enough money to do anything they thought was necessary, whenever they wanted.

It was enough to start a war.

The AHF initially had only nine full-time employees. They were a tight-knit group who were evangelical in their zeal. They believed in what they were doing. They were the ones keeping America on track, and there wasn't anything they wouldn't do to ensure it stayed that way.

Over the years, their employee numbers had grown to twenty-seven—still a small group, in part because their standards were so rigorous and the application process so involved that few worthy candidates ever stayed the course long enough for serious consideration.

You can find twenty-six other people you could trust with your life. You cannot find two hundred and twenty-six. At least, not in the civilian world.

The other reason they had been able to maintain such a small payroll was the ever-increasing efficiency of technology. One man with $10,000 of technology today could do what one hundred men with $50 million of equipment back in 1975 often couldn't. What used to require an army now simply required the right person, the right technology, and the financial resources to hire whatever independent contractors were necessary to execute any particular job.

The American Heritage Foundation had all three.

They had used hundreds of independent contractors over the years for a variety of tasks, but even this group was kept to a bare minimum to ensure that the Foundation's very existence remained off the grid.

If you controlled the grid, it was possible to keep yourself off it.

In its entire forty-two-year existence, no one had ever left the American Heritage Foundation except to retire or die. This was not because of the compensation, which was adequate but nothing great. And it wasn't because of the benefits package or perks or any of the other usual measures of what makes one job more desirable than another. Everyone who worked in this office thought they had the greatest job in the world because it was their mission. They effected real change in the real world on a regular basis, and no one outside them had a clue.

They were the puppet masters.

Elected officials, political appointees, committees, cabinets, intelligence directors, and everyone else who made Washington their personal playground did so for only limited periods of time. What could a person, even a really talented one, truly accomplish in renewable four-year chunks of time? The answer was *very little*, at least according to American Heritage doctrine. And most politicians were not very talented. The vast majority of them were little more than children who needed guidance and direction, not unlike movie stars. *Give them a part to play, and if they play it well, reward them. But if they don't, get rid of them.*

Ronald Reagan was their shining example; God rest his soul.

The current director of the American Heritage Foundation, Bob Stenson, revered Reagan almost as much as his predecessor and mentor had. Lawrence Walters, one of the original seven founders, had a knack for spotting talent before anyone else. He was one of the first to suggest to the modestly talented actor that he would make a great politician. Walters also recognized the talent in Stenson when he was still only a midlevel CIA agent. Walters handpicked him. Recruited him. Trained him. And gradually brought him up through the Foundation's ranks, over nineteen years, to the point where he inherited the mantle in 2005 when Alzheimer's forced the last of the founders to step aside.

If kings could select their princes instead of simply bearing them, it would be done like that.

As in all father-son relationships, things weren't always smooth between Walters and Stenson. Tensions arose when opinions differed, such as in the case of Henry Townsend. Stenson had urged Walters as early as 2002 to end their relationship with the derelict representative from New York. But Walters insisted that the younger Townsend's proclivities could be useful tools to keep him in line. Over time, however, it became apparent that the man-boy congressman simply couldn't control his adolescent urges.

When the old man finally decided to retire, due to increasingly poor health, he privately admitted that he should have done something about the derelict senator long ago. Walters had allowed his history with and affection for the embarrassment's father to cloud his judgment. Stenson stated with absolute candor that he was not about to put another jackass in the White House. One idiot son was enough for a generation. With that, Walters left his office for the last time, confident that the American Heritage Foundation was in good hands.

Stenson sat behind his Steelcase tanker desk, reviewing the day's communications to make sure there wasn't anything he had missed. He was reading messages on his encrypted device, which matched the ones carried by Corbin Davis and Gloria Pruitt, as well as dozens of others. There was nothing out of the ordinary. Everyone who was supposed to check in had done so. It was just another day at the office. Stenson called his wife, Millie, to let her know he would be leaving soon. She was always so happy when he came home at a reasonable hour. Dinner would be on the table. His favorite, pork loin.

CHAPTER 24

Tisch School of the Arts, New York University, May 24, 9:07 a.m.

Professor Jacob Hendrix entered his office to find that a dozen envelopes and messages had been slipped under the door. Some were flyers about student productions. The rest was administrative junk from the dean's office or invitations from other faculty members. He plopped all of it on his desk without looking at it and turned to his computer. He logged in and pulled up *Wikipedia*, where he typed a search for *acoustic archeology*.

((•))

The moment Jacob hit "Enter," an alert triggered on one of the many screens in the basement office of Michael Barnes. Certain keywords immediately triggered an alert if typed at one of the many IP addresses he was tracking. With a few keystrokes, Barnes could now see exactly what was on Jacob's computer screen. Barnes read the *Wikipedia* entry right along with Jacob, about the "garden variety" of acoustic archeology that had been featured in several investigative shows. The listing included the mention of "the future possibility of being able to re-create any type of sound wave," but that "such technology remains in the realm of science fiction."

Barnes had been doing this kind of work long enough that he didn't believe much in chance. Almost nothing happened purely out of coincidence. Still, it was a possibility here. The search could be nothing more than the result of an innocent conversation with Skylar.

That possibility was removed the moment Jacob typed *Edward Parks*. There was no *Wikipedia* entry for the name. A Google search for it brought up three entries: an attorney who was a partner at the DC law firm of Hogan Lovells; a twenty-four-year-old baritone who was currently studying at the Yale School of Music; and an orthopedic surgeon in Denver.

There was nothing about Eddie, and there never would be. The same was true of the search for *echo box*. There would never be any information available about the device of Eddie's creation. There was, however, an abundance of data regarding another device with the same name. This echo box was a device used to check the output power and spectrum of a radar transmitter. Anyone who was curious could learn all they wanted about that particular machine.

Barnes picked up the phone in his office and dialed a two-digit extension.

((•))

Stephen Millard recognized Michael Barnes's extension and immediately picked up the phone. "Good morning, Mr. Barnes. What can I do for you?"

"I need to see him."

"I'm afraid Dr. Fenton is tied up in meetings all afternoon."

"Tell him it's urgent."

Dr. Fenton had given Stephen strict instructions, when he was first hired, that if Mr. Barnes ever needed him urgently, Stephen was to interrupt him no matter what. In seven years of working here, that had never happened. This was the first time that Michael Barnes had ever said something was urgent. "One moment, please." He placed Barnes on hold, then quickly jotted down a note, which he carried to Dr. Fenton's door.

Stephen knocked lightly, then sheepishly poked his head inside. Dr. Fenton was sitting with a prospective new patient, a red-haired teenage girl whose hands constantly twitched. She sat nervously next to her mother, who looked utterly exhausted and like she couldn't wait to hand over her daughter. Among the reasons was that the girl had blown up their garage trying to achieve cold fusion. What the mother didn't realize was that with proper equipment, her daughter just might succeed.

Fenton looked angrily at Stephen and turned apologetically to the mother. "Privacy is normally a top priority among our staff."

"Please pardon the interruption." Stephen walked briskly to the doctor and handed him the note, which he had folded in half.

Fenton read the note and turned to his assistant. "Were these his exact words?"

"Yes, sir," Stephen answered nervously. "I wouldn't have interrupted otherwise."

Dr. Fenton stood up and spoke calmly. "Stephen, this is Betina Winters and her lovely daughter, Rachel. Why don't you show them around our facility? It shouldn't take me more than a few minutes to rejoin you."

Fenton picked up the phone as soon as Stephen ushered out the mother and daughter. "Get up here."

CHAPTER 25

Harmony House, Woodbury, New Jersey, May 24, 11:32 a.m.

Lunch on Wednesdays was hot dogs and tater tots. Eddie rated today's a four and a five, respectively. The vegetable was corn, which he found too soupy. He spit out the one bite he took and only gave it a one. Dessert was a choice of green Jell-O or vanilla pudding. Eddie took both. He sampled the Jell-O, but thought it too firm. Two. He shoved it away. The pudding, however, was so good that he gave it a rare five plus. He licked the small dish clean and returned to the service line.

When Jerome saw him coming, he turned and quickly started to walk away. After the last incident, he had adopted a policy of avoiding Eddie, if possible.

"Hey, Jerome, why are you walking away so fast?"

"Got dishes to clean."

Eddie made his BUZZER sound. "Not true. Definitely not true."

Jerome paused. "How would you know, man?"

"Dr. Fenton says I'm a walking polygraph."

The man from Harlem bugged out his eyes. "For real?"

"For real."

Jerome decided to give Eddie a test. "My birthday is April 19."

Eddie made his BUZZER sound. "Not true. Definitely not true."

Jerome was impressed. "I was born the day before. April 18."

"True."

Jerome decided to go another round. "My middle name is Malikai."

"True."

"I'm the youngest in my family."

Eddie made his BUZZER sound. "You are not the youngest."

Jerome shook his head. "I got four younger sisters." He thought about what a power Eddie possessed. And what a burden. "Goddamn."

Eddie looked puzzled. "Are you angry, Jerome?"

"No, Eddie. Look, I just better go, okay?"

"Okay. But I wanted to tell you the vanilla pudding got a five plus, and I almost never give any food a five plus."

Jerome nodded his appreciation. "Is that your highest rating, five plus?"

"Yes. It's only the second five plus I've given this year. The first one was for the green beans served for dinner on Wednesday, February 22, because they were the best green beans I have ever tasted."

Jerome moved closer to him. "You know who made the pudding today?"

"The same person who always makes the pudding. You, Jerome."

"Give the man a booby prize."

"What's a booby prize?"

"It's something you win."

"Why is it called a booby?"

Jerome shrugged. "Got me."

Eddie looked confused. "Got you what?"

Jerome noticed his boss, Ida Peroni, moving toward them from across the cafeteria. She was shaking her head with displeasure. Jerome spoke quickly. "I got one last pudding. I was kinda saving it for myself, but you can have it if you like."

"For real?" Eddie asked the question like Jerome had.

"For real."

Eddie looked thrilled as Jerome handed him the pudding. He held it like a prized trophy as Ida arrived. Trying to hide her concern, she asked, "Eddie, is everything okay?"

"Everything is a lot better than okay, Ida. Jerome is the best vanilla-pudding maker in Harmony House. You should give him a booby prize because it's something you win." He brushed by her, finishing the pudding before he reached his seat, where he was surprised to find Skylar waiting for him. There was pudding all around his mouth. She offered him a napkin as he licked the dish clean.

"I guess that pudding was pretty good."

"Your guess is correct, Skylar. It was five plus."

"You look like you slept well."

"I did. For over sixteen hours. How long did you sleep last night?"

"A little over four hours."

"Do you feel tired?"

"A little."

He made his BUZZER sound.

"Okay, a lot. I'm very tired, if you want to know the truth."

"You can take a nap in my bed if you want to. I can tuck you in like you tucked me in. My pajamas will be too big for you, though."

"Thank you for the kind offer, Eddie, but no thanks."

"Why did you only sleep for four hours?"

"Because I was reading about you."

"Why were you reading about me?"

"Because I think you are one of the most fascinating people I have ever met."

"I think you are one of the most fascinating people I have ever met, Skylar. Can I read about you?"

"I'm afraid there hasn't been much written about me."

"If you wrote your autobiography, I could read that."

"I'll make you a promise. If I ever write my autobiography, I'll give it to you to read."

"Then I will put it on my bookshelf right next to my Book of Questions, because I think your autobiography will have a lot of answers to the questions in my book."

She smiled at him with genuine affection. "One of the things I learned about you last night is that you think too much about the echo box."

He stared at her. "I think about it a lot because I am very close to figuring out why it won't work."

"Eddie, how long have you been very close?"

He blinked several times. "Eleven years and three months."

"That's a long time to try to think about only one thing."

"I've thought about it for a lot longer than that, but that's how long I've been very close."

"How much progress have you made in all that time?"

"Fourteen percent."

She nodded. "Just over a percent a year."

"One point two four repeating."

"At this rate, you'll need another seventy years to finish it."

Eddie corrected her. "Sixty-nine point one zero nine."

"That's a long time, Eddie."

"Yes, it is. A very long time. I don't want to have to wait that long to hear my mother's voice."

"Which means in order to finish it, you're going to have to come up with a completely different approach. Something new. It might be surprisingly simple, but it also might be terribly complicated. There's no way to know what it is right now, but to reach a different destination, you first have to change the journey."

Eddie looked confused. "How do I change the journey?"

"It helps to first clear your head."

"I don't want to clear my head."

"I didn't mean literally. It's only an expression."

"I don't like expressions."

She marveled at how easy it was to forget his limitations. "When I want a fresh start, I like to take a walk."

"Where do you walk?"

"Somewhere I haven't walked before."

"Antarctica. I have never walked in Antarctica."

"Neither have I, but I was thinking somewhere a little more accessible."

"Miami Beach, Florida, is more accessible."

"It's beautiful outside. Why don't we go out in the yard?"

(((•)))

A gentle afternoon breeze greeted them as they exited the building. The sun shined brightly as they walked onto the rolling lawns surrounding Harmony House. Eddie paused, closing his eyes. He slowly rotated his head from side to side.

Skylar watched him. "What do you hear?"

"Everything." He focused on a bird flying overhead and watched it land in a nearby tree. It was an American goldfinch, the New Jersey state bird. The goldfinch chirped. Eddie chirped back. Looking reassured, he continued walking. "Where are we going on our walk, Skylar?"

"Nowhere in particular."

"That's a strange destination."

"Haven't you ever walked just for the sake of walking?"

"No." He kept walking. Listening to his footsteps. And to traffic somewhere off in the distance. Staring at the ground in front of him, he was trying to process the notion of walking nowhere in particular. "This is kind of like when you were communicating nonverbally, isn't it?"

"How do you mean?"

"We are doing one thing, but we're really doing a lot more than that."

"That is very perceptive of you."

"This is also very memorable, just like that was."

"I think walks are good for people."

"So are eating fruits and vegetables, and not smoking, and drinking only moderate amounts of alcohol."

"Those are all true."

"According to the surgeon general, women should not drink alcoholic beverages during pregnancy because of the risk of birth defects."

"That is also true."

"Have you ever been pregnant, Skylar?"

She hesitated slightly. "That's a very personal question, Eddie."

"Dr. Fenton says I should not ask very personal questions."

"Unless you know someone very well, that's probably a good idea."

"I don't know anyone very well." They kept walking.

This was an important opportunity, and she knew she had to take it. "Yes, Eddie, I was pregnant once." Her voice quivered almost imperceptibly. On her list of memories she'd rather forget, this was number one.

"Was it a boy baby or a girl baby?"

"Neither." She thought about how to admit to an abortion without actually saying it, but without lying, either. "The pregnancy stopped. I never had the baby."

He took a moment to process the answer. "Will you try to have another one?"

She shook her head. "I don't think so, Eddie."

"Why not?"

"Because it's just not something I can ever see myself wanting."

He studied her. "My mother wanted me, but she died when I was born."

"I am sure she wanted you, too." She briefly thought of how little her own mother had wanted her or her brother. How else could a woman abandon her small children?

"I'm going to hear my mother sing one day."

"I believe you will." She was firmly reassuring.

Eddie stopped suddenly, rotating his head slightly.

"What's wrong?"

"The mystery man is walking to his car."

Across the yard, she saw the man, whom she did not recognize. He was walking through the parking lot toward his beige Impala. He moved with purpose. "Why do you call him the mystery man?"

"Dr. Fenton told me he's none of my concern."

"Why did you ask Dr. Fenton about him?"

"I know the job of everyone else who works at Harmony House. I know their names, their job titles, when they arrive, when they leave, when they go on vacation, and many other things about them. I know that Nurse Gloria has a son named Cornell who graduated from Yale Law School. I know that Jerome in the cafeteria has a wife named Marla who is going bald, but he tells her she looks beautiful every night."

She watched the man drive out of the parking lot and past the driveway-gate guard. "What makes you so sure he works here?"

"He's here almost every day, but sometimes he doesn't come inside the building. Sometimes, he just sits in his car."

"That's a little strange."

"Yes, it is a little strange. That's what he was doing last Friday when you left Dr. Fenton's office feeling excited for the foreseeable future."

"He was just sitting there?"

"Then, after a while, he drove away."

"When the opportunity presents itself, I'll ask Dr. Fenton about him."

"How will you know when the opportunity presents itself?"

She glanced at him and resumed walking. "Years of practice."

"Will you teach me how?"

"I'll do my best."

He did not make his BUZZER sound. Because Skylar was telling the truth.

((•))

It was well into the evening before Skylar noticed the sun had already gone down. She was on her fourth storage box of materials on Eddie, and still felt like she was only getting started. She made all kinds of notes of things to check on further. The acoustic tiles. The boot soles. His love of birds. And the earliest incarnations of the echo box, which predated his arrival at Harmony House. According to his pediatrician's notes, Eddie first mentioned the device when he was only eight years old. The notes included a sketch Eddie had made at the time, which was quite similar to the existing prototype. Skylar shook her head in awe. *What kind of an eight-year-old thinks of reconstructing partial wave fragments to generate sounds made long ago?*

"Eddie's father has never once come to visit in the entire time he's been here." Fenton stood in the doorway to her office. "He simply seems to want no further connection with Eddie."

"Some parents just prefer to wash their hands." She was thinking of her own mother, and the pain her absence had caused Skylar for so many years. As a child, she had often wondered what she had done wrong that caused her mother to leave. As a teenager, Skylar imagined confronting her, particularly after Christopher's death. And as an adult, she mostly preferred not to think of her at all, because while she had intellectually come to terms with her mother's decision, Skylar knew that deep down, she still carried a genuine hatred for the woman.

"It's tragic, really. For both parties." He entered her office slowly, noting the few personal touches she'd put around the room.

"I'm convinced that Eddie's lack of intimacy has been a major barrier to his progress."

He chuckled. "That's true for all of us, isn't it?"

She smiled briefly. "Most of us don't have to memorize what a smile means."

Fenton nodded appreciatively. "How do you intend to connect with him?"

"By making him feel safe with me. I want him to know it's okay to take chances."

Fenton looked out her window. "The walk outside today was a good idea. He's been spending far too much time cooped up inside."

"One of my goals is to do as many new things as he will tolerate. I want to expand his comfort zone."

"Be careful not to stretch it too much. Without his many routines, he absolutely falls apart."

"Once he trusts that I won't let him fall, you'll be amazed what happens."

The moment was interrupted when Skylar's cell phone rang. It was Jacob. She answered the phone, saying, "Honey, hang on for just a second." She turned to Fenton, cupping the phone. "He was expecting me for dinner. I have some explaining to do."

"By all means. I should be getting home, as well. Have a good night." He backed out of the office and closed the door.

CHAPTER 26

Christopher Street, New York City, May 24, 7:08 p.m.

Jacob was walking down the sidewalk, which was always crowded, especially at rush hour, when he called Skylar. He was heading toward the subway station at Sheridan Square with his student Barry Handelman, the billionaire's son, and Barry's rather stunning girlfriend. Jacob waited for Skylar to finish whatever she was doing.

She finally got back on the line. "I thought you were supposed to be going to some art-house flick with your students?"

"I am. All my students bailed on me except one. His girlfriend is joining us, and I was wondering if I could convince you to make it a foursome."

"Wish I could, but I'm still at Harmony House."

"Okay, just thought I'd ask. Don't work too late." Jacob, Barry, and his girlfriend, Tatiana, who happened to be a model, descended into the station.

Tatiana asked Barry, with a slight Argentinean accent, "Do we really have to take the subway? Why don't we just take the car?"

The professor interjected. "He's traveling with me, not the other way around. Professors don't do limos. Especially when they belong to their students."

Jacob could see that both his student and his girlfriend truly hated the subway, but neither said anything further. The professor regretted his insistence almost immediately when he noticed the homeless guy following them. The man was in really bad shape. He walked with a severe limp. His tattered clothing was filthy. Jacob figured the guy had probably targeted them because of Barry's girlfriend. Not that she was his objective, but no woman like this would be with a guy like Barry if he wasn't filthy rich.

They turned a corner as they made their way through the station. Jacob used the opportunity to glance behind them to see if the bum was still following them. He wasn't. Jacob was just being paranoid. At least, that was what he told himself.

Arriving at the uptown platform, he glanced at Tatiana. "Have you ever seen a French film?"

She responded in French. *"Professeur, ce n'est pas parce que je suis mannequin que je suis inculte."* (Professor, just because I am a model does not make me illiterate.)

He responded in kind. *"Je n'ai jamais dit ça. La majorité des Americains n'en ont pas vu un seul."* (I never said you were. Most Americans have never seen a foreign film.)

Barry interjected. "English, please, or I'm going to start getting jealous." He smiled playfully.

Tatiana glanced at him, then at Jacob. "I am not American."

"Yeah, I gathered that. I was only offering to give you some background in case you weren't familiar with what we're about to see." Jacob said it without any airs. He was genuinely trying to be helpful.

"I have seen many French films, but never an avant-garde one."

"Well, you're in for a treat," he said loudly over the cacophony around them. "That or you're in for the most god-awful time you've ever experienced, in which case I'll buy you both a drink."

Barry chimed in, practically yelling over the noise of the approaching train. "In that case, I'll be calling a car."

"Maybe then you'll have to bring the professor out clubbing with us."

"Who said we were going out?"

"Who said we weren't?" she purred.

Considering the possibilities of where this night might go, Jacob didn't notice the homeless guy making his way toward them again.

Ever since the Twin Towers went down, New York City had been on constant vigil for the next terrorist attack. The subway system was widely considered one of the most likely targets, simply because of the scale of the thing. There were 468 different stations along 842 miles of track. Over five million passengers rode the trains every weekday, making it the seventh-busiest subway system in the world, behind Beijing, Shanghai, Tokyo, Guangzhou, Seoul, and Moscow. The points of vulnerability were simply too many to count.

Jacob, Barry, and Tatiana listened as a train neared the station. Local trains slowed their approach and weren't nearly as piercing as express trains, which zoomed right on by. The approaching train was clearly not going to stop.

The homeless guy yelled as loud as he could above the shrill of the approaching train. "It is time America paid for its sins!"

Nobody gave much attention to him until he put on a gas mask, which had been hidden beneath his tattered coat. The gas mask looked brand new.

By the time he held a canister high above his head, he had the attention of every single person on the crowded platform.

Most were frozen with panic. One woman screamed. Another man raced up the stairs, knocking over several kids. A businessman close to the bum charged toward him, trying to tackle him. But not before the homeless guy pulled the pin on the canister and dropped it to the cement floor.

Fssssssss. It was a horrifying sound.

The gas dispersed rapidly. This was really happening.

Smoke immediately filled the subway tunnel as the screeching express train entered the station. It was hard to see anything. People's eyes were burning. So were their lungs. So were their minds.

They thought they were dying.

Passengers scrambled over each other to get out of the station. Many went the wrong way. It was pandemonium.

In the middle of the melee, just as the express train reached the platform, the bum lunged for Jacob, grabbing the back of his coat. The grungy man's grip was incredibly strong. Much stronger than it should have been.

In one swift, violent motion, he hurled Jacob onto the tracks in front of the express train traveling at thirty-eight miles per hour.

CHAPTER 27

Sheridan Square Subway Station, New York City, May 24, 7:13 p.m.

The screech of the express train passing in front of the platform jumped several decibels the moment the conductor hit the emergency brake. He'd worked for the MTA for twenty-three years and conducted for the last eleven. The only other time he'd pulled the emergency brake was also for a body on the tracks. That one was a suicide. This one was different.

He'd pulled the brake on instinct. And immediately wished he hadn't. Had he thought about it a moment longer, he would have kept right on going, because he was sure the rapidly spreading white gas cloud was lethal.

They were all going to die.

The squeal of the brakes was punishing. Sparks flew off the tracks where the giant steel wheels skidded down the rails.

The passengers inside the train were thrown violently forward as the train rapidly slowed. Several would later require hospitalization, one in critical condition. Their screams were loud, but not as loud as the hundred or so people on the platform.

Almost no one saw the man get thrown in front of the train. Most weren't sure what had happened. They were too busy running away from the ever-expanding cloud of noxious white smoke. Only those nearest Jacob actually saw him tumble to his death. The gas cloud was too thick. Everything was too chaotic.

In total, thirty-seven New Yorkers would be treated for injuries sustained during the stampede. The unfortunate were trampled, including Tatiana, who was screaming at the top of her lungs. She was one of the few who had seen Jacob fall to the tracks and watched the train cut him in half. Her eyes were glazed. She was going into shock, and mumbled incoherently.

The gas was everywhere. "Hold your breath!" Barry screamed at his catatonic girlfriend. He grabbed her hand and pushed and shoved his way through the throng struggling to get out of the danger zone. She moved like a zombie, but somehow managed to hang on.

$$((\bullet))$$

The paranoia worked in favor of the homeless man who had pushed Jacob to his death. He was not among those worried about a chemical attack. Because he knew it wasn't lethal. It wouldn't be until eleven hours later that a joint task force of federal, state, and city officials would determine the smoke was only tear gas, probably stolen from the NYPD. The entire event wasn't anything more than a stunt, a desperate act by some crazy guy who wanted attention. It was not unlike the fake bomb incident that had shut down LaGuardia for seven hours in the summer of 2009.

Only no one had died in that one.

The killer was gone before anyone gave much thought to pursuing him. He had disappeared among the fleeing hordes by concealing his gas mask and acting like the rest of the herd running for their lives. The homeless man bounded up the steps swiftly, with no sign of a limp. He quickly reached the top of the stairs and continued along with the swell of other terrified passengers, until he ducked inside a men's room.

He locked himself in a stall and removed his disgusting, matted wig. It wasn't until he pulled off his fake beard that Michael Barnes became recognizable.

He removed his tattered coat and pants, revealing a Brooks Brothers suit beneath it: Mr. Businessman. He stuffed the ratty garments, along with the gas mask, into a nylon sports bag, which had been folded up inside a pocket. When he stepped out of the stall, no one would suspect that he was the crazy bum who had faked a terrorist attack and pushed an innocent man to his death.

Barnes moved to the sink, where he splashed cold water on his face. He showed no emotion whatsoever. The assignment was not finished. He still had to get out of the station, but that was the easy part.

He stepped out of the bathroom, coughing into his hand like so many others around him. He looked just like every other New Yorker caught up in the chaos at what was supposed to have been the end of another ordinary workday. The nylon gym bag he was carrying suggested he had been on his way to Equinox or some other fashionable gym to work off the stress of the day, before the incident occurred. Like everyone else, he now acted more like he was heading to a bar.

Michael Barnes exited the station, just one of a herd of terrified people. Some dropped to their knees to catch their breath, or to thank God that they were still alive. Most were on their phones, letting loved ones know what had happened and that they were unharmed. That was the pose Barnes adopted, appearing to be on his phone for the entire walk to his beige Impala parked near New York University, which now had one less professor than it had at the start of the day. As he pulled into traffic, he passed the first of dozens of emergency vehicles that would be arriving on the scene.

CHAPTER 28

Jacob Hendrix's Apartment, Greenwich Village, New York City, May 24, 10:57 p.m.

It was almost eleven o'clock that evening by the time Skylar walked up the two flights of stairs to Jacob's apartment on Bleecker Street. It had been several days since she'd done any Pilates, and her body was craving some exercise. These stairs weren't much, but they would have to do for the moment.

When Skylar reached the third floor, she was surprised to find a weathered man in a wrinkled suit standing outside Jacob's door. He was sticking his business card in the crack by the lock. He was in his late thirties, but looked more like fifty. "Can I help you?"

He turned to face her. "Is this Jacob Hendrix's apartment?"

She eyed him suspiciously. "Who wants to know?"

He removed his business card from the door and offered it to her. "I'm Detective Butler McHenry, NYPD."

She studied his card, then took out her keys. "Yes, this is Jacob's apartment. For the moment, it's mine, too. What's going on?"

"Could I see some identification, please?"

She nervously took out her wallet and handed him her Massachusetts driver's license. "What's this all about?"

"Ms. Drummond, this says you live in Cambridge."

"I just moved. I haven't had time to change it yet." Her pulse quickened as she became nervous. "What's going on?"

He handed her back her license. "May I come inside for a moment?"

She hesitated. "I guess so." She led Detective McHenry into the apartment. Inside, McHenry noted the many photographs featuring Jacob and Skylar.

"You're kind of freaking me out, Detective. Would you tell me what's going on?"

"I think you might want to have a seat."

"I don't want to sit." She started to panic. "Did something happen to Jacob?" McHenry took a deep breath and looked at her sadly. "He's okay, isn't he?"

His eyes told her everything, and then he confirmed it. "No."

"Oh my God." She sat down at the kitchen table, practically collapsing in the chair. Her hands were shaking.

McHenry sat down across from her, swallowing hard as he struggled to say the words properly. "Jacob Hendrix is gone."

She wasn't sure she had heard him correctly. She couldn't have. Her words came out rapidly. "What do you mean, 'gone'? What kind of gone?"

McHenry stared at the table, then slowly raised his gaze to Skylar. "Jacob is dead."

"*What?*" She didn't believe it. She couldn't. It was too much to process. She started to feel light-headed.

He paused to let her catch her breath. "There was a terrorist incident in the Sheridan Square subway station."

All she could think was to blame herself for not listening to the radio on her way home. For not wondering why so many streets had been blocked off nearby, making it nearly impossible to get home. She should have put two and two together. *Dammit!* "What happened?"

"It appears to have been some kind of gas attack. We're not sure."

"How many people died?"

"We don't know yet. A lot of people are being treated in area hospitals. Mr. Hendrix is one of two confirmed fatalities so far. It appears he tripped or was pushed in all the commotion. It's too early to know for sure. But, somehow, he ended up on the tracks in front of an oncoming train." He said it as gently as he could, but it still came out like a diesel-powered sledgehammer.

Tears streamed down Skylar's face as her mind went reeling. She refused to believe it. "How can this . . . I was just talking to him as he was walking into the station. We got cut off."

"We're still interviewing witnesses, trying to determine exactly what happened."

The blood drained from Skylar's tear-soaked face. She went numb, trying to remember their last conversation. What was the last thing she said to him? What was the last thing Jacob heard from her? It was all jumbled. In this moment, she could only remember bits and pieces.

Detective McHenry continued. "All we know at this point is that there were two students with him. One was pretty badly shaken up."

Skylar stared vacantly at the surface of the table. Her voice was distant. "Only one of them was his student."

McHenry looked at her. "Excuse me?"

"Only one was his student." She sounded a thousand miles away.

"How do you know?"

"Jacob told me on the phone."

McHenry nodded. "Ms. Drummond, I'm so sorry."

"It's doctor. Dr. Drummond." She turned and looked him directly in the eyes. "I'm such an asshole." She sobbed heavily as guilt, sadness, and regret began to overwhelm her. There was so much she hadn't said. So much she hadn't done. Jacob was devoted, loving, intelligent, sexy, and fun. Everything. All he had wanted was to make her happy. All he had asked for was a modest commitment in return. *What is wrong with me?* she wondered. *What the hell is wrong with me?!*

McHenry knew not to say anything. Almost everyone regretted not saying or doing something after a loved one died. It was only natural.

"Do you know if he died right away?"

McHenry nodded. "I can assure you he didn't suffer."

Skylar stared at him vacantly, barely able to process what she was hearing. "I can't believe this."

"I can only imagine how hard this must be." He stood, pointing to his business card on the kitchen table. "This has all my numbers. You can reach me anytime, day or night."

She nodded mechanically. She couldn't imagine why she would ever call him.

"May I have a phone number in case I need to reach you?"

"Why would you need to reach me?"

"You never know if you might be able to help us with the investigation."

She jotted down her number on the back of an envelope and handed it to him.

He pocketed the envelope. "Again, I'm very sorry for your loss."

It was only after he closed the door that she really allowed herself to feel what had just happened. Skylar burst into tears and cried like she hadn't cried since her younger brother died, over ten years ago.

CHAPTER 29

Early the next morning, Bob Stenson walked briskly toward the conference room inside the American Heritage Foundation. He carried three newspapers, all of which featured multiple stories about the apparent terrorist attack in the New York City subway station. The *New York Times*, the *Wall Street Journal*, and the *Washington Post* all had extensive coverage, with wide-ranging theories, but nothing conclusive. The incident was too fresh. The investigation too new.

Stenson had three lieutenants who reported directly to him: Caitlin McCloskey, Daryl Trotter, and Jason Greers. McCloskey was the eldest daughter of one of the Foundation's original partners. She wasn't the visionary her father had been, but Caitlin was both extremely sharp and completely committed. She was also damn good in a crunch. The woman shined in a crisis. There was never any question she would be a Foundation lifer.

Trotter was the deep thinker of the three. He was a chess player who had achieved a FIDE rating over 2600 and the rank of Grandmaster by the age of nineteen, which only 123 other people in the world had ever accomplished. Had he not found a much better game to devote his considerable faculties to, he almost certainly would have gone on to reach the status of a Garry Kasparov or Magnus Carlsen. But from the first moment he got to play with real pawns and real rooks in the real world, from inside the confines of the American Heritage Foundation, Trotter knew he'd found his game. He never played competitive chess again.

Jason Greers was the most well rounded of the three. He was also the most ambitious. There was never much question as to which of them would get Stenson's office when he decided to retire. The other two seemed to have accepted it—a good thing, because a fluid transition would be important when the time came.

All three were already seated at the conference table, waiting for Stenson, as he entered the room and tossed the three newspapers on the table. "Talk to me."

Jason Greers spoke first. "It's peculiar."

"Why?" Stenson knew why, of course, but wanted to hear what they were thinking, just like his mentor, Walters, used to do with him.

McCloskey spoke matter-of-factly. "It was a well-coordinated strike. Well planned. Well executed. This was not the work of an amateur."

"If it was a professional, everyone in that station would be dead."

Trotter jumped in. "Suicide bombers are not professionals." His thoughts were often so far ahead of what he was saying he would forget to complete a statement.

"This was not a suicide bomb."

Trotter snapped himself back to the present. "No, it wasn't. Which means we can rule out an amateur."

Greers helped connect the dots that Trotter was leaving out. "Whoever the guy is, he's good. Undoubtedly, someone we know knows him. The question we should be asking is why a professional would go through all this trouble for such a nominal result."

Bob Stenson stated the obvious: "You're assuming he achieved his objective. He may not have."

"He accomplished exactly what he set out to," McCloskey said with a degree of admiration.

"What makes you so sure?"

"There wasn't a single useful witness description of him, and not one clean image on any surveillance camera. You have to admit that's impressive."

Stenson nodded. It was.

Trotter continued. "We've found nothing to suggest that anything went wrong. Therefore, whatever was achieved was his objective, as nominal as it might seem."

The boss was perplexed, which was rare. "What was achieved?"

Greers smirked. "He got everyone's attention."

"Which could mean this was a preamble."

Trotter shook his head. "No. Someone with this skill set acts, and then disappears. They do not draw attention to themselves before a major play. It takes away the element of surprise."

"So if this was a one-off, what could the objective possibly have been?"

"To show that he can," McCloskey replied. The room went quiet, because her reasoning was sound. McCloskey sat up a little straighter.

Stenson considered the thought. "You think this was a demonstration?"

"I'm saying it could have been. We don't have enough information to know what it was. But we certainly cannot rule it out."

Stenson nodded in agreement. One of them always came up with something he hadn't considered. "Keep it back burner. Something's going to turn up that will make it all make sense. It always does. Until then, focus elsewhere."

CHAPTER 30

Jacob Hendrix's Apartment, Greenwich Village, New York City, May 27, 7:55 a.m.

Skylar didn't leave the apartment for over forty-eight hours. She watched the developing news coverage of the subway gas attack in mind-numbing repetition. No legitimate terrorist organization was stepping forward to claim responsibility. The determination that the gas released in the subway was not lethal sarin or VX or ricin, but only common tear gas, explained why. The news was a relief, but also infuriating. Jacob didn't die because some group of extremists was attempting to wage war on the United States. He died because some crazy asshole in need of attention decided he didn't care who got hurt in the process. *Selfish bastard.*

Eventually, she turned off the television. Nothing new was being reported. The police still had no leads, and it didn't look like they would anytime soon. Skylar already knew all she needed to know. Jacob was gone. She would never have the opportunity to make things right with him. She would never be able to reassure him like she knew he wanted her to. She would never be able to say yes, that deep inside, she wanted the same things he did, but was just too damn afraid.

She would never be able to admit to him her deepest fears. The ones that kept her away from him and everyone else. She couldn't tell him that it was her, and not him. She loved him; she really did. At least, as best she could.

She wanted him to know that she never meant to keep him at arm's length—she really didn't—but that she didn't know how to overcome the barriers she had erected so long ago. She didn't know how to fill the void that had always been there inside her. He had deserved better, and she wished she could have given it to him.

She would have to spend the rest of her life knowing that she hadn't.

Skylar didn't sleep at all that first night. She called Fenton's office about the time she would have normally arrived at Harmony House to tell him she would not be coming in for work the rest of the week.

At the news of Jacob's death, Fenton sounded empathetic. "My God, you poor dear. Is there anything I can do to help?"

She said there wasn't, and that she'd be back to work next week.

"Take all the time you need."

Skylar started to plan Jacob's funeral, but didn't get far. It was too soon. Thinking about him lying dead in a casket was too much. His bloodless face. His lifeless eyes. She kept breaking down. Jacob's parents wanted to make the arrangements, anyway. They were giving him the burial plot they'd been saving for themselves. The funeral was still three weeks away, to give family members time to make their travel arrangements. Skylar thanked them for their help. His mother asked Skylar if she wanted company in Jacob's apartment, but Skylar declined the offer. She wanted to be alone.

By Saturday morning, the walls were closing in. She needed to get out, but didn't know where to go. Shu Han Ju? She couldn't. And it was too bright and sunny outside to go to Central Park. She didn't want to be around all those cheerful, happy people. She even thought about going to the Met, but didn't want to break down in front of a bunch of stuffy art lovers and tourists. Maybe a vacation would do her good. Mexico? Italy? Paris? None of it sounded remotely bearable.

That left Harmony House. *When all else fails, work.* She couldn't stand the thought of sitting in her office with the one photograph of her and Jacob on the shelf, but she could at least bury herself in another box of materials on Eddie. His files were the only things she thought she could focus on.

((•))

She arrived at the Harmony House driveway gate later that morning and showed the guard her ID. She parked in the lot, taking a moment to collect herself. The beige Impala was parked in its usual spot, but there was no sign of the mystery man. Upon entering the building, Skylar veered toward Fenton's office before heading to her own. She thought it would be a good idea to check in with the boss before retreating to her office. To let him know she was okay. That this wouldn't interfere with her work. In fact, all she wanted to do was disappear into it. Nineteen hours a day, seven days a week, for the next ten years. Maybe then she would be ready to move on.

She found it curious that Stephen Millard, Dr. Fenton's faithful secretary, was not at his desk, when it suddenly occurred to her that it was Saturday. Only a skeleton support staff worked on the weekends. Fenton probably wouldn't be there, either. She turned to exit, when she heard a voice from inside Fenton's office. It was not the old man's. It was Eddie's. He had recognized her from the sound of her footsteps. "Skylar, come here. I'm in Dr. Fenton's office."

She entered to find Eddie sitting exactly as he had been the last time he was in here. The echo box sat on Fenton's coffee table, connected to Eddie's laptop. The eight one-inch satellite microphones were moving in perfect unison as they pointed around the room.

"Hi, Eddie." She tried to sound as cheerful as she could, hoping to conceal the incredible sadness overwhelming her from Eddie, as well as from herself.

"Dr. Fenton isn't here today, because today is Saturday and he doesn't usually work on Saturdays. At least, not anymore. He used to, but after his wife died, he started to garden because that is what his wife liked to do, and Dr. Fenton says gardening reminds him of her. Her name was Ruth. They were married a long time." Eddie never once looked at Skylar. His eyes were glued to his laptop screen.

"Are you sure it's okay for you to be in here?"

"Dr. Fenton gave me permission to come into his office anytime I thought it was really important, and I thought it was really important."

"What's going on?"

"I came up with a new approach, just like you suggested." He said it quite like the way she had spoken the phrase to him, but he still didn't look at her.

"I'm glad to hear it." Skylar was barely holding it together.

"It was surprisingly simple, also just like you said."

"What was?" Eddie pointed to the echo box. She turned toward the device. "You mean to tell me it's working?"

"Almost." He innocently turned back to the laptop screen, where he watched the loading progress bar below the three-dimensional image of the office. "Eighty-three percent, eighty-four percent . . ."

She moved closer toward the laptop screen to see for herself. *Ninety-one percent. Ninety-two.* She was stunned. "Oh my God."

He knew that phrase meant shock, surprise, or dismay, but he couldn't tell which. "Are you okay, Skylar?"

"Yes, I'm fine."

He made his BUZZER sound, but never looked away from the laptop screen. *Ninety-five percent. Ninety-six percent.* Eddie seemed much more calm than he had previously. Like he knew this time was different.

He seemed to know he'd done it.

Skylar glanced around the room, checking for sharp objects, then toward the door, hoping that Nurse Gloria was in the immediate vicinity when things didn't go as planned.

When the counter read *one hundred percent*, he looked up at Skylar with a spectacular smile, which he'd been practicing for years. For the very first time in his life, Eddie seemed to be expressing himself emotionally. But, given the circumstances, neither he nor Skylar paid much attention. "What would you like to hear, Skylar?"

She remained calm, as well as dubious. "Eddie, I think you should choose."

He thought about it for a moment. "It would probably be a good idea to start with a recent date. There will be considerably less distortion and white noise to filter out."

"Okay." She prepared for the upcoming tantrum.

Eddie studied the recent Timeline of Wave History for Dr. Fenton's office. He moved a designator from the end of the timeline (the present) to yesterday (Friday), then pinpointed the most clearly identifiable sound waves. He looked up to Skylar. "Are you ready to hear something that no one has ever heard before?"

She inched closer to Eddie. The more he built up the moment, the more she prepared herself to spring into action. "I think so." She immediately began to doubt whether she could restrain him by herself. She envisioned him thrashing about, hurting her as well as himself, and, worse, damaging the echo box. She dreaded the thought of having to explain the incident to Fenton. Skylar considered trying to stop Eddie from proceeding, but didn't act quickly enough.

"These are the first sound waves ever re-created." He hit "Play."

CHAPTER 31

Harmony House, Woodbury, New Jersey, May 27, 10:10 a.m.

At first, all that could be heard was low-decibel HISSING and WARBLE. Skylar immediately grew concerned, expecting Eddie to explode.

But, surprisingly, he didn't. "Now that I've been able to rebuild the waves, I should be able to clean up most of this harmonic distortion by running it through a series of filters."

She nodded, pretending to understand, when she suddenly froze. The impossible became possible as Fenton's voice was heard through the laptop's speakers: *"Stephen, I don't remember who my ten thirty is with. God, I really am getting old."*

Skylar's eyes bugged out with disbelief. She forgot to breathe. "Holy shit."

"That expression confuses me," Eddie replied.

Fenton's voice continued after a brief pause. *"Reschedule it. Next week, or, better yet, the week after."*

Skylar recovered quickly. "Sounded like he was on the phone with his assistant."

Through the laptop, Skylar and Eddie heard the sound of a phone hanging up.

"Give the lady a booby prize." He tried to sound like Jerome had in the cafeteria. Eddie worked his laptop, running the reconstructed sound waves through several more filters.

When he played Fenton's phone conversation with his assistant again, it sounded considerably crisper. The dialogue was distinct.

Skylar wanted another demonstration before she was really going to believe what she was hearing. "Can you find a conversation he had with someone in person?"

"Yes." Eddie moved the time designator to the day before yesterday (Thursday), but the waves were only single sets, which meant they were one-sided phone conversations, like the one they'd just heard.

Eddie was looking for two sets of overlapping waves, which meant a conversation between two people in the same space. He slid the designator to Wednesday, where he found what he was looking for. "This was a conversation Dr. Fenton was having with someone else in this office. It was approximately the time we took our walk in the yard to nowhere in particular, which I still think was a strange destination." He hit "Play."

Through the laptop, they heard a light knock. Fenton said, *"Come in."* The door opened and closed. The sound reproduction was a bit garbled but still distinct enough. Someone had entered the office, but Eddie couldn't make out the footsteps.

Fenton asked his visitor, *"Mr. Barnes, to what do I owe the pleasure?"*

Barnes answered, *"Your new doctor's boyfriend has been looking into Eddie."*

Skylar's face dropped. She didn't recognize the man's voice, but realized Barnes must be the head of Harmony House security. She couldn't believe he was talking about Jacob.

Eddie turned to her. "I don't recognize who Dr. Fenton is talking to. Do you?"

She shook her head no. Her mind was already reeling.

Eddie said, "I think he must be the mystery man, because he's the only one who works here whose voice I have never heard."

"Shh." Skylar listened intently.

Dr. Fenton's was the next voice heard: *"What have you got?"* The sound of documents being reviewed was clear. Evidence was being examined.

> BARNES: *Either she's got loose lips or he's been sticking his nose where it doesn't belong.*

Goose bumps became visible on Skylar's arms. She was barely breathing.

> BARNES: *Could be nothing, but I thought you should be made aware.*

There was a momentary pause.

> FENTON: *I don't like it.*

His voice was cold. Emotionless.

> BARNES: *My real concern is that there is at least one op being run out of NYU, and possibly several. I haven't confirmed it, but I'm pretty damn sure. If I'm right, the professor may not even know what he's done.*

There was another pause, this time even longer. Fenton was clearly thinking through his options.

> FENTON: *We can't afford a breach. Not now. Not even the possibility of one.*

This was the kind of conversation where the most important things were the ones not said. But there was no misunderstanding. Barnes seemed to know exactly what Fenton meant.

BARNES: *You sure about this?*

FENTON: *Yes, I'm sure. Skylar is too valuable. She's already made more progress with Eddie in days than the others made in years.*

A pause. Presumably Barnes was deciding on a course of action.

BARNES: *Will you want to know the details?*

FENTON: *Nothing in his residence. Make it look like an accident.*

BARNES: *He takes the subway.*

Skylar blurted out, "Oh my God." Her hands were trembling.

Eddie pressed "Stop." The playback halted. "That's the second time you've said 'Oh my God,' Skylar."

Tears started streaming down her face. She was shaking.

"You're crying." He said it descriptively, not compassionately. He wasn't sure how to respond.

Skylar nodded.

"Are you crying in a good way?" He thought of how people had explained that his mother's voice had brought them to tears.

"No, Eddie. I'm upset."

"Why are you upset?"

"Because of what I just heard."

"I thought it would make you happy. Why did it make you upset?"

"I can't tell you that right now."

"Because it involves the mystery man and he is none of my concern?"

She nodded.

Eddie looked around the room, imagining all the sound waves bouncing all around them. "Would you like to hear something else?"

"Not . . . now." She had trouble getting the words out. Skylar had lost control of her breathing.

"Okay."

She got up and started pacing around the room. Her head was spinning. She had no idea what she was going to do. *Think, Skylar. Think! Do something!* The only thing she was certain of was that her world was collapsing around her.

Nothing would ever be the same again.

"Do you know what I want to hear?" he asked innocently.

"No, Eddie." She continued to pace. *Should I go to the police? The FBI? The CIA?*

"I want to hear my mother sing."

She stopped dead in her tracks. It was suddenly crystal clear. Skylar knew what she had to do. And that was to get Eddie and his echo box the hell out of Harmony House. Beyond that, she didn't have a clue. But she did know what the first step was. "You know what, Eddie?"

"No, I don't." He had no idea what he was supposed to know.

"I want you to hear your mother sing, too."

"My father used to tell me she sang a lot when I was inside her stomach. Will you see if Dr. Fenton will give me permission to go to the house I grew up in?"

"I think we should go there right now."

He looked confused. "Right now?"

"Right now." She sounded certain. Defiant, even.

"Dr. Fenton said I should never try to leave without his permission."

"What if I told you he already gave me permission?"

He made his BUZZER sound. "Not true, Skylar." She had forgotten who she was talking to.

She spoke very carefully. "Eddie, what if I told you I didn't think it was safe for you here anymore?"

He listened intently. The statement was true. And, therefore, upsetting. "Why isn't it safe here anymore?" He glanced around nervously.

She looked him directly in the eyes. "You need to trust me on this for a little while. Can you do that?"

He thought for a moment. "Yes."

"I would never ask you to do anything I didn't think was in your best interest."

He nodded. *True.*

"Good. Let's go." She spoke quickly, deciding that time was of the essence. She immediately helped him pack up the echo box and the laptop.

"Are we going to walk there, Skylar?"

"No, I think it would be better if we drive."

"I don't know how to drive."

"That's okay. I do."

"Do you have a license?"

She nodded. "I do."

"Have you ever gotten a ticket?"

"Yes."

"What did you do wrong?"

"I was speeding."

"How fast were you speeding?"

"I don't remember, but it was faster than the posted limit."

Eddie took a moment to consider what he should do. "I have been told many times that everybody makes mistakes."

"Some more than others." She was thinking of her faith in Dr. Fenton.

He watched her with interest. "You are moving very fast. Are we in a hurry?"

"Yes, we are."

"Why?"

"Because I don't want anyone to try and stop us. The sooner we leave, the better."

Realizing it wasn't a true-or-false statement but a judgment, he took a moment to consider his response. He didn't like judgments. They were too hard to understand. But he did like Skylar. That much he was certain of. "Okay." Together, they quickly carried the echo box and laptop out of Marcus Fenton's office and headed toward the front entrance. "Skylar, do you know the address of where we are going?"

She paused. "No, but I have it in my office. Would you like to see it?"

"Yes, I would. Private spaces reveal much about people. My room is a good example. At least seventeen people have told me they've learned a lot about me just by being inside my room. I would like to know more about you, so, yes, I would like to visit your office."

They veered up the stairs. Eddie counted each one. Seventeen steps to reach the second floor. Thirty-one steps down the hall. Skylar's was the fifth office on the left. It looked out onto the yard where they had taken their walk to nowhere in particular. Eddie stared out the window as Skylar riffled through the papers in the many file boxes labeled *Parks, Edward*, searching for his childhood address. She couldn't find it. "Shit."

He practiced saying the word just like she had said it. "Shit. Shit. Shit."

She kept looking.

Eddie said, "Three seventeen West Susquehanna Avenue, Philadelphia, Pennsylvania, 19122."

"What's that?"

"The address."

"Why didn't you tell me you knew it?"

"You didn't ask. You asked if I wanted to see your office."

"Let's go." She led him quickly out the door and down the stairs.

Eddie counted the same number of steps in the hallway and down the stairs that he had counted on the way up. Thirty-one and seventeen. Nothing had changed. That was a relief.

They carried Eddie's equipment out the door and to her car. Skylar glanced toward the beige Impala, which remained empty. *Thank God.* She placed the echo box and the laptop supercomputer in her trunk, then opened the front passenger's door for Eddie.

"I haven't been inside a car in eight years, four months, and eleven days when I was taken to a dentist's office for minor oral surgery."

"There's no time like the present." She helped him into the seat.

"No, there is not. Every moment is unique and can never be repeated." She made sure he was buckled in before getting in the driver's seat. "Won't the security guard try to stop us, Skylar?" Eddie stared at the driveway guard, whose back was toward them, as Skylar pulled out of her parking space.

"I'm pretty sure he's only concerned about keeping people away." Her voice quivered. She was nervous.

And Eddie could hear it. Which made him uncomfortable. He clenched his hands and started to fidget, particularly when he saw the security guard's holstered sidearm. "Did you know the security guard has a gun?"

"Yes, I did."

"I will be scared if he tries to shoot us."

"I will be scared, too." The guard continued facing out, but Skylar decided not to take any chances. "Eddie, would you do me a favor, and put your hands over your ears for a minute?"

"Okay." He covered his ears and started counting seconds as Skylar hit the gas. *VROOM!* She accelerated past the gate before the guard ever had time to close it.

It took him a moment to process what had just happened. Then he grabbed his emergency phone. "Mr. Barnes, we have a problem."

CHAPTER 32

Michael Barnes's Office, Harmony House, May 27, 10:27 a.m.

The call from the Harmony House gate guard was nothing to panic over. Sitting in his office, Barnes asked the obvious question. "Why didn't you stop them?"

Barnes was not a man who riled easily. Over the course of his various careers in the military, law enforcement, intelligence, and security, he'd been shot at too many times to count. He'd been hospitalized from injuries sustained on seven different occasions, two of which were life threatening. He had pulled his own trigger more times than he could remember. Three different people he cared about had died in his arms. One was the only woman he ever really loved. That was thirteen years ago. It was only after she was gone that he'd been free to become the machine he was now.

The guard answered nervously. "I didn't see the vehicle until it was too late. My focus was on approaching traffic, not departing." He tried not to sound too guilty, or too apologetic, either. After all, it was his boss who had instructed him to focus on external threats and not internal ones.

Barnes was angry. Not at the gate guard. At Fenton. Barnes had warned him that something like this could occur. Warned him repeatedly. But Fenton refused to listen. He felt that too much internal security might make their patients feel threatened, which could inhibit their progress. And, after all, progress was the only reason they were there. So Barnes took the less visible approach of thoroughly investigating every single employee of the facility, as well as keeping tabs on each of them.

Barnes believed this current situation would be cause to change their security measures going forward, but this was a consideration that would have to wait. Now was a time for action. "Was the echo box in their possession?"

"Unknown, sir. The device was not in view, but they could have placed it inside the vehicle before I saw them."

Barnes turned to one of his many computers and typed in a series of instructions. An electronic map of Harmony House and the surrounding area appeared on the screen. Courtesy of the transmitter affixed to the right rear wheel well, a blip representing Skylar's Honda was seen moving away from Harmony House toward I-295. Barnes didn't worry about where she was going. He would find her no matter where she went. He speed-dialed Marcus Fenton at his home number.

Fenton was in the garden when his phone rang. "What?"

Barnes's voice was without emotion. "Something's happened." He went into the details, describing Skylar's exact arrival time and departure time with Eddie.

Dr. Fenton did not respond the way Barnes had expected him to. There wasn't even a hint of anger in the old man's voice. "You realize what this means, don't you?"

Barnes didn't feel like guessing. "Why don't you tell me, sir."

"It means the echo box is working."

This took Barnes by surprise. "How can you be sure of that?"

"Why else would she have taken him with her?"

"I can think of a number of reasons." He was principally thinking of grief and revenge, but was certain he could come up with a half dozen other motivations if he cared to.

"You don't know her like I do."

Barnes shook his head, deciding not to challenge his employer's hubris. "Enlighten me."

"There is no way she would put Eddie at risk unless something extraordinary occurred. She thinks either he's in danger, or that he can help her. The only reason she would think either was because he'd gotten the box to work."

Barnes didn't give the theory much credence, but didn't care to engage his superior on the matter, either. All he cared about was getting the patient and the doctor back where they belonged. That was his job, one he was so very good at. "I'm tracking her vehicle. I'll be dispatching a team to retrieve them and the device."

"Make sure they do it without upsetting Eddie or damaging the box."

"Copy that." He said it with sharp intensity. His mission parameters were clear: handle the doctor and the patient with kid gloves. With everyone else, use a chain saw, if necessary. Collateral damage was tolerable. Loose ends were not. Time was of the essence. He glanced at the electronic map where Skylar could be seen continuing toward I-295 as he contacted his two-man team, Charlie and Danger.

Charlie was Abraham Hirsch, a Tennessee boy who had been a budding MLB prospect until he threw out his arm during his senior year of high school. Danger was Merrill Lutz, a third-generation Army Ranger from Maryland who'd seen more than his fair share of special operations by the time he was approached by Michael Barnes.

This would be their first field test together. Each had accomplished a great deal in the clandestine arts separately before going to work for Barnes, but none of that mattered now. All that mattered was how they performed for him. In this moment. On this task.

The game was on.

CHAPTER 33

I-295 North, Outside Bellmawr, New Jersey, May 27, 10:29 a.m.

Skylar gripped the steering wheel tightly, repeatedly glancing in the rearview mirror of her Accord to see if anyone was following them as they sped north, following the signs to I-95. No one was. At least, no one she could see.

"Fifty-six . . . fifty-seven . . ." Eddie's hands were still over his ears as he finished counting seconds to one minute. He had been doing so ever since Skylar had asked him to put his hands over his ears for a minute as they sped past the Harmony House gate guard. As Eddie put down his hands, he cringed. "Does your engine always sound like this?"

"Like what?"

"Very high pitched and whiny and unpleasant."

She looked down to her speedometer to see that she was going almost a hundred miles per hour, and quickly slowed down to eighty. "I didn't realize how fast we were going."

"Why not?"

"I was distracted."

"By what?"

"I've got a lot on my mind." She thought of Jacob, and what he must have looked like lying dead on the subway tracks, cut in half; of

Dr. Fenton, and how fatherly he'd come off during their first interview. *What a bastard. What a cruel and heartless bastard.*

Eddie looked at the top of Skylar's head, searching for what was on her mind. "I don't see anything."

She glanced briefly toward him. "It's just an expression, Eddie."

"I don't like expressions."

"I meant to say that I was thinking about something else and got distracted."

"What were you thinking about?"

"A lot of different things."

Eddie nodded. "If you want help reading the speedometer, I can do it for you."

She nodded. "Great."

He leaned over to watch the fluctuations of the speedometer. "Eighty-two. Eighty-three. Eighty-four."

"Once a minute would be fine."

"I can also keep a log of the speeds, if you would like me to. Do you have a notebook and a number-two pencil I could use?"

She shook her head. "I don't."

"I have extra notebooks and pencils in my room at Harmony House. We could use those."

"No, Eddie. The logs can wait."

"I'll just memorize them, then." He nodded reassuringly. Once a minute for the rest of their drive, he would glance at the speedometer and mentally log their speed. He stared at the passing countryside out his window. He wasn't admiring the beauty so much as looking for something familiar. Something to latch on to. But most of the houses and buildings and malls were built after Eddie had arrived at Harmony House, and he had never left the grounds. Not once. The lack of familiarity was disconcerting. Things were different. That made him uncomfortable. And that was not good.

"Eddie, are you okay?"

"I want to go back to Harmony House." His hand started to twitch, like he was getting ready to slap himself.

"To get your notebooks?"

"I don't recognize any of these buildings." He pointed out the window. "Those offices weren't there before. Or that Burger King. Or that Shell station. None of this was here."

She took a deep breath and spoke with authority. "Eddie, please look at me."

"Why?"

"Because I am familiar to you. Look at me and nothing else. Can you do that?"

"I can try." He leaned closer to her so that she was all he could see. He couldn't look at her for very long, and certainly not in the eyes, but he was able to keep bringing his gaze back to her.

"Is that better?" She already knew the answer.

He blinked repeatedly. "You're pretty."

She remembered the first time they met. That was the second thing he ever said to her, right after he asked what she'd been feeling when she left Dr. Fenton's office after being hired. "You've said that before."

"People who are pretty get told that a lot. Do you get told that a lot, Skylar?"

"By you, I do." She smiled.

He kept staring at her as they got on the interstate. They quickly reached an interchange indicating that those traveling to Philadelphia should keep left. Eddie noticed the signs out of the corner of his eye as Skylar remained in the right lanes. "We're going the wrong way, Skylar."

"We need to make a stop first."

"Where?"

She hesitated for just a second. "New York City."

"I don't want to go to New York City. I went there once when I was six years old. It was too loud. People in New York City yell too much.

And honk their horns more than is necessary. The buildings are tall, and everything echoes. It's much louder than Philadelphia."

"We won't stay there very long, but there is someone in New York who can help us."

"How long is very long?"

"I don't want to give you a specific number, because I never want you to think I lied to you."

Eddie nodded, satisfied with her answer. "Why do we need help?"

"That is another thing you are going to have to trust me on."

"That is now two things."

"Yes, it is."

"Will there be more things you will ask me to trust you on, Skylar?"

"I don't know, Eddie. Probably."

He nodded, as if processing the information, but he was only responding that way because he'd seen other people do it. It was one of the many physical responses he'd practiced a great many times. "There is one good thing about New York City."

"What's that?"

"Carnegie Hall. Many people believe it has the greatest acoustics in the world. I can't say for sure because I have never been there, but I do know it was designed by an architect named William Tuthill in 1890. He was an amateur cellist who had what many people called a golden ear, which meant that he could hear things other people couldn't."

"Kind of like you."

He paused to consider the similarity. He had never thought of himself as having golden ears. He tried to look at his ears in the rear-view mirror. "Do you think I could build a concert hall like William Tuthill one day?"

"I think you could build an even better one."

"I should probably go to architecture school first. Then learn to play the cello and serve on the board of the Oratorio Society of New York, because that is where William Tuthill met Andrew Carnegie. He's the person who gave William Tuthill the money to build the hall, which is why it's called Carnegie Hall. Have you ever been there, Skylar?"

"Yes, I have."

"You're lucky."

Skylar could only shake her head. Lucky was the last thing she felt right now.

"Did you know the main hall has two thousand eight hundred and four seats?"

"No, I didn't."

"Did you know it was one of New York City's last big public buildings constructed entirely of brickwork with no steel frame, until one was added in the 1900s?"

"I do now."

"After we stop in New York City, can we still go to my old house in Philadelphia? I want to hear my mother sing."

"I promise we will."

"A promise is a promise."

"Yes, it is." She reached into her purse and fished for something. She withdrew a business card, which Eddie read.

"Who is Detective Butler McHenry?"

"A policeman. He's the person we're going to see in New York City."

"Are we in trouble?"

"No, Eddie."

He made his BUZZER sound.

She clarified. "We are not in trouble with the police."

"Who are we in trouble with?"

"People who are not the police."

Eddie's eyes opened wide with concern. "All of them?"

"No, Eddie. Only a few people."

"How is the detective going to help us?"

"I want him to hear the conversation you replayed in Dr. Fenton's office."

"Why?"

"Because I think he will be interested to hear it."

"Why?"

"I think it reveals that Dr. Fenton and the mystery man were involved in a crime."

His eyes perked up with curiosity. "What kind of crime?"

"I'd rather not say."

"Because the mystery man is none of my concern?"

"For now, Eddie. Only for now."

She dialed the number for the detective's mobile phone.

CHAPTER 34

Red's Sports Bar, Queens, New York City, May 27, 11:11 a.m.

Saturday was Butler McHenry's day off. At least, it was supposed to be. He couldn't remember a Saturday in months when something hadn't called him to duty, but he had a good feeling about today. He'd already taken a six-mile run at a respectable eight-minute-mile pace, in order to balance out all the beer he was going to drink the rest of the day. He had every intention of spending the next ten hours on his favorite stool in his favorite sports bar, drinking his favorite beer.

The name of the place was proudly announced in appropriately colored neon in the window. *Red's*. It was named after the bear of a proprietor, who was 6'5" when he stooped. Red, whose given name was Jameson Dulaney, got his nickname while playing defensive tackle at Wisconsin. Most of his family members hadn't been sure exactly where Wisconsin was before Jameson started sending home all kinds of red Badger gear. But soon enough, the only color his family could be seen wearing was red, which was how their son got his nickname.

Butler loved the place for its authenticity. It wasn't some fake TGI Friday's or one of those other prefab chains. The walls were decorated with all kinds of genuine Badger memorabilia and pictures from Red's

Badger career. Red falling on a Hawkeye fumble. Red crushing a Wildcat quarterback. Red standing over a fallen Wolverine. The bar was the kind of neighborhood joint where you stepped down half a flight of stairs when you entered. The old wooden floors were covered in peanut shells. Most of the patrons were cops, or former cops, which was the other reason Butler liked it. Red's father was a cop, and helped establish the bar's regular clientele. If you were a cop and lived in this part of Queens, this was where you did your drinking. And cops around here did a lot of it.

Butler was surveying the numerous televisions showing a variety of sporting events—including the third round of some golf tournament he'd never heard of, college softball, dirt-track auto racing, and bowling—when his cell phone rang. He hadn't even had his first sip of Rolling Rock, and he would soon be glad he hadn't. "Detective McHenry."

"Detective, this is Skylar Drummond. We met Wednesday night at Jacob Hendrix's apartment."

McHenry immediately recognized her voice. "Of course. What can I do for you?"

"I have some information I would like to share with you."

"What kind of information?"

"I'd rather not say over the phone."

He could hear that she was frightened, as well as desperately trying to hide it. "When would you like to meet?"

"Right now." Her voice quivered ever so slightly.

"Skylar, you sound scared. Are you in any danger?"

"I'm honestly not sure. I might be."

He sat upright. She had his full attention. "Tell me where you are."

"I'm driving northbound on the I-95."

"Why don't you find someplace to pull off, and I can meet you there."

"I'd rather keep going, if it's all the same to you. Can I come to you?"

"I'm in Queens."

"What's the address?"

((•))

As Butler McHenry gave her the location, she repeated the street number for Eddie to memorize. What neither Skylar nor the detective realized was that three other individuals had been listening to their conversation. One was Barnes, inside his basement office at Harmony House. The other two, Lutz and Hirsch, were listening on speakerphone as they accelerated toward Queens. Lutz was behind the wheel. Hirsch jotted down Butler's address on a notepad next to the computer on his lap. The screen showed the same map Barnes had in his office, which was tracking Skylar's present location.

He clicked off the speakerphone when the conversation ended. Hirsch spoke into another phone, which was connected to Barnes. "We're about seven minutes behind them."

"Get your ass in gear. I don't want her talking to this cop." Barnes hung up the phone, confident that Dr. Skylar Drummond, Edward Parks, and his device would be back on the grounds of Harmony House within the hour.

CHAPTER 35

Harmony House, Woodbury, New Jersey, May 27, 11:17 a.m.

On her afternoon rounds, Nurse Gloria had stopped by room 237 to check on Eddie, as she often did. There was no sign of him or the echo box. This was no cause for concern, until a quick stop by the cafeteria showed no sign of him there, either. She approached Jerome behind the counter. "Have you seen Eddie?"

"Not today."

Nurse Gloria was surprised. "You sure?"

"Sure as I can be. He's kind of hard to miss."

She nodded and headed to the two other places she thought Eddie might be: Dr. Fenton's office and Dr. Drummond's. Finding him in neither, she picked up a facility phone and dialed the extension for Security, to report the missing patient. Michael Barnes reported that Security was aware of the situation. "The patient was complaining of stomach pain and taken to a local hospital for observation."

"When did this happen?"

"Ten thirty-seven." He picked that time because he knew the nurse's workday had started at eleven.

"Why wasn't I notified?"

"It isn't protocol to notify you."

Nurse Gloria had never liked these security people. It was their combination of intensity and loyalty that made her uncomfortable. That, or just her innate fear of being discovered, which resulted in her approach to dealing with them: as little as possible. Today was an anomaly, just like the message she was going to send her secondary employer from the grounds of Harmony House. Her instructions were to send her communications at the end of the day from the confines of her residence, unless the matter was urgent. Gloria figured that Eddie and the box being off grounds qualified.

Her message read: EP & box off grounds. Location unknown. From the moment she hit "Send," it took less than fourteen seconds for notice of the encrypted transmission to appear on one of the screens in Michael Barnes's office. What Nurse Gloria could not have known was that any transmission that originated from or was received within the grounds of Harmony House was logged by the last man she would ever want to see it.

While the encryption might prevent him from reading the body of the message, the very fact that an encrypted transmission originated from within Harmony House immediately following her phone call to him was enough to set off all kinds of alarm bells.

Barnes saw the recipient's number, but knew that the number would be a dead end. Anyone clever enough to have engaged the nurse so surreptitiously would use a relay to forward the message again and again until the trail ran cold. The ultimate recipient could be anywhere in the world, and would never be known. But that didn't matter.

Nurse Gloria had made his job easy. And Michael Barnes was going to make sure that she paid for it dearly.

CHAPTER 36

American Heritage Foundation, Alexandria, Virginia,
May 27, 12:03 p.m.

Bob Stenson normally arrived at the American Heritage Foundation before seven in the morning, but he played doubles tennis on Saturday mornings, and then treated himself to a ninety-minute deep-tissue Swedish massage, so he didn't pull into the parking lot until after noon. He parked his Chrysler 300C, enjoying the crisp afternoon air as he entered the building. He was immediately approached by his most promising lieutenant, Jason Greers. "Sir, I tried reaching you on your cell . . ."

Stenson kept walking toward his office. "You know I take personal time on Saturday mornings."

"Yes, sir, I do." He followed his boss into his utilitarian office.

Stenson sat behind his desk. "So?"

"We got a message I thought you would like to know about right away." Barely able to contain his excitement, Jason handed him a copy of Gloria's text message.

Jason now had Stenson's attention. "You're correct." He read the brief message again, remaining perfectly calm.

Stenson had learned over the years never to get excited, because there was no such thing as checkmate in this never-ending game of chess. There were only moves and countermoves, day in and day out. Some had much greater significance than others, but the game would always continue. Which was why he could allow himself to play his weekly tennis and deal with any crisis when he got back to the office.

The echo box might be the exception to this, but Stenson agreed with the majority of the government scientists: he doubted the technology would ever work. Was it significant that the device was off Harmony House grounds? Possibly. But there were other things that were far more certain. "Did you happen to note the time the message came in?"

"Yes, 11:19." Jason Greers had a photographic memory.

"Do you know why that is significant?"

Jason thought for a moment. "Gloria Pruitt's shift started at 11:00, so Parks probably left the grounds sometime before she arrived. She must have immediately noticed Eddie and the box were missing, and texted us right away. Which was exactly what we had instructed her to do."

Stenson nodded. "Her diligence will also be her downfall. Barnes has that facility wired every which way to Sunday. He may not have been able to read the message, but I can promise you he now knows someone on their staff is playing for another team. It won't take him long to figure out who it is, if he hasn't already."

"There's no question he'll take her out." Greers spoke with certainty.

"He won't do it himself, but you're right." There was no emotion in Stenson's voice, because he had no emotional issue with letting Gloria Pruitt die. She was a chess piece about to be taken off the board, nothing more. And a pawn, at that. "He'll have it done tonight. Which means we have a choice to make."

"If we intervene, Barnes will recognize the scope of what he's up against and further fortify his position. It will require a great deal more effort to establish a new foothold inside Harmony House."

"Barnes is now aware that he has a security problem. He's going to batten down the hatches no matter what we do."

Greers grinned slyly, like he was about to reveal something big. "Have you considered the possibility that the echo box now actually works?"

Stenson cleared his throat. No, he hadn't. Jesus, he was slipping. "Jason, if we could confirm that, we would devote the entirety of our very considerable resources toward retrieving it."

Jason smiled with wonder. "It really would be astonishing, wouldn't it? If the echo box works, I mean."

"So astonishing that it's also highly unlikely."

The apprentice was determined to impress his mentor. "I've been thinking about how Edward and the box could have managed to leave Harmony House grounds."

"He didn't just walk off by himself."

"No, he didn't. He must have had help. And there is only one logical candidate."

"The new resident. Dr. Skylar Drummond."

"If our nurse's reports are accurate, he wouldn't trust anyone else enough to venture off facility grounds. This is the first time he's left."

"You're assuming Parks was conscious."

"If he wasn't, he could have been taken by anyone at Harmony House. But if he went willingly, there is only one person he would have left with."

"Have you confirmed that she was living with the victim of the subway event?"

The ambitious lieutenant nodded, certain that he had found the missing piece of the puzzle. "Quite a coincidence, don't you think?"

Stenson nodded, recognizing where Jason was going with this. "It's still a bit of a stretch."

"Michael Barnes is a psychopath. I wouldn't put it past him."

"He's a pit bull. He only does what Fenton tells him to. What reason could the good doctor have given him?"

"I can think of three. One is emotional. One is paranoid."

"What's the third?"

"That Fenton isn't paranoid. The professor might have exposed something, intentionally or otherwise."

The man in charge of the Foundation scratched his chin, recognizing the probability of a connection, which almost always meant there was one. "You think someone might have been running the professor?"

"Things had been going awfully smoothly for him," Greers suggested.

"They sometimes do without anyone's help. By all accounts, the young man was a star." He looked pointedly at Greers.

"Well, something seems to have put him on Fenton's radar."

Stenson considered the young medical resident who had just started working for Fenton. "The new resident didn't give herself much of a mourning period, did she?"

"The walls start to close in on you pretty quickly after a loved one passes."

Stenson was lucky. He'd never cared for anyone who'd died suddenly. He imagined that he wouldn't take it very well. That was one reason he'd been so impressed with Jason during his background check. The young man's fiancée had been killed by a drunk driver committing his fourth offense. Jason handled the loss stoically, which contributed to his being hired at the Foundation. Stenson had the offender killed as a little signing bonus for his new hire. To this day, Stenson had never acknowledged the deed.

He pieced the day's events together. "So she comes up for air, and decides to go to the office. But, as soon as she gets there, she does something that might end her career with Fenton. Why would she risk her dream job?"

"I've come up with several scenarios, but each involves Edward Parks successfully demonstrating the echo box. I believe he played something for her."

Stenson folded his arms behind his head. "What could she have heard that would make her want to risk everything?"

"The only way to answer that is to listen to the device for ourselves."

"That would kill two birds with one stone, wouldn't it?" Proving the box worked, and hearing what Skylar had heard.

"I believe the fact that she took Eddie Parks and his device off Harmony House grounds proves that the echo box is now functional."

Stenson shook his head in disagreement. "Edward Parks is known to have extraordinary hearing. He could have overheard something, which he then told the doctor. She could have taken Edward and his device to use as leverage."

Jason nodded. "Dangerous game. She has no idea what Fenton's capable of."

"She will soon enough."

Jason returned to the previous matter. "What do you want to do about the nurse?"

"What concerns me is how losing his mother might affect her son, Cornell." Gloria Pruitt's son was the X factor. While Bob Stenson still considered the echo box a long shot, he saw Cornell as a sure thing. He believed with complete confidence that Cornell could be the next great African American leader of the country.

That is, if the American Heritage Foundation had anything to do with it.

"She's all the family he has."

Stenson didn't care about the family issue. Strategically, anyway. "It could be an opportunity to bring a handler into his life."

Jason knew he meant a woman they controlled. "He isn't ready to settle down yet. He has too many oats to sow."

Stenson grinned slightly. "Yes, he does, doesn't he?" The man in charge of the American Heritage Foundation admired Cornell's prowess with women. Every great leader possessed it.

"I believe it's too soon to introduce ourselves to him directly."

"He doesn't have enough skeletons in his closet."

"Perhaps it's time we put some there."

Stenson immediately liked this idea. Liked it a lot. "Nothing too major, but something with enough gravitas that it would tarnish his otherwise-sterling reputation if it ever got out."

Jason jotted down a quick note. "Without the mother as our conduit, this could get messy."

"I don't like messy."

"Then the matter of intervention on her behalf is settled."

The boss nodded. "Send a team. Have them follow Ms. Pruitt home from Harmony House. Barnes might become impatient and act the moment she's off the grounds. They are to shield her from any knowledge of the threat, if possible."

Jason nodded, jotting down more notes. "Any preference who we use?"

"Get the baseball fans. The National League East guys. They shouldn't be more than a couple hours' drive."

"You do realize we could be stirring up a hornets' nest. There's no telling how Barnes will react when his people don't return."

Bob Stenson stared directly at the subordinate he viewed as a younger version of himself. "I'm of the opinion that Mr. Barnes is requiring more of our attention than he deserves." It was clear that Stenson had something in mind.

"I agree." His promising young lieutenant didn't yet know what his boss was thinking, but he was about to.

Stenson gave him a hint. "What do you do when a pit bull turns rabid?"

"You put him down." Jason now understood.

Stenson looked out the window, reflecting. "The most elegant solutions are always the simplest, aren't they?"

CHAPTER 37

I-295 South, Throgs Neck Bridge, May 27, 12:17 p.m.

Skylar and Eddie drove over the East River from the Bronx toward Queens on the Throgs Neck Bridge and then finally found their destination on Jamaica Avenue. Skylar parked in front of Red's, then quickly got out and checked to see if anyone had followed them. She didn't see anyone. She had no idea that the transmitter in her wheel well and the one inside her phone were broadcasting their location loud and clear.

Eddie got out of the passenger's seat and closed his eyes, slowly rotating his head from side to side. He didn't realize he was standing in the middle of the street until an oncoming car just barely avoided hitting him. HONK! The driver yelled out his window at the top of his lungs, "Freakin' moron! Get outta the road!"

Eddie panicked and started slapping himself. "Freakin' moron! Freakin' moron!"

He was on his fourth refrain by the time Skylar reached him. She gripped him firmly, holding his arms tightly until the fight left him, as Gloria would have said. "It's okay. Just take a few deep breaths."

He did so, then said, "I don't like it here. I want to go back to my room."

"We can't do that just yet. I need to speak with Detective McHenry for a few minutes."

"How many is a few?"

"I can't give you an accurate estimate until we see how this goes."

"Until we see how what goes?"

"My conversation with the detective. I want you to play for him what you played for me in Dr. Fenton's office. Would you do that, Eddie?"

He furrowed his brow and exhaled audibly, because that was what he'd seen people do when they acquiesced reluctantly. "Yes, I would do that."

She popped open the trunk and took the laptop supercomputer. Eddie took the echo box. Together, they approached the entrance.

"What is Red's, Skylar?"

"It's a sports bar."

"What's a sports bar?"

"A place for guys with nothing better to do."

They entered, walking down the half flight of stairs to the main floor. Eddie grimaced at the cacophony. Four different sports broadcasts fought with a dozen different conversations and a jukebox playing distorted Bob Seger. The oversized proprietor immediately moved toward the two strangers in his bar. Red addressed Skylar. "What's wrong with your friend?"

"I have been diagnosed with Asperger's syndrome, which falls within the high-functioning end of the autism spectrum."

Red looked like he'd just heard Mandarin. Skylar translated. "It's too loud for him in here."

"Why'd you bring him, then?"

"We're looking for Detective Butler McHenry." Red eyed her suspiciously. She added, "He's expecting us."

After a moment, he motioned down the bar. "He's the ugly guy who looks like an asshole."

"Not mine," Eddie said.

Red was speechless as Skylar and Eddie made their way toward Butler. "Hello, Detective."

He studied her quickly. "Hello, Skylar. What's going on?"

"This is Edward Parks, one of the patients at the facility where I work."

Eddie interjected. "Harmony House is a special place for special people."

"Hello, Edward. I'm Detective McHenry." Butler extended his hand to shake.

Eddie did not extend his hand. He just stared awkwardly at the detective's.

Skylar intervened. "Eddie doesn't shake hands. He's not comfortable with most forms of physical contact."

Butler nodded as pleasantly as he could. "Okay."

"Is there somewhere more private we can talk?"

The detective turned down the bar to Red. "You mind if I use the office for a minute?"

Red shook his head. "Don't mess anything up. I just had it cleaned."

Eddie made his BUZZER sound.

Red wasn't sure how to take it. "What was that?"

Butler answered, "He said your momma was good last night."

"That is not true, Detective. I've never even met his mother."

McHenry led Skylar and Eddie through a door marked "Private" at the rear of the bar. The small office was an absolute pigsty, but at least it was more quiet than in the bar.

"Not cleaned. Definitely not cleaned. You see?" Eddie ran his finger along the dusty desktop, just like Skylar's little brother, Christopher, used to do around the surfaces of their childhood home. With her mother out of the picture so early, and her father not much of a domestic, it was left to Skylar to keep the house clean. By Christopher's standards, she usually failed miserably, but did her best because dust made her brother uncomfortable, just like it was putting Eddie ill at ease now.

"I do see." Her tone was soothing, intended to calm Eddie down. It worked, at least to some degree.

Eddie watched the grainy black-and-white images on two old surveillance monitors. The video flickered through badly scratched glass. One angle showed the cash register. The other showed the bar's entrance. "Are places for guys with nothing better to do always so loud?"

McHenry stifled a smile. "For this place, that's actually quiet."

Skylar turned to Eddie. "Would you play him the last conversation you played for me when we were in Dr. Fenton's office?"

"Because he's a detective who is going to help us?"

"That's what I'm hoping for."

He stared at Butler for a moment and turned back to Skylar. "Yes." Eddie turned on the laptop, which took a moment to boot up.

Skylar explained to Butler, "What you're about to hear is a conversation that took place on Wednesday afternoon, approximately four hours before the incident in the subway occurred." She said it in such a way that the detective understood Eddie did not know about Jacob Hendrix's death, and that she did not want him to.

"Where did this conversation take place?"

"In my boss's office at Harmony House. His name is Dr. Marcus Fenton."

"Was he aware the conversation was being recorded?"

Eddie chimed in quickly. "The conversation was not recorded."

"You lost me."

Eddie immediately launched into his lecture. "The basis for sound-wave retrieval and reconstruction, which is called acoustic archeology, has existed since 1969. We just haven't had equipment sensitive enough to acoustically map an enclosed space or the computing speed necessary to re-create the original sound wave." He paused for emphasis, just like he had in the recreation room at Harmony House. "Until now."

Detective McHenry turned to Skylar. "What the hell is he talking about?" He didn't notice the two men who could be seen entering the bar on the two old black-and-white monitors.

((•))

Red's was a locals-only bar. And it was a cop bar. If someone new wasn't either, every set of eyes in the place was on them until an acceptable explanation as to their presence was given. Red knew when he approached Skylar and Eddie that they weren't going to be trouble. The opposite was true when he moved toward Lutz and Hirsch. "Can I help you?"

Hirsch eyed the massive bartender. "We're looking for Detective Butler McHenry."

The bar quieted ever so slightly, but Red didn't flinch. "Never heard of him." He returned to cleaning glasses behind the bar.

Lutz didn't appreciate the lack of cooperation. "Are you the proprietor?"

Red positioned himself next to one of the photographs on the wall in which he was clearly identified. "Good guess." He glanced behind the bar, where his trusty baseball bat was located. From the dings and dents in the bat's surface, he was obviously not afraid to use it.

Down the bar, another off-duty detective quickly typed in a text message on his phone: You've got company.

((•))

Inside Red's office, Butler felt his phone vibrate as Eddie babbled. When the detective read the message, he glanced at the security monitors.

The two strangers were talking to Red. He interrupted Eddie's lecture, addressing Skylar. "Do you know who those guys are?"

Skylar's face went white. "They work at Harmony House. In security."

Eddie looked confused. "How did they know we were here, Skylar?"

"I had a feeling we were being followed."

"What kind of feeling?"

"I'll explain it later. Eddie, just play the conversation you played for me earlier."

He nodded and clicked "Play" on the laptop. Eddie had managed to clean up some of the harmonic distortion, which made the conversation sound clearer than it had previously:

FENTON: *Mr. Barnes, to what do I owe the pleasure?*

BARNES: *Your new doctor's boyfriend has been looking into Eddie.*

McHenry looked to Skylar. "By *new doctor*, is he referring to you?"

Skylar nodded.

"Who's the guy talking to your boss?"

"We believe he's head of Harmony House security."

Eddie chimed in quickly. "His name is Mr. Barnes, but I call him the mystery man because he's very mysterious."

FENTON: *What have you got?*

Papers could be heard flipping.

BARNES: *Either she's got loose lips or he's been sticking his nose where it doesn't belong.*

Skylar grew increasingly nervous. "Eddie, skip forward a little."
He did so.

BARNES: *Will you want to know the details?*

FENTON: *Nothing in his residence. Make it look like an accident.*

BARNES: *He takes the subway.*

FENTON: *All kinds of bad things happen in subways these days. I'm sure you'll figure something out.*

"Eddie, that's enough." Skylar's hands were trembling as she turned to McHenry. "What do you think?"

The detective stared at the echo box in amazement. "I think it's going to be a while before I get to enjoy any Rolling Rock." He paused. "This is for real?"

She nodded. "I need your help."

McHenry believed her. "First things first." He typed a response to the text message: Get them out of here.

On the surveillance monitor, the detective who received the message looked directly into one of the security cameras and nodded.

$$((\cdot))$$

In the bar, the detective made his way through the crowd of fellow officers, patting them on the shoulders. "Hey, Red, why don't you give the fellas a couple on the house?" He might as well have said, "Lock and load, boys."

Six off-duty officers and detectives joined him, surrounding the strangers.

Red answered the detective. "I did. Said they weren't interested."

"Then what are they doing here?"

"Looking for a Butler McHenry. Ever heard of him?"

"Can't say that I have. Any of you?" He turned to the others, who all shook their heads. "Looks like you two are shit out of luck."

It was a standoff. Hirsch and Lutz knew they weren't going to get anything from these guys. Cops were a tight fraternity. Almost as tight as former intelligence operatives. Hirsch never broke eye contact as he and Lutz backed toward the door. "Luck changes."

Outside the bar, they walked toward their vehicle. Lutz was not pleased. "You know they're in there."

"Of course they are."

"Assholes thought they were cute."

"We would have done the same thing."

"How do you want to handle it?"

"We wait. They have to come out sometime." They moved to the rear of the car.

"And if they don't?"

"We go back in." He opened the trunk, revealing a rather astonishing arsenal. Instead of weapons, they grabbed protein bars and energy drinks, preparing to wait as long as it took.

CHAPTER 38

Red's Sports Bar, Queens, New York City, May 27, 1:01 p.m.

Eddie studied Skylar as she stared at the security monitors inside Red's office. "Skylar, why are your hands shaking?"

"Because I'm a little nervous."

"Why are you a little nervous?"

"There's a lot going on, Eddie."

"You mean, more than us standing with a New York City Police detective in a cramped and dusty office?"

"Yes."

Butler turned to Skylar. "Does he always talk like that?"

She nodded. "Pretty much."

Eddie was confused. "Talk like what?"

"The detective was commenting that you have a unique way of communicating, and I was agreeing with him."

Eddie nodded, imitating her. "Pretty much." He turned to the detective. "I am not very good at nonverbal forms of communication, but that is something Skylar has been trying to teach me. We walked to nowhere in particular."

"How long did it take you to get there?"

Skylar stifled a smile as Eddie answered, "I don't know. We didn't time it."

Butler waited for him to get the joke, which, of course, he didn't. Skylar jumped in. "I think he was teasing you, Eddie."

The detective corrected her. "No, I really want to know how long it took."

Eddie made his BUZZER sound.

Skylar explained, "If you say something that isn't true, he does that."

Butler's eyes widened. "Every time?"

She nodded. "Every time."

Butler shook his head. Just what he needed. He texted the detective in the bar: They still out there?

His friend nodded toward the security camera, then nodded toward the entrance.

Butler typed: Distract them.

His NYPD brother nodded again, then turned to the off-duty officers around him.

((•))

Sitting alone in his government-issued vehicle, Lutz grew increasingly impatient as he waited outside Red's. It had been over an hour. Hirsch was around the corner, standing in the alley behind the bar, watching the only other exit. He checked in with his partner in the car. "Anything?"

"Nada."

"How soon do you want to make a move?"

"Soon as boss man says so." Lutz hung up and listened to sirens passing as he dialed Michael Barnes. Some were far off in the distance, others within a few blocks. Maintaining sanity in Queens meant learning to tune out the erratic but never-ending urban cacophony.

Barnes answered the phone in his office on the first ring. "Any change?"

"Negative. They're still inside."

"Continue holding your position. I want this thing contained."

"Copy that." Lutz clicked off the phone, still ignoring one of the approaching sirens, until the New York City Fire Department ambulance pulled up right alongside his car and parked, blocking him in. Two paramedics hopped out and opened the rear doors to remove a gurney. They quickly wheeled it toward the entrance to Red's.

Lutz stepped out of his vehicle, speaking loudly. "What the hell?"

The ambulance driver glanced over briefly. "Medical emergency." He continued into Red's.

Lutz speed-dialed his counterpart in the alley. "We have a situation."

"You want company?"

"Stay there." He walked briskly inside Red's, moving toward the crowd circled around someone lying on the peanut-shell-covered floor. It was one of the off-duty officers, who was being tended to by the two paramedics. "What happened?"

One of the more senior detectives turned toward Lutz. "None of your business."

The former intelligence operative stared him down. "I can make it my business."

Red stepped toward him, baseball bat in hand. "You sure you want to do that?"

One of the paramedics screamed rather convincingly as he worked on the fallen cop. *"He's having a heart attack!"*

The escalating drama was visible on the security monitors inside the private office. Lutz could not see that, behind him, the detective who'd arranged the whole thing was quietly exiting the bar.

Eddie turned to Skylar. "Why did you give that man your phone and keys?"

(((•)))

Outside the bar, the detective unlocked Skylar's Honda and got into the driver's seat. He put her phone on the passenger's seat and took off quickly.

Lutz could not see the car speeding down the street. His cell phone rang. It was Barnes. "Yes, sir."

"Why aren't you following them?"

"They're still here."

On the electronic map inside Barnes's office, Skylar's car was speeding away from the bar. "No, they're not."

Lutz glanced out the window to see that the Honda was gone. Determination filled his voice. "They won't get far." He bolted out of the bar and jumped into his car, which was still blocked in by the ambulance. But not for long. *Wham!* He slammed into the car parked in front of him, pushing it forward a foot. *Wham!* Then he did the same thing to the car behind.

Hearing the collisions, Hirsch came barreling out of the alley as Lutz maneuvered onto the sidewalk. Hirsch jumped into the passenger's seat. "What the hell?"

Lutz motioned to the empty space where Skylar's car had been parked.

"How'd they get out?"

"Fuck if I know." He punched the gas, and the car screeched back onto the street as they resumed their pursuit of Skylar's vehicle.

(((•)))

Inside the bar, one of the cops who'd been acting concerned over his fallen comrade tapped one of the paramedics on the shoulder. "Show's over."

The guy who'd been faking the heart attack opened his eyes and started dusting the peanut shells off his flannel shirt. "If my car is one of the ones that prick just rammed, he's gonna be awful sorry."

Red moved to the office door and knocked twice. McHenry opened the door, giving a nod of appreciation to all in the room. No words were exchanged.

Skylar and Eddie followed him out of the office. They carried the laptop and the echo box with them. Eddie paused, staring blankly at the paramedics. "Why did you pretend to help him if you knew he wasn't having a real heart attack?"

The paramedic clearly did not appreciate Eddie's lack of gratitude. "As I understand it, we were saving your ass."

Eddie looked behind himself, trying to see his own backside.

Skylar apologized to the paramedics. "Eddie, just say thank you to these nice men for helping us."

Eddie did so. The paramedic turned to McHenry. "This guy for real?"

Eddie chimed in. "I am flesh and blood and teeth and bones and—"

Skylar jumped in. "They were only acting, Eddie."

"Acting is pretending, and pretending is lying, and lying is not something paramedics should do because they are like doctors and doctors shouldn't lie."

"I'm a doctor, and sometimes I lie."

Eddie seemed genuinely shocked. "You do?"

"Everybody has to lie sometimes."

"I don't."

"If you spend enough time outside Harmony House, you will, trust me."

Butler could feel his colleagues' frustration rising. "Dr. Drummond, we need to get your patient out of here before one of my guys kills him."

She and Eddie followed the detective out the door. "Skylar, have you ever lied to me?"

"No, Eddie, I haven't. And I hope I never have to."

"Why would you have to?"

"Because things get complicated."

"Why?"

"They just do."

Crossing the street toward Butler's Chevy Tahoe, Eddie remained extremely cautious. He looked both ways, then took a step. Then looked both ways again. He was doing everything he could to avoid another near miss.

Butler turned to Eddie in disbelief. "You mind speeding it up a little?"

Eddie continued moving along with incredible caution. "I don't like it here at all."

The detective was quickly reaching his threshold, Skylar recognized. "Eddie, the sooner we get out of here, the sooner you can hear your mother's voice."

Eddie jumped into the back seat of Butler's SUV. Skylar buckled him in and got in the front passenger's seat. Butler punched the gas, SCREECHING out of the parking space. Eddie covered his ears. "This car hurts my ears."

Skylar turned to Butler. "Where are we going?"

"My precinct. I want my lieutenant to hear what—"

Eddie interrupted. "Skylar, I'm hungry. Is it time for afternoon snack yet?"

She checked her watch: 1:07 p.m. Afternoon snack at Harmony House had been served seven minutes ago. "Yes, it is, Eddie. We'll get you something at the police station."

"Saturday-afternoon snack is graham crackers and milk."

Skylar knew the answer to the question she was about to ask the detective, but went ahead anyway. "They wouldn't happen to have graham crackers and milk at your station, would they?"

"You're kidding, right?"

Eddie imitated him. "You're kidding, right?"

Butler managed to contain himself. "No, there aren't any graham crackers and milk."

Skylar tried to be helpful. "There must be some kind of snack."

"Only what's in the vending machines. Candy bars, and whatnot."

"Candy bars are high in sugar, high in calories, and low in nutritional value. They are not an appropriate snack, Detective McHenry."

Skylar intervened. "Is there somewhere we can stop on the way?"

He eyeballed her incredulously. "You're not serious."

"Any deviation from his regular routine is a genuine hardship for him."

"Whoever those guys are coming after you, they're out here looking for you. Right now. You get that, right?"

"I do." Realizing she was never going to reach him with compassion, she took a more practical approach. "It'll only take a minute, and you'll find him a lot less annoying."

Butler couldn't help but shake his head, eyeing the road ahead for the nearest convenience store. The New York Police Department had finally caught a break in their investigation of the subway gas attack, the headline story of every national paper for the last three days, and the lead detective on the case was about to stop and buy graham crackers and milk.

CHAPTER 39

Barnes watched the pursuit from his office. Hirsch and Lutz's car was quickly closing in on Skylar and Eddie.

Inside the pursuit car, Lutz finally got close enough to catch a glimpse of the driver. It was not Skylar. "Son of a bitch." He slowed down quickly and cranked a U-turn, heading back to the bar.

Barnes called within eight seconds. Hirsch answered, "It was a decoy. We're heading back to the bar."

"Don't waste your time. They're already gone." Barnes's tone was ice. He glanced at his computer screen, where an array of personal information about Detective Butler McHenry appeared. Former US Army Ranger, 1998–2004. Member of the NYPD since 2005. Decorated twice. Suspended once. The more Barnes read, the more he didn't like it. McHenry had both training and experience. Barnes needed to find Skylar and Eddie now, before this situation escalated any further. "If cops are driving her car, McHenry is now driving them. Keep your eyes out for a blue Chevy Tahoe, New York plate George-David-Romeo-six-seven-zero-three. I'm sending you directions to his residence."

"You really think he's that dumb?"

"He's a cop, isn't he?"

CHAPTER 40

Eddie followed behind Skylar and Detective McHenry as they walked quickly up and down the narrow aisles inside Jorge's Quick Stop, looking for graham crackers. They were still in Queens. The bare fluorescent tubes above them flickered intermittently. Eddie was the only one of the three who didn't seem to be in a hurry. "Where are the graham crackers, Skylar?"

Skylar tried to break the news gently. "I think they're out of them."

"This is bad. Very bad." His breathing grew more rapid as he started to panic. McHenry watched with increasing concern.

Skylar knew Eddie was about to lose it. She moved so that she could look him directly in the eyes. He tried to look away, but she managed to keep his gaze. "If they don't have them here, we will find them somewhere else. I promise."

Eddie veered abruptly away from a grape-juice display, keeping his distance from the stacks of purple beverages.

Butler picked up a box of Nilla Wafers. "How about these?"

"Those are not graham crackers."

"I know they're not graham crackers. I was offering you an alternative."

"I don't want an alternative. I want graham crackers. And milk."

The detective had lost his patience. "Well, that's just too bad."

Eddie paused uncomfortably. "I don't like it here."

"Then we'll go to another store," Skylar reassured him.

"I won't like it in there, either, Skylar. I don't like it anywhere outside Harmony House." His hands twitched. Ready to claw himself.

Skylar moved abruptly toward him. "Eddie, look at me. Right now. Look at me and nothing else." She was right in his face. Studying him. But not touching him. She kept his gaze until the tension finally left his body. "Better?"

Eddie nodded, only to realize, "I'm still hungry."

Butler went up to the Puerto Rican clerk behind the counter; his name tag read *Jorge*. Butler confirmed what he already knew. The store had plenty of booze and cigarettes, but not the one item they needed. Butler turned to Skylar. "Does it have to be graham crackers?"

Eddie corrected him. "Graham crackers and milk."

At least they carried milk, so Skylar quickly paid for a carton. It was larger than the ones served inside Harmony House, but Skylar assured Eddie she would pour him the proper serving.

Butler shook his head. "Let's go."

CHAPTER 41

American Heritage Foundation, Alexandria, Virginia,
May 27, 1:22 p.m.

Caitlin McCloskey's office inside the American Heritage Foundation displayed the kinds of images typical of a young working mother: photos of her two small children and her lawyer husband, and their family Christmas card from last year. She looked like an accountant or a private-school teacher or a corporate communications director. In fact, early in life, before she came to understand what her father actually did for a living, Caitlin was quite certain she was going to be one of those things. But from the moment her father, one of the seven original founders of the Foundation, pulled back the curtain and revealed what he did—and the opportunity she had within the firm—there was never a thought about another career. The power and control were addictive. Especially on days like today.

She was on the phone with a man whose real name she did not know. She did not want to know it almost as much as she didn't want him to know hers. Because this man killed people for a living. He and his partner had done the job for them at least a dozen times that she knew of. The two men had no idea who their employers were, because it was inconsequential, as long as they were paid. Half upfront, the other half upon completion.

The pair's former general had made the anonymous introduction shortly after both were honorably discharged from the United States Army, using only code names the assassins had chosen: Phillies fan was "Giles," and Mets fan was "Murphy." One party had an urgent need; the other party had a unique skill set that could fill that need, which was all either side wanted to know. The general had suggested a standard fee of $50,000, which both parties accepted. The pair's first assignment for their unknown employer was a relatively easy breather: a troublesome investigative reporter needed to disappear on a camping trip in Canada. They were told who the subject was and when and where the job was to be done. The mission went off without a hitch, and thus began an exclusive relationship that was going on eight years now.

The general had made it clear to both parties that, going forward, special circumstances could warrant a loftier price tag. New York congressman Henry Townsend was a good example. Due to the high-profile nature of the subject, and the urgency with which the job had to be handled, the price was $250,000.

Every job would start like this: A call was made to a particular encrypted mobile phone in the killers' possession, which was never used for any other purpose. No one else had this number. The caller would describe the job and all pertinent details. The service providers would evaluate the task and respond with a price. There was never any negotiation.

Both sides of the transaction had a simple understanding: if the employer was not comfortable with the price, the call would be terminated, as would the relationship. The same would be true for any failure on the contractors' part. There was no room for error in this line of work. Failure was simply not an option.

For this evening's efforts, they had quoted their standard rate of $50,000, even though there was a strong likelihood of multiple subjects being involved. The pair kept the price to their minimum because they felt they'd recently pushed their employers a bit too far by pricing the New York congressman at a quarter of a million dollars. Yes, they had their client over a barrel. Yes, there really wasn't anyone else their patron could have turned to in that moment. But even killers knew not to get greedy. There were at least half a dozen other teams operating in this part of the world, and they didn't want to ruin a good thing. They only had one employer. It was all they needed. The pair wanted to keep this client, whoever it was, happy. So they priced tonight's work at base level, which was correctly viewed as a giveback and immediately accepted.

Caitlin watched real-time satellite views on her numerous computer screens. One showed the Harmony House grounds and surrounding vicinity. A vehicle had stopped on the side of the road one hundred yards from the facility entrance. The driver had popped the hood of his sky-blue Jeep Wagoneer and appeared to be checking the engine. As Caitlin zoomed in her view, the Philadelphia Phillies cap of the driver became visible. The resolution was astonishing. She could even make out some sort of player's signature on the brim. It looked like the last name was Nola, but she couldn't be sure. Baseball had never interested her much. She told the man, "You should receive confirmation from your bank any second."

On-screen, Giles checked his regular cell phone, an iPhone 8. He had just received a message from his Swiss bank, Banque Pasche, confirming that his account had received a wire originating from the United States for $25,000. "Good to go." He hung up, then called his partner, who was parked outside Gloria Pruitt's modest but well-kept home. Caitlin did not have nearly as clear a view of him, because of the dense trees around Gloria's house, but she knew he was there. His Mets cap had been momentarily visible when he got out of his car.

Jason Greers poked his head inside Caitlin's office. "Show about to start?"

"Not until tonight. Giles is outside Harmony House, just in case. Murphy is scoping out Gloria Pruitt's house, doing recon." She pointed to the screens with the various views.

"Where do you think Barnes will make his move?"

"Inside her home. No question."

"Why do you think?"

"He'll want to send a message that the gloves are off. Inside, they'll have more privacy." She said it without emotion. Because she told herself it was just business. How long she could keep telling herself that was a matter of conjecture.

Jason nodded. "Absolutely. No question." She was smart, and he wanted to make sure she knew he appreciated it. "You going to tell them that?" He smiled ever so slightly.

She smiled right back. "I thought I'd leave that suggestion to you." *Tell two of the world's best assassins how to do their job. Yeah, right.*

CHAPTER 42

Ninetieth Avenue, Queens, New York City, May 27, 1:45 p.m.

Detective Butler McHenry gripped the wheel tightly, repeatedly glancing in his rearview mirror to make sure they were not being followed. Eddie stared out his window at the row of dilapidated, old houses that were once fine middle-class homes.

The area was ripe for gentrification. Developers were just waiting for the elderly owners to kick the bucket so they could swoop the properties up from the heirs. Detective McHenry would eventually be one of those former owners, but he hoped it wouldn't be anytime soon.

Eddie noticed a dead bug on the rear passenger's window of McHenry's Tahoe. He tried to clean it off, only to smear its entrails, making it worse. He rolled down the window, and decided the button was far more interesting than the urban squalor around them. Up, down. Up, down. He'd stick his head out the window, then pull it back in. Out, then in. The difference in sound would be striking to anyone. To Eddie, it was like two different worlds.

The detective glanced at Eddie, struggling to get a handle on the adult who was acting like a preschooler in his back seat. "You mind if I ask how old you are?"

"Twenty-seven years, three months, twenty-five days, and what time is it?"

Butler glanced at his watch. "About one fifty."

"And five hours and fifty minutes, approximately. How old are you, Detective?"

"Thirty-eight and change."

"What kind of change?"

"I meant a little older than thirty-eight."

"Why didn't you say that?"

McHenry shook his head, reminded why he didn't like kids—and liked adults who acted like them even less. He vowed to talk to Eddie as little as possible.

Skylar turned back to her patient as he continued sticking his head out the window. "Eddie, please don't do that."

"I like the way it feels on my face."

"It isn't safe."

"Why isn't it safe?"

She decided not to mention that there were highly trained members of Harmony House's security staff out there looking for them. "You could accidentally press the button the wrong way, and your head could get stuck."

"What would happen if my head got stuck?"

"It would hurt a lot. And I don't want that to happen."

"I don't, either." He rolled up the window.

Skylar stared out her window at the well-worn neighborhood. "Detective McHenry, where are we going?"

"To get his graham crackers, so we can get to the station."

"And then we're going to Philadelphia, right?" Eddie leaned over the front seat between them.

Skylar answered, "Not just yet, Eddie. But soon."

"How soon?"

"I'll be able to give you a specific answer as soon as I have a private conversation with Detective McHenry."

"Because it involves the mystery man, and he is none of my concern?"

"Yes, Eddie. For the time being."

The detective was curious. "What's in Philly?"

"He wants to hear his mother sing."

McHenry nodded, adding it to the list of things he would be asking her as he pulled into the narrow driveway of his own mother's house.

"Is this your place?" Skylar asked.

"Do I look like I would have graham crackers in my cupboard?"

"Right next to the Budweiser."

In the back seat, Eddie began humming the brand's old jingle.

"It's my mother's house."

"This is where you grew up?" said Skylar.

Butler nodded. "We're only staying here long enough to get him his crackers." He got out and walked briskly toward the house, only to realize Eddie was not following. He was standing still in the driveway, doing his usual head rotation with his eyes closed. Wind WHISTLED through the branches of a dying elm tree. An old swing set that had been rusting for thirty years SQUEAKED lightly in the yard. Traffic could be heard all around them, including a lot of big rigs. The Cross Island Parkway was only a few blocks away.

McHenry was becoming annoyed. "He does realize we're in a hurry, doesn't he?"

Skylar explained, "He has to familiarize himself with every new environment."

Eddie had heard enough. "I don't like it here."

Skylar watched him closely. "Why not?"

He kept his eyes closed as he answered. "I don't hear any birds. Not a bluebird, not a sparrow, not even a starling."

"What do you hear?"

"A squeaky swing set. Old dogs. Four of them. There is a highway approximately five blocks away. There are a lot of trucks on the highway. Most of the trucks are at least ten years old. Some of them are much older."

McHenry looked at him with interest. "How can you tell how old the trucks are?"

"New trucks sound different from old trucks, just like young people sound different from old people." Eddie stopped rotating his head and opened his eyes.

"Are you comfortable yet?" Skylar knew not to push.

"I'm hungry."

Skylar nodded slightly. "I'll take that as a yes." Eddie carried his precious devices and followed McHenry into the house.

The detective picked up several days' worth of mail, which was strewn around the faded hardwood floor of the entryway below the mail slot. The home's decorations and furnishings were from another era. Wallpaper that was once white was now a mild yellow. The Formica countertops were well worn. The dining-room table was noticeably warped, and the rug in the kitchen had dozens of stains of all variety and vintage. The house was a time capsule. "I just had to put my mother in a home. She couldn't take care of herself after she broke her hip."

"I can't take care of myself, either."

McHenry led them into the kitchen and searched through the cupboards until he found a box of graham crackers. "Bingo."

"What does *bingo* mean?"

"It's something you say when you find what you're looking for."

Eddie turned toward Skylar. "Bingo."

For just a second, he looked her in the eyes. Not because he was instructed to, like he had been in so many practice exercises with so many different doctors over the years. He did it because he wanted to see her reaction. Because it mattered to him. Because he felt connected to someone for the first time in his life.

Skylar caught it. Felt it in her spine. She had been on alert for such a moment ever since their walk to nowhere in particular, but she honestly hadn't expected it this soon. She had once shared a similar moment with her younger brother, Christopher, but that had taken years. It happened just before she went to college, which was incredibly unfortunate. Skylar had reached him just before she had to leave him, and he never recovered from it. Skylar never forgave herself for his death, which had everything to do with the emptiness she'd felt all these years.

As she returned Eddie's gaze, she promised herself she would not allow the same thing to happen to him. In fact, she swore on her life. She would rather die than see anything happen to him. Because if she couldn't save him, she could never save herself. And she'd been living in a cell of her own making for quite long enough.

That, and, given the circumstances, she needed someone to cling to.

Butler handed Eddie the box of graham crackers. "Can we go now?"

"I haven't eaten my afternoon snack yet."

"You can eat in the car."

Eddie stared at him. "Is that a joke, Detective McHenry?"

"Do I look like I'm joking?"

Eddie studied the man's face closely. "I have difficulty interpreting facial expressions."

Skylar put her hand on Butler's shoulder. "Just . . . let him eat here. We'd only have to pull over, anyway. Trust me."

She asked the detective if there was a glass Eddie could use. He gave her one, and she carefully poured Eddie a six-ounce serving of milk. She then removed two graham-cracker sheets from the box and handed them to him. Eddie broke one of the large rectangular pieces into two squares, then broke each of the squares into two smaller rectangles. He did the same with the second sheet and neatly stacked the eight small rectangles on top of each other. After placing a napkin on his lap, he took a bite of graham cracker and chewed it carefully. "Three. Not fresh." He took another bite and a sip of milk. "Four. This milk is just the right temperature. Nice and cold."

Skylar was about to explain, when Butler cut her off. "I don't even want to know."

She smiled slightly. "Eddie, I would like to speak to Detective McHenry privately for a few minutes. Would you mind staying here?"

"How many minutes is a few?"

"Not more than fifteen."

He scanned the kitchen for any visible signs of purple food. There were none he could see. "No, I would not mind."

They left Eddie alone in the kitchen with the echo box to enjoy his graham crackers and milk while they spoke in the hallway. Skylar glanced at the numerous family photos on the walls. She focused on several of Butler with two small children. "These your kids?"

Butler nodded. "Clayton's my son. He's thirteen now. Katherine's nine."

"They're beautiful."

"They live with their mother in Colorado Springs." His voice was tense.

"How often do you get to see them?"

"Not as much as I'd like." It was clear he wanted to change the subject.

She turned to an older picture, which featured Butler when he was about the same age as his son was now. He stood beside a muscled, stern-looking man. "Your father?"

"Stepfather." His eyes went cold. "How about you start from the beginning so even an idiot like me can understand what the hell is going on."

CHAPTER 43

Butler McHenry's Townhome, Queens, New York City,
May 27, 2:06 p.m.

Lutz and Hirsch peered inside the windows of Butler's town house. The lights were off. No car in the driveway. Didn't look like anyone was home. They walked around back to the kitchen door. Lutz scanned the neighbors' houses as Hirsch went to work on the lock. They were inside McHenry's residence in less time than it took most people to find their keys.

With well-rehearsed precision, they fanned out through the house. Butler wasn't there. Lutz called Barnes. "Nobody's home."

"Enough hide-and-seek. Let's make him come to us."

"How, sir?"

"I'm reporting to Homeland Security that New York Detective Butler McHenry is harboring fugitives in possession of stolen classified technology. Federal warrants will be issued for all three."

"Hard core. Love it." Lutz actually thought it was dumb as hell, but a little ass kissing seemed to be in order.

"It won't take long for McHenry's lieutenant to contact him and ask what the hell is going on. The detective will try to explain and get nowhere. He'll be ordered to report to his precinct, which he'll agree to because he'll want to play the box for them."

"Doesn't it concern you what they might hear?"

"Anything they hear would be inadmissible. But they're not going to hear anything, because you'll intercept them outside the precinct and take them into your custody."

"On our way." Hirsch and Lutz exited the way they came, locking the door behind them. McHenry would never know anyone had been there.

CHAPTER 44

McHenry's Mother's House, Queens, New York City,
May 27, 2:09 p.m.

Skylar had been talking to Butler for just over twelve minutes when she completed her account of recent events. He hadn't stopped pacing the entire time. The more he heard, the more anxious he became. Detective McHenry was now sure of only one thing. He was in way over his head. "The only shot you have at going after your boss will be to prove this mystery guy acted under his instructions, but that's never going to happen."

"Why not?"

"He killed Professor Hendrix in front of eighty-seven people, and no one can describe him any better than 'He was a homeless guy with a beard.' Whoever he is, he's a professional. We'll be lucky to ever find him, much less arrest him."

"If you're trying to scare me, it's working."

"I'm not trying to scare you, just trying to help you realize what we might—"

He stopped talking as they heard glass breaking inside the kitchen. Quickly followed by screaming.

Butler responded on instinct, lightning fast. "Stay here." He had his weapon out and was racing down the hall before Skylar could react.

"Like hell." Going after him, all she could think of was that if any harm came to Eddie, she would never forgive herself.

She arrived in the kitchen a moment behind Butler to find Eddie sitting calmly by himself at the table. His graham crackers and milk were gone. Eddie became terrified when he saw McHenry pointing his gun around the room. Eddie started screaming, "Don't shoot! Don't shoot!" The food in his mouth sprayed everywhere as he slapped himself repeatedly. SLAP! SLAP! SLAP!

The detective was dumbfounded as Skylar rushed to Eddie, wrapping her arms around him as tightly as she could. "Shh."

Eddie was hysterical. "Don't shoot! Don't shoot!"

She continued holding him, trying to sound as reassuring as she could. "He wasn't going to shoot you, Eddie."

"Don't shoot! Don't shoot!" His eyes remained fixated on the gun.

Skylar glared at Butler. "Would you holster your weapon, please?" The way she said "please" made it sound more like *you goddamn idiot*.

Butler wasn't ready to put away his weapon just yet. He'd heard glass breaking. And someone screaming. The voice was not Eddie's. He was sure of it. Someone else was there.

Butler quickly surveyed the windows around the room to see which ones had been broken. Strangely, all the panes remained intact. The room was just as he had left it. There was no sign of damage anywhere. So what the hell was going on?

Skylar continued holding Eddie until his breathing finally slowed. His arms went limp. Nurse Gloria would have nodded with approval. Skylar released her grip gently and looked directly into his eyes. "We heard screaming. Detective McHenry and I were worried."

Eddie's voice was weak. "I'm tired."

Skylar spoke gently. "Who was screaming, Eddie?"

"I don't like it here."

Her voice remained soothing. "I know you don't. But we need to know who was screaming."

"I'm—" Eddie cut himself off. He took several long, deep breaths, and gradually regained his composure. He turned to Butler. "Detective, did you recognize the voices?"

"No."

Eddie looked puzzled. "Are you sure?"

Talking to Eddie required a patience the detective was fresh out of. He responded tersely. "Why, should I have?"

"Yes, you should have." Eddie waited, still expecting the detective to realize the obvious. "One of the voices was you."

The detective froze. He slowly turned to Skylar, who was now focused on the laptop, which was connected to the echo box. The eight one-inch satellite microphones slowly stopped moving. Their work was done. The laptop screen showed a three-dimensional rendering of the kitchen. The progress counter read: *100 percent*. The timeline went back thirty years.

Through the laptop came HISSING and all kinds of DISTORTION, but a man could be heard YELLING: *"Who the . . . think . . . talking to, boy?"*

McHenry's face dropped. Particularly when he heard the next voice.

LITTLE BOY: *I swear . . . I'll kill you . . . hit her again!*

MAN: *You threatening . . . ?*

LITTLE BOY: *. . . goddamn right!*

The sound of a fist hitting a face was clear. The thud was sickening. So was the sound of a body falling to the floor. A small body.

McHenry stared at the exact spot on the floor where he had collapsed as a young boy. He hadn't thought about the many times his stepfather had hit him—particularly this incident—in a very long while. Pain flashed across his face. The hurt he'd felt when it happened was all too clear in his mind. Sense memories often are. "Turn it off." Eddie did.

The detective sat down at the kitchen table, staring at the eight satellite microphones extended from the echo box. Skylar sat down across from him, appreciating how he must be feeling. She thought of the moments from her childhood that would be most painful for her to hear. She studied the detective. "That was you?"

He nodded, speaking slowly. "Bastard used to hit my mom. I couldn't stop him." He paused, unconsciously scratching his head where he still bore the scar. "Thirty-seven stitches."

Skylar saw his pain clearly. He hurt like he did as a boy, not as a man remembering it. "I'm sorry." Her voice was soothing. Genuine. Affecting.

Butler now understood how she could reach Eddie the way she did. There was just something about her. She made him feel better. At least a little. "He's why I became a cop. First thing I planned on doing out of the Academy was putting the son of a bitch away, but he died before I got the chance."

Eddie glanced at the detective. "Are you angry with me, Detective?"

Butler shook his head. "No, Eddie. But I think I get it now."

"Get what now?"

"The importance of your box."

"I'm going to hear my mother sing." Eddie smiled innocently.

"I hope you do."

"Detective, would you like to hear more?"

He shook his head. "That's all right. I'm good."

"You don't look good, Detective. I can tell because you are not smiling."

"I'm okay. But you know what?"

"No, I don't."

"You're not as bad at reading people's expressions as you think." Butler turned to Skylar. He paused to make sure the weight of what he was about to say was clear. He motioned to the echo box. "This thing is going to change the world. You get that, right?"

She looked him squarely in the eyes. "Yes, I get that."

"I mean like the car. The phone. The plane. It's going to change everything." The possibilities were blowing his mind.

She nodded with understanding. "Kind of overwhelming, isn't it?"

He nodded slowly. But she was relieved that the man she had turned to for help now genuinely appreciated the importance of Eddie and his echo box.

Skylar had an ally, and that was a start.

CHAPTER 45

Williamsburg Bridge, New York City, May 27, 2:47 p.m.

Butler's cell phone rang as he drove across the bridge toward Manhattan. It was his boss, Lieutenant Victoria Daniels. "What the hell is going on?" She sounded more tense than usual. Butler would soon learn that it was because the highest-ranking officer of the Sixth Precinct, Deputy Inspector Anthony Nataro, was beside her.

"Good afternoon to you, too, Detective Lieutenant." He glanced over to Skylar, sitting next to him. She was keeping an eye on Eddie in the rearview mirror. He had tissue paper sticking out of his ears, but otherwise seemed to be doing okay. He clutched the echo box, which was now contained in a weathered old backpack Skylar correctly guessed was Butler's from his school days. Eddie held the backpack tightly, like a security blanket, as he looked out the windows. He slowly rotated his head back and forth, trying to make himself feel comfortable.

Daniels wasn't amused. "You're on speakerphone with Deputy Inspector Nataro. We would both like to know why a federal warrant has been issued for your arrest."

Butler realized he should have anticipated this. "I can explain."

"I'm listening."

"I have the first solid lead on the subway gas attack, with evidence to back it up."

"How did you come by this evidence?" The detective lieutenant sounded surprised. Clearly, this was the last thing she expected to hear.

"It walked in the door of my favorite sports bar."

Nataro and Daniels could be heard whispering. "You're telling me it just walked in the door?"

"Yes, that is exactly what I'm telling you. I have a dozen witnesses who will confirm it."

Anthony Nataro chimed in. "Detective, this is Deputy Inspector Nataro. What kind of evidence?"

Butler was glad he asked. "It's something I'd like you both to hear."

"A recording?"

"Something like that."

"Bring it to the station."

"I'm on my way to you now. I'm crossing the Williamsburg as we speak."

Again, Nataro and Daniels whispered to each other before he asked, "Are Skylar Drummond and Edward Parks with you?"

"They are. Would you like to speak with them?"

Eddie shook his head as he continued looking out the windows. "She is a stranger. I don't talk to strangers."

The lieutenant could hear him. "Was that Edward Parks?"

"He prefers to be called Eddie."

"Were you aware he and Dr. Drummond are in possession of stolen classified technology?"

"I was not aware that it was considered stolen."

Eddie made his BUZZER sound. The statement wasn't true.

Lieutenant Daniels was not amused. "What the hell was that?"

"That was Eddie, who can shut up now."

"Detective, why are you helping these people?"

"It's not like that. I'm working the subway attack."

"I'm not following."

"You will when you hear what I have to play for you."

Daniels hesitated. "I'm not sure that's going to be possible."

Butler stared through the windshield, thinking. "They're waiting for us, aren't they?"

The deputy inspector didn't hesitate. "With the promise of a whole lot more of them if we don't provide full cooperation."

Butler spoke clearly and concisely, so there was no chance of mis-understanding. "Sir, the subway gas attack was not random, and it wasn't some nutjob. It was a hit on the professor, designed to look like a terrorist incident."

There was a long moment of silence. Butler knew it sounded far-fetched. Far-fetched as hell. Which was why he continued. "The people waiting to arrest me are either involved or covering up for those who were, but I cannot prove it unless I'm allowed to play the evidence for you."

Through the phone, Butler could hear Nataro tell Daniels, "It's your call."

She addressed Butler. "Park away from the station. Enter through the west emergency stairwell."

"What about the alarm?" Butler asked.

"I'll make sure it's disconnected. Go to Interrogation Five. Call me when you're there."

She hung up the phone and turned to her boss. "Before we give them up, I'd like to hear whatever it is McHenry has to play for us."

"You and me both." Nataro removed something from his pocket and slid a device across the lieutenant's desk. It was a handheld recorder. "Just be careful."

CHAPTER 46

Bob Stenson looked up from his desk inside the American Heritage Foundation as he heard three sets of footsteps approaching rapidly from down the hallway. They weren't exactly running, but they weren't exactly walking, either. "Easy there, people."

Daryl Trotter, Jason Greers, and Caitlin McCloskey slowed their gaits as they reached their superior's door. Trotter spoke first. "A federal warrant's been issued for Skylar Drummond and Edward Parks for the theft of classified materials."

Stenson slowly sat up in his chair. "Calm down, Daryl. I can barely understand you when you talk so fast." He glanced at Jason as if to say, *From now on, you do the talking.*

Daryl Trotter handed his boss copies of the two federal warrants.

Stenson skimmed the documents, looking puzzled. "Why the hell would Barnes go and make his housekeeping public?"

"I believe the answer lies with an additional warrant, which was issued for a New York Police detective named Butler McHenry." Daryl handed him the third warrant.

Stenson didn't read more than the detective's name. "Who is he, and what does he have to do with anything?"

"He's wanted for harboring Drummond and Parks."

Stenson paused to digest the information. "Why would a New York City detective harbor two federal fugitives?"

"Because he's one of the detectives assigned to the subway gas attack that killed Dr. Drummond's boyfriend, the professor."

Stenson scratched his chin, letting this sink in. It took him a moment to catch up to what the former chess Grandmaster had put together.

Jason chimed in. "People go to the police because they want help."

Caitlin was not about to be left out of the conversation. "Or because they have information they think would help in an investigation."

Even Stenson was opening his eyes a little wider now. The pieces of the puzzle were falling into place. "For the detective to risk his own career, he must have heard something rather extraordinary."

Jason added, "Just like Edward's doctor."

Daryl connected the dots. "I believe whatever they heard is something that links either Dr. Fenton or Michael Barnes to the incident in the subway."

Stenson smiled ever so slightly. "Or both." He couldn't help but think of how efficient it would be if both parties were involved. He turned to his young protégé, Jason. "Well, I'll be damned, Mr. Greers. It looks like you were right. There is a connection."

Jason grinned slyly, careful not to show too much emotion. Mr. Stenson wouldn't appreciate that. Neither would his peers. "Thank you, sir."

"And, more importantly, it looks like the echo box is a reality."

"It looks that way, sir." Jason said it with all humility. He knew to let his earlier discovery that day speak for itself.

Stenson looked around to the four corners of his office. "My God, can you imagine the secrets this room could give up?" His expression of wonder and amazement turned quickly to one of foreboding and concern. "We must acquire the device at all costs."

His three lieutenants turned to each other, wheels spinning. The expression *at all costs* was used rarely within this building, especially by Bob Stenson. With all the resources at their disposal, the statement was significant. Caitlin asked, "How many assets do we have in the immediate New York area?"

Jason answered with commanding certainty. "Think bigger. We should pull in everyone from the entire Eastern Seaboard."

Daryl read a text message on one of the several handheld devices he carried with him at all times. "NYPD is reporting McHenry is en route with the device to the Sixth Precinct, along with the other two fugitives."

Caitlin could see what was coming. "Barnes's security personnel will be waiting for them, where they intend to take possession of Edward, the doctor, and the device."

Stenson still managed to remain perfectly calm as he picked up the phone. "That's not going to happen."

CHAPTER 47

Crooked Stick Golf Club, Carmel, Indiana, May 27, 3:07 p.m.

Senator Davis was playing his best round of the year. He was on the eleventh hole at Crooked Stick, his favorite course. His last couple of rounds had been truly dreadful, but his ball was currently smack-dab in the middle of the fairway on the eleventh hole. It was a 457-yard par four, and the senator had just hit one hell of a drive. He was not known as much of a big hitter, but he had most definitely gotten all of this one. The ball carried a good 220 yards and didn't stop rolling for another 30, in part because of the downward slope of the fairway. His playing partners were certain he'd been taking private lessons, and demanded to know from whom. Davis swore he hadn't had time for lessons. He was just on his game today.

The pin was 175 yards away. His caddie suggested a five iron, but the senator was feeling strong. He was going with a six. A nice, firm six. He'd taken several practice swings when he felt a vibration in his pants pocket. It was his new phone. The one he had just received and was instructed to keep on his person at all times. "Shit," he muttered under his breath. He turned away from the rest of his foursome as he flipped open the device. "Good afternoon."

"Senator, good afternoon. Bob Stenson calling. I'm sorry to interrupt your round. How's Crooked Stick treating you?"

Davis couldn't believe it. *How the hell does he know I'm in the middle of a round at Crooked Stick?* The senator looked around, wondering who the hell was spying on him. He saw no one but the other three golfers he was playing with and their caddies. He answered, uncomfortably, "Not too shabbily."

It didn't occur to the senator to look straight up, not that it would have done any good. Stenson's vantage point was 423 miles above the earth. The same one Caitlin McCloskey had been using to follow the National League East fans. The GeoEye-1 Reconnaissance Satellite was the world's most advanced commercial imaging satellite. Its publicly available images were impressive, but it was the classified abilities of this satellite that were simply astonishing. Stenson, of course, was watching these.

GeoEye-1 had been funded primarily by the National Geospatial-Intelligence Agency (NGA) to the tune of $478 million. The decision had been made by the NGA's new director, Lieutenant General James Culpepper, who happened to be an acquaintance of three of the Foundation's seven founders. They had called in some favors to get Culpepper the job, so when the original puppet masters contacted him on behalf of GeoEye, Culpepper was not about to say no. To that request, or anything else. Culpepper readily committed half a billion dollars of taxpayer money.

It took one phone call.

In exchange for that one phone call, GeoEye granted the American Heritage Foundation unlimited access to the classified portion of the satellite. It turned out to be costing the company roughly $53 million a year in lost revenue, but no one in the company ever complained. Particularly since the chairman was about to ask for the Foundation's help to secure the funding for their next satellite, GeoEye-2, which was going to cost over a billion dollars.

Stenson talked to the senator warmly, like they were old friends. "Give Justice Barkley my best, won't you?"

"I'll do that." It somehow made the senator feel better that he wasn't the only one under the thumb of the American Heritage Foundation.

"Allow me to get right to the point, Senator. It appears Dr. Marcus Fenton's patient has managed to make his echo box work. Acoustic archeology is real."

The head of Corbin's six-iron club dropped to the fairway as his arm went limp. "I don't believe it."

"We were dubious as well, but circumstances lead us to believe otherwise."

"What circumstances?"

"Fenton's head of security has issued a federal warrant for the arrest of a doctor and patient who left hospital grounds in possession of the echo box."

Davis remained skeptical. "Could be just another one of his ploys."

"True. But if the echo box is working, we believe Fenton's objective in reacquiring the device will be to take it underground."

Davis was flabbergasted. He'd never trusted the arrogant son of a bitch, and sure as hell wasn't about to start now. "He'll never get away with it."

"Senator, all he'd have to do is claim the device still doesn't work, and no one would be the wiser."

It was so obvious. Davis didn't have to be convinced of what Marcus Fenton was capable of. "If this technology is real, it should be in the hands of the NSA or NRO. Certainly not Fenton's."

"We believe that, as chairman of the Senate Select Committee on Intelligence, you need to hear a demonstration for yourself to confirm its legitimacy."

Davis liked this idea. He liked it a lot. "How would you suggest I go about arranging such a demonstration?"

Senator Corbin Davis had just asked the right question. "The New York office of Homeland Security is at your disposal. National Director Merrell will do whatever you tell him. He doesn't need to know the specifics. All he needs to know is that the device is classified, and that his agents are to take possession of it from the NYPD."

"Won't Fenton's people have something to say about that?"

"It's private security guards in the employ of a government-funded psychiatric facility versus federal agents from the Department of Homeland Security. Who do you think will flinch first?"

Davis smiled, glad as hell that Stenson and he were on the same side. "I'm calling Director Merrell now."

"Let us know if we can be of any assistance."

After hanging up with Davis, Stenson turned to his protégé, who had been allowed to remain in the office as he spoke to the senator. "Any questions?"

Jason Greers was humbled. All he had strategically considered was how quickly they could get their independent contractors to converge on New York City. It hadn't occurred to him that the far more elegant solution was to get others to do the work for them. It only took one phone call and wouldn't cost them a dime. And it further cemented their new relationship with the Indiana senator.

It was the American Heritage Foundation who would take the echo box underground, not Dr. Fenton. The old windbag had surely planned to use the device to tout his own genius and keep his facility funded in perpetuity. The Foundation, however, was going to keep the echo box all to itself. They would know even more than they did now, and no one would be the wiser.

But a few specifics still needed explaining. "You don't actually intend to allow Senator Davis to hear the device, do you?"

Stenson smirked. "Absolutely." From behind his desk, he studied Greers, who looked confused until Stenson finished mapping out the upcoming steps in detail.

If there was ever a doubt in Jason Greers's mind about his chosen career, Stenson knew it was long gone. "If we have the echo box, and no one else does, that would be . . . a very good thing for us."

"That's rather an understatement, don't you think?"

Greers nodded. "I thought you would appreciate it."

"I do," Stenson acknowledged.

The protégé considered what was to follow. "Eventually, Edward Parks will try to build another prototype."

"If he is given the resources, of course he will."

"Fenton could manage to find someone else to step in."

"He could." The mentor wanted his charge to see it for himself. The move was obvious.

"Doesn't that concern you?"

"Does it look like it concerns me?" Stenson locked eyes with Greers. *See it, already. See it.*

It took only another moment before Greers understood. "We're not going to let that happen."

"Of course not." Stenson smiled. Greers had passed yet another test. "The moment we are in possession of the echo box and confirm that it's operational, Edward Parks becomes a liability."

CHAPTER 48

Sixth Precinct, New York City, May 27, 3:11 p.m.

Interrogation Room Five was pretty much the same as the other four interrogation rooms inside the Sixth Precinct. A windowless box with a metal table and two chairs in the middle. The table was scratched with graffiti. The chairs repaired with duct tape. Eddie stood, slowly rotating his head back and forth as he made himself comfortable. They had parked two blocks away on Beach Street, and entered the station through the west emergency exit, just as the lieutenant had instructed. "Detective McHenry, why is this room called an interrogation room?"

"Because it's where we interrogate suspects."

"Why do you interrogate suspects?"

"To see what they will reveal about a particular crime."

"Do they ever lie?"

"Only when they open their mouths."

Eddie looked around the walls of the room. "There are probably a lot of very interesting echoes bouncing all around us."

Skylar chimed in. "I bet there are, too."

"Why would you bet, Skylar?"

"Because I believe you are correct. And if you believe something is correct, people sometimes make a wager on that belief."

"I don't have any money."

"Would you like me to lend you some?" she asked with her usual warmth, which kept Eddie at ease.

"Five million dollars, please."

She was reminded that money had no meaning for him. Skylar took out a bill. "I don't happen to have that much on me at the moment. How about one dollar?"

"Is that enough to bet with?"

"Yes, Eddie. It's plenty."

"Okay. One dollar." Eddie accepted the currency, staring at it with interest. He wasn't exactly sure what to do with it, or even how to hold it. "I bet one dollar."

"I bet one dollar, too." She placed a bill on the table. Eddie copied her action, putting his dollar next to hers.

"That's two dollars in the pot," she told him.

"What pot?"

Skylar clarified, "Whoever wins the bet gets to keep both dollars."

"Forever?" Eddie asked with a degree of amazement.

"You can do whatever you want with them."

"Can I buy a car?"

"No, Eddie, you cannot buy a car."

"You said, 'You can do whatever you want with them.'" Butler was visibly amazed at Eddie's imitation of Skylar.

"You can do anything that only costs two dollars."

"What costs only two dollars?"

"Well, a pretzel, for one thing."

Butler interrupted, "Could we please get on with this?"

Skylar nodded to Eddie. "I will tell you some things you can buy for two dollars after you win the bet. Let's hear the echoes."

CHAPTER 49

Main Entrance, Sixth Precinct, May 27, 3:42 p.m.

Lutz and Hirsch had been standing in front of the station for fifty-seven minutes. There had been no sign of Dr. Drummond or Edward Parks, and the two former intelligence agents were beginning to doubt there would be. Hirsch scanned the passing pedestrians. "This is a jerk-off."

Lutz agreed. "They're either already inside, or holed up somewhere."

"If they're inside, we're going to need help getting them out."

"I think the cavalry just arrived." Lutz was staring at two black Suburbans, which screeched to a halt in front of the station. Six Homeland Security agents got out of each van, moving quickly toward the entrance to the station. "Thanks for coming."

The lead agent was more amused than annoyed. "Who the hell are you?"

"We work for Michael Barnes at Harmony House."

The agent stared at them blankly. "Who the hell is Michael Barnes?"

Hirsch and Lutz waited for the agent to crack a smile and let them in on the joke. But the federal agent was dead serious. Lutz didn't like being toyed with. "He's the one who sent you here, asshole."

"No, he didn't. The director of Homeland Security, Arthur Merrell, did. I'm Agent Harold Raines. Step out of the way."

Lutz didn't move. "Call your boss. You were sent here to assist us."

"You've been misinformed." Agent Raines turned to his associates. "Arrest him if he doesn't move." The agents eyeballed Lutz, waiting. After a moment, Lutz stepped backward, allowing Raines and the others from the Department of Homeland Security to enter the police station. All except two, who remained by the entrance with the Harmony House security personnel.

Hirsch stepped away from them as he dialed Michael Barnes. "Sir, we have a situation."

(((•)))

The station went eerily quiet as Raines led the parade of Homeland Security agents toward the office of Deputy Inspector Nataro. Every cop, perp, lawyer, victim, witness, and loved one stared with curiosity as the dark-suited men marched past them. What the hell was going on? Everyone had a guess. It must have something to do with the subway gas attack. Did the agents know who did it? Was the perpetrator in the building?

Suddenly, everyday adversaries were united against the enemy that had ripped open the wound this city would never recover from. They readied their cell phones to snap pictures or tweet the news. Some didn't even bother to wait, and speculated on the proceedings. If they guessed right, they might even become famous. Sadly, no one was ever punished for being wrong these days. And no one was rewarded for coming in second. All anyone cared about was breaking a story, whether they broke the right one or not.

(((•)))

Deputy Inspector Anthony Nataro acted surprised as Agent Raines was led inside his office. "What can I do for you?" Of course, Nataro knew

215

damn well what the agent was there for, but the deputy inspector was never one to tip his hand.

"I'm here to transfer the federal prisoners you have in custody."

"Which prisoners would those be?"

Agent Raines handed him the transfer order, which was signed by Department of Homeland Security Director Arthur Merrell.

Nataro reviewed the document. "If we had them, I'd give them to you. But we're still waiting for Detective McHenry to turn himself in." He lied incredibly well. Which was why he was going to make a great politician.

Raines was clearly getting frustrated. "When is the last time you had any communication with him?"

"About forty minutes ago."

"Mind if I wait with you?" It came out like more of a statement than a request.

"Be my guest." He gestured for the agent to sit on the couch, which he did, stretching out in a way that made it clear he wouldn't be leaving anytime soon. Not without what he came for.

Raines got on the phone with his people. Nataro did the same, connecting with Detective Lieutenant Victoria Daniels. "Do we have an update on the McHenry situation?"

((•))

Victoria was inside Interrogation Room Five, standing next to Butler McHenry. She was still trying to process the lecture on acoustic archeology she had just been given as she stared at the echo box performing its synchronized ballet. "Momentarily," she told her boss into the phone. "Let me call you back." She hung up, turning to Skylar. "Forgive me, Doctor, but I was never much for science."

Butler chimed in. "It'll make more sense once you've heard something you would remember. Eddie, if the detective lieutenant gives you a date and time, can you play that back for her?"

Eddie was uncomfortable around the stranger, never looking up from his computer screen. "How will she give it to me?"

Butler turned to Skylar for help. She translated for Eddie. "Detective McHenry believes that Ms. Daniels will better understand how the echo box works after you play her a demonstration. If she tells you a date and time, will you play those echoes for her?"

"Why didn't Detective McHenry just say that?"

Butler was unable to bite his tongue. "I did."

Skylar intervened. "Detective Lieutenant, when were you most recently in this room?"

Victoria answered, "Last Monday, the twenty-second. About three thirty."

Without looking at her, Eddie asked, "Morning or afternoon?"

"Afternoon."

Eddie plugged in the date and time, studying the particular waves originally produced at that time. There were four distinctly different waves visible. "There were four people in this room."

"That's correct," Victoria responded, clearly impatient.

"Was one of them a suspect you were interrogating?"

"Yes." The detective lieutenant was quickly concluding this was a waste of time.

"Did the suspect tell you the truth?"

Skylar jumped in. "Eddie, please just hit 'Play.'"

He nodded and hit "Play." The voices came through clearly, with little distortion, due to the characteristics of the room: it was small, the surfaces were hard, there were no windows, and the echoes were recently produced.

SUSPECT, crying: *I swear to God, I don't know where she is!*

Eddie made his BUZZER sound.

"Shh." Skylar motioned for him to remain quiet. He nodded apologetically.

VICTORIA: *Tell me where she is, Henry.*

The lieutenant's voice in the recording was neither intense nor threatening. It was utterly devoid of emotion, which was what made it so frightening. Skylar watched the diminutive woman closely as she listened to herself and couldn't believe what she was hearing. Victoria now understood the science, or at least the importance of it.

SUSPECT: *I don't fucking know! What are you, deaf?!*

Eddie winced. The screaming hurt his ears.

VICTORIA: *If this little girl dies, I will do everything in my power to have you put to death. And on the day your miserable life ends, I promise I will be there, because I will want to watch you beg, and have absolutely nobody care.*

Skylar glanced at Eddie. "That's enough." Eddie hit "Stop."

Victoria Daniels glanced around the room. "Where's the bug?"

Eddie started scanning every square inch of the floor, looking for the insect she must be referring to.

Skylar answered the detective lieutenant. "There isn't one. Neither of us has ever been inside this room until a few minutes ago."

Butler McHenry addressed his superior, emphasizing every word. "Any room. Any conversation. Ever."

All Victoria Daniels could say was, "My God."

"Exactly." Butler now had the same expression Skylar had had when she'd watched him first understand the gravity of the situation. He had an ally, and that was good.

Skylar addressed Eddie, who was still searching the floor. "I should have told you that the bug Ms. Daniels was referring to was a recording device, not an insect."

"The detective lieutenant should have been more specific, then." He turned toward Victoria without looking at her. "You were not very nice to Henry."

Victoria stared at him, dumbfounded. "Henry wasn't a very nice person."

Skylar was curious. "Did he tell you where the little girl was?"

The detective lieutenant nodded. "He did." She turned to Butler, motioning toward the echo box. "This thing is for real?"

Butler nodded slowly. He understood that it was a lot to process.

"No wonder there's a federal warrant out for your arrest."

Eddie looked confused. "Why is it no wonder that there is a federal warrant out for his arrest?"

Skylar quickly jumped in. "Ms. Daniels wasn't talking to you, Eddie."

Eddie kept his head down. "You mean it's none of my business?"

"That's correct."

"Just like the mystery man?"

"Yes."

Butler turned to Eddie. "Play the first thing you played for me in the bar."

Eddie looked at Skylar, who nodded her approval. He clicked open the file containing the restored sound waves from inside Dr. Fenton's office, and hit "Play."

Victoria reached inside her pocket and clicked the "Record" button on the pocket recorder Deputy Inspector Nataro had given her.

Whatever she was about to hear, he would hear, too.

CHAPTER 50

Dr. Marcus Fenton's House, Pine Hill, New Jersey, May 27, 4:11 p.m.

Inside the home office of his ramshackle farmhouse, Dr. Marcus Fenton clenched the phone so tightly that his knuckles turned white. He had just gotten the most disturbing news from Michael Barnes, which was confirmed by an immediate call to the Department of Homeland Security. Their agents were interfering with a Harmony House security matter, and Fenton wanted an explanation. He'd been sitting on hold for over five minutes, waiting for Senator Corbin Davis to pick up the phone and explain why he'd issued the order to Homeland Security Director Arthur Merrell. *How dare this midwestern pretty boy treat me with such disrespect?*

The senator finally came on the line, trying to sound more like he'd just stepped out of a meeting than off a putting green. "I've only got a minute, Doctor. What can I do for you?"

"Call off your dogs."

"Excuse me?" The senator was clearly amused.

"Homeland is interfering with an internal security matter, and I want it stopped."

Davis actually struggled not to laugh out loud. "Federal warrants were issued for the arrest of one of your employees and one of your patients. How is that an internal security matter?"

Fenton knew Barnes had made a mistake the moment warrants were issued. It was uncharacteristic of him to invite outside attention. How could he have been so dumb? Fenton decided to cut to the chase. "What is this really about, Senator?"

It was so rare that anyone asked the politician a direct question. Perhaps because he simply held all the cards, Davis decided to give an equally direct answer. "I want to hear it for myself. The box."

Fenton was dumbfounded. "Why didn't you just ask me for a demonstration?"

"Because I don't trust you." A long pause followed.

The senior doctor scrambled, summoning every bit of charm at his disposal. "What reason have I ever given you not to trust me, Senator?"

"Doctor, I'm not going to get into this. Homeland is going to take possession of the device, and then I am going to listen to it. If it works, it will be given the protection it deserves. You and your patient will have continuing access, but under their auspices, not yours. If, however, the device does not work, it will be returned to your facility for further development."

Fenton slumped in his chair, defeated. "You can't just take the echo box away from me."

"It was never yours to begin with. Good day, Doctor."

The moment the call ended, Marcus Fenton phoned his head of security. The doctor would have threatened him if he wasn't truly afraid of Michael Barnes. "Senator Davis said Homeland Security is going to take possession of the echo box. The senator wants to hear it for himself."

"I'd like to know how he found out so fast." The head of Harmony House security sounded curious.

Fenton exploded, "Because you issued goddamn federal warrants!"

Barnes remained dangerously calm. "The warrant never specified what kind of technology was stolen."

"It named Edward Parks, didn't it?"

"The senator was calling Homeland Security to intervene less than two hours after the warrant had been issued. Unless he was sitting there, monitoring New York Police Department chatter, it should have taken him days, if not weeks, for this to come on his radar."

"What are you getting at?"

"Someone is feeding him information."

"Who?"

"We have a mole."

Fenton fell silent. He could feel his blood pressure skyrocketing. He closed his eyes, struggling to continue the conversation. "My God."

"I found out earlier today."

"Who?" Fenton tried to mentally run through his list of employees, but his mind was racing. He wasn't even sure he wanted to know.

"Your head nurse, Gloria Pruitt."

Fenton shook his head. "I don't believe it."

"That's your choice, sir." Barnes shook his own head, still perfectly calm.

The senior doctor felt like he'd been stabbed in the back. The physical pain was very real. "You're sure?"

"When have I ever told you anything I wasn't sure about?" He let the question linger for a moment, then asked, "It's curious, don't you think?"

"What?" Fenton snapped back.

"We have a mole, and Homeland is the one who capitalizes on the information."

Fenton thought the notion was preposterous. "You think Homeland has been spying on us?"

"I think Homeland may have been compromised. Whoever was spying on us is using Homeland to acquire the device for themselves."

"I don't follow."

"It's the only thing that makes sense."

"With all due respect, you sound paranoid, Mr. Barnes."

"Within every intelligence agency, there are internal factions with specific agendas. One of them has obviously been made aware of Eddie and his echo box."

The doctor suddenly didn't think his security director sounded so off base. "If you knew about these factions, why would you have issued federal arrest warrants?"

"Because if local law enforcement became aware of the echo box, it would only be a matter of time before federal agencies were notified. It was our best move."

Fenton sighed as he slumped in his office chair. "What the hell are we going to do?"

Barnes remained perfectly calm. "We actually have a number of options, Doctor."

"Like what?"

((•))

Senator Corbin Davis approached the seventeenth tee with the confidence and swagger of a dragon slayer. Any lingering doubts he had held about his involvement with the American Heritage Foundation had been swept away. At the end of the day, no one succeeded in politics without getting into bed with at least one eight-hundred-pound gorilla. The trick was picking the right one.

The senator from Indiana had picked very well.

CHAPTER 51

Sixth Precinct, New York City, May 27, 4:23 p.m.

NYPD Detective Lieutenant Victoria Daniels struggled to digest what she had just heard, as Eddie stopped playing back the reconstructed conversation between Dr. Fenton and Michael Barnes at Harmony House. She couldn't quite wrap her head around it. Daniels reached into her coat pocket and turned off Deputy Inspector Nataro's micro-recorder, gazing around the walls of Interrogation Room Five, which somehow now looked different. She realized the walls of every room she ever entered would never look the same. Because now she knew what was bouncing around every one of them: the history of each space. Every action. Every word. Every crime. Every lie. Every room was now its own historical document. Its own recording. All that had to be done was to have the record re-created, and the evidence was there for anyone to hear.

There would never again be any more "He said, she said." There would only be "Here is what was said."

That was, if the device ever saw the light of day.

Victoria was now a believer, which was what scared her. It was evident in her face.

"Now do you blame me for helping them?" asked Butler.

"I would have done the same thing." There wasn't a doubt in her mind. Not about her answer to the question. Nor how this was going to play out.

"Now what?"

She knew Butler wasn't leading her. He really didn't know the next move—that was why he had come in.

"Step out with me for a second." She exited with Butler into the hallway, closing the door behind them. They spoke very quietly, just above a whisper.

Inside Interrogation Room Five, Skylar moved to Eddie, motioning toward the door. She also spoke quietly. "Can you tell me what they're saying?"

Eddie nodded, turning his head toward the door. He closed his eyes, which helped him focus exclusively on what he could hear. He cupped his hands behind his ears to amplify whatever sound waves were audible. He repeated the conversation occurring in the hallway, doing rather decent imitations of Butler's and Victoria's voices: "You've got no choice. You know that, right? . . . I want to make sure nothing's going to happen to them . . . you can't. Accept it . . ."

Eddie was confused by the conversation, and turned to Skylar. "What are they talking about?"

"Us." Skylar crossed her arms tightly across her chest and turned away from Eddie. All she could think was, What had she done? Detective McHenry was going to be forced to turn them over to Fenton's security team, and there wasn't anything she could do about it.

"Why doesn't Detective McHenry have a choice?"

"Because the government isn't going to give him one."

Eddie resumed listening to Butler and Victoria's conversation, repeating every word. "They killed her boyfriend . . . I appreciate that, Detective. But what exactly do you think you can do for them? This is way above either of our pay grades."

Eddie turned to Skylar as she started to cry. "Is he talking about your boyfriend, Skylar?" She nodded. "I didn't know you had a boyfriend. I'm sure he must have been nice. What was his name?"

Skylar was barely able to answer. "Jacob."

"Who killed him?"

"Dr. Fenton and the mystery man." She struggled to get the words out.

"It's wrong to kill someone. It says so in the Bible. 'Thou shalt not kill.'" Eddie paused, trying to process the information. "Skylar, why did Dr. Fenton and the mystery man kill your boyfriend?"

Skylar couldn't respond. Her face was buried in her hands.

Eddie wanted to help her, but didn't know how, so he did the one thing he could do. He continued repeating the conversation in the hallway: "The least I could do is help them get out of the city. What good would that do? . . . They want to go to Philadelphia. Why Philly? . . . The only reason Parks invented the thing was to hear his mother's voice. She died giving birth to him."

Eddie showed no emotion. He continued, sounding like Detective Lieutenant Daniels: "You know what I hate? I hate knowing that this thing exists, and what it could do for every case we've ever had, or ever will have."

In the hallway, Butler didn't follow. "Why do you hate it?"

"Because there is no way on God's green earth that anyone at our level is ever going to get the chance to use it."

Repeating their words, Eddie turned to Skylar. "Who is 'anyone at our level'?"

"I think she means police officers."

"Why won't police officers ever get the chance to use the echo box?"

Skylar answered quickly. "I'll have to tell you later."

Eddie listened, then repeated the continuing dialogue between Daniels and McHenry. "He's spent his entire life working on this. He deserves to hear his mother. You're right. He does. If I don't help him, who will?" There was a pause in the hallway. Eddie spoke like the detective lieutenant: "You were never here."

Eddie made his BUZZER sound.

Skylar quickly turned to face him, listening intently. "Shh." She watched Eddie, waiting for him to continue repeating their conversation. He said nothing. "Did they stop talking?"

"You told me to 'shh.'"

Skylar spoke urgently. "Tell me what they're saying."

"I never saw you." Eddie was about to make his BUZZER sound again, but he could see that Skylar was already gesturing for him not to. Eddie managed to stop himself, and continued repeating what Victoria was saying: "I'll give you two minutes. Call and tell me the suspects fled right before you got to the station and that you are in pursuit."

Victoria's footsteps could be heard walking away as Butler returned to the interrogation room. "Time to go."

Eddie looked confused. "Where are we going, Detective?"

"You want to hear your mother sing?"

"Yes, very much."

"Then move your ass."

CHAPTER 52

Deputy Inspector Nataro's Office, Sixth Precinct, May 27, 4:31 p.m.

Deputy Inspector Nataro looked up as Victoria entered his office. "Detective Lieutenant Daniels, this is Homeland Security Agent Harold Raines. Agent Raines, Detective Lieutenant Daniels." The agent stood up and shook hands with Victoria.

She clenched her teeth. This thing was getting bigger fast. Too big. Too fast.

Agent Raines kept his eyes on her. "Where are the suspects?"

"They're on their way here."

"They should have been here by now."

"Yes, they should have." Her face gave away nothing.

The veteran agent studied her. Somehow, he just knew he was being played. He spoke into his headset microphone as he moved toward the door. "Search the building top to bottom. I have reason to believe the suspects are in the building." He joined the other agents as they fanned out through the building with experienced coordination.

The deputy inspector glanced at Daniels. "You better have one hell of a story to tell."

She placed Nataro's pocket recorder on his desk. "The doctor's boyfriend was the victim thrown in front of the subway train."

"The professor?"

She nodded. "Her boss apparently had him killed for snooping into Parks, who is her patient. The professor stuck his nose where he shouldn't have."

"What's the big deal with this patient?"

"It's something you need to hear."

He looked down at the small recorder in his hand. "Whatever's on this tape will back that up?"

"No judge will ever hear it, but yes." Victoria Daniels then began to explain science that she herself was only beginning to grasp.

CHAPTER 53

Hudson Street, New York City, May 27, 4:39 p.m.

Butler led Skylar and Eddie away from the station down Hudson Street, toward a park named after James J. Walker, the two-term New York City mayor in the 1920s—known as "Beau James" because of his flamboyant lifestyle—who resigned amid scandal in 1932 and fled to Europe with his movie-star lover. The park featured an elaborate playground, bocce courts, and a synthetic-turf soccer field, which caught Eddie's attention. He had never seen artificial grass in person before. He stared at it through a fence surrounding the play area, slowing down considerably. "That's not real grass, is it?"

"No, Eddie, it's not. It's called artificial turf." She could see that he was fixated.

"Can I touch it?" He stopped to reach through the fence.

"We don't have time for that right now." She gently nudged his shoulder, which caused him to suddenly recoil.

Eddie looked around nervously, rotating his head from side to side as he tried to become comfortable with these new surroundings. He clutched the backpack containing the echo box and laptop supercomputer tightly to his chest. "Are you sure this is the way to Philadelphia?"

Skylar reassured him. "Yes, Eddie."

"Do we have to walk all the way there?"

"We're only going to walk a little farther."

Butler gave them some advice. "If you do walk anywhere, find the largest group of tourists you can and stay in the middle of them."

"I don't like crowds."

"Deal with it."

Eddie looked around for tourists, but there were none to be seen. "Why should we stay in the middle of tourists?"

"So no one sees you."

"The tourists would see us if we were walking in the middle of them."

"They're not the ones trying to take your box away."

Eddie paused suddenly, clutching the echo box and laptop tightly to his chest. "Who is trying to take the echo box from me?"

Butler floundered. "The people looking for you."

Eddie turned to Skylar, desperate for reassurance. "Does Dr. Fenton want to take the echo box away from me?"

She wanted to lie to him. But she also knew she couldn't. Skylar glared at Butler briefly before reluctantly answering Eddie. "Yes, Eddie, I think that is what he intends to do."

"The echo box is mine!" Eddie attempted to slap himself, but both his hands were mercifully occupied with clutching his devices. He could not strike a clean blow. "I have to hear my mother's voice! I have to!"

Skylar grabbed his arms and clenched them tightly. She spoke to him in a voice that was soothing but matter-of-fact. "I'm afraid the echo box is property of Harmony House."

Tears welled up in Eddie's eyes. "It's my property. It's mine!"

"They're the ones who paid for it."

"It's mine!" Eddie started to cry. Butler looked anxious, because they didn't have time for this.

Skylar had to think quickly. She knew what the echo box meant to Eddie. And what it would do to him if it were taken away. Skylar looked him squarely in the eyes. "Eddie, I promise I will do everything in my power to stop anyone from taking the echo box away from you."

Eddie took several long breaths, wiping his tears on his sleeve. He believed her. After several more moments, she released him, and they continued through the park.

Butler stopped abruptly as they reached the park's south side. "This is as far as I go."

Eddie looked around them to see if there was any kind of physical barrier preventing the detective from going farther. "Why?"

"Because I'm in enough trouble as it is because of you two." He pointed east toward Varick Street, where dozens of taxicabs were passing in both directions. "Catch a cab uptown. After that, you're on your own." He took out his phone.

"Thank you, Detective. For everything." Skylar's gratitude was apparent.

He nodded, dialing Detective Lieutenant Daniels as he turned and raced toward his car.

Eddie struggled to keep up with Skylar as they walked quickly to the corner. "Do we have to walk so fast?"

"You don't want them to catch us, do you?"

Eddie clenched his hands tightly and managed to walk faster, staying by her side. "Why is Detective McHenry in trouble?"

"Because he helped us."

"Isn't that what police officers are supposed to do?"

"In this case, it was against the rules."

"So why did he help us?"

"Because sometimes, to do what you think is right, you have to break the rules."

Eddie nodded—not because he understood, but because he wanted Skylar to think he did. "Detective McHenry gave me graham crackers and milk at his mother's house. He shouldn't get in trouble for that."

"I don't think he should, either." That was when Skylar saw him. Lutz. On the hunt. He was only a block away, frantically scanning the area. Skylar concentrated, trying not to let panic seep into her voice. "Have you ever ridden inside a taxicab, Eddie?" She waved at passing cabs, praying one would stop.

Eddie nodded. "Yes, when I was younger. I have ridden inside twenty-seven taxicabs, except for the ones I can't remember as a baby." He imitated her actions, waving at the passing cabs. It wasn't subtle.

That was when Lutz spotted them. The former special operative started running toward them with impressive speed.

Skylar could see Lutz closing in from behind Eddie. A shark locked on its prey. Fortunately, Eddie could not see him.

A cab quickly stopped in front of Skylar and Eddie. "Would you like to ride in your twenty-eighth cab?"

"No. Twenty-seven is three squared, which makes it a much better number than twenty-eight, which is four times seven, or two times two times seven, and not nearly as interesting."

Lutz was closing in. He was less than half a block away.

"What if I said please?" Skylar pleaded.

He shook his head. "The answer would still be no."

She was on the verge of losing it. "Would you get in the cab if I asked you to do it for me anyway?"

Eddie stared at the sidewalk. "Yes, I would do it for you anyway, Skylar."

Thank God. She quickly opened the door and helped Eddie get inside the cab. Skylar rushed in the other side and gave the driver a very simple command: "Drive!"

The Afghan driver may not have understood much English, but he did understand this particular instruction. His passengers' heads were thrown back into the seat as he stepped on the gas.

Lutz came within eight feet of the rear bumper as he ran after the cab. He did not give up the chase for another two blocks. The man was incredibly fast. But man versus automobile was never much of a contest. Whoever had the better technology would always win this race, or any other.

Through the rear window, Eddie watched Lutz fade into the distance. Surprisingly, Eddie was not concerned. "This is kind of a game, isn't it?"

"Yes, it is."

"Like tag?"

"Like tag."

"I don't like tag, because people touch you when they tag you, and you're it."

"Then I'll try to make sure no one tags you."

Eddie stared out the windows, marveling at the many tall buildings all around them. "What if someone tags you, Skylar?"

"I won't like it, either."

"Then I will try to make sure no one tags you, either."

CHAPTER 54

Varick Street, New York City, May 27, 4:47 p.m.

Lutz and Hirsch had split up when Homeland began their search inside the Sixth Precinct. Hirsch had remained by the precinct entrance while Lutz searched the perimeter, which was how he had come upon Skylar and Eddie. As the cab waded into a sea of others, Lutz focused his gaze on the vehicle's license plate. It was a combination of four letters or numbers, as opposed to the usual seven required on passenger vehicles. These four letters or numbers also appeared on the vehicle's top light, which was mounted on the roof beneath a Nautica advertisement featuring a nicely tanned man on a boat.

Unfortunately, Lutz could only make out two of the four identifiers on the license plate: 5E. He quickly punched the letter and number into his phone; he would later transmit them to Barnes, with the full knowledge that without at least one more digit, those two were practically useless, because they led to 1,296 license-plate possibilities. There was barely enough time to narrow it down from thirteen cabs, much less thirteen hundred.

Lutz quickly ducked into a Popeyes and waited in line as Homeland Security agents and NYPD officers rapidly expanded their perimeter around the station. The other customers all turned toward the street to see what the commotion was about. The agents and officers paid no attention to him or the other customers, or to the particular cab containing Skylar and Eddie, among the hundreds of others in view. It was just one of many other yellow metal fish swimming toward Midtown. Lutz may have only had half of the cab's license plate, but it was still more than they had.

CHAPTER 55

Detective McHenry had just finished giving his fictionalized account of the suspects' escape to his superiors and DHS Agent Raines inside the deputy inspector's office. Butler knew the agent wasn't buying a word of it, but he had no intention of offering any more than he was asked to.

Raines looked amused. "Is that it?"

"That's all I can tell you." Butler glanced calmly at Nataro and Daniels. Poker players at a table, except that they were all standing. Nobody was giving away anything.

"And this recording they played for you. You believe it's legitimate?"

"I do." Butler had to restrain himself from clarifying that what they had heard was not a recording.

"What makes you so sure?"

"Because she risked a great deal to bring it to me."

"Skylar Drummond isn't the only one who risked a lot today." Agent Raines paused, allowing the threat to sink in. "What I don't understand is why you helped them flee."

"I don't know what you're talking about." Butler's voice didn't waver. He was a better liar than Victoria was.

"No?"

"What I did was hear evidence I thought my superior officers should also hear, but as I was bringing in my witnesses to this station, you idiots had to issue federal warrants and scare them off." Butler eyed Victoria and Anthony, just to make sure they were all clear on the story. "Agent Raines, some asshole out there single-handedly paralyzed the city for the last three days, and killed an NYU professor who had a great future ahead of him. This investigation may not be your primary concern, but it is mine. Now if you don't mind, I'd like to get on with it."

The agent studied him for a moment, then spoke with clear disdain. "By all means, Detective, I wouldn't want to interfere with your investigation."

Raines watched McHenry through the window as he left the station. "Where do you think he's going?"

"No idea," Lieutenant Daniels lied. She knew exactly where he was going.

DHS Agent Raines surprised her by asking, "May I see your phone?"

"Excuse me?" She had heard him clearly, and knew exactly why he was asking, but didn't want him to know that.

"I want McHenry's number. It's the last number that called you."

She did not hand him her phone. She scrolled through her most recent calls and read him Butler's number. Agent Raines entered the digits into his phone and hit "Send."

CHAPTER 56

New York Office, Department of Homeland Security,
May 27, 5:09 p.m.

In less than a second, the numeric text message arrived on a screen inside 633 Third Avenue, home of the New York State office of the Department of Homeland Security. The office, a secure beehive, was even more active than usual because of the recent subway event. In the seventy-two hours since the attack occurred, every last bit of security-camera footage from the area had been pored over frame by frame. Every witness statement had been reviewed. The personal information of every individual identified as having been in the area was checked against the DHS's vast database, which was now integrated with the other intelligence-agency systems. Of the 347 personnel housed in the New York office, over two hundred had been assigned to the subway investigation. So far, they had collectively come up with a grand total of nothing, which explained the tension hanging over the rows of analysts' cubicles. And the candy wrappers around the floor.

Max Garber was like many of the other analysts housed in the dozens of six-by-six partitioned work areas: he was Ivy League–educated (Penn), in his early thirties, and begrudgingly wore the uniform of a lightly starched white-collar shirt and tie because it was required for the job, just like the background checks and the random drug testing. He knew he could be making a lot more money in Boston or Northern California, but nowhere else would he have the access to systems and data that he did here.

For someone who thought of his workstation as a "data cockpit," DHS was the mother ship. Particularly for someone like him, who had lost his father in 9/11.

He had become Agent Raines's analyst of choice eleven months ago, when Garber had stayed up for three straight days data mining credit-card purchases in the Brooklyn area, looking for suspects in a newly discovered Islamic fundamentalist cell. Garber's work not only resulted in the capture of two suspects, but also uncovered a sophisticated offshore financing operation that had funneled more than $27 million to ISIS.

In his current investigation, he was focusing on a promising connection with a Farsi-speaking British citizen who'd happened to be on the subway platform when Jacob Hendrix was killed. Raines's text message containing Butler's cell number now appeared on his screen. Garber texted back: Whose #?

Raines's answer appeared immediately: NYPD Det. Priority 1.

Garber sat up in his chair and minimized the window of what he'd been working on. Goodbye, Mr. Farsi-speaking Brit. Hello, Detective whoever-you-are. Priority 1 was not a designation Agent Raines used often. It meant *urgent. Right now. Drop everything.* And a priority-1 instruction that involved tapping the phone of a New York City Police detective meant all kinds of higher-ups were going to get involved, because of obvious legal and jurisdictional issues. They would need a lot of information at their fingertips to make immediate decisions. Garber wasted no time. He texted Raines, On it, and went to work. Within fifteen minutes, they would know exactly where the detective was, and every word he spoke into his phone for as long as they cared to listen.

Which put them fifteen minutes behind the American Heritage Foundation.

CHAPTER 57

American Heritage Foundation, Alexandria, Virginia,
May 27, 5:16 p.m.

Jason Greers looked over Daryl Trotter's shoulder as they watched the world's best reality television show on several different screens. From three different angles, Detective McHenry could be seen driving out of the Sixth Precinct garage, where he had only recently parked his car. The American Heritage Foundation had been tapped into the detective's phone from the moment they learned of the federal arrest warrant being issued. Unlike official government agencies, the Foundation needed no approval or justification. There was no oversight and no review. The terrifying reality was that there wasn't a satellite view or surveillance angle or phone number or online account they couldn't access faster than anyone else. "Where's he going?"

Daryl answered like it should have been obvious. "Pine Hill, New Jersey."

Jason was puzzled. He didn't have a clue. "What's in Pine Hill?"

Daryl typed in a set of longitude and latitude numbers that zoomed his satellite view to a ramshackle farmhouse built in 1931. "The home of Dr. Marcus Fenton."

Jason nodded. *Of course.* "McHenry's got no jurisdiction or admissible evidence."

"Precisely why he's going there now. Because he still can." One of Daryl Trotter's skills was to think like the players involved in any situation. "He wants to make Fenton sweat."

"Think it'll work?"

Daryl turned to face Jason. "Only if we want it to."

CHAPTER 58

Sixth Avenue, New York City, May 27, 5:19 p.m.

Skylar and Eddie's cab was approaching Fifty-Sixth Street. Its progress slowed as the cab hit construction traffic that had been snarling things for weeks and had become the bane of many Midtown residents. If there was one thing the city did not need, it was another glistening residential high-rise, at least as far as those who already lived in one were concerned.

The cabbie, who dealt with this and every other New York City traffic challenge on a daily basis, knew exactly how to circumnavigate it. He forced his way through three lanes of traffic and veered west on Fifty-Seventh. He would take Eighth Avenue to Columbus Circle, and his passengers would never know the difference.

As their cab waited at a red light on Fifty-Seventh Street, Eddie suddenly saw something out his side window. It caused him to momentarily forget about everything else in the world. Seeing the thing from a distance through the dirty window of a cab was not enough. He had to see it clearly for himself. And, more importantly, he had to hear it for himself.

Without warning, Eddie opened the left rear cab door and jumped out into traffic before Skylar realized what was going on. She tried to grab his arm, but it was too late. Eddie was already running into oncoming traffic. Right in front of a town car. It was horrifying.

The SCREECH of the approaching tires completely drowned out Skylar's attempt at a scream. "Eddie!"

The black sedan missed him by less than a foot. Probably closer to six inches. The side-view mirror practically grazed his left cheek. The sedan's driver angrily blared his horn at Eddie throughout the next block.

Eddie never noticed him or his sedan. In fact, he never even flinched. He remained transfixed, a junkie chasing the ultimate high, and continued running through traffic, away from the cab, with his laptop and echo box in hand.

"Eddie, stop! *Stop!*" But he kept right on going. In a panic, Skylar scrambled after him into traffic, leaving the driver enraged.

She, too, was nearly killed in an instant. A delivery truck narrowly avoided her as it sped on by. Drivers, it seemed, just weren't prepared for random pedestrians running in front of their vehicles without any warning whatsoever. The bigger problem with this oversized vehicle, for Skylar, was that it completely obstructed her view of Eddie. Which would have been okay, except that it was followed by another truck. And another one. *"Eddie!"*

By the time the small convoy ended, Eddie was nowhere to be seen. She bolted across the remaining three lanes of traffic, looking everywhere. "Eddie!" It was only pure luck that kept her from being run over. Reaching the other side of the street, she didn't understand where Eddie could have gone. Or why he would have bolted away. She was spinning in circles, beginning to panic, when something dawned on her. She realized why Eddie had bolted from the cab.

She turned around to face one of the most revered American buildings ever constructed.

CHAPTER 59

Carnegie Hall, New York City, May 27, 5:21 p.m.

Eddie's expression was one of pure wonder as he walked through the lobby of the hallowed confines. Not unlike children driving up to Disneyland, or adults looking out an airplane window and seeing the Las Vegas Strip for the first time, it was something people never forgot. He had imagined this location more times than he could remember. He was already looking forward to regaling anyone who would listen with every detail of his visit to Carnegie Hall. In the foyer, the Florentine Renaissance decor and the tinged marble floor—gently worn from the millions of footsteps that had crossed over it through the years—were just as he had pictured them. So were the round-headed archways of white plaster and gray stone. And the Corinthian pilasters. And the vaulted ceilings hanging over the gold-and-white interior.

On one side of the lobby was the box office, where a line of twenty people hoped to buy tickets to an upcoming event. Alas, each of them was being told by the two salespeople behind bulletproof Plexiglas that every show was sold out.

On the other side of the lobby, a German tourist group was setting out on their guided journey into the main hall, the Isaac Stern Auditorium. As their guide opened the door to the hall, utterly lustrous MUSIC wafted through the opening. Conductor Charles Dutoit was rehearsing the Philadelphia Orchestra as they readied for their performance of Hector Berlioz's *Symphonie Fantastique* later that evening. The sounds were some of the most beautiful Eddie had ever heard, but they only lasted a few seconds, because the doors then closed. There was no question in his mind. He simply had to hear more. Eddie quickly caught up with the tour group and remained in the middle of them, just as Detective McHenry had suggested. He apparently looked sufficiently German, because none of the tourists even glanced twice at him. The lone security guard on duty at the entrance didn't, either, so Eddie was allowed to move with the group into the auditorium.

Inside the hall, Eddie immediately stopped moving. Even momentarily stopped breathing. He closed his eyes as the most blissful smile crept over his face. He bathed in the thunderous music flooding over him. Everything he'd read about this place was true. The acoustics were simply astonishing. Architect William Tuthill did, indeed, have a golden ear.

The rest of the tour group continued quietly through the hall, but without Eddie. He sat down at the rear of the auditorium, slowly rotating his head from side to side as he listened to the sumptuous SOUNDS. His level of bliss was one few would ever know. He hoped he could stay there for days.

Unfortunately, his visit was about to be cut short.

$$((\cdot))$$

Out of breath, Skylar raced into the lobby, frantically scanning every face for the one she was looking for. *"Eddie!"* Nobody paid much attention to her. This was, after all, New York. She rushed to the front of the ticket line, pressing her face to the protective partition. "Excuse me—"

The salesperson never bothered to look up and spoke in a mono-tone. "You'll have to wait in line like everybody else."

Skylar put her mouth right next to the slots of the circular opening. "I'm a doctor. I'm looking for my patient."

Now the clerk glanced at her. "Why would your patient be here?"

"Because I think he ran in here."

"Is he dangerous?"

"No, he's not. But he's lost. I need to find him."

"If you don't see him, then I haven't seen him, either." She turned back to her computer screen.

Skylar surveyed the others in the lobby, moving toward the entrance to the main hall. The security guard approached her. "Ma'am, you can-not go into the auditorium without an escort."

"Will you escort me?"

"Next tour starts in an hour. You can wait over there." He pointed to an area off to the side.

"I can't wait." She continued through the doors without stopping as the orchestra rehearsed. The guard quickly caught up with her as she surveyed the thousands of auditorium seats. She knew Eddie had to be here somewhere.

The guard got right in her face and whispered intensely, "Leave now, or I will call the police."

"Good. Do it. Ask for Detective Butler McHenry."

The security guard hadn't expected this. "What is this about?" There was more than a hint of concern in his voice.

She answered tersely. "I'm a doctor looking for a patient who has escaped from a mental institution." She kept scanning the empty seats, wondering where the hell Eddie could be.

The guard's eyebrows raised. "A mental patient?"

She nodded for emphasis, allowing the guard's fears to run ram-pant. "He's about five foot ten, Caucasian, with brown hair. He's carry-ing a blue nylon backpack. Have you seen him?"

"What's in the backpack?" The guard was clearly concerned about the possibility of weapons—or worse—in the possession of a mental patient inside the building.

"Electronic equipment. Nothing that could hurt anyone, if that's what you're worried about."

He breathed a sigh of relief. "Why would an escaped mental patient be here?"

They were apparently talking too loudly. At the conductor's direction, the musicians stopped playing, and the auditorium fell silent. The maestro turned to glare across the expanse of the hall at the source of the distraction. "Do you mind?"

The guard blushed. He held up his hand as if to say, *Sorry, won't happen again.* He pointed toward the door. "Let's continue this outside."

Skylar took one last look around the auditorium before leaving. *Where the hell could Eddie have gone?*

((•))

At that moment, Eddie was being escorted out of the building by another guard, who had been dispatched the moment Eddie had taken a seat in the great hall. The act was strictly forbidden. Upon entering the building, his every movement had been followed through a well-concealed security system, because of the way he had been carrying his backpack. It clearly contained something of weight, and could very well be an explosive device.

The guard had approached Eddie quietly, hoping not to disturb the rehearsal, and asked if he had a guest pass, which would have allowed him to attend the rehearsal. When Eddie replied that he did not know what a guest pass was, the guard asked Eddie to follow him.

As they exited through the nearest doorway at the rear of the hall, Eddie asked if the guard was taking him to get a guest pass. The guard replied no, he was going to get him an exit pass. The statement was not technically a lie, so Eddie didn't recognize it as such. He said that he had never heard of an exit pass before.

The guard said that exit passes were very special and that only very special people ever got them. Eddie told the man that he lived in Harmony House, which was a special place for special people. With an unsympathetic smirk, the guard said that everything must be right with the universe, and he led Eddie out of the building onto the sidewalk along Seventh Avenue.

When Eddie asked where the exit pass was, the guard said he just gave it to him. Eddie looked confused, because the statement rang true—which in the guard's mind, it was—but Eddie was also certain that the statement was not true. The man had not given him anything, at least that Eddie was aware of.

He looked even more confused as the man quickly retreated back inside the building and locked the door. Eddie moved to the door, knocking politely. There was no answer. There was no door handle, either. He tried knocking again, but to no avail. Wondering if he might have misplaced his exit pass, he checked his pockets, as well as the ground he stood on, in case he had dropped it. He hadn't. There was no sign of a pass anywhere.

Eddie looked up from the sidewalk at the city around him, which suddenly seemed very large. And loud. And scary. It only now dawned on him that Skylar was nowhere in sight. He was alone in New York City.

"Skylar?"

CHAPTER 60

Main Lobby, Carnegie Hall, May 27, 5:28 p.m.

Skylar and the security guard had been joined in the lobby by the guard's superior, the director of Carnegie Hall security. Skylar wasn't quite screaming at the top of her lungs, but she was close. The security director did his best to maintain his composure. "Ma'am, would you mind lowering your voice?"

"I want help finding my patient!"

"Doctor, if you would stop yelling, we will be glad to assist you."

She paused to collect herself, and nodded. No more yelling.

The director of security appeared satisfied. "One of my guards just escorted someone who fits your patient's description out of the building."

"Why was he escorted out?" Skylar's concern grew.

"He had gained unauthorized access to the hall during a closed rehearsal."

Skylar took charge. "Show me where he was escorted out."

((•))

They were joined on the sidewalk by the guard who had led Eddie out of Carnegie Hall. The guard looked repeatedly to his boss, wondering what he had done wrong.

Skylar scanned around them in every direction, but Eddie was nowhere in sight. She turned to the guard who'd led Eddie out. "How long ago was he here?"

The guard shrugged. "About four or five minutes."

Skylar resumed searching around them, wondering which way he would have gone. She looked for markers—anything that might have attracted Eddie's attention. There was nothing. Until she saw the trees four blocks away. Central Park. Compared with the rest of New York City, the park was quiet. And trees meant birds. There was no question which way he was headed.

Skylar took off running.

CHAPTER 61

New York Office, Department of Homeland Security,
May 27, 5:31 p.m.

Max Garber followed the GPS blip on his screen as it moved through the Lincoln Tunnel heading for New Jersey. Garber was impressed that they could get such a clear signal through forty feet of water that was practically radioactive. The sad fact was the Hudson River was so polluted it had been declared a Superfund site after General Electric was found guilty of having dumped more than one million pounds of polychlorinated biphenyls into it over the previous thirty years.

In the fifteen minutes it had taken to get approval from the Homeland higher-ups for tapping Detective Butler McHenry's phone, Max Garber had brought himself up to speed with the day's events. He glanced at Agent Raines's location; he was now moving westbound on Desbrosses Street in his search for the doctor and patient who were believed to be in possession of stolen classified technology. Garber sent Raines a message: Det. heading to NJ. Lincoln Tunnel.

Raines responded immediately: Keep me posted. Want to hear calls.

Garber typed: Done.

CHAPTER 62

Hudson Street, New York City, May 27, 5:34 p.m.

Agent Raines rode shotgun in a blacked-out Suburban, scanning pedestrians when he wasn't working his phone. There were three other vehicles cruising the area around the Sixth Precinct, and they were soon to be joined by more. The search for Dr. Skylar Drummond and Edward Parks was rapidly becoming an all-out manhunt.

The agent behind the wheel got a message over his radio headset, which he immediately related to Raines. The NYPD had just received word from the head of security at Carnegie Hall that there had been some kind of disturbance involving a doctor and an escaped mental patient.

The Suburban was stuck in gridlock, so the driver screeched a U-turn into the middle of oncoming traffic. New Yorkers didn't care that the vehicle had bubble lights flashing through the grille or sirens wailing. They only knew that some asshole cut them off, and they were going to express their feelings about the matter. At least a dozen cars started honking.

The Suburban immediately came upon more gridlocked traffic. The driver didn't hesitate to veer up onto the sidewalk. Within half a block the traffic was moving again; the Suburban hopped off the sidewalk curb and back onto the street, running through red light after red light.

((•))

What Agent Raines didn't realize was that he, too, was being pursued. After Lutz's brief encounter with Raines in front of the Sixth Precinct, Michael Barnes had instructed his men to place a transmitter in the wheel well of the Homeland vehicle. Barnes knew he didn't have the manpower to locate Skylar and Eddie before the government agents did. But he had the manpower and know-how to take the doctor and her patient from them once the fugitives were in Homeland's custody. It was a dangerous game, but it wouldn't be the first time Barnes had played it. Sometimes, you just needed to show people how many dangerous threats there were out in the big, bad world.

Somebody was using Homeland for their own agenda, so Barnes decided he would, too. He only planned to briefly detain Skylar and Eddie before he and his men would then "rescue" them. Barnes would come off as a hero, the duo humiliated at the sports bar would have the last laugh, and Dr. Fenton would be able to take the credit he deserved for the echo box before riding off into the sunset. After all, the device was the man's swan song. The grand finale on a long and illustrious career. Barnes wanted his boss to go out on a high note—both because he deserved it, and because the revelation that an unknown faction had temporarily kidnapped his staff doctor and her patient from federal custody would guarantee increased funding for Harmony House security for years to come.

That, and Barnes simply wanted to show whoever these bastards were not to mess with him.

((•))

Hirsch and Lutz followed Raines's blacked-out Suburban from a safe distance of several blocks. They would not make the mistake of moving in too soon; there was no margin for error. They had already suffered one failure. They could not afford another. They would wait until Dr. Drummond, Edward Parks, and the echo box were securely in Homeland's possession. Then, with sudden swiftness, they would strike with brutal efficiency.

For now, they would wait.

CHAPTER 63

Harmony House, Woodbury, New Jersey, May 27, 5:39 p.m.

Inside his basement office, Barnes had just finished giving instructions for another mission to Able and Baker, his other two-man team. Able was Conrad Strunk, the smallest of Michael Barnes's team, and also the meanest. Alaskan trailer trash. Strunk had absolutely no problem with dirty work, which was the nature of this mission. He saw the world as a battlefield, and terrible things happened in battle. It was that simple. Baker, his partner, whose proper name was Joe Dobson, knew that only too well. The man had survived an eight-week kidnapping ordeal in Baghdad that left him with only one testicle and permanent emotional detachment, as a result of torture methods that could accurately be described as medieval.

Barnes told Strunk and Dobson exactly how it should go down. Barnes wanted it done later that night. The deed was not only intended to stop the leak; it was also designed to send a message to Nurse Gloria's handlers. Whoever she was working for needed to know the gloves were off. The stakes had been raised. Barnes wanted these bastards to know he would be looking for them, and their next recruit, every second of every hour he remained head of security at Harmony House. Michael

Barnes did not like to be played, and he was going to make damn sure the offending party knew it.

He was going to make the nurse suffer.

((•))

Fenton passed Strunk and Dobson as they exited Barnes's office. The senior doctor barely acknowledged them. Normally, he didn't like being down in this basement, and liked becoming directly involved in facility security matters even less, but today wasn't normal. Very far from it, in fact. He entered his security director's office without knocking, something he'd never done before. "Delineate our options."

Barnes, surprised to see his boss inside his office, paused before answering. "I don't think that's such a good idea."

Fenton put aside his fear of his security director and snapped, "I didn't ask what you think."

Barnes remained calm. "It would seem that a previous conversation we had in your office is what set all this in motion." He paused for emphasis. "If the echo box is working, we both need to be a great deal more careful about what we say in enclosed spaces."

Fenton had momentarily forgotten how much the world was about to change. *Anything you say can and will be used against you in a court of law.* The oft-repeated statement would have to be amended to something like, *Anything you have said can now be used against you, so you might as well fess up and get on with it.* People were going to have to learn to be as careful about what they said as they now were with what they transmitted. The American public was going to have to learn restraint, which Fenton thought would be a good thing in the long run. More like things used to be.

No one could retract what had already been spoken. Those echoes were already there, bouncing around, waiting to be reconstructed. Like blood evidence left at the scene of a crime, it never disappeared completely. A permanent record remained for anyone with the proper technology to retrieve. Fenton considered the future. "Eddie has said that eventually, the box will even work outdoors."

Barnes shook his head. "I guess it doesn't much matter where we incriminate ourselves, then." It took him a moment to wrap his head around the notion that anything ever spoken anywhere could one day be heard. It was truly stunning to consider, particularly in his line of work. Barnes quickly asked himself what he would hear first if given the choice. He knew right away that he would take the box to the Soldiers' National Cemetery in Gettysburg, and listen to Lincoln's address. It had been given at three p.m. on November 19, 1863, and was widely considered to be the greatest speech ever delivered in the English language.

Certain technologies were capable of winning battles before they ever started. In the Information Age, the echo box was going to be one of them. Fenton returned to the question at hand. "What is your plan?"

Barnes paused, deciding just how little he could get away with saying. "You are personally going to deliver the device to the president of the United States."

Fenton blinked several times as he digested the simple directive. "I'm what?"

"We can't trust anyone else to hand it over." Barnes watched the glimmer of a smile slowly appear in Fenton's face, just as Barnes knew it would.

"How will you regain possession of the device?"

Barnes just stared at him, and then looked pointedly at the four corners of his office. There was no way in hell he was going to answer that question.

Concern appeared in Fenton's face. "We cannot afford another mistake."

Barnes resented the statement. "The reason we are in this situation, Marcus, is not because of a mistake. You always knew the world was going to change the moment the box worked. It just so happened that moment occurred today."

Fenton nodded, both because his chief of security had a point, and because Fenton knew not to push the man too far.

"Immunity would be a good idea before you hand over the box. For both of us." Barnes was thinking about the crimes he was about to commit more than the ones he already had.

Fenton didn't hesitate. "Get me the echo box, and I will get us immunity."

After Fenton left, Barnes turned his focus back to the screen, pleased with the distance Lutz and Hirsch were maintaining from the DHS agents. He reached into his drawer and popped some antacid. The stabbing pains in his stomach were clear reminders of the extraordinary risk he was taking. This was the endgame. Michael Barnes was going all in. He liked his cards, but couldn't be entirely certain what his opponents were holding. He wasn't even sure who they were. But somebody had been playing him for far too long. Whoever it was needed to be taught a lesson. And Michael Barnes was going to teach them a doozy.

CHAPTER 64

Eddie looked scared. He had no idea how far he had walked, or for how long. He had just been walking to "nowhere in particular," which he still found to be a very peculiar destination.

He had given up trying to find the exit pass that he was supposedly given by the Carnegie Hall security guard, because he had no idea what the pass looked like. Eddie also didn't know why the man had locked him out of the fabled concert hall. It was all very confusing, and it made him feel uncomfortable, which was never a good thing.

Immediately after being locked out of the hall, he had trouble breathing. Then his vision became blurry. He put his hands on his knees because he thought he might fall over. But as his world started spinning and he was on the verge of slapping himself, something unexpected happened: Eddie imagined himself becoming completely helpless in this massive city of strangers. And the thought so terrified him that it somehow helped him to calm down. Because there wasn't anyone around who would help him. No doctors. No nurses. No anyone. Worst of all, no Skylar. He could relax when he was once again with her, but not until then. For the time being, he knew he needed to help himself. So he did. Counting footsteps, mapping the city visually, as well as acoustically. He differentiated the great many SOUNDS being produced all around him, and he intended to catalog them all from memory at the earliest possible opportunity. He was going to need a lot more notebooks.

There was no way Eddie could recognize what a developmental leap he had taken: Eddie was in control of himself. Not completely, but enough so to manage. He was on his own, and he was doing okay. It wouldn't last long. It couldn't. But these were some of the most important minutes of his life.

He was surprised to realize he had become surrounded at an intersection by a group of elderly people who had just gotten off a bus labeled "Skyways." He didn't understand why a bus, which traveled on the ground, would be called Skyways. An airplane, maybe, or even a helicopter, but not a bus. It made no sense.

The old people were waiting to cross the street when Eddie remembered what Detective McHenry had said: "Find the largest group of tourists you can and stay in the middle of them." So that's what Eddie did. He wasn't sure that these people were tourists, and was about to ask one of them, when he remembered that they were strangers. Mostly because he wasn't sure what else to do, Eddie stayed within the group until they arrived at a theater where a musical called *Chicago* was being performed. Why a group of tourists would come to New York to see a musical called *Chicago* was another thing that made no sense to Eddie. *Is there also a musical called* New York *being performed in Chicago?* The world was so confusing.

In any event, a heavyset woman in a yellow vest was handing each of the senior citizens a ticket that allowed them to enter the theater for the musical's next performance. The woman in the yellow vest did not hand Eddie a ticket, so he was not allowed to enter with them.

Alone once again, Eddie looked for another group to stay in the middle of. The next group he saw consisted mostly of men in dark business suits with either red or yellow ties. He had no idea what the significance of their tie colors was, but guessed each color must refer to a particular type of job. In Harmony House, different types of employees wore different types of outfits. The nurses wore tan. The cafeteria workers wore blue. The doctors wore white. Dr. Fenton sometimes wore a tie, but there was no consistent pattern to the colors of them. Eddie would have noticed if there was.

This particular group walked much faster than the older group from the Skyways bus. Eddie wanted to ask them to slow down, but didn't speak to them because it wasn't safe. He observed them, finding it curious that none of these men talked to each other. The old people in the other group didn't stop talking to each other the entire time he was with them, but all of these men talked into devices to people who were somewhere else, or typed on devices with their thumbs.

Eddie had never talked on a mobile phone, or typed with his thumbs. He had never sent a text message or an email, never updated a social-media page. He understood that these things existed and more or less how they worked, but it was strictly against Harmony House policy for patients to contact the outside world without permission. He had asked Dr. Fenton on numerous occasions, but the doctor always said the same thing: there were a lot of bad people out there, and the only way Eddie could be protected was to prevent the bad people from getting to him. He looked at those around him, wondering which of them were the bad people. Some of them? All of them? How could he tell? It was all very scary.

His world started to spin as Eddie became increasingly uncomfortable. New York City was too loud and too crowded and too different from Harmony House. He didn't belong here. He wanted to go home, but didn't know where Skylar was. He was surrounded by strangers, and Eddie knew he shouldn't be alone. It wasn't safe. Something bad could happen. He might get hurt, and the thought of that frightened him. There were so many ways a bad person could hurt him. He knew that people got robbed and stabbed and raped and murdered and tied up and tortured, all the time. None of these things ever happened inside Harmony House. He had only read about them, or watched them on television. These were things that only happened in the outside world, which he was now in the middle of. And it suddenly all became much too much.

SLAP! SLAP SLAP! SLAP SLAP *SLAP*!

Most of the businessmen around him didn't even notice, but those who did kept right on going. Except for the guy closest to Eddie. The investment banker stopped to ask if he was okay. Eddie slapped himself several more times until his entire cheek was bright red. It looked like a nasty patch of sunburn. Catching his breath, he answered that he didn't talk to strangers. The investment banker shook his head, wondering why he had even bothered, and quickly moved on. The freak could slap himself right into the emergency room for all he cared.

Eddie stood alone on the sidewalk for quite a while, wondering which way he should go, when he felt something he hadn't in years. A rumbling in his stomach. It was well past Harmony House dinnertime. The day's excitement and the unusual amount of walking had made him feel particularly hungry. He thought of his brief attempt at a hunger strike many years ago, and how much he'd disliked the feeling. To no one in particular, he said, "I'm hungry." No one answered. Or even bothered to glance at him. Eddie briefly wondered if he had become invisible, but then dismissed the notion. Invisibility wasn't possible. Not yet, anyway. But the gnawing in his stomach persisted, so he repeated himself. "I'm hungry."

The soft-pretzel vendor was at the other end of the block when Eddie first smelled the man's wares. Eddie breathed in deeply through his nose as his feet led him toward the scent. "I'm hungry." He'd repeated the sentence another six times by the time he reached the pretzel man.

"Two dollar." The man's accent was Egyptian.

Eddie was again confused. "Two dollar what?"

"Two dollar." He pointed to his handwritten sign, which read: "PRETZELS—$2."

"You mean two dollars."

The pretzel guy sneered with disgust at the arrogant American correcting his English. "Two dollar."

Eddie remembered the two one-dollar bills Skylar had given him after their bet in the police station, and reached into his pants pocket. He pulled out the two bills and held them up for the pretzel man to see. "This is two dollars."

The vendor quickly snatched the bills from Eddie's hand and replaced them with a freshly baked good. "This is pretzel."

It was the first item Eddie had ever purchased in his life. He enjoyed the warmth of the baked, twisted bread in his hand. It was comforting. Not too hot, and not too cold. He hesitantly took a very small bite, chewing with just his front teeth. Eddie had clearly never tasted one before.

"You never have pretzel?"

"Not one like this. The only kind of pretzels I have eaten are small and hard and crunchy."

The pretzel guy grinned widely. "Then you never have pretzel."

Eddie looked confused. "I just told you that I have only eaten pretzels that are small and hard and crunchy."

The Egyptian man motioned to the pretzel in Eddie's hand. "You like?"

Eddie took a moment to chew the small bite he had taken. He took his time like a connoisseur. "Three."

"Three what?"

"I give this pretzel a score of three. It could very well be a four, or even a four plus, but I have never tasted another pretzel like this one, so I don't have anything to compare it to. That's why I cannot give it a higher score. But I promise that when I eventually write down the score in my notebook, I will revise the number accordingly after I have a sufficient number of comparisons, if the revision is warranted."

The vendor nodded, not understanding a word Eddie had said after "three." But the man was pleased when Eddie took a large second bite, and an even larger third.

Eddie shoved the rest of the soft pretzel into his mouth, causing his cheeks to bulge and nearby pedestrians to maintain their distance, as he continued on down the sidewalk. Keeping his head down, looking at the cracks in the pavement as he stepped over them, he had no idea where he was or where he was going. Eddie knew only that he should keep walking. *To nowhere in particular.* So he continued counting his footsteps. Seven thousand four hundred and eighty-three. Seven thousand four hundred and eighty-four. Seven thousand four hundred and eighty-five.

CHAPTER 65

Central Park South, New York City, May 27, 6:43 p.m.

Skylar ran along the southern edge of the park, repeatedly calling out Eddie's name like a parent looking for a lost child. She grew more desperate with every passing moment. Looking. Looking. *Where the hell could he be?* It was her fault Eddie was off Harmony House grounds. And it was her fault he'd been allowed to slip out of the cab. She had already been living with the guilt of her brother's death after she left for college; a second death of someone equally as special, and perhaps even more, was something she couldn't bear. It would end her. She had to find him. *"EDDIE!"*

Skylar saw him in the distance. A man carrying a nylon bag clutched tightly to his chest. He was surrounded by a large group of tourists, moving away from her. She only caught a brief glimpse, but it was enough. Skylar took off running like she hadn't since her lacrosse days. The woman could really run. Even at an all-out sprint, she remained graceful. *It has to be Eddie. It just has to.*

But well before she ever reached him, she saw the man's face. He was at least fifty, and graying. The man was not Eddie. *Dammit!*

She continued looking all around her, turning her gaze up into the trees, hoping to find birds like the ones Eddie sang with at Harmony

House. One of these beautiful creatures might very well lead her directly to him. But where were they? There were no such birds in Central Park. The only birds that Skylar could see were pigeons. Dirty, nasty, flying rats that did not chirp or whistle. The sound pigeons made was more of a coo, and that was generous. The sound was ugly, and nothing Eddie would try to make music with.

Skylar kept running.

CHAPTER 66

Sixth Avenue, New York City, May 27, 6:56 p.m.

Agent Raines wasn't more than three blocks from Skylar. And rapidly getting closer. He had worked out a well-coordinated search grid en route to Carnegie Hall, which divvied up the sixteen-square-block area around the hallowed hall among the twelve search teams now taking his lead. He was a veteran. He knew this city. And he wasn't going to allow these suspects to escape. Especially now that he had learned from agents who had interviewed the Carnegie Hall personnel that the patient and doctor had been separated. The doctor wouldn't flee until she rejoined her patient, because she was responsible for him. She was looking for him while they were looking for her.

CHAPTER 67

New York Office, Department of Homeland Security,
May 27, 7:01 p.m.

The temperature inside 633 Third Avenue was rising, or so it seemed from the beads of perspiration on the foreheads of the eight Homeland Security analysts feverishly working their computers to catch a glimpse of the two fugitives. Max Garber was still tracking Detective Butler McHenry's southbound progress on the New Jersey Turnpike, but he was also now lead analyst on the fugitive-task-force support team, because of Raines. Garber clearly relished the hunt. He and his seven compatriots were scanning the unique biometric features of every face in view around Carnegie Hall. Well, most of them, anyway.

The program needed at least seven facial markers to positively identify someone, and it took a minimum of half a second to lock these in. Translation, the software missed every fourth or fifth person. This included the athletic woman who had been briefly running through the crowd along Central Park South. She just happened to be one of the fourth or fifth persons whose identity the software missed before she disappeared from view. And none of the analysts were even bothering to check any faces themselves. They were too busy tallying probables and weighting candidates for further investigation. Given the number of other possible simultaneous sightings, and that the woman they were looking for was less important than the man, neither Garber nor any of his people gave Skylar a second look.

CHAPTER 68

Bird Shop, New York City, May 27, 7:23 p.m.

As it turned out, Skylar was right. Eddie was talking to the birds. Three, in fact. A monk parakeet, a green singing finch, and a blue-fronted amazon. But he wasn't in Central Park. Or anywhere close to it. He was in a bird shop, one of only three in New York City. After walking 11,327 steps, Eddie saw the sign for the bird shop. It was colorful and friendly, and Eddie knew instantly that was where he should go. Because birds were good. So were people who liked birds.

A small crowd inside the store had gathered to watch him WHISTLE, CHIRP, and WHIR with his avian friends. The onlookers' expressions said it all. No one had ever seen anything like it. Not even the gray-bearded owner, who'd been in the bird business for over forty years. When there was a momentary lull in the conversation between Eddie and the birds, the proprietor asked, "You mind if I ask you something?"

"I don't talk to strangers."

The old man nodded as if he'd just been charmed by a precocious child. "Well, let's fix that, then. I'm Rupert Kreitenberg, and this is my shop. We're not strangers anymore, are we?"

Eddie made his BUZZER sound, startling the proprietor. "We are most definitely still strangers, Rupert Kreitenberg." Eddie kept his eyes on the monk parakeet.

Kreitenberg studied him with admiration. "You're the first person I've ever met who seems to love birds as much as I do."

"How much do you love birds?" Eddie asked.

"More than I've ever loved anything else."

"More than people?"

The owner smiled. "Definitely more than people."

"What is your favorite bird?"

"Can't say that I have one. I honestly love them all."

"Every single one?"

"Indeed."

"Even pigeons?" Eddie knew that most people did not like pigeons, especially people who lived in New York City.

"Yes, even pigeons."

Eddie turned to the old man without emotion. "I love birds more than people, too. Well, all except one."

"That person must be very special."

"Yes, she is. She is very special."

"Is she your girlfriend?" Rupert asked with a certain charm that was disarming.

"She's my doctor. But I don't know where she is right now." Eddie thought for a moment before continuing. "My name is Edward Parks, but I ask people to call me Eddie because it is the familiar of Edward and I am familiar with everyone I know."

"Hello, Eddie. My name is Rupert."

"Yes. Rupert Kreitenberg. You already told me that."

"So I did." He smiled warmly.

"We have something in common, which means we aren't strangers anymore."

"I'm glad we're not strangers anymore, Eddie."

Eddie closed his eyes, rotating his head slowly back and forth as he listened closely for any hint of falsehood. There was none. He turned his attention back to the birds.

"Do you mind if I ask where you learned to communicate with birds like that?" The proprietor couldn't stop smiling.

"No, I do not mind."

Rupert waited for an answer, then realized Eddie had already given him one. Rupert asked the question again, but this time more directly.

"Harmony House."

"What is Harmony House?"

"A special place for special people."

The proprietor's suspicion about Eddie was confirmed. He'd read about people with mental disorders who could do all kinds of amazing things, like memorizing phone books or counting cards. Apparently, talking with birds could now be added to this list. "Is that where you live?"

Eddie nodded. "I have lived in Harmony House since I was eleven years old, two months, and twelve days." The birds CHIRPED at him. Eddie responded.

"Do you understand what they're saying to you?"

"Yes."

"You mind telling me?"

"No, I do not mind telling you." Eddie WHISTLED, CHIRPED, and WHIRRED to the man, repeating the sounds he had just made to the birds.

Kreitenberg nodded. "Fair enough."

"What is fair enough?"

"I believe what you meant to say is there is no translation. It's music. How do you translate music, right?" Eddie CHIRPED some more. The old man smiled with astonishment. He was like a veteran music teacher unexpectedly coming upon a prodigy of unfathomable talent. It was how Beethoven's father, who was a decent composer himself, must have felt. "You know, I've spent my whole life around birds, and I've never seen anyone do what you can do. Did someone teach you?"

"No."

"Then how did you learn?"

"I have golden ears like William Tuthill."

"Who is William Tuthill?"

"He is the architect who designed Carnegie Hall."

The shop owner nodded, now remembering that little bit of New York history. "Yes, Eddie, I believe you do have golden ears."

Eddie returned his focus to the birds. "They do not like to be kept in cages, you know."

"No, I don't suppose they do."

"If you love them more than people, why do you keep them in cages?"

"Selling them is how I make my living."

Eddie looked confused. "How does selling birds make you live?"

"It's the way I earn money. Selling birds is how I keep a roof over my head."

Eddie looked up. "Structural support beams keep this roof over your head."

"This shop is how I put food on the table."

"I carry mine on a tray."

The owner could only stare in wonder. This young man was unlike anyone he'd ever met. Rupert knew this was one day he would never forget.

CHAPTER 69

West End Avenue, New York City, May 27, 7:44 p.m.

Skylar was exhausted. She'd been searching for miles. The shadows on the buildings were growing longer. There wasn't much daylight left. And she was no closer to finding Eddie than when she started. In fact, she was further away than ever. Somehow, she could sense it. She was looking for a needle in a haystack. The best way to help him might be to turn herself in and help Homeland find him before something unforgivable happened.

She moved to a graffiti-strewn pay phone mounted on a wall, only to find the receiver had been smashed long ago. There were no other pay phones in view, because so few people used them now, but there were dozens of cell phones in use all around her. Everyone she approached, asking to borrow their phone, looked at her with mild annoyance, moderate disdain, or outright disgust, if they acknowledged her at all. Skylar was beginning to dislike New York almost as much as Eddie did.

She walked to a newsstand, where she pleaded with the proprietor to borrow his phone. Engrossed in his own conversation, he pointed across the street to the dilapidated Jones Marquis Hotel. She darted through traffic and into the hotel lobby, where the elderly front-desk clerk flat-out refused Skylar's request, even when she explained it was a police emergency. He pointed to the 1970s-era phone booth on the other side of the lobby and told her to call 911.

Skylar collapsed inside the booth and pulled the glass doors closed. She enjoyed the moment of privacy, then collected herself before calling to turn herself in. Skylar glanced out through the glass doors at the elderly clerk as she dialed 911. The clerk leaned down behind the front desk to pick up something off the floor. It turned out to be a rusty little birdcage containing a yellow parakeet, which he placed on the counter. It was apparently dinnertime for the tiny creature. It flitted about excitedly in the cage as the elderly clerk scooped out a small portion of seeds, which he poured into a rectangular dish at the bottom of the cage.

Through the phone, the police operator spoke the six words she repeated several hundred times each eight-hour shift. "Nine one one, what's your emergency?"

Skylar hung up the receiver. She was no longer ready to give up her search for Eddie. Not yet. Skylar still had one more trick up her sleeve. She grabbed the well-worn yellow-pages book dangling from a metal chain inside the phone booth. The book was missing its cover and a considerable number of other pages. She prayed the one she needed was still intact. After flipping through the eight and a half pages of listings for "Beauty Supplies," she came to the listings for "Bird Shops."

In all of New York City, there were only three. Total page space was less than one-quarter. Only one of the shops, Flight, on East Eighty-Seventh, had any kind of ad at all. The other two, Give 'Em the Bird and Beautiful Birds, on Amsterdam, simply had their addresses and numbers listed. Skylar didn't know New York all that well, so she wasn't entirely sure which of the three shops was closest, but she thought it was the one on Amsterdam Avenue. And she had to start somewhere, so she left the hotel, after tearing out the yellow page containing the three bird shops, and hailed a cab.

CHAPTER 70

New York Office, Department of Homeland Security,
May 27, 7:55 p.m.

What Skylar couldn't have known was that the Jones Marquis had only five months ago been a popular address for prostitution. The New York City Police had successfully raided the establishment on several occasions, and had installed a camera directly across the street, providing a clear view of every individual who entered or exited. The ACLU had tried to force its removal, like they had so many others, but the matter was successfully tied up in the courts and the camera had already caught all the working girls and johns it was going to, so the matter seemed to simply fade away. While the hookers had moved on to another area, the camera remained, mostly because it was cheaper to leave it up than take it down.

The city was full of such surveillance refuse, which now included over 127,000 cameras. The law-enforcement and intelligence communities had only recently figured out how to utilize them in real time. Part of the solution was the new facial-recognition software being used inside 633 Third Avenue. Three of the eight Homeland analysts using it were currently engaged in a debate over whether a recent "catch" with a 55-percent-probable identity match for the female suspect as she entered a particular hotel several minutes ago was worth forwarding to the agents in the field.

The analysts had studied the profile image as closely as the particular camera's resolution would allow. Three hundred and fifty horizontal television lines (TVL) was on the low end of surveillance-technology resolution, and not nearly as useful as cameras with 480 TVL or higher. The three analysts did the best they could with what they had to work with, enhancing the footage to a nominal degree. When they brought the possible catch to Max Garber, he refused to act on it. Seventy percent was their threshold. Anything less sent field agents on too many wild-goose chases.

As the three analysts continued brainstorming how to improve the image to give them an actionable probability rating, none of them did what Max Garber did, which was to simply watch the ongoing real-time footage from the same camera. The same blonde woman in the same outfit who had only been seen in profile entering the hotel a few minutes ago could now be seen exiting the hotel, hailing a cab. This image was not in profile. She was looking directly at the camera. It was only moments before *87% Probable Match—Skylar Drummond* appeared across the bottom of the screen.

"Hey, guys." He pointed to the image, leaving the other three analysts speechless. Within seconds Max was on the phone with Agent Raines, who immediately directed four field teams to go after the cab Skylar Drummond had just gotten into. They were going to form a perimeter around the moving vehicle and immediately close in as soon as it stopped moving. Max contacted the New York City cab-dispatch office, and coordinated with them to track the cab's progress without alerting the driver. The dispatcher would also steer other cabs away from the immediate vicinity.

Agent Raines was right to have singled out Max. He was their quarterback, and the other DHS analysts were only too happy to follow his play call.

CHAPTER 71

Amsterdam Avenue, New York City, May 27, 8:03 p.m.

As Skylar's cab pulled to the curb, she asked the driver to wait for her. She said she'd only be a minute. Before the driver could protest, she was already rushing inside Beautiful Birds. Skylar entered the store and quickly moved through the overcrowded rooms. There were cages of every conceivable size stacked on top of one another. Big ones. Small ones. Wood ones. Hanging ones. And ones that looked like modern art. Prices ranged from forty-seven dollars to several thousand dollars. There weren't many birds, though. As far as Skylar could tell, there were three cages of canaries, two parrot cages, and several containing birds she didn't recognize. Not finding Eddie, she quickly bypassed a line of customers waiting for the proprietor, and asked if he'd seen anyone matching Eddie's description. The shop owner said he had not. When she asked if he was sure, he said yes, he goddamn was. And if she didn't mind, he had paying customers to attend to.

Skylar headed back out the door. One bird shop down, two to go. She stopped suddenly on the sidewalk. On any other day, she wouldn't have noticed them, but the black Suburbans arriving at either end of the block caught her eye. The vehicles were identical. It could be no coincidence.

She turned around and raced back inside the store. She went to the rear of the shop, passing floor-to-ceiling stacks of bird food, which looked like they were going to fall at any minute. She approached a door marked "Employees Only." It was locked. Skylar knocked urgently, but no one answered. She was cursing to herself, when the door cracked open.

An overweight teenage boy, whom Skylar took to be the son of the owner, poked his head out of the door. "Can I help you?"

"Does this place have a rear exit?" she asked urgently.

"No." He tried to close the door and return to playing *Ultra Street Fighter II* on his Nintendo Switch, but Skylar blocked the door with her foot.

"How about a bathroom? Is there one back here? I really have to go."

"I guess." He reluctantly opened the door and pointed inside to a bathroom. Skylar raced inside it, locked the door, and turned on the faucet full blast.

CHAPTER 72

Beautiful Birds, New York City, May 27, 8:07 p.m.

Agent Raines rushed inside the bird shop moments later. There was no sign of Skylar, so he quickly made his way toward the back and the "Employees Only" door. He banged on it loudly. After a moment, the teenage boy opened the door, clearly annoyed. "What?"

Raines flashed his badge and spoke urgently. "Homeland Security. I'm looking for a woman in her late twenties."

Before the agent could provide any further description, the boy's eyes went wide. He dropped his game controller and pointed toward the bathroom, where the faucet could still be heard running. He was barely able to speak. "She's in there."

Raines immediately drew his weapon and advanced swiftly toward the bathroom door. "Skylar Drummond, this is Homeland Security. Come out now." There was no response. The agent checked the door handle and confirmed it was locked. "Open the door. I won't ask again." Getting no reply, he kicked in the door. Wham! The door splintered readily.

He rushed inside the small bathroom; a window above the toilet was open. Peering out, he saw that one of the exterior metal security bars had completely rusted, allowing Skylar to bend it just enough to squeeze by. There was, however, no way in hell his 6'3", 220-pound frame was ever going to make it through, no matter what kind of shape he was in. He caught sight of Skylar as she ran out of the alley. "Son of a bitch!" Raines raced back into the store.

((•))

Skylar barreled out of the alley onto Sixty-Eighth Street, where she carefully peered around a wall of plywood surrounding a construction site plastered with posters for upcoming movies she would never see based on graphic novels she had never heard of. She didn't know how Homeland had found her, but realized they probably had dozens of agents out there looking for her. Skylar was also vaguely aware of the vast number of security cameras around the city. She knew she had to be more careful. But when opportunity presented itself, she wasn't about to hesitate.

A cab pulled over halfway down the block next to a petite woman attempting to carry shopping bags from various retailers. Fortunately for Skylar, the load was too much for the shopper. By the time the woman had given up trying to carry her haul all at once, intending to place her bounty into the cab several bags at a time, Skylar had already slipped into the cab, shut the door, and instructed the driver to hit the gas. As the cab sped away, the shopper raised the middle finger of her right hand and yelled at the top of her ample lungs, "Selfish bitch!"

CHAPTER 73

Harmony House, Woodbury, New Jersey, May 27, 8:09 p.m.

The Department of Homeland Security was back to square one, which meant Michael Barnes was, too. But he was calm by comparison. In fact, as the Harmony House security director received updates from his two men in the vicinity, Barnes enjoyed learning of Raines's outbursts. It meant he was an amateur. Had he even half the patience or experience Michael Barnes did, Agent Raines would have asked one simple question: Why had the doctor gone to a bird shop, of all places? Why not a hair salon or a bank branch or a fast-food restaurant? The answer was simple: Edward Parks had a thing for birds.

Michael Barnes was now sure of one thing: Skylar Drummond didn't know where Eddie Parks was. She had made an educated guess, and a good one at that. Because New York City had only three listings for bird shops. With only two left, Barnes had a fifty-fifty shot of guessing which one Skylar Drummond was going to next. He liked his odds, and placed his bet.

CHAPTER 74

Upper East Side, New York City, May 27, 8:16 p.m.

Lutz drove with reckless abandon. Hirsch navigated for him. By sheer luck, they made every traffic light en route to East Eighty-Seventh Street. Good fortune, it seemed, was on their side.

They arrived outside Flight in just under seven minutes, less than half the time it should have taken. The two security specialists bolted from their double-parked car and raced to the bird store's entrance.

To find the doors locked. The lights were off. According to the sign listing the store's hours, they had closed at eight o'clock. Hirsch peered in the storefront window as Lutz banged on the door loudly. The birds inside shrieked, but nothing else moved. There was no one there.

They quickly doubled back to their vehicle, hoping for similar luck with the traffic lights as they raced to the last bird shop on their list.

CHAPTER 75

Give 'Em the Bird, New York City, May 27, 8:33 p.m.

Skylar arrived first. She banged on the windows of Give 'Em the Bird, whose door was also locked. It, too, had closed at eight. *"Is anybody in there?"* She banged some more, but still there was no answer. Skylar was losing faith. She was on a wild-goose chase and knew it. The longer she delayed turning herself in, the longer it would take to find Eddie. Who was she kidding?

"There is nobody in there, but there is somebody in here." Skylar spun around to see Eddie looking at her through the open passenger's-side window of a late-model Volkswagen Jetta.

"Eddie!" Her joy was pure and unbridled. Skylar rushed to him, kneeling beside the car's open window. She instinctively reached out to touch his arm, which made Eddie flinch. Skylar quickly withdrew her hand as if to apologize for encroaching on his physical space. She knew better than to attempt physical contact, but just couldn't stop herself.

Eddie then did something Skylar could not have expected. He awkwardly reached out and hesitantly touched her arm. For only the briefest moment. It was all he could manage. But he wanted her to know that he wanted to touch her, too.

The enormity of the gesture wasn't lost on Skylar. It was more than she was ever able to elicit from her little brother. Try and try as she might, as a teenager, she was never able to help Christopher feel comfortable enough to initiate any contact. Skylar took a moment to find just the right thing to say, certain that it was the most physical contact Eddie had ever initiated in his life. "Thank you."

Eddie looked at her inquisitively. "For what?"

She answered with her eyes. For taking a chance. With her. Right then. In the middle of all this. For extending himself. And validating her belief in him. For comforting her as best he could. "For being okay."

"I am okay, Skylar."

She couldn't stop smiling. "I can see that."

"You're crying."

She nodded. "Happy tears."

"How can you tell the difference between happy tears and unhappy tears?"

"You have to look at the rest of the person's face. If they're smiling, they're happy tears." She used her hand to wipe her cheeks.

The bearded man in the driver's seat couldn't stop from beaming, either. He was immediately taken with the one person Eddie liked more than birds. "You must be Skylar."

"Who are you?" There was an edge in her voice. Her protective instincts were up, like a mother who was talking to the stranger who'd just invited her child into his car.

Eddie answered for his new friend. "He is Rupert Kreitenberg, who loves birds more than people."

Rupert tried to allay Skylar's understandable concern. "Eddie came into my shop and started talking to the birds. I've never seen anything like it. After a while, we started talking, and he explained how he got separated from you. I didn't think I should leave him alone, so I was going to take him back to Harmony House."

She studied him suspiciously. "It's a hell of a favor to do for someone you just met."

He nodded, understanding her skepticism. "I've never done anything this nice for anyone in my life."

Eddie interrupted, making his BUZZER sound.

Kreitenberg smiled and continued. "I've also never met anyone quite like Eddie."

Skylar softened, smiling briefly. She knew the feeling. "Most people haven't." She studied the man, who genuinely seemed harmless. "Mind if I get in?"

"By all means." He unlocked his doors so that Skylar could get into the back seat, where there was birdseed all over the seat and floor. "You'll have to excuse the mess."

Skylar climbed in, using her hand to sweep off the seat. "What mess?"

He smiled at her in the rearview mirror. "So where would you like to go?"

CHAPTER 76

Gloria Pruitt's House, Parsippany, New Jersey, May 27, 9:28 p.m.

Nurse Gloria's legs were tired, particularly her feet. Her heels throbbed. So did her knees, which typically swelled a good inch during the work-day. A nurse's job was to be on her feet, and by the end of an eight-hour shift, Gloria's were ready to call it quits. She was still quite curious as to the whereabouts of Eddie Parks, but had decided not to stick her nose where it didn't belong. The head of security had given her an answer, and that was supposed to be good enough.

Given her primary allegiance to her true employer, Gloria did not want to draw undue attention to herself. She needed to be careful. Her instinct for self-preservation had kicked in when she'd sent the text earlier that day. She genuinely cared about Eddie, but nowhere close to how much she cared about her son, or her own well-being.

Her drive home typically took thirty-five minutes, but required a little extra time today because she made stops at the grocery store for a pork tenderloin and the pharmacy to refill her Lipitor prescription. She never once noticed the sky-blue Jeep Wagoneer following her.

The nurse parked in her driveway as the sun set over the horizon. It was darker than it should have been, because the exterior lights weren't on. They were supposed to go on automatically, but, like everything else in life, they didn't always work as they should. She carried her dinner and medicine into her kitchen, turned on the radio, which she kept tuned to her favorite easy-listening station, and rinsed off the pork in her sink. Eating alone used to depress her, until she decided to make an occasion out of her meals. Now, every dinner she prepared was something special. A date with herself. It took time and focus, and was a far better way to spend an evening than watching the day's investment news. Jim Cramer's advice had never much helped grow her retirement fund, anyway. The repetition had also turned her into one heck of a cook, at least according to her devoted son, Cornell, who came home every chance he could.

Gloria was thinking about pouring herself a glass of white zinfandel when she thought she heard something outside. Well, not so much heard it as felt it. Something or someone was in her backyard. She couldn't quite make out what it was, but something wasn't right.

The hairs on the back of her neck stood up as everything got very quiet. The air was suddenly perfectly still. Too still. Looking out the window, she couldn't see a thing. It was nearly pitch black. There was no light outside except for the moon, and even that was obscured by the dense trees around her yard. She flipped the switch on the wall by the back door, but all her outdoor lights seemed to have gone on the fritz at the same time. A trip to the hardware store was now on her agenda for the following morning, right after church. God always came first on Sundays.

At least, that was her plan.

((•))

Crouched in Gloria's backyard, Strunk was fidgety from adrenaline. "Let's do this."

Dobson nodded. He didn't have quite the appetite his partner did for this type of work, and he wanted to get it over with.

The two lethal silhouettes moved swiftly across the yard toward the kitchen door. One carried a crowbar. The other a roll of duct tape. They were going to make it look like dangerous predators were on the loose. Morris County residents would be double locking their doors for years to come after reading news accounts of what was about to occur. *First she was robbed. Then tied up and beaten. And then far, far worse.* Sales of firearms and security systems would go up for months, as they always did after a heavily reported crime. Because Michael Barnes's two-man team was going to leave an ugly mess. Whoever Gloria was working for would get the message, loud and clear.

CHAPTER 77

Backyard, Gloria Pruitt's House, May 27, 9:29 p.m.

Through Leupold Mark 6 tactical night-vision scopes, Strunk and Dobson, Michael Barnes's two-man team, looked like greenish apparitions. The lenses were zoomed to 8X, which was close enough to make the targets' expressions clear. The taller man was gritting his teeth, like he was here for business that he was eager to be done with. But the smaller one appeared to be smiling ever so slightly. He was excited. There was no question he was looking forward to whatever he was about to do.

That expression was about to change.

(((•)))

The two baseball fans had their Phillies and Mets caps turned around backward. Not as any kind of fashion statement, but so that the bills of their caps didn't obstruct their views through the night-vision scopes of their matching suppressed SR-25 sniper rifles. Most would argue that this weapon was the finest ever designed by Eugene Stoner (SR stood for *Stoner Rifle*) and manufactured by the Knight's Armament Company. The SR-25 was a work of industrial art. Functional, beautiful, and lethal. The baseball fans carried the same weapon not only because they both preferred it, but also because redundancy was a good idea in any system. If one cog goes down, another is available to take its place, and the machine can keep right on functioning.

The baseball fans were lying prone on the ground about forty yards apart. Murphy, the Mets fan, had been here for hours, demonstrating masterful patience, but the Phillies fan, Giles, had only just arrived, shortly after the nurse. He had followed her from Harmony House to make sure she got there. Murphy had worked out their kill zone, which was generous by their standards, and directed his partner into position by speaking into the bone-conduction tactical headset positioned snugly against his larynx. Giles wore a matching headset. Both men could whisper at nearly inaudible volumes and still hear each other clearly.

Murphy moved his right index finger onto the trigger, gently applying consistent tension before he prepared to fully squeeze. He spoke almost silently. "One."

Giles used a slightly different technique to prepare for firing his weapon: he gently pulsed his finger on the trigger in synch with his heart rate. This allowed him to make sure he pulled the trigger in between beats. A sniper learns never to fire on the beat, which can be unpredictable. No one's heart beats perfectly every time. Exactly one second after he heard his partner's voice, he responded quietly. "Two."

Neither man said "three." Instead, they simultaneously fired their .22-caliber suppressed sniper rifles. *Fffwwt!*

The muzzle flashes on either side of Michael Barnes's men told them they were under attack, but Strunk and Dobson didn't have time to react. They were taken by complete surprise. The two men were thirty feet from Gloria Pruitt's kitchen door when their chests exploded.

The entrance wounds were small compared with the gaping holes that exploded out their backs.

The gunfire was impressively quiet, and demonstrated recent improvements in suppression technology. In fact, the sound of the two bodies collapsing to the ground had created more of a ruckus than the guns. Branches cracked. Leaves crackled.

Was that thunder she heard? Did something fall out of a tree? Whatever it was, there was some kind of commotion going on outside Gloria's window. She went to the back door and yelled out through the screen, "Is anybody there?"

Strunk didn't move. He was already dead, lying on his back. But to the surprise of the baseball fans, who were watching through their infrared scopes, Dobson's eyes were still blinking. His mouth was moving, but no words were coming out because his lungs, what was left of them, were full of blood.

Determined to find out what was going on, Gloria retreated inside her house to look for a flashlight. In the pantry, she opened the toolbox she kept for such emergencies. Of the three flashlights inside, only one worked, and this one barely. She took the dim flashlight and walked fearlessly out into her backyard. "Anybody back here?" She flashed the light around, moving it across the shrubs and trees until something on the ground caught her eye. Something red, which looked like blood. As she moved closer to the area, she became sure it was blood. There were two pools of it right next to each other, like two animals had just been killed there. Big animals.

But where were the bodies?

It occurred to her that whatever killed the two animals was still out there, and might still be hungry. There were confirmed recent sightings of coyotes in New Jersey. For all she knew, there might even be wolves. Gloria suddenly forgot all about the pain in her legs, and ran the ten yards to her kitchen door faster than she'd run any distance in years.

She locked and bolted the door. She shook her head while catching her breath, thanking the Lord for not punishing her bravado. He must have known she'd be going to church the next day, and decided to cut her some slack.

She didn't drink hard liquor very often, but tonight's dinner was definitely going to be accompanied by three or four fingers of scotch. Maybe five.

CHAPTER 78

American Heritage Foundation, Alexandria, Virginia,
May 27, 9:32 p.m.

The human body begins to cool immediately after the moment of death, which was why the heat signatures of the two bodies being carried from Gloria Pruitt's property were different from those of the baseball fans carrying them, as indicated by the thermal-imaging technology being used to observe them. From her office, Caitlin McCloskey watched along with Daryl Trotter while they enjoyed deli sandwiches from Jersey Mike's. She pointed to the dead bodies as they were carried to the Jeep Wagoneer. "They were killed at the same time, but their body temperatures are different. Why?"

Daryl corrected her. "They were shot at the same time, but both didn't die right away. It took him several minutes longer." He pointed to the brighter one.

"Nasty," she said with a noticeable lack of emotion.

Daryl asked, "How will they get rid of the bodies?"

"Fish food, if I had to guess," Caitlin answered with her mouth full of turkey and provolone.

Daryl concurred. "Cliché, but effective."

Bob Stenson briskly entered Caitlin's office. "How is our nurse doing?"

"Alive and well, thanks to the baseball fans."

"Where are they now?"

"Disposing of the bodies."

Satisfied, Stenson nodded. That was all he needed to hear. "I want you both to put all your focus back on the echo box. Homeland has no idea where either Drummond or Parks is. For all we know, they've left the city."

"Only if they're together," said Daryl. He was thinking strategically. "The doctor wouldn't leave without her patient unless she was forced to."

Caitlin nodded in agreement. She was thinking emotionally. "She'd turn herself in before leaving him alone on the streets this long."

Stenson spoke definitively. "She has not turned herself in."

Daryl spoke quickly as his mouth tried to keep up with his brain. "The only conclusion is that they are together. The question is, did they leave the city, or are they hiding?"

Caitlin jumped in. "She has few other close relationships with people in the city."

Daryl blinked rapidly as he factored in the additional data. "Edward's behavior is unpredictable, and might draw unwanted attention. Her goal will be to get him out of the city, probably somewhere nice and quiet."

Caitlin turned to Daryl. "Where?"

Daryl paused, his biological supercomputer running through an awesome number of calculations per second. He didn't like his answer. "I don't know."

Stenson made sure to look genuinely surprised. "That's disheartening."

"Let me give it some more thought." Trotter left the office quickly.

Stenson glanced at Caitlin, who couldn't stop herself from smirking. Human beings, even the smartest of them, were very easy creatures to manipulate if you knew which buttons to push.

CHAPTER 79

***Dr. Marcus Fenton's House, Pine Hill, New Jersey,
May 27, 9:35 p.m.***

Butler McHenry sat in his car, which was parked in front of Marcus Fenton's farmhouse. He had clearly been there for quite a while by the time the veteran doctor arrived home. Fenton seemed genuinely surprised to find that he had a visitor. "Can I help you?"

"Dr. Fenton, I'm Detective Butler McHenry with the New York City Police." Butler watched the older man closely.

Fenton didn't bat an eye. "Good evening, Detective. You're a long way from the city. What brings you all the way out here?"

Butler said pleasantly, "I'd like to ask you a few questions, if that would be all right."

"About what?" Fenton smiled innocently.

"I'd prefer we talk at the station." It was, of course, a bluff. A big one. But he wanted the doctor on McHenry turf, not Fenton turf.

"You must be joking."

"Not even slightly." The hint of a smile crept into his face as he saw the frustration build in Fenton. The trip here was now officially worth it, even if the doctor called his bluff.

"And if I decline?" The contempt in Fenton's voice couldn't hide his anxiety.

McHenry knew he had him. "I'll return with a warrant."

Fenton's face filled with rage. "You son of a bitch."

Butler opened the rear door of his car and patted the roof as the doctor moved to get in. "Watch your head. I wouldn't want you to hurt yourself."

CHAPTER 80

Max Garber stared at the blinking yellow dot on his screen as it started to move. The dot was the location of Detective Butler McHenry— or, more specifically, his phone. The detective was now retracing the route he had taken to the Pine Hill residence, which meant McHenry was returning to New York. What Garber had no way of knowing was whether he was returning to New York alone or with Dr. Fenton.

A simple Google search had revealed that Fenton was the founder and director of Harmony House, which was a government-funded facility in Woodbury. It seemed to be some kind of psychiatric hospital where Edward Parks was a patient, and where Dr. Skylar Drummond had started working less than two weeks ago. Garber, a closet gumshoe, wondered how a doctor and a psychiatric patient could have come into possession of classified technology. It was curious.

Detective McHenry was one of the lead investigators in the recent gas attack in the subway, which meant there was a connection between the fugitives and the attack.

But what?

He called Agent Raines to relate that Detective McHenry was returning from New Jersey. Raines responded that he didn't care about the detective at the moment. Until the fugitives were in custody, they were to be Max's one and only priority.

Max stood up, asking his ever-growing team of analysts keeping real-time watch over the city if anyone had anything worth relating. There was no response, other than shaking heads. Nobody dared to bring up any more low-probability catches. Nothing under 70 percent would be mentioned. Max spoke into the phone to his superior. "Sir, if they were still in the city, we'd have seen something by now."

"I'm inclined to agree." Agent Raines's voice was reassuring. He seemed to want Garber to know that he still had complete confidence in him. "Focus your people's attention on the subways, particularly the major stations. Get their images out there wide."

Max smiled, because he had already done so. Every street cop and transit-authority officer had already received high-resolution images of the two fugitives.

CHAPTER 81

Secaucus Junction, Secaucus, New Jersey, May 27, 9:41 p.m.

Eddie had never been on a train. Given the number of firsts he had already experienced in the last ten hours, Skylar was reluctant to introduce him to another. But there they were, parked outside of Secaucus Junction, trying to prepare Eddie for his first train ride. He was tired, both physically and emotionally, but managed to keep his growing sense of panic at bay by memorizing a printed train schedule.

He was hungry. Night had fallen, and he should have eaten dinner four hours ago. Saturday was fish-stick night at Harmony House, and it was among the most consistent meals offered by the institution. While Eddie had never given any serving of fish sticks the prestigious rating of five, he had also never given one a score lower than three, and it was the only Harmony House entrée to hold that distinction. Fish sticks were consistently a three or a four, and consistency was what Eddie craved now more than ever.

"How much longer do we have to wait?" he asked Skylar as they waited for Kreitenberg inside his car, which was parked in a handicapped space near the station's main entrance. The bird-shop owner had a ninety-three-year-old mother he occasionally drove to doctor appointments, and that gave him the legal right to possess the handi-capped placard now dangling from the rearview mirror.

"As long as it takes Rupert to buy us the train tickets to Philadelphia."

"Does it always take this long to buy train tickets?"

"It depends how many people are in line, and how many tellers are open." The slightest hint of concern crept into her voice. Rupert was taking longer than expected.

"Does everyone who rides on a train need someone else to buy their tickets?"

"Only people who are playing tag like we are."

"Because they don't want anyone to say, 'Tag, you're it'?"

"Exactly." Skylar kept a close eye on their surroundings. The parking lot around them was dimly lit. There was a nonstop parade of cars pulling up, with people getting into or out of them quickly.

The only sign of the authorities was a vacant police car that had already been parked by the main entrance when they had arrived. It was this vehicle that had prompted Skylar to ask the bird-shop owner to buy their train tickets for them.

To her surprise, Kreitenberg didn't ask for an explanation. In fact, he answered with fatherly understanding that he'd be glad to help them. What shocked Skylar even more was that he refused to allow her to pay for the tickets. He told them he'd be right back, and then left them in the car, adding that there were granola bars in the glove box if either of them got hungry.

Eddie opened the compartment and devoured one of the bars. He cringed somewhat, but that didn't stop him from eating the whole thing. "Two. Not good. Stale. Too crunchy. This granola hurts my teeth."

"Didn't seem to bother you too much," she said, continuously scanning the area around them.

Eddie paused, staring at the empty wrapper in his hands. She was right. "Skylar, why do you keep looking around?"

"I'm wondering where Rupert is."

As authoritatively as he could, he answered, "It depends how many people are in line, and how many tellers are open." His imitation of her was getting better.

Skylar smiled until a shadow suddenly appeared outside her window. Panic set in. She quickly glanced around the car, wondering how to get her and Eddie safely out of the vehicle, until the shadow held two train tickets to Philadelphia up against the window. She sighed with relief as Rupert opened the door.

"Sorry if I startled you."

"You came out a different exit."

"I did." He nodded, motioning to the empty police car. "I counted six officers and what looked to be the same number of agents, but they are harder to pick out. I saw at least one holding a phone with pictures on it, and I'm pretty sure they were yours."

Eddie turned to Skylar. "Why would officers and agents have phones with our pictures on them?"

"Because they're looking for us."

"Are they playing tag, too?"

"Yes."

Eddie asked, "How many people are playing tag with us?"

"More than I care to think about." She glanced briefly at Rupert, who continued to surprise her. "Why aren't you asking any questions?"

"If you were comfortable telling me what's going on, you would have already done so." She got out of the car, and he handed her the train tickets, along with two New York Mets caps and oversized T-shirts. "They're looking for a doctor and her patient, not two baseball fans. The Mets are playing the Phillies tomorrow in Philadelphia. Now you two will fit right in." He motioned to other fans making their way into the station. "Next train leaves at 10:22."

She studied him, realizing her faith in New Yorkers had just been restored. "Did you really tell Eddie that you like birds more than people?"

He answered sincerely, "Not everyone is lucky enough to know someone like you."

Skylar shook her head. "I'm not as nice as you think."

Rupert smiled warmly. "All I need to know is the effect you have on him." He gestured to Eddie as he got out to join them. "You know how special he is. What you don't know is how special you are."

((•))

From the moment Skylar and Eddie entered the crowded station, it was apparent that Kreitenberg was correct about the number of law-enforcement personnel looking for them. There seemed to be officers and agents around every corner, glancing at phones, which Skylar was certain displayed their images.

Skylar held her breath and kept her eyes on the ground as Eddie paused to cup his hands to his ears and rotate his head, familiarizing himself with the sounds of the gleaming station. The main concourse was over forty feet high and featured a thirty-foot-tall steel-and-glass cat-tail sculpture as its centerpiece. The sculpture was supposed to remind New Jersey Transit passengers that they were in the Meadowlands, where cattails were prevalent. At least, they had been before the open spaces were bulldozed and turned into a train station featuring statues of them.

The sculpture was ringed with neon, which emitted a slight but audible BUZZ. Eddie focused on it, along with every other noise echoing around the cavernous space. Footsteps, conversations, ringing devices, squeaking wheels, and never-ending arrival/departure announcements all bounced around the space's surfaces of granite, limestone, steel, and glass. The collective white noise formed a continuous RUMBLE, which Skylar knew was going to be a challenge for Eddie.

This explained the tissue paper sticking out of his ears. Not much, thankfully, but it was there, for anyone who looked closely enough.

Perhaps Skylar should have been less concerned with appearances, because Eddie's hands started shaking. "I don't like it here."

"The faster we keep moving, the less time we have to spend here."

"It's too loud."

"Breathe, Eddie."

"I am breathing. Otherwise, I would be dead."

"Focus on your breathing. Try to slow it down."

"Why?"

"Because I'm asking you to." She had learned to stop trying to explain things, much like parents do by their second or third child.

It only took Eddie a moment to act on the request. He began breathing slower. As the new rhythm became more automatic for him, Skylar watched as he turned his attention to the many passersby. He focused on one person at a time. Many of these people wore Mets garb, just like Skylar and Eddie. Kreitenberg was right. They were blending in, and that was good. They appeared to be nothing more than two small parts of the Mets collective moving toward a common destination. She gave people slight nods, or looks that compatriots give each other. They were united in common purpose. They were one.

It was working right until Eddie started to moo like a cow. He was focused on a heavyset woman walking by in well-worn cowboy boots. "Moo."

Skylar considered them fortunate that the woman didn't hear him. "Why are you mooing?"

"This space makes people sound like cattle." He stared at a particularly large, unshaven man, who was drinking from a large bottle wrapped inside a paper bag. He was at least 6'4" and over three hundred pounds. "Moo."

The man stopped abruptly and stared down at Eddie. "What the hell you say?"

"Moo."

Skylar quickly jumped in. "Please excuse my friend. He has Tourette's, and can't control certain impulses."

Eddie made his BUZZER sound. "I do not have Tourette's. I have Asperger's syndrome."

Skylar got right in Eddie's face and looked him directly in the eyes. "I'm your doctor. If I say you have Tourette's, you have Tourette's. Now let's go."

She would have dragged him away by the arm if she could, but knew that would only make things worse. So she did the only thing she could, and that was to walk away, desperately hoping that he would follow.

Thankfully, Eddie did follow her, repeating what the large man was saying behind him as he did. "Shoulda beat that punk-ass bitch to the ground. Don't care if he's no retard. Sumbitch needs to learn some respect." Eddie's tone and intonation were dead-on.

After turning a corner, confident that they were a safe distance away from the man-beast, Skylar paused, breathing a deep sigh of relief. She waited for Eddie to catch up to her. "You do not have Tourette's."

Eddie looked upset. "Then why did you say I do?"

"Because I felt like I had to."

"Why?"

"Because I didn't want him to hurt you."

This got his attention. "You really think he was going to hurt me?"

She nodded. "I'm quite sure of it."

Eddie glanced at various parts of his body, imagining a serious injury. "So it's okay to lie if you don't want someone to get hurt?"

She didn't know what to say. "It's okay if you don't have any other alternatives."

"How do you know if you don't have any other alternatives?"

"You do your best to consider all other possibilities."

Eddie nodded as if he understood, which he didn't. It was all quite confusing, and left him feeling uncomfortable. "I want to go back to Harmony House."

Skylar nodded. She knew this was hard for him, but she wasn't about to give up yet. "I thought you wanted to hear your mother's voice."

"I do."

"If I take you back to Harmony House, you may never get to." She would also lose any chance of ever getting retribution for Jacob's death.

"Because Dr. Fenton might take my echo box away?"

She nodded. "Yes. And I made you a promise to stop anyone from taking it away from you."

"Yes, you did."

"But I need your help to keep that promise."

He thought for a moment and reached his decision. "I will help you keep that promise." He counted his footsteps under his breath as he and Skylar made their way down two flights of stairs to the lower departure level. They were joined by an increasing number of Mets fans heading for the same train, who all shared the same thought: there was nothing more fun than staying up all night making fun of Phillies fans on their home turf the night before a good shellacking.

Eddie continued quietly counting to himself. "Two hundred and thirty-two. Two hundred and thirty-three." He stopped abruptly to scratch his neck where the newly purchased Mets T-shirt collar was rubbing against it. "I don't like this shirt. It itches my neck." He started to take it off.

"You only have to wear it until we get on the train."

"It makes me uncomfortable." He pulled the shirt over his head.

Skylar glanced at an officer in the distance, and spoke conspiratorially. "If a police officer tags you, it will be even more uncomfortable."

Eddie looked around. He also saw the officer down the platform. "I do not want to be tagged. I want to hear my mother sing."

"Then keep walking and do your best not to draw attention to yourself."

He put the Mets jersey back over his head as he resumed walking toward the train. "Two hundred and thirty-four. Two hundred and thirty-five."

CHAPTER 82

Harmony House, Woodbury, New Jersey, May 27, 10:11 p.m.

The distraught call from his boss was not Michael Barnes's main concern. It was understandable that Fenton resented being in the back of a squad car. Of course he was livid about being taken in for questioning. Detective Butler McHenry was a nuisance, but not a legitimate threat, not to either of them. McHenry had no jurisdiction nor evidence he could use against Fenton. The detective was fishing, hoping the old man would slip. In Barnes's professional estimation, that was highly unlikely. Possible, because anything was possible, but the odds were low. Fenton would lose a few hours being questioned, but that would be the extent of it. McHenry was nothing more than a frustrated detective who knew justice would never be carried out. His only move was to pester and annoy.

Barnes's bigger concern, the one causing the knot in his stomach to grow increasingly tight and resistant to the over-the-counter remedies he'd been gobbling down, was that the team he'd sent after the nurse had not been heard from. Strunk and Dobson should have checked in over an hour ago, but both of their phones had stopped transmitting GPS signals at Gloria Pruitt's residence. Which meant something had happened.

But what?

Barnes ran through a variety of scenarios, and the most likely involved the local police showing up at the nurse's house while Dobson and Strunk were engaged in the activities he'd prescribed. But even that was a stretch. A neighbor would have had to have seen something suspicious and called the police, or possibly even intervened directly. But his team's response in either scenario would have been to eliminate the witnesses. They would have had no qualms about it, and neither would Barnes. Far better to have collateral damage than anything even potentially leading investigators back to Harmony House.

So what was the holdup?

He called his team again. Both calls went right to voicemail. Something was very wrong. As he imagined various locations where his two men might be, Barnes never considered anywhere remotely close to their actual location. Which was the bottom of the Atlantic Ocean.

Parts of them were there, anyway.

CHAPTER 83

Peaceful Easy Feeling, 5.3 Nautical Miles off the New Jersey Coast,
May 27, 10:14 p.m.

The GPS coordinates were N 39°37′51.44″, W 74°05′56.59″. The National League East fans had jointly purchased the Albemarle 360XF three years ago, mostly because of the Volvo Penta IPS engine that came with it. IPS stood for *Inboard Performance System*, and that was what set this fishing boat apart.

At the moment, however, the Volvo Penta IPS wasn't being asked to give them anything, because the engine was turned off. The boat was still, except for the gentle rocking caused by the ocean currents beneath it. They had picked this location because of the three-hundred-foot vertical wall that was directly beneath them. The wall teemed with carnivorous life that didn't seem to care about whether its food came from land or water. Whatever the sharks didn't eat, the marlin, cod, mackerel, and Atlantic barracuda would. And whatever they declined would be savored by the bottom-feeders, which never rejected anything remotely edible. The absence of sunlight apparently made everything look good.

The key to getting these fish to feed on human remains was to chop up the bodies into pieces small enough to look appetizing. This was exactly the activity the boat-owning assassins were engaged in. And it explained the blood spattered all around the back of the boat, including over its beautifully scripted name.

The partners accomplished their work with matching Henckels carbon steel eleven-inch meat cleavers. The blades were razor sharp. Neither man showed any emotion about the work. It was just part of the job. The mess would all be hosed away within minutes after the last chunk of human flesh had been tossed overboard.

Giles paused as his phone rang. Not his regular phone. The encrypted one used exclusively for communication with their employer. They were probably calling for a progress report. He answered by saying, "The job is complete."

"I had no doubt," Stenson replied. "That's not why I'm calling. I have another job for you."

"I'm listening," Giles responded, which was what he always said when Stenson called. Murphy paused to listen in.

"It needs to be done tonight."

To the National League East fans, this only meant one thing: their boat was going to be paid off a lot sooner than they had anticipated. And if they got lucky, they would still make it to Citizens Bank Park the following day to watch their favorite teams battle each other for divisional supremacy.

CHAPTER 84

American Heritage Foundation, Alexandria, Virginia,
May 27, 10:15 p.m.

Realizing how long this night was about to become, Stenson was thankful he had taken the time to play doubles and get a massage earlier that day. It took serious conditioning to stay sharp and alert for twenty-four continuous hours, and sometimes much longer. Such marathons were rare, but they arose without warning. Any given day could turn into one, which was both an exciting part of working at the American Heritage Foundation and a frustrating one.

Foundation employees were on call 24/7/365. They were emergency-room doctors. The world was their patient. One who could go into cardiac arrest at any moment. Or suffer a cerebral hemorrhage. Or think it had when it had merely bumped its forehead. Most patients had no idea what they really needed, and the same was true for the world.

At least, that's how Bob Stenson saw it.

He had been administering critical care to a patient on and off life support for the greater part of three decades. The patient was far better off now than when their unique program of intervention began operations, and that was all the proof Stenson needed to validate his efforts.

He keenly watched the infrared images on his computer screen as the National League East fans discussed the specifics of the new assignment they had just been offered. Stenson had transmitted the subject's name (Michael Barnes), along with his relationship to the subjects of the just-completed assignment (their superior), and highlights of his military and civilian record (the list was long and impressive). The baseball fans needed to know exactly who and what they would be going up against.

They were taking considerably longer than usual to arrive at a price, which Stenson had expected. He had never tasked them with going after such a well-trained subject. By now, Barnes had certainly realized his two-man team was gone. Which meant someone had eliminated them. Whoever did the deed had recognized what Barnes's next move would be, and preempted it. Barnes would now be on the alert for an attack. This assignment required outthinking one of the best in the game, and success was by no means guaranteed.

"Five hundred thousand." The number hung in the air, both over in the boat 5.3 miles off the New Jersey coast, and inside Stenson's office in Alexandria, Virginia. It was ten times their standard rate. Twice what they had charged for Senator Townsend.

Stenson didn't reply for a good twenty seconds. He had decided before he made the call not to respond right away no matter what figure was quoted. He wanted his killers to sweat a little.

He had doubted they knew just how big a number he was comfortable with, and their price was a reflection of that. It was half. One million dollars would not have made him flinch. Perhaps they wanted him to think they were giving him another bargain. Or perhaps it was because Stenson was more familiar with Barnes and what he was capable of. Barnes had been a thorn in the side of the American Heritage

315

Foundation for too long, and Stenson was prepared to pay greatly for that thorn to be removed.

"The terms are acceptable." Stenson hung up the phone and watched on-screen as Giles delivered the news to his partner. They high-fived, then began chopping up what was left of the two bodies as quickly as they could. They had a lot of preparations to make.

CHAPTER 85

Secaucus Junction, Secaucus, New Jersey, May 27, 10:20 p.m.

It took Eddie another 317 steps to reach the Philadelphia-bound train, which brought the total to 552. This number included two flights of stairs, which contained thirty-two steps each. Eddie had remarked after descending each staircase that thirty-two steps was an unusually high number for one flight of stairs, but perhaps not for train stations, which Eddie could not comment on because Secaucus Junction was the first one he had ever been inside.

Skylar led him into the car farthest from the stairs, which happened to be the first car, the one directly behind the locomotive. They sat at the rear of the car, because no one standing on the platform could see them, and it gave them a tactical vantage point on the car doors. They would see anyone entering the car before they saw Skylar or Eddie.

Settling into their seats, Eddie immediately took off his Mets jersey and handed it to Skylar. "You said I only had to wear it until we got on the train."

"Yes, I did." She smiled warmly as Eddie closed his eyes, rotating his head back and forth to familiarize himself with the SOUNDS of the train car. Skylar did her version of the same, turning her attention to the other passengers. There were seven: two couples, one threesome.

One couple was elderly and spoke in either Swedish or Norwegian; Skylar couldn't be sure. The other was a married couple in their thirties, energetically discussing a performance they had just seen. Whatever it was, the wife thought the show was revelatory. The husband, however, had hated it, and said he would prefer to pay for the privilege of never having to sit through such garbage again. The threesome was a father and two teenage sons decked out in Mets garb, only their jerseys were well worn compared to Skylar's and Eddie's. They were genuine fans on their way to the Greatest Show on Earth.

None of the other passengers was cause for concern. *Thank God.* Skylar paused to catch her breath as the doors closed and the train started to move. They had made it out of Secaucus Junction, thanks to a little luck and the kindness of a stranger. She glanced around at the other passengers again, making sure she had properly assessed them the first time.

It only now occurred to her that she was thinking like a fugitive, and not like someone grieving the loss of a loved one. Skylar hadn't thought of Jacob in several hours. She knew she had more grieving to do, but it would have to wait. And for that, she was grateful. Skylar removed one of the granola bars she had taken from Rupert Kreitenberg's glove compartment and offered it to Eddie. "Hungry?"

Eddie did not respond. Because he didn't hear her. His fingers were flying across the keyboard of his laptop supercomputer. He must have turned it on while she was surveying the other passengers.

"Eddie?" She waved the granola bar in front of his face. "Would you like another granola bar? Because I'm going to eat it if you don't."

Again, he didn't respond. He kept his focus on his computer and continued working at a frenzied pace. Eddie was gone.

Skylar remembered Nurse Gloria saying, "He gets a certain kind of idea in his head, and wild elephants can't stop him from seeing it through." Watching him, she realized he, too, was feeling relief. He wasn't thinking about being away from Harmony House or being tagged, or even being hungry. All he was thinking about was whatever was currently occupying him, and that was a good thing.

But what was it? What was he thinking about? Skylar glanced over his shoulder at the computer screen and realized she was looking at another language. Eddie could be writing improvements to the echo-box algorithms, or he could be working on something else entirely. There was no way she could tell. It reminded her of her younger brother, Christopher, and the hundreds of pages of equations he had left behind that she had tried to decipher over the years. Most were complete gibberish, but some actually seemed to be the start of something, at least according to the theoretical physicists she had shown his work to.

She glanced out the windows at the moonlit Meadowlands as she ate the stale granola bar. She was surprised to see a few cattails waving gently in the night air. How nice that there were actually a few left. It really must have been a beautiful area before all the stadiums were built.

The train was due to arrive in Philadelphia at 12:39 a.m., exactly two hours and seventeen minutes from now. She couldn't leave Eddie, so she'd have to occupy herself as best she could. Her thoughts immediately went to Jacob, and Skylar now realized this train ride was going to be a very long one.

CHAPTER 86

Sixth Precinct, New York City, May 27, 11:19 p.m.

Marcus Fenton had never been inside a police station before and, after tonight, was determined to never be inside one again. How dare they bring him in for questioning? Who the hell did this detective think he was? And how dare McHenry leave him alone in a windowless interrogation room for over twenty-five minutes?

He was confident that there were people studying him through the two-way mirror that dominated one of the walls. They were watching him for signs of guilt. For something that could be used against him. Because nothing they had to date could be. As long as he remained calm, they wouldn't have a shred of usable evidence.

McHenry had brought him to this room, then immediately left without a word. Fenton had considered contacting his lawyer, who, in turn, would contact an attorney who handled this sort of thing, but decided against it unless they arrested him. He also briefly considered contacting Senator Davis to arrange for his release, but decided he would rather sweep this little incident under the rug as soon as it was over. He would grin and bear the momentary inconvenience, and then move on. After all, how long could this take?

((•))

Butler McHenry sipped the last bit of two-day-old coffee from a Styrofoam cup as he stared through the mirror at Fenton, who sat quietly at the table in the interrogation room.

Detective Lieutenant Victoria Daniels entered the observation room. "Has he asked for a lawyer yet?"

"Nope."

"Have you asked him anything yet?"

"Nope."

"How long do you plan on keeping him here?"

"As long as you'll let me."

"We've looked into the man's records. He's a big-shot doctor with big-shot connections and the federal government behind him. The moment you ask him a question he doesn't want to answer, he'll get lawyered up and be released. You'll never get anywhere near this man again."

Butler nodded. "I know."

Daniels shook her head. "So what the hell are you doing?"

"Enjoying the moment. The shitbag is guilty. I confirmed it the moment he agreed to come here. But I couldn't exactly stop and say, 'Well, thanks for your confession. I know there's nothing I can do about it, so I might as well turn around and take you back home.'"

"No, but you might as well say it now. I'll make arrangements for someone to take him."

As Butler got up to begin his interrogation of Fenton, he noticed Daniels removing something from her pocket, but paid little attention to it.

"Sorry to keep you waiting," he said, sitting down across from the doctor.

Marcus clasped his hands on the table in front of him. "No you're not."

Butler nodded. "I was trying to be polite."

"It doesn't suit you."

The detective looked him squarely in the eyes. "Would you like to make a confession?"

"Are you a priest?"

"Do I look like a priest?"

"If you're not a priest, I have nothing to confess."

Before Butler could respond, static came over the dusty intercom speaker at the top of the two-way mirror, close to the ceiling. The next sound to come through the intercom was the voice of Michael Barnes: *"You sure about this?"*

Fenton looked puzzled, but Butler recognized the acoustic reconstruction instantly. He'd heard it twice already. The detective turned back toward the mirror and glanced where he knew Victoria was standing. This was one of those rare moments when someone does exactly the right thing at exactly the right moment. He nodded with heartfelt gratitude.

The detective lieutenant held Deputy Inspector Nataro's pocket recorder next to the intercom microphone as the reconstructed conversation continued to play.

FENTON: *Yes, I'm sure. Skylar is too valuable. She's already made more progress with Eddie in days than the others made in years.*

Marcus Fenton's face tightened as he now recognized the conversation.

BARNES: *Will you want to know the details?*

FENTON: *Nothing in his residence. Make it look like an accident.*

BARNES: *He takes the subway.*

The click of the "Off" button could be heard over the intercom as Victoria stopped the playback. She stood so close to the two-way mirror, watching Fenton, that her breath steamed the glass.

Butler studied the doctor across the table, enjoying every second. If the NYPD ever made a Mastercard commercial, this was a moment that could fairly be described as priceless.

"I want to speak to my lawyer." Fenton's voice quivered. He was clearly rattled.

"I figured as much." Butler stood up from the table. "You're free to go. Transportation will be arranged for you."

Surprised, the senior doctor immediately got to his feet and moved toward the door. He paused. "You'll never be able to use it, you know."

"We just did."

Fenton steamed. "In a court of law."

"That may be. But now you know we know. And you will never be able to forget it." He held the door open for Fenton as the doctor stormed out of the room.

CHAPTER 87

New York Office, Department of Homeland Security,
May 28, 12:07 a.m.

Max Garber had followed Agent Raines's instructions to the letter, focusing his analysts' efforts on the area's five major train stations: Penn, Grand Central, Hoboken, Newark, and Secaucus Junction. All were reachable by subway. Penn and Grand Central were the obvious choices, but for that reason alone, Garber knew not to overlook the other three. The two fugitives had managed surprisingly well thus far to elude capture, and while part of their success could be attributed to luck, not all of it could. The doctor and patient were making smart choices. And the smart choice in this instance would be to avoid the two most obvious ones.

Garber split up his analysts into five equal teams, each assigned to one of the stations. They played catch up, reviewing surveillance footage from the last two hours—a guesstimate as to the earliest time the doctor and patient could have reached one of the train stations—to the present. Making full use of Homeland's facial-recognition system, they methodically studied every train passenger's face they could. Anyone with a rating of 70 percent or higher received closer, human inspection. It was this small percentage of "possibles" that required the analysts' complete attention. And was why most of them were looking bleary eyed and chugging as many Red Bull and Rockstar and 5-Hour Energy drinks as they could get their hands on.

In each of the train stations, a majority of travelers wore either Yankees or Mets paraphernalia. This was, after all, baseball season. And the Mets were playing their National League East rivals the following afternoon. Whether going to the game or not, every legitimate fan was required to wear their colors. And in New York, the Yankees and Mets had a lot of fans. Max Garber was a fan of the latter. Later, if he wasn't in the office, he'd be watching the game. If he was still in the office, which was looking increasingly likely, he'd sneak glimpses of the game on his phone.

Passing through the five analyst teams, Garber took note of the ones focused on Grand Central and Secaucus Junction, because those stations seemed to have the highest concentrations of Mets fans passing through their terminals. A quick search of train routes revealed why: those two stations had the most express trains to Philadelphia, site of the following day's matchup. The problem was that all five analyst teams had already completed their searches of the available footage, and none had come up with a single actionable lead.

Garber scratched his head. He dreaded the thought of reporting no progress to Agent Raines. So what to do now? In part because he didn't have any other ideas, and in part because his gut was telling him that somebody missed something, he randomly reassigned each team a different train station. Each was going to review the same footage another team had pored over. Garber wanted to be sure.

The government is known for redundancy. It's expensive and inefficient, but, every now and then, critical. This was one of those rare times that justified all the wasted taxpayer dollars. Because the second team to review the footage from Secaucus Junction needed less than fifteen minutes to spot the fugitives standing near the cattail sculpture in the station's main concourse. The time was 10:09, just over two hours earlier. Skylar Drummond and Edward Parks were both dressed in Mets jerseys and caps, which was probably why they were missed the first time. Max Garber was once again impressed with a choice the fugitives had made. He quickly called Agent Raines to inform him of their findings as all five analyst teams attempted to track Skylar and Eddie's progress through the train station.

The agent's question was simple and direct. "Where were they headed?"

"We're working on it now, but currently have no conclusive evidence. I can only make an educated guess."

"I'm listening."

"Both were wearing New York Mets jerseys and caps."

"They play the Phillies tomorrow, don't they?"

"They do. An express train for Philadelphia left Secaucus six minutes after the last time we spotted them."

"When is that train due to arrive?"

Garber checked the clock at the lower-right corner of his monitor. "In seventeen minutes."

In the time it took the analyst to hang up the phone, Agent Raines had already clicked off, speed-dialed the main Homeland switchboard, and asked to be connected to the Philadelphia office.

Raines had no idea that another party located in Alexandria, Virginia, would be listening to the call, just as they had been listening to his conversation with his favorite analyst.

CHAPTER 88

American Heritage Foundation, Alexandria, Virginia,
May 28, 12:12 a.m.

That particular phone call to Agent Raines regarding the fugitive sighting in Secaucus Junction had triggered a flurry of activity inside the American Heritage Foundation. Jason Greers listened to the call and quickly related the information to his superior. Bob Stenson promptly placed his second phone call of the day to Senator Corbin Davis, who was entertaining the last of the four hundred guests who had attended a fund-raiser in his honor. The senator excused himself from his well-heeled donors and stepped outside the garish home of his third-largest campaign contributor to listen to a set of detailed instructions. Davis then dialed Homeland Security Director Arthur Merrell and proceeded to give one of the country's three most powerful law-enforcement officers explicit orders as to how and where the fugitives should be apprehended, and, perhaps even more importantly, who should be allowed to come in contact with them and the echo box once they were in custody.

Merrell managed to overlook the disrespect he was being shown, because of his rising curiosity. "Senator, just what the hell is this thing these two are in possession of?"

"I'm not at liberty to say."

The Homeland Security director shook his head. "You don't know, do you?"

Corbin Davis grinned slyly. "Tell yourself that if it will make you feel better."

Merrell hated being kept out of the loop. "Must be a real game changer."

Davis paused, deciding to give the top cop just a tiny crumb to nibble on. "That would be an understatement."

CHAPTER 89

New Jersey Transit Train, Approaching Philadelphia,
May 28, 12:33 a.m.

When Eddie's fingers finally stopped flying across his laptop keyboard, he looked up to realize he had no idea where he was. All he knew was this wasn't his room. *Where am I?* He started to panic until he turned and saw Skylar sitting next to him. She was sound asleep. Just the sight of her helped calm him down. He now remembered that they were in a train. Headed to Philadelphia. To hear his mother sing.

Eddie glanced out the window, but couldn't see much. Silhouettes of apartment buildings and factories and gas stations and junkyards. A never-ending blur of streetlights and park lights and brake lights. It was not enough detail to give him any idea where along the route they were.

Skylar must have fallen asleep a while ago. She looked so peaceful. He was about to say her name when he stopped himself. And just watched her. Listening to her breathe. Eddie matched his breathing to hers, inhaling and exhaling at exactly the same pace. Then slowly reached out to touch his finger to her skin. He wanted human contact. Maybe only a fingertip's worth, but it was still a giant leap.

Skylar suddenly jolted awake, which made Eddie jump, too. "Sorry, I must have fallen asleep."

Eddie immediately pulled his finger back, pretending to scratch his forearm. "Why are you sorry?"

"I tried to stay awake."

"You were tired."

She nodded, glancing at his laptop supercomputer to see that it was turned off. She was about to ask him what he'd been working on, when the train lurched forward, slowing noticeably.

Eddie was worried. "What happened? Did the train come off the tracks?"

She checked her watch. It was 12:33, which meant they were just about to pull into 30th Street Station. "We're almost there."

Eddie looked confused. "Almost where?"

"To 30th Street Station."

"We're in Philadelphia?!"

She paused a long moment before saying, "Yes, Eddie. Welcome home."

CHAPTER 90

Harmony House, Woodbury, New Jersey, May 28, 12:42 a.m.

Michael Barnes was now certain that a third party had entered the game. Or, rather, a third party who had always been in the game, watching in silence, lurking in the shadows, had decided to reveal itself by entering the field of play. There was no other possible explanation for the sudden disappearance of his two-man team sent to Gloria Pruitt's residence. Barnes had ruled out every other possibility. Someone knew they were coming. Which could only mean Barnes's communications had been compromised. *My God, for how long?*

Barnes was impressed. Such a move required patience. Discipline. Resources. And experience. Which meant whoever had caused the disappearance of his team was a formidable adversary. Perhaps, even, an unbeatable one. But Barnes had been in unwinnable situations before. It had been decades since he'd faced such a daunting challenge, but he was confident he still had the chops.

There was, however, one critical difference. In those earlier situations, all of which had occurred outside US borders, there was no walking away. Failure meant death. That was not the case today. He could just walk away. Disappear. It was an option he'd prepared for years ago. While Michael Barnes was indeed fiercely loyal to Marcus Fenton, he was not willing to rot in a cell for him. If the ship was sinking, Barnes would jump and jump fast, and never look back.

But this ship wasn't sinking just yet.

The irate calls from his boss were the least of Michael Barnes's concerns. So what if the venerable doctor had been humiliated at the hands of a New York City Police detective? All Butler McHenry had done was confirm one very crucial piece of information: the echo box was now working. Acoustic archeology was real. The detective had played a recording for Dr. Fenton. Which explained why the third party had stepped out of the shadows.

The two questions burning in Barnes's mind were: Where was the echo box currently, and what did the nurse have to do with Edward Parks and his device?

As to the first matter, Lutz and Hirsch had never lost visual contact with Homeland Security Agent Harold Raines. Barnes's team had done exactly as they were instructed, maintaining a safe distance from the subject. Barnes had expected them to report that Raines was returning to the Sixth Precinct to gain possession of the device. Instead, Michael Barnes was informed that Agent Raines had returned to the Homeland regional office at 633 Third Avenue. Which could only mean one thing: Homeland was giving up the chase, at least in New York. Edward Parks and Skylar Drummond were no longer in the city. They had gotten away. When Lutz and Hirsch asked what they should do, Barnes ordered them back to Harmony House.

As to the second matter, regarding the nurse, the previously unknown party would have only protected her because she had value to them. They wanted her to continue working for them. They wanted to maintain the status quo. Their status quo. Which couldn't possibly include someone who had just tried to have her killed. Michael Barnes could almost see the bull's-eye materializing on his forehead as he stared at his own reflection in his computer screen. They would be coming after him, and when he least expected it.

Barnes was surprised at how quickly he reached his decision. Perhaps it was the wisdom that comes with age. Or that deep down, he doubted that he truly still had what it took. Whichever the case, after nearly two decades of loyal and dutiful service to Dr. Marcus Fenton and Harmony House, Barnes simply got up and left his office. He didn't take a single personal item with him. Not a photo. Not a pencil. Not even one of the many stomach remedies he always kept on hand. He exited the building, walked across the parking lot, got in his beige Impala, and drove off the grounds of Harmony House without so much as a word.

The only things he would be taking with him on his journey were contained in two thirty-six-cubic-foot, vacuum-sealed aluminum storage lockers buried side by side beneath a wooden toolshed in his backyard. Because that was the plan. He'd carefully stocked the lockers years ago. The metal boxes held everything he'd need to live on for years in any number of environments. Michael Barnes was going off the grid. He just needed to get his carefully packed supplies, and he would be gone. *Pffft!* The world would never see him again.

Unless he wanted it to.

CHAPTER 91

Eddie was once again wearing his baseball jersey as he and Skylar walked through 30th Street Station with the other Mets fans. Some people in the distance booed, which wasn't entirely unexpected. New Yorkers would have greeted arriving Phillies fans similarly. Skylar took note of several Philadelphia police officers gathered in the main concourse. There was a notable lack of urgency about them. It was clear they had not been put on tactical alert for two federal fugitives in possession of stolen classified technology. Not yet, anyway. But Skylar veered away from them, just to be safe.

"Are we still playing tag?" Eddie asked.

"Yes, we are."

"Do we have to?"

"I'm afraid so."

"Why are you afraid so?"

"Because they're still playing." She nodded toward the police officers.

Eddie paused. "I don't ever want to play this kind of game again."

"I don't, either." She smiled at him as they made their way out of the building with the flow of Mets navy blue and orange. They moved down the sidewalk toward a line of cabs, where a man with dreadlocks, wearing a bright-orange vest, was coordinating who got into which cab.

Skylar turned to Eddie and asked, "Would you be okay taking cab ride number twenty-nine?"

Eddie studied the line of cabs, along with their license-plate numbers. "Twenty-nine is a prime number. I like prime numbers, because they can't be divided by anything but themselves. Do you like prime numbers?"

"Love them." She answered playfully, knowing what his reaction would be.

He made his BUZZER sound.

"Will you take cab ride number twenty-nine because it's a prime number?"

"No, I will because you asked." He smiled at her briefly.

The man in the vest pointed them toward the cab at the front of the line. Skylar moved toward it, opening the door for Eddie to get in, only to discover that he had moved to the cab behind it. "He wants us to ride in this one, Eddie."

"I don't want to ride in that one." He pointed to the cab behind it in line. "I want to ride in this one."

"Do you mind telling me why?"

"No, I don't mind."

Skylar waited for an explanation as the man in the vest told her they needed to get a move on or lose their turn. It took her another moment to realize she needed to ask Eddie, "Why?"

He pointed to the license plate of the first cab. "All the numbers are even."

"What's wrong with even numbers?"

"Other than the number two, even numbers cannot be primes. Twenty-nine is a prime number. It is odd."

Two of the cabbies farther back in line started to HONK impatiently. Eddie covered his ears in pain. "Tell them to stop honking their horns. It hurts my ears."

Skylar pleaded, "They will stop honking if you get in the cab. Eddie, please." To her surprise, he climbed in the door she was holding open for him. Skylar joined him in the back of the cab, which smelled like stale, cheap beer.

Eddie cringed. "This cab smells like that place for guys with no place better to go, except there are no peanut shells on the floor."

The driver was apologetic, saying that somebody had spilled beer on the floor earlier that night, and he hadn't had time to clean it up.

Skylar asked Eddie, "Would you like to go directly to your old house, or would you rather get something to eat first?"

Eddie answered without hesitation. "I would like to go directly to my old house. I have only been hungry for a few hours, but I have been waiting to hear my mother's voice my whole life."

Skylar gave the driver the address, and he headed for it. She kept a close eye on Eddie, who wouldn't stop fidgeting. "I don't want you to get your hopes up too much."

"How will I know if my hopes are up too much?"

"You need to consider all the possibilities."

"What are all the possibilities?"

"Well, for example, one possibility is that your father no longer lives there."

Eddie nodded. "I understand that my father may no longer live there. But the echoes of when he and my mother did live there will still be there."

"If someone else now lives there, they may not be comfortable allowing us inside, particularly at one in the morning."

"Why wouldn't they be comfortable?"

"Would you be comfortable letting a perfect stranger snoop around your room at Harmony House?"

"We are not going to snoop around my old house, Skylar."

"I know that. But whoever may live there now might not. And we can't explain exactly what we're going to do there, either, so as far as any new resident might be concerned, we'll be snooping around."

"Why can't we explain exactly what we are doing there?"

"This is another thing you're just going to have to trust me on." She smiled ever so slightly.

Eddie briefly thought about the growing list of things Skylar had asked him to trust her on. "Yes, I understand that if someone else now lives there, they may not be comfortable allowing us inside."

Skylar nodded reassuringly. "But don't worry. If that's the case, I'm sure I can find a way to convince them."

Eddie smiled and nodded, because he knew the statement was true. "I'm sure you can convince them, too. Look how many things you have convinced me to do that no one has ever been able to convince me of before."

She nodded. "That's because you trust me."

"How do you know I trust you?"

"Through your actions."

"My actions communicate that I trust you?"

She nodded. "Actions speak louder than words."

Eddie stared out the window. "No they don't."

"It's a figure of speech."

"I don't like figures of speech."

"This one is actually a good one," Skylar assured him. "If someone tells you they care about you, they might mean it, but they also might not. But if someone shows you through their actions, then you know they mean it."

Eddie noticed the cabdriver was nodding in agreement, so he nodded, as well. "I will continue showing you through my actions that I trust you."

She looked him in the eyes. "I'm glad, Eddie. That makes me feel good."

He looked away. "Why does it make you feel good?"

"Because I want you to trust me."

"Do you trust me?" he asked with all sincerity.

"Eddie, I trust you one hundred percent."

"That makes me feel good, too." He said it with the exact same intonation she had used.

For the first time since she'd known Eddie Parks, Skylar couldn't be sure of whether he was merely regurgitating what he had just heard or actually meant it. So she asked, "Why does it make you feel good?"

"Because I want you to trust me." The slightest hint of a smile crept across his face.

The cab headed north on Broad Street, passing the main campus of Temple University before heading west on Susquehanna Avenue. The driver pulled to the curb in the 300 block and announced that they had reached their destination. The meter read: $17.30. Skylar paid him with a twenty, and got out of the cab, along with Eddie.

He stared at the door to 317, but did not move toward it. "Eddie, what's wrong?"

He just stood there, pointing toward the home's entrance. "That's the wrong door."

"Are you sure it's the right address?"

"It's the right address: 317 West Susquehanna Avenue, Philadelphia, Pennsylvania, 19122. But it is definitely not the right door."

"What's wrong with it?"

"The door is the wrong shape and wrong color. It should be brown and splotchy, not black, and it should be curved on top."

"Maybe it was just painted."

"No, it was not just painted. Nothing is the same. The whole building is wrong. It's not the same at all."

Skylar only now noticed how new the redbrick structure looked. In fact, the entire block looked new. Like it had all been recently rebuilt and gentrified, much like developers were intending to do with Butler McHenry's mother's neighborhood. Dread filled her voice. "Eddie, do you remember if the building used to be made out of brick?"

"It was not made out of brick. It was made out of wood. Yellow-painted wood. Some of it had termites, and those parts were more gray than yellow."

Skylar moved to him carefully. "Eddie, do you know that when they build new buildings, they often tear down old ones first?"

"Yes, I do know."

She waited for him to connect the dots. He didn't. "I think that's why the building looks different now."

Eddie looked like he'd had the wind knocked out of him. "You think they tore down my house?" She nodded. Eddie was devastated. "If they tore down my house, the echoes will be too dispersed. If the echoes are too dispersed, I won't be able to reconstruct enough of the original sound waves to hear my mother's voice!" SLAP! SLAP! SLAP!

Skylar quickly grabbed his hands and held them tight as he flailed against her. "You will hear her, Eddie. I don't know how, but I promise you will hear your mother sing."

His face turned red as he fought against her with all his might. It took considerably longer than usual for him to calm down. Skylar did not release him until she was certain all the fight had left him.

And that was when all hell broke loose.

CHAPTER 92

317 West Susquehanna Avenue, Philadelphia, Pennsylvania,
May 28, 1:01 a.m.

Eddie tensed suddenly. His entire body went rigid. Skylar had no idea why until she saw the six heavily armed federal agents moving swiftly toward him. Weapons drawn. Safeties off. Eddie started screaming hysterically. The Philadelphia-based Homeland Security agents had been waiting for them in the shadows. They were now less than twenty feet away. Eddie and Skylar were completely surrounded. *How could I not have seen them?* Skylar thought.

"FREEZE!" barked the lead agent. "FEDERAL AGENTS!"

Skylar pulled Eddie in tight, clutching him with every bit of strength she had as his body started to convulse.

The lead agent barked, "PUT YOUR HANDS IN THE AIR!"

Skylar kept a firm grasp on Eddie, and screamed, "If I let go of him, he'll harm himself!"

His tone did not waver. "RAISE YOUR HANDS AND KNEEL, OR WE WILL OPEN FIRE."

There was no question in Skylar's mind that he and his associates would follow through on the threat. So she complied. The echo box and laptop supercomputer tumbled from Eddie's grip, falling to the street as he started seizing violently. He collapsed near his precious devices, SLAPPING himself as hard as he could. Ten times. Twenty times. There would be no stopping it this time.

Skylar looked on helplessly as the agents closed in. She pleaded, "He needs to be restrained!"

The agent was now standing directly in front of her. "Happy to oblige." He smirked. "I'm Agent Kendricks." He nodded to one of his subordinates, who cuffed her left wrist, and then her right, behind her back. It was the first time Skylar had ever been in restraints, but all she could think of was Eddie.

He had slapped himself almost fifty times by the time the agents managed to restrain him. His face looked raw. His cheek was bleeding. It took four agents to hold him down long enough to get his arms behind his back and cuffs around his wrists.

Skylar tried to sound reassuring. "Eddie, I'm still here. I'm right here with you. Try to focus on my voice. Pretend that I'm still holding you."

He continued writhing helplessly in the middle of the street, even after they had released him. The handcuffs dug into his wrists. The silver cuffs quickly became stained with blood as the metal bit into his skin. He couldn't stop himself, seemingly oblivious to the pain.

Skylar struggled to keep from crying. Her eyes welled with tears. "Eddie, can you hear me? You're hurting yourself. Stop. Please, stop . . ."

And then, without warning, he did. Eddie stopped moving altogether. He was no longer even blinking.

Agent Kendricks immediately moved to him, getting on his knees, checking Eddie's pupils. They were dilated. "He's gone into shock."

"Take his goddamn handcuffs off!" Skylar screamed.

Kendricks did so. Eddie just lay there limply.

Skylar pleaded, "Please, let me help him. I won't go anywhere."

Kendricks rebuffed her without emotion. "He is no longer a danger to himself. An ambulance is on its way." A siren could be heard approaching in the distance.

"Where are you going to take him?"

"That's none of your concern." The agent's tone was authoritative.

"Like hell it's not! *Where are you going to take him?*"

He eyeballed her. "If I were you, I'd be more concerned about where we're taking you." She eyeballed him right back.

He then turned to one of his subordinates, who was bending down to pick up the echo box. "Sir, what should we do with—"

Kendricks suddenly drew his weapon and took direct aim at his fellow agent. "Back away! NOW!"

The young agent jumped back, bewildered. "Sir, I was only trying to—"

"Our orders are that no one touches either machine. Is that clear?"

"Yes, sir." The young agent took several more steps away from the echo box, assuming that contamination might be a factor. He was only too happy to get the hell away from the thing.

Skylar kept her eyes glued to Eddie as the ambulance arrived on the scene. Its siren was deafeningly loud. She realized that if he hadn't gone into shock, Eddie would now be in tremendous pain. Several agents surrounded the paramedics as they tended to him. Skylar no longer had a clear view of what was being done to him. It was killing her. "I'm still with you, Eddie."

"He's in shock," said one of the paramedics. "He can't hear you."

"You have no idea what he can hear!" she snapped.

Every agent immediately turned his or her attention to Philadelphia Director of Homeland Security Albert Shoals, as he arrived. There were four other agents with the director, two on each side. One of each pair carried a large metal case handcuffed to his right wrist. Shoals approached Agent Kendricks. "Where is the device?"

Kendricks moved to the echo box and supercomputer lying in the street. "Nobody has touched either item since we apprehended the fugitives, sir."

Director Shoals studied them. "They look like they were dropped."

"They were, sir. The fugitive Edward Parks dropped them when he was surrounded."

"Whatever the hell this thing does, you better hope it still does it." Shoals nodded to the men with the cases, who approached the echo box and laptop lying in the street. One unlocked his case, placed the echo box inside it, locked it, and gave the key to Director Shoals. The other agent did the same with the laptop, locking it up and giving the key to the director.

The five men left as abruptly as they had arrived, and in the exact same formation. The men with the cases remained on either side of Shoals. The second agent in each pair flanked them on the outside, remaining a half step behind their counterparts. They got into a waiting blacked-out Suburban, the middle vehicle in a caravan of three. As the vehicles sped away in close formation, Skylar was certain that neither she nor Eddie would ever see the echo box again.

She turned back to Eddie as the paramedics moved him onto a gurney and started wheeling him toward the ambulance. "Eddie, I promise I will find you."

He did not respond. Eddie had already been sedated. The gurney was placed in the rear of the ambulance. The doors were closed. And the ambulance sped off. Skylar did not look away until it was completely gone from view.

And all at once, Skylar felt as alone as she'd ever felt in her life.

Agent Kendricks stepped toward her. "Follow me." He led her to a waiting vehicle.

"Please tell me where they're taking him." The agent did not respond. She quickly grew frustrated. "What harm will it do to tell me?"

He paused outside the vehicle. "The more accurate question is, Doctor, what good will it do? My understanding is that you're never going to see your patient again."

CHAPTER 93

Michael Barnes's House, Swedesboro, New Jersey, May 28, 1:19 a.m.

Michael Barnes's cell phone vibrated, sliding around the tan Formica counter of his small kitchen as the device rang and rang, just like it had the dozen other times Fenton had called recently. Once again, the call went through to voicemail. Barnes did not answer the phone because he could not hear it. He was busy with a shovel in the storage shed at the rear of his property, digging up the second of two storage containers he had so carefully packed years ago.

Barnes had purchased the home when he first started working for Dr. Marcus Fenton, because it was cheap, it afforded him the privacy he required, and Swedesboro and Woolwich Township were close, but not too close, to Woodbury and Harmony House. Seventeen minutes, door to door, and there was never any traffic. It didn't bother him that the place was a dump.

The property was dimly lit by design. Barnes liked it that way. It gave the impression that the home's resident was careless, and gave him a tactical advantage against most types of threat. The only light at the rear of the property came from the temporary work light Barnes had strung up across one of the storage shed's beams. He had backed his Impala to the shed's sagging entrance in part to block any view of his activities, as well as to reduce the distance he'd have to carry the unearthed containers. The first box was already in his back seat. The container had just barely fit, which was no coincidence. It was the largest container that would fit through the door. The second box would similarly squeeze into the vehicle's trunk.

Barnes was sweating as he hoisted the second container out of the ground. It had only been buried two feet beneath the ground's surface, and the box weighed no more than 150 pounds, but it felt to him like twice that much. Barnes thought to himself that maybe he really was getting too old for this shit. Given how radically his life was about to change, he found the notion reassuring. He had made this choice because it was his only choice. In a universe of one option, you take it.

Barnes dragged the container to the rear of his car, and paused to take a breath. That was when he saw it: a single, partial boot print in the driveway dirt, which had never been paved for exactly this reason. He had visitors. Barnes's tactical neural computer instantly cranked up to an uncountable number of calculations per second, and went something like this: The print was the right heel of a combat boot made by Altama or Belleville, both of which were military approved, AR 670 compliant. The size was approximately twelve, which meant the size of his enemy was approximately 6'1" and 190 pounds. The adversary most certainly had training similar to his own, which meant he wouldn't have come alone. He had at least one associate with him, and possibly more. Barnes was outnumbered.

These were elite hired professionals working in a clandestine service few knew existed. And at least one of them could see him at this very second. The only piece of the equation that didn't add up was why he was still alive. It was a matter that would be resolved in the next three seconds.

(((•)))

The target looked like a greenish apparition through the Leupold Mark 6 tactical night-vision scopes trained on him from opposite sides of the property. The National League East fans had arrived shortly after the home's owner had returned, but it had taken them longer than expected to get into desirable firing positions. The property was a ramshackle obstacle course: storage bins, stacks of tires, a dilapidated greenhouse, rusting lawn furniture, and a broken-down canned-ham trailer that looked like it hadn't been touched in decades. There were old strings of Christmas lights strung up around the property, some sagging so badly they almost touched the ground. It was all so haphazardly scattered about that there was no way they could possibly know that everything had been placed for very specific reasons known only to the maze's designer.

The baseball fans, however, would find out soon enough.

Thirty yards from his partner, Murphy whispered into his bone-induction tactical headset, gently applying consistent tension in preparation for squeezing the trigger of his SR-25. "One."

Giles pulsed his trigger finger on his identical weapon. "Two." As the two men fired in perfect unison exactly one second later, something unexpected happened. Barnes ducked. He dropped to the ground as if his legs had suddenly given out, collapsing right behind the storage container, which was bulletproof. Barnes's instincts had saved his life, but hadn't saved him from being wounded. Murphy's .22-caliber bullet clipped Barnes's right ear, removing the upper portion of it, which fell to the ground like an undercooked piece of chicken sausage. Giles's hollow point ripped through Barnes's left shoulder, causing enough structural damage that replacement would be his only option for returning to full function. That was, if he survived the night. But it was his nonshooting shoulder, so at least he had a fighting chance.

The National League East fans watched him hide behind the storage case, which was large enough to conceal his body. Murphy said quietly, "Son of a bitch got lucky."

Giles never blinked. "Not for long."

Murphy carefully scanned for a glimpse of the target. "We have that same case."

Giles recognized it, too, remembering that the reason they had selected it was the reason it was being used now. "No point trying to shoot through it, then."

Neither took any action. In this game of chess, it was their opponent's move.

((•))

Barnes was in excruciating pain. But the searing sensation only seemed to further sharpen his senses. The game was on, and it was being played on a field of his design. He had a true advantage. He knew exactly where on the property grid the two shots had been fired from. He also knew exactly how best to approach them.

Barnes's first order of business was to neutralize their night vision, which he assumed they were using, because it was what he would do. Employing the storage container as a shield, he pulled it with him as he crawled backward, deeper into the shed. Reaching the rear wall, he grabbed a section of pipe from a stack of them, and used it to reach up and flick an old light switch. With the click of the mechanism, the entire property lit up like a Christmas tree, quite literally. The old, sagging strings all worked perfectly. They might not have been stadium lights, but they were enough to temporarily blind anyone not expecting them. Barnes took out his handgun.

((•))

By the time the National League East fans had adjusted their eyes, Barnes could no longer be seen. "Target's on the move," said Giles. He scanned his half of the property, knowing his partner would be doing the same on his side.

"Copy." Murphy scoured the rear of the property. There was no sign of Barnes. So he closed his eyes and listened. There was no indication of movement. Crickets were chirping, but that was about it. The air was still. Tense. "He's good."

"We're better." Giles continued scanning around him, methodically looking from left to right, then back again. He was a machine. Patience was the key. And they could wait all night. Sooner or later, the target would reveal himself. And if he could see them, they could see him. It was their advantage, two-to-one.

((•))

What the National League East fans hadn't counted on was how well Barnes knew his property, which had more in common with a paintball combat zone than a traditional backyard. He literally knew every angle. Which meant he was playing chess and his hostiles were playing checkers. If either one of the shooters had moved, Barnes would have heard it.

The shooter on the west side was closest to him. The hostile had taken his shot from behind the canned-ham trailer, which was located twenty yards from Barnes through poorly tended hedges. This shooter's bullet was the one that had removed part of Barnes's ear. That meant the shooter had probably been standing. Barnes guessed the assassin was still within six inches of the trailer corner he had used to steady his sniper rifle.

The trailer walls were a combination of clapboard and aluminum siding. A bullet's trajectory would deviate less than one degree if fired through it. The hedges wouldn't affect the projectile's trajectory at all. Barnes decided to fire three shots in quick succession. Each would be six inches apart horizontally and twelve inches apart vertically, because it was possible the target had decided to kneel. Barnes rehearsed the quick three-shot several times, and then fired without pause. BOOM! BOOM! BOOM!

((•))

Giles, whose position was between a stack of tires and a swing set, could see the muzzle flashes in the distance, and immediately returned fire. He would soon learn none of his shots had found the mark.

Murphy, however, never saw the gunfire, because the trailer blocked his view. The three shots ripped through the wood and metal siding like it was Swiss cheese. The first bullet missed him, but the second and third did not. The second shot punctured Murphy's abdomen, perforating his descending colon and shattering his pelvis. The third shot hit him in the leg, obliterating his right femur, along with his quadriceps and adductor muscles. He collapsed instantly. He grimaced, clenching his teeth. "I'm hit."

"How bad?" his partner asked urgently.

"Doc's gonna earn his pay." He was referring to the emergency-room doctor they had on retainer. First, they needed to reach him, but there was no way Murphy would be able to move on his own. All he could do was lie there, writhing.

Giles needed to help his partner, but couldn't until Barnes was neutralized. He knew this was no time to get emotional. He needed to think clearly and strategically. His enemy would expect him to give his partner aid. That was why he couldn't. But what wouldn't Barnes expect? Giles quickly considered his options. Then dialed 911.

((•))

Barnes had no way of knowing the severity of his opponent's injuries. He heard the body collapse behind the trailer, so he knew at least one of his shots had found its mark. He got into position in case the second shooter attempted to help his partner, and then waited for his enemy's next move.

Barnes liked his odds better now that it was one-on-one, but he was injured, and his remaining opponent wasn't. He couldn't afford to be as patient as the other shooter could. His advantage was his knowledge of the terrain, and Barnes needed to capitalize on it while he still could. As he devised his strategy, he heard a siren in the distance. Then two. And more. They were getting louder. *Son of a bitch,* he thought. *Now that was clever.* He had to give his opponent props. What was once an open-ended game would now be decided in less than sixty seconds.

He thought fast. Ghosts weren't supposed to draw attention to themselves, but this one just did. Whoever was employing these two wouldn't be pleased. Even if they completed their assignment and he didn't survive the night, this would be viewed as unacceptable. It might even mean the end of their chosen careers. In fact, the more Barnes thought about it, the more sure he was they had decided this was their swan song. Which meant they were in the same situation he was. They would disappear before the night was over. The only question now in Barnes's mind was how much pride they took in their work. He was about to find out.

Barnes retraced his steps, moving quickly toward the Impala. Using only his right arm, he stood the storage container on its narrow side, leaning it against the open trunk of the car. He somehow ignored the searing pain shooting through his left shoulder and used the vehicle as leverage to lift the back end of the heavy container and slide it into the trunk; it just barely fit. Keeping his eyes on the driveway in front of him for any movement, he hopped into the driver's seat and started the engine. He saw no movement through the windshield. *Are they actually letting me go?* It didn't matter. Barnes did not intend to exit via the driveway, anyway. Behind him, along the rear of his property, ran an old wooden fence about six feet high that kept the neighbors from getting too curious about what he did back there. It also created an emergency exit if the need ever arose. Barnes put the transmission in reverse and slammed his foot on the gas.

((•))

From the moment the assassins had arrived and seen what Michael Barnes was unearthing inside his storage shed, they knew they needed to have a Plan B. Plan A was a repeat of their performance from earlier that night. But Michael Barnes was most certainly well armed, and one slight misstep could lead to a messy firefight. That would lead to a thorough investigation, and their employers would not like that. Plan B would be similarly displeasing to their bosses, due to the attention it would later bring, but it would have the benefit of a plausible explanation. Emergency kits such as Barnes's always contained six things: a variety of clothing, freeze-dried foodstuffs, a water-filtration system, medical supplies, a large amount of cash, and an even larger number of weapons. This often included explosives. After all, theirs did.

Giles had required less than two minutes to affix orange-colored Semtex to the car's front left wheel well as Michael Barnes dug out the first of his storage cases. Four pounds of the waterproof putty would have been sufficient. Ten pounds would have eviscerated the body. But the National League East fans had decided to go with twenty pounds of the Czech-made explosive, because Barnes would have had at least that much in his survivalist stash. And everybody knew that explosives were dangerous, especially when they were moved.

Giles watched Barnes get inside his car and start the engine. As he put the car in gear, Giles flicked off the safety of the remote detonator in his hands. He then said quietly to his partner, "Fire in the hole," and pressed the button beneath the blinking red light.

BOOM!!!

The jolt would measure as a magnitude-3.1 earthquake in a seismic-activity-measuring station seven miles away. In Barnes's yard, Giles was thrown hard to the ground with the wind knocked out of him. Murphy, already on the ground, momentarily lost consciousness.

At ground zero, Michael Barnes was vaporized. The largest piece of him that would be recovered measured less than two inches long. He was scattered across his entire fourteen-thousand-square-foot lot, as well as several of his neighbors' yards. Some of him would remain lodged in another homeowner's gutter for months.

CHAPTER 94

American Heritage Foundation, Alexandria, Virginia,
May 28, 1:53 a.m.

The heat signature of the explosion flashed so brightly on the American Heritage Foundation's high-definition monitor that Daryl Trotter thought the screen might have to be replaced. Caitlin McCloskey sat next to him with her eyes glued to the screen. "So much for subtlety."

Jason Greers stood behind them, looking over their shoulders. "All that matters is that Barnes will no longer be a problem." He texted the news to Stenson, who was not on American Heritage grounds.

"He won't be happy if Forensics finds anything."

Jason scoffed. "If they do, we can make that disappear, too."

Caitlin shook her head. She hated when testosterone got the better of her counterparts, especially Jason. She focused her attention on the monitor, where she could now see something fluttering in the air. "What is that?"

"What?" Jason looked closer, but couldn't tell what she was looking at.

She pointed to the screen. "There. In the air. It looks like confetti." The thermal-imaged sky above Michael Barnes's residence became filled with what looked like thousands of pieces of large confetti.

Daryl smiled. "I'll give you both a clue. It was inside the cases Barnes had loaded into his car."

Caitlin kept studying the screen. It looked like paper. "Pages from a Bible?"

"You've got to be kidding." Jason snickered. "Michael Barnes never opened a Bible in his life."

Caitlin disliked being embarrassed. "Then what?"

Daryl answered quickly, intent on defusing the tension between them. "Cash."

Jason was stunned by the sheer volume of money fluttering around in the air over Swedesboro. "That's got to be a couple hundred grand."

"At least." Daryl nodded. "I think I can tell you why our guys used so much explosive . . ."

Caitlin wasn't about to ask another dumb question, so she let Jason do it for her. "Why?"

"A small amount would look exactly like what it was. A hit. A large amount will give investigators the impression that a stockpile accidentally ignited. Anybody who kept that much cash on hand was preparing for something. Extremists often include a variety of weapons and ordnance in their stashes. Further investigation into Barnes will reveal the disappearance of two of his employees earlier last night. While those cases will go unsolved, the presumption will be that Barnes snapped, was somehow involved with their disappearance, and then accidentally blew himself up while setting out to make himself disappear."

Jason was truly impressed. "Goddamn, they're good."

Caitlin had a different thought. "I just pray we never do anything to piss them off."

CHAPTER 95

Philadelphia Office, Department of Homeland Security,
May 28, 2:17 a.m.

Homeland Security Agent Kendricks led Skylar down a corridor lined with cells inside the Philadelphia office. "When do I get my phone call?" she demanded.

"You're joking, right?" The agent smirked.

"Do I sound like I'm joking?"

They paused outside a cell at the end of the hall, where the agent removed her handcuffs. The cell door opened electronically. "Doctor, you were in illegal possession of classified technology. If the technology is deemed to have been a threat to national security, you will be classified as an enemy combatant. That means you will lose your rights as a United States citizen. We can hold you indefinitely. So if I were you, I wouldn't hold my breath for any phone call."

CHAPTER 96

The hospital known as CHOP was the closest hospital to Eddie's childhood home. Director Shoals's office had already notified them of Eddie's impending arrival. He was described as "an extremely high-value patient," so Eddie was greeted by a large team of doctors and nurses as the ambulance pulled up in front of the emergency-room doors. An even larger security team from Homeland surrounded the medical staff as they performed their duties. The agents would be accompanying this patient wherever he was taken.

The doctors and nurses had never seen so much security around any patient. His symptoms were obvious and few, but the doctors checked and rechecked everything before making any formal diagnosis. There were minor abrasions to the patient's face and wrists. Straining against his handcuffs had clearly caused the latter damage. The doctors were surprised to learn the facial injuries were self-inflicted. This led them to believe the patient might have a history of mental illness, which would be helpful to know in order to properly prescribe a course of treatment for whatever trauma had caused him to go into shock.

While no other symptoms were present, the doctors ran a lengthy battery of tests to rule out every conceivable possibility. They performed a variety of blood work, as well. Seven vials' worth. A CAT scan. MRI. X-rays. Then more blood tests, just to double-check the first set of results, which all came back negative.

All the while, Eddie remained unconscious. He saw nothing. Heard nothing. His breathing was steady. His vitals were normal, and wavered little. The only question was how long it would take for him to come out of shock. When one of the agents asked the question, CHOP's chief of emergency surgery answered authoritatively, "It's a wild card. We just never know. Sometimes, the patient can return to relative normality within a matter of minutes. But some patients can remain in shock, or some variant of it, well, indefinitely."

CHAPTER 97

I-295 North, Bellmawr, New Jersey, May 28, 2:39 a.m.

The National League East fans sped north along a dark stretch of I-295 at over a hundred miles per hour. Giles drove. Murphy was lying across the back seat, applying as much pressure as he could muster to his wounds, but it wasn't working. Pools of blood covered the seat. He was dying. His voice was weak. "How much farther?"

"A couple minutes. Stop being such a pussy." Giles glanced in the rearview mirror, pleased to see the glimmer of a smile pass over Murphy's face.

"You should . . . check in."

His partner nodded, and dialed their employer.

The man they had never met, and would never meet, answered after the first ring. "Yes?"

"The job is complete."

"Final payment will be processed." Click. Their employer disconnected the line. The $250,000 would be received in their account less than five minutes later.

Giles dialed another number for the second time that night. It was their emergency doctor. Tonight was the first time in three years they had needed his services. Until this point, he had been handsomely paid for doing almost nothing. Now, they intended to get their money's worth. "We're five minutes out." The doctor said he was ready.

CHAPTER 98

Lutz and Hirsch were dreading their return to Harmony House. They had failed, pure and simple. Their boss, Michael Barnes, was an unforgiving man. He did not tolerate failure at any level, but especially when so much was at stake. All Lutz and Hirsch could do was face whatever consequences were awaiting them.

Which was why they were so surprised by what greeted them. There was nobody manning the front gate. No security personnel patrolling the grounds. Lutz and Hirsch considered the possibility that Harmony House was under siege. That the facility had been taken over. The two men grabbed as much firepower as they could carry from the portable arsenal in their trunk, and set out to defend their home base. But all they accomplished was to terrify several nurses and a member of the cafeteria staff playing a quiet game of poker at the end of their shift. As far as these people knew, it was just another night at this special place for special people.

Strangest of all was the absence of Michael Barnes. Their boss wasn't in his office, or anywhere on the grounds. His car was not in the parking lot. And he was not answering his phone. They had never once known their boss not to answer his phone. Something was wrong.

Lutz and Hirsch quickly discussed their options. One was honorable: stay and defend the fort until they found out what the hell had happened. The other was self-preserving: flee and don't look back. The latter went against all their years of training, but Barnes was most likely either long gone or dead, which meant he wasn't coming back. If Barnes was gone, somebody must have given him a very good reason to make himself disappear. If somebody had taken him out, they were next.

Lutz and Hirsch would later wonder what took them so long to reach the obvious conclusion. They didn't slow down until they were somewhere in Iowa, where they dumped their car in exchange for a new one, and kept right on going.

CHAPTER 99

Industrial Park, Haddonfield, New Jersey, May 28, 2:44 a.m.

Dr. Reggie Portman had started his medical career as a combat medic, a 68 Whiskey, during the Gulf War, and knew right away that he had found his calling. He thrived on the combination of overwhelming pressure, incredible danger, and never-ending chaos. It was quite simply the best drug he'd ever found. Reggie re-upped for a second tour and intended to sign up for a third when his wife got pregnant with twins. She threatened to divorce him if he wasn't around to help with all the diapers, so he spent the next two decades performing and teaching others emergency medicine at Pennsylvania Hospital, the oldest hospital in the country.

It was here that he became acquainted with the National League East fans, when Murphy's appendix burst three years ago. They appreciated his experience and skill, and recognized a kindred spirit. It was clear that he missed the rush of working in a combat zone, and they needed someone they could trust in the event of a medical emergency. Like now. He had been on private retainer ever since. Not for the money, but for the rush—or, at least, the promise of it. Until this point, all the good doctor had done was set up an ad-hoc emergency room in an old warehouse in an aging industrial park on the outskirts of Haddonfield, where the three met once a month to replenish the National League East fans' personal blood supplies. Donated blood had a shelf life of forty-two days, and Reggie knew that if his services were ever needed, blood would be the key determinant of success or failure.

The two assassins were about to find out just how well their money had been spent.

Giles screeched to a halt next to the warehouse, where Dr. Portman greeted him and helped carry in the wounded killer. Murphy was placed on an operating table, where the doctor assessed his injuries. His patient looked up, watching him closely. "Why the hell are you smiling?"

"Because I live for this shit." The doctor had him stabilized in less than seventeen minutes. Without a fresh supply of the patient's own blood, it might have been a different story. But, as with most tests, preparation was the best indicator of outcome. As soon as the patient was resting comfortably, Dr. Portman explained the outlook for his recovery. His shattered pelvis would need four to six months to heal. Same for his right femur, but the rehab would take considerably longer, depending on the level of performance he hoped to return to.

The baseball fans knew there was no such thing as returning to this game after taking time off. There was no off season. They were done, whether they wanted to be or not. This was the first and last time they would ever need the good doctor's services.

CHAPTER 100

Philadelphia International Airport, Philadelphia, Pennsylvania, May 28, 2:48 a.m.

Philadelphia Director of Homeland Security Albert Shoals and his caravan sped onto the tarmac, where a CH-47 Chinook military transport helicopter awaited them. National Director of Homeland Security Arthur Merrell paced in front of it. He had insisted on personally taking possession of the technology. Shoals resented the implicit lack of trust, but Merrell was not going to allow anyone else to handle it. He might not know what it was, but he was damn well sure going to be part of its delivery.

Shoals handed Merrell the two keys in his possession. Director Merrell and the two men cuffed to the cases boarded the helicopter, which immediately took off for Joint Base McGuire-Dix-Lakehurst, commonly known as JB MDL. The massive complex was a base for the army, air force, and navy, as well as the largest federal prison in the country. The base was as close to an impenetrable fortress as existed in the modern world.

The helicopter landed somewhere in the middle of the sprawling complex, touching down next to a nondescript warehouse with no visible signage. Two men in plain uniforms exited the building and approached Merrell. There was no way to tell which branch of the military they were part of. Or if they were part of one at all. Only one of them spoke. "Director, we will take possession of the packages."

Merrell took out the two keys and unlocked the cases from the agents' wrists. The agents handed over the locked cases, along with the keys. Merrell was surprised when the two men in nondescript uniforms immediately turned to go back inside. The director of Homeland Security asked, "Don't you have anything for me to sign?"

They paused. "What would you like to sign?" one of the men asked.

The director of Homeland Security didn't appreciate the man's tone. "Something that acknowledges transfer of this technology to your possession."

The two men in the plain uniforms glanced at each other, as if they found the statement amusing. "Sir, the ground you are now standing on does not appear on any map of this facility. There was no transfer because there is no technology." They carried the two cases into the nondescript building as Merrell and his party returned to the waiting Chinook.

((•))

Bob Stenson watched the helicopter take off into the night sky. He waited calmly inside his Chrysler until the helicopter's running lights disappeared from view, then pulled up to the well-lit, windowless building whose use his predecessor had arranged with the elder Bush while he was still director of the CIA. Stenson couldn't even remember now what favor the founders had done for the then-aspiring politician, but it most certainly involved future residency in the White House.

Bush's thank-you was to have all official records of the building expunged. The massive facility had gone through so many operational changes over the last decade that no one individual was aware of all that went on at JB MDL, except in their assigned area. This nondescript building was just one of so many others. Nobody knew what went on inside it, and nobody really cared.

Stenson had instructed Indiana senator Corbin Davis to select this site to store the echo box because it was the most secure building on the Eastern Seaboard. It was also the best place for the senator to test the technology, which was set to begin first thing in the morning. Stenson knew that the building being part of JB MDL would give the senator a false sense of comfort because it felt so official.

It worked every time.

CHAPTER 101

Philadelphia Office, Department of Homeland Security,
May 28, 6:26 a.m.

Skylar paced her cell like a caged animal. She guessed it was somewhere around six thirty a.m. She hadn't slept more than forty-five minutes. No one had spoken with her yet. The female guard who delivered her breakfast never said a word. The guard simply slid the tray through the opening in the cell door and exited.

The food was awful, but the coffee was good. A four, in Eddie's vernacular. After finishing her breakfast, she paced back and forth, counting her steps before she even realized it. Which made her feel better and worse at the same time. Skylar didn't know where Eddie was. Or what kind of shape he was in. But she knew he would be scared. Terrified, in fact. Which only further fueled her determination. Skylar's one and only goal was to see Eddie again. It was her fault he was in this mess. And she would do whatever it took to get him out of it.

She continued to pace. Ninety-six, ninety-seven, ninety-eight . . .

CHAPTER 102

Eddie stared at the ceiling. At least, that was the direction he was look-ing. Straight up. He was lying on his back inside Children's Hospital of Philadelphia. The patient room number was 423. It was at the end of a hall. Two agents were stationed by the door. One by the elevator bank. And one outside the hospital's main entrance.

Eddie didn't seem focused on anything at all. He was barely blink-ing. And hadn't moved since waking up sometime in the middle of the night. A squat nurse from the Dominican Republic sat by his bedside, asking every so often if he'd like anything to eat or drink. Her voice was gentle, and her accent was comforting. It was no coincidence she had been selected for this assignment. But he had yet to respond to her. He was hooked up to an IV drip, so at least his body was getting fluids.

The hospital's chief of emergency surgery, who had treated Eddie upon his arrival the night before, entered the room with one of the agents stationed outside the door. The doctor checked Eddie's charts and asked the Dominican nurse, "How's he doing?"

"Same as before. No change."

The doctor nodded, pleased. "Has he spoken yet?"

The nurse shook her head. "Not a word."

"Has he been offered anything to eat or drink?"

"Every fifteen minutes." She showed him the notepad where she kept detailed records.

The doctor leaned down toward Eddie, smiling warmly. "How are you feeling this morning, Edward?"

Eddie stared at the ceiling.

"Can you hear me?"

Eddie did not answer. His jaw remained clenched.

The doctor studied him, speaking with reassurance. "There's no rush. Take all the time you need. Just let us know if there is anything we can do to make you more comfortable."

Eddie stared blankly at the ceiling as the doctor left with the agent, who stopped him in the hall. "How long do you think it will be before he talks again?"

"Hard to say."

"Try."

The doctor realized the agent needed something to report to his superiors. "The good news is the patient is no longer in shock. Pupil dilation and autonomic responses are back within normal range. The patient also no longer appears to be a danger to himself or others. As to when he'll communicate, there's really no way to know. In cases like this, time is the best healer. He needs to want to talk. If we try to force him, it will probably only make things worse. It could even retraumatize him and send him back into shock. All we can do is be patient, and let nature take its course."

CHAPTER 103

Joint Base McGuire-Dix-Lakehurst, Trenton, New Jersey,
May 28, 7:37 a.m.

Senator Corbin Davis watched with eager interest as his world-class experts studied the two devices inside the nondescript building in the middle of JB MDL. The scientists' names were Pembrose and Landgraf. Both were familiar with the device and the science behind it. Both were also skeptical the technology would ever work. They were only too happy to debunk whatever nonsense was afoot, or to be the first ones to hear reconstituted echoes. The trio had been escorted directly inside a small conference room. As soon as the scientists completed their work, they and the senator were to be escorted out of the building and off the grounds.

The scientists clearly knew how to operate the device, having tested it on several previous occasions. They readily caused the box to spring open, revealing the eight one-inch satellite microphones, which performed their perfectly synchronized ballet.

The senator asked, "What's it doing?"

Pembrose, the younger of the scientists, answered, "Acoustically mapping the room."

Landgraf, the veteran, added, "In theory."

Pembrose replied, "We'll know soon enough." They both kept their eyes glued to the progress bar that appeared below the three-dimensional image of the space. The counter quickly climbed: *Three percent . . . six percent . . . nine percent . . .* , but then started to slow. *Eleven percent. Twelve percent* took longer. *Thirteen* was even slower than that. After another two minutes, the counter had still not reached *fifteen percent.*

Corbin Davis studied the differing expressions of his two experts. Pembrose looked disappointed, like a child who didn't get the present he wanted for his birthday. Landgraf grinned smugly, like he knew this would happen all along.

The senator grew concerned. "Is it supposed to take this long?"

The younger scientist reluctantly replied, "No."

"So what does this mean?"

The older scientist cleared his throat, then answered bluntly. "The device doesn't work."

The senator had trouble remaining calm. "Son of a bitch. You're sure?"

Landgraf nodded. "Yes."

Davis turned to the younger brainiac, hoping for a different opinion. "There's no way you could have missed something?"

The scientists glanced at each other. Pembrose replied, "Give us thirty minutes, and we'll be able to tell you beyond a shadow of a doubt."

The senator mumbled under his breath as he moved toward the door. "I'm going to gut Marcus Fenton like a squealing pig." Corbin Davis stepped outside the small conference room, where he was promptly met by the two guards in plain uniforms. "I need some privacy." He glanced around at the handful of unmarked doors, expecting to be led into one.

The guards in the plain uniforms didn't move. The taller one replied, "You will have to step outside the building, sir."

The senator stared angrily, then stormed outside as he took out his shiny, new encrypted phone. The guards couldn't help but notice that it matched their own.

CHAPTER 104

American Heritage Foundation, Alexandria, Virginia,
May 28, 7:48 a.m.

Bob Stenson sat calmly in his office as he listened to the Indiana senator yelling over the phone. "Slow down, Senator. I need time to process
this." He paused for dramatic effect. "Your scientists are sure?"

"They're confirming it now, but that is correct. The damn thing
doesn't work."

Stenson exhaled loudly, playing his part with aplomb. "What the
hell is Fenton up to?"

"I don't know, and I don't care. I want him gone."

Stenson, the master puppeteer, smiled ever so slightly. "It's your
call, Senator. We will support whatever action you see fit." And like that,
it was done. Senator Davis would convene the Senate Select Committee
on Intelligence on an emergency basis, and Fenton would be terminated
within the week. There was the obvious question of his replacement,
but that was a matter that could wait. There was no urgency. Which
was why Stenson leaned back in his chair and smiled.

This was, without a doubt, the greatest moment of his professional life. It made the whole hanging-chad business in 2000 pale in
comparison. He was now in possession of the single most important

technological advancement in intelligence in the last forty years, and no one knew he had it. Within a matter of hours, no one would believe the echo box even worked. The rest of the world would think they'd been led on a wild-goose chase by a blustery, old windbag hell-bent on bolstering his legacy. The good senator from Indiana would demand retribution, and Stenson would allow him to satisfy his bloodlust because Fenton would no longer be of any use to them.

What no one else knew was that after watching Homeland Security Director Merrell deliver the devices to the nondescript building at JB MDL, Stenson had replaced the devices with his own. These duplicates included every one of Eddie's previous specifications. Namely, the ones that didn't work. These facsimiles had been produced at Stenson's request over a year earlier, when he'd decided to give some other brilliant minds a crack at acoustic archeology. While their efforts proved unsuccessful, Stenson had a feeling even then that his duplicates might one day serve a purpose. He just hadn't imagined how important a role they would play.

All he had to decide now was which of the world's greatest secrets he would listen to first. He had a president to bring down. And another one to install. There were enemies to destroy. And fence-sitters to bring into line. Bob Stenson and the American Heritage Foundation were about to know anything they wanted, and no one would have a clue how they got their information. They would be unstoppable.

First, there was the matter of Edward Parks, who was officially now a liability. He could not be allowed to create another echo box, nor pass along the algorithms to anyone else capable of doing so. There was only one way to guarantee neither would happen. Stenson had no qualms about proceeding, and intended to initiate the order before leaving the office.

His private moment of glory, however, was interrupted by the sound of footsteps racing down the hall toward his office. "Slow down, Jason."

Jason did not slow down. He ran straight into his superior's office. "Sir, we have a problem."

CHAPTER 105

Dr. Marcus Fenton's House, Pine Hill, New Jersey,
May 28, 8:33 a.m.

A police car parked in Marcus Fenton's driveway for the second time in less than twelve hours. Prior to these two visits, the last time a law-enforcement vehicle had entered the property was in 2002, to inform Fenton of a string of nearby burglaries. He was not about to take any more nonsense from the NYPD, and he stormed out to the uniformed officer. "I'm not going anywhere, or saying a goddamn thing, without my lawyer."

The officer looked confused. "Sir?"

Fenton stood his ground. "Unless you have a warrant, I'm not going anywhere."

The officer shook his head. "I think there must be some misunder-standing. Are you Dr. Marcus Fenton?"

Only now did he notice the car was not NYPD. It had local mark-ings. The officer was a local sheriff. Fenton answered, "Yes, I'm Marcus Fenton. What can I do for you?"

The sheriff paused for a moment, as he had been trained to do when delivering bad news. "Did a Michael Barnes work for you?"

CHAPTER 106

American Heritage Foundation, Alexandria, Virginia,
May 28, 8:58 a.m.

The conference room inside the American Heritage Foundation was dead silent. Bob Stenson stood next to the large mahogany table, staring down at the devices sitting in the middle of it—the laptop supercomputer and the echo box, which had until last night been in the possession of Edward Parks and Skylar Drummond. There was also a second, commercially available computer, which belonged to the balding scientist Stenson had brought in to test Edward Parks's device. The scientist's computer was wired to Parks's supercomputer, running system diagnostics.

The scientist, Carter Harwood, was the only person Stenson had ever trusted to work on Edward Parks's devices. Like all Foundation employees and independent contractors, Harwood had come to their attention through strong personal recommendations. He had also survived their exhaustive background check. A great many leading scientists, it turned out, had a flag or two in their personal histories that disqualified them from further consideration by the Foundation. Such was the case with Pembrose and Landgraf, the scientists Senator Davis had brought with him to JB MDL. One was a former heroin addict. The other had started undergoing hormone therapy for gender reassignment.

When Stenson had cleared Harwood, twelve years ago, the Foundation director knew his man might never be capable of completing Edward Parks's research, should it go unfinished for one reason or another, but Stenson was certain that Harwood could be trusted. And, ultimately, that was more important. Because what Stenson really needed in this position was a forger, not an artist. It was Harwood who produced the duplicate machines that had just been tested in the nondescript building on the grounds of JB MDL. He knew the devices better than anyone except for Edward Parks himself. Which was why Stenson listened when Harwood said there was a problem.

On the laptop supercomputer's screen, there was an incomplete three-dimensional rendering of the conference room space. The progress counter read: *13 percent*. The counter hadn't changed in twenty-two minutes.

Stenson was immediately thankful he had not yet ordered the end of Edward Parks, who still might have a purpose to serve, after all. "Why isn't it working?"

"I don't know yet. I can't give you an answer until I finish running the diagnostics." Harwood, calm and clinical, motioned to his own computer, which was connected to Eddie's. Harwood's $3,000 machine was going to reveal what was wrong with the $300,000 machine.

Stenson looked around the table to his three lieutenants, who seemed equally dumbfounded. "Any ideas?"

Caitlin McCloskey pointed to the scratches from where Eddie had dropped the devices. "Maybe they were damaged when they were dropped."

Harwood shook his head. "That was my first thought as well. But it's not the case. I'm sure of it. Whatever the problem is, it's not hardware related."

Jason Greers asked, "So why would it work yesterday, but not today? Something has to have changed."

Daryl Trotter made a comment that caused everyone to stiffen. "Only if the device was actually working yesterday."

Jason took immediate offense, because this entire wild-goose chase had essentially started with him. "What are you suggesting, that the doctor and her mental patient faked the recordings?"

Daryl couldn't stop himself from correcting Jason. "Technically, they're echo reconstructions, not recordings."

Jason snapped, "Whatever they are!"

Caitlin smiled briefly, knowing how much their boss disliked emotional outbursts. Jason was losing his cool.

Daryl remained completely even-keeled. "I'm not suggesting anything, Jason. I'm clarifying that there are two possible scenarios. One scenario is that the three reconstructions stored on the device—the one with Dr. Fenton and Michael Barnes, the one with the boy being hit, and the one of the kidnapping suspect being interrogated—are legitimate. In that case, you are correct. Something had to have changed. But if they're not legitimate, the logic doesn't follow."

Stenson chimed in. "They're legitimate. We know too much about Skylar Drummond and Edward Parks. Neither is capable of the kind of forethought to have intentionally set all this in motion. It's simply too far-fetched."

Vindicated, Greers glared smugly at Trotter, who shrugged. He was only trying to help. He wanted to make sure they considered every alternative. "So what changed?"

Harwood looked up as the diagnostics concluded. "Nothing."

Jason stared at him. "Not possible."

The scientist stared right back. "Machines don't lie. I'm telling you I've compared every line of code from the previous version I tested, which I had stored on my machine, to the present version on the Parks machine. Not a single character in a single line of code changed."

Caitlin McCloskey was dumbfounded. "So how do you explain it?"

Jason Greers didn't know. Neither did Bob Stenson. Then Daryl Trotter got an idea. "Does each reconstruction include a separate file of the original degenerated sound waves that served as the basis for the reconstruction?"

Harwood knew the answer, but double-checked just to make sure. "All three folders include files with the original fragments, as well as each reconstructed version."

"Why?" asked Stenson.

Trotter smiled. "I know what changed."

CHAPTER 107

The Remains of Michael Barnes's House, Swedesboro, New Jersey, May 28, 9:15 a.m.

Following the local sheriff, Marcus Fenton was allowed to pass beneath the yellow crime-scene tape that now stretched around the entire perimeter of Michael Barnes's property. It wasn't long after sunrise when the first of Barnes's neighbors had noticed the currency fluttering into their properties. A few Facebook updates and tweets later, hundreds of people from all over the area had raced to the property, trying to grab whatever cash they could. Homeland had initially assigned a dozen agents to the scene, but quickly added another two dozen to maintain security and, more importantly, collect all the cash. By eleven forty-five a.m., their count had reached well over $400,000, and they were barely through half of what they had found.

Much of the debris was still smoldering as the sheriff led Fenton toward the back of the property. The hood of Barnes's car was lodged in his kitchen window. Articles of clothing, ranging from an olive-green winter parka to bright-orange swim trunks to white running shoes, dangled from tree branches in every direction. The two men were met by the Homeland agent in charge (AIC), Arlo Gunn, who was coordinating the cleanup. After brief introductions, Fenton asked, "What the hell happened?"

Gunn smiled. "We were hoping you could tell us."

Fenton looked around at the devastation surrounding them, realizing how quickly his situation was going from bad to worse. "I have no idea."

"Michael Barnes worked for you, didn't he?" He asked it casually, without any hint of suspicion.

"He did. He was my head of security."

"Where is that?"

"Harmony House. In Woodbury."

"What kind of facility is it?"

"It's a government-funded assisted-living facility for patients with particular gifts."

Gunn scratched his sideburns, as if making mental notes for later. "How long had he worked for you?"

"Well over a decade. Almost fifteen years."

Gunn nodded, apparently satisfied with the answer. "How would you have characterized your relationship with the deceased?"

"Professionally, he was a trusted employee. But we had no personal relationship outside the workplace."

"Had he ever mentioned that he kept a stockpile of cash and explosives on his property?"

"No, he never did. Honestly, I still find all this hard to believe."

"Really?"

Fenton cleared his throat. "I mean, that he could have been so paranoid. And stupid. I had no idea."

Gunn nodded. "Had the two of you gotten into any kind of argument yesterday?"

Fenton could feel his shirt collar sticking to the back of his neck. He was starting to sweat. "I wouldn't describe it as an argument. We were managing a patient crisis."

"What kind of patient crisis?"

Fenton was quite certain Gunn already knew the answer. He was more interested in how Fenton answered than what he said. "A patient had fled the facility."

"Which was Barnes's job to prevent from happening."

"It was among his responsibilities, yes."

"So in other words, he had failed you."

"Not him personally, but members of his staff."

The agent in charge crossed his arms over his chest. "Barnes failed to return this patient to your facility, did he not?"

"In that regard, yes, he did fail."

The AIC smiled ever so slightly. He was enjoying this. "Were you aware that your missing patient, Edward Parks, has been in the custody of Homeland Security since approximately midnight last night?"

Fenton gritted his teeth. "No, I was not aware. That's very good news."

The AIC glanced at someone approaching in the distance. All Fenton could see was a man in a suit. The senior doctor hadn't brought his distance glasses, and couldn't make out any further details.

The agent in charge asked Fenton, "Why did the New York Police Department bring you in for questioning last night?"

Fenton's jaw tightened noticeably. "As best as I could determine, to harass me with inadmissible evidence."

The AIC turned to the man approaching them, who was now close enough for the doctor to recognize. "Detective, was the purpose of your interrogation last night to harass this man with inadmissible evidence?"

Detective Butler McHenry shook his head innocently. "No, sir. Where did you get that idea?"

The agent in charge studied Fenton. "Doctor, what evidence were you referring to?"

CHAPTER 108

Daryl Trotter stood behind the scientist as he worked Edward Parks's computer inside the conference room. Bob Stenson and the other two American Heritage Foundation lieutenants looked on impatiently from the opposite side of the mahogany table. Harwood removed a pair of headphones and turned to Daryl. "I've gotten all I'm going to get out of it."

Daryl nodded, then turned to his colleagues. "Okay, what I want you to do is listen to the difference between these two reconstructions produced from the same original wave fragments. I had him pick the file with the lowest amount of white noise, which was the interrogation of the kidnapping suspect. The characteristics of an interrogation room are ideal for this purpose, and the echoes are also the least decayed due to age."

Stenson was growing annoyed. "Get on with it."

"Right. Okay, this first one is the reconstruction that was already stored on Parks's machine, presumably made yesterday."

He nodded to Harwood, who hit "Play" on Edward Parks's computer. The voices came through clearly, just as they had the first time the reconstruction was heard inside the Sixth Precinct.

SUSPECT: *I swear to God, I don't know where she is!*

DETECTIVE LIEUTENANT VICTORIA DANIELS:
Tell me where she is, Henry.

SUSPECT: *I don't fucking know! What are you, deaf?!*

Stenson shook his head. "We've already heard this, Daryl." The scientist stopped the playback.

Daryl nodded. "Right. I know. It's important for the sake of comparison." He turned to Harwood. "Now play the one you just made using the more recent version of Edward Parks's program."

The scientist again hit "Play." The voices were completely inaudible. All that was heard was shrill screeching. Daryl hit "Stop" on the supercomputer. "Quite a difference, wouldn't you say?"

Stenson shook his head. "What's the point?"

"Unless something was overlooked, a newer version of a program should be more advanced than the one that preceded it. Revised software should work better, not worse."

Caitlin McCloskey wasn't following. "What is it, a glitch?"

Harwood shook his head. "No. Edward Parks doesn't make little errors. Only big ones."

McCloskey shrugged, still in the dark. Jason Greers was right there with her, but he wasn't going to be so obvious about it.

Bob Stenson, on the other hand, suddenly saw the light. "Well, I'll be damned."

Trotter smiled. "Exactly." He knew Stenson would be the first of the others to realize what had happened.

Caitlin couldn't help herself—she blurted out, "Exactly what?"

"He saw it coming," Trotter replied.

"Who?"

"Edward Parks."

Stenson added, "Dr. Drummond must have given him the suggestion."

Now Caitlin was getting frustrated. "Suggested what to him?"

The scientist now caught up with Trotter and Stenson. "That he regress his work. She realized Parks was going to lose possession of his device, so she had him revert his program to the previous version."

Greers was furious. "He what?!"

Harwood struggled to fathom the brinksmanship. "It's . . . it's . . ."

Stenson completed the sentence for him. "Brilliant." He said it in an ice-cold tone that made two things immediately clear: he had genuine appreciation for the fugitives' unanticipated move, and Stenson was already certain what the American Heritage Foundation was going to do next.

CHAPTER 109

Skylar had been served dinner inside the Homeland holding cell the same way she had been served breakfast and lunch. In silence. As if her very words could be wielded like venom. Which she found kind of flattering.

Skylar continued to eat every last bite of food she was given, because she knew eventually she would need her strength. They were going to have to talk to her sometime. And when they did, she wanted to be ready.

Still, Skylar was surprised when Kendricks, the humorless agent who had arrested her, appeared outside her door. "Approach me with your back toward me. Place your hands and wrists through the opening so I can cuff them."

She did so. "Where are we going?"

"You'll find out when you get there." He locked the cuffs around her wrists and led her out of the building.

((•))

Skylar had never been to Children's Hospital of Philadelphia before, so she didn't recognize the building until they pulled in front of its sign. Skylar knew she wouldn't get an answer, but asked anyway. "What are we doing here?"

Kendricks didn't say a word. He parked the car in a red zone, where he was met by the Homeland agent stationed outside the main entrance. He escorted them to the elevators, where they were instructed to go to the fourth floor. Stepping out of the elevator, they were met by an agent who escorted them to the end of the hall, where two more agents were stationed outside the door to room 423. These two studied Skylar with interest. She was too young and attractive to be the woman they were expecting. The shorter one, Ziggler, addressed her. "Dr. Skylar Drummond?"

"Why do you sound surprised?"

"I suppose I was expecting someone older."

She was in no mood for flattery. "Why am I here?"

The two agents turned to Kendricks. Ziggler asked, "You haven't told her?"

Kendricks answered matter-of-factly. "Weren't my instructions."

The shorter agent decided to make it clear exactly who was in charge. "Remove her handcuffs."

Kendricks took out his handcuff keys and removed the restraints from Skylar's wrists. She nodded to the shorter agent with appreciation. "Thank you."

Ziggler felt three inches taller. "Would you like to see your patient?"

She momentarily forgot to breathe. "Eddie's here?"

He nodded. "Other side of this door." She immediately moved toward it, when the agent stepped in front of her. "There's something you should know before you see him."

((•))

Skylar entered room 423 with great excitement and even greater trepidation. CHOP's head of emergency medicine had been correct: there was no telling how long traumatized patients could remain "locked in." Or what would reconnect them with the world again. The only thing Skylar knew was that she wanted to see Eddie. And touch him. And reassure him that everything was going to be okay, even if he couldn't hear her.

She broke into tears upon seeing him. He was staring at the ceiling. "Eddie." She placed her hand on his cheek, and kissed his forehead. He did not respond.

The shorter agent had followed her into the room. "Would you like a moment alone with him?"

She nodded gratefully. "Please."

"Take as much time as you need." The agent looked to the replacement nurse and motioned for her to leave the room as well. She made a note on her time chart, and exited into the hallway with her materials. Ziggler followed her, pausing in the doorway. "I'll be right outside if you need anything."

Skylar waited for the door to close, then pulled a chair up next to Eddie and continued to cry. All she could think was how helpless he looked. So docile. So innocent. He reminded Skylar of her brother, Christopher, who never did anything in his life to hurt anyone. Neither had Eddie. They weren't capable of it. All Eddie had ever wanted was to hear his mother's voice. Was that too much to ask? He had devoted his entire life to the pursuit of it. And now his only hope for that dream coming true had been taken away from him. The world cared nothing for him or his wishes. It only cared about his device, and what it could do. The mysteries it could solve. The answers it would reveal. And it was all her fault. Because she was just as guilty as everybody else. Right along with the rest of the world, Skylar had placed her needs above Eddie's. She should have never taken him off Harmony House grounds.

She would never forgive herself, just like she would blame herself for her brother's suicide for the rest of her life. Tears slowly rolled down her cheeks. "Eddie, I'm so sorry. I'm so, so sorry."

His eyes remained fixed on the ceiling, even as he whispered in a barely audible voice, "Why are you so, so sorry, Skylar?"

She stared at him in disbelief, certain that she must have just hallucinated. Until he slowly turned his head toward her and looked at her briefly. "Eddie, you spoke."

"Yes, I did." He sounded terribly sad and distant, and then he looked away.

She trembled with a mixture of excitement and confusion. "How . . . how is this possible?"

"In human beings, voicing occurs when air is expelled from the lungs through the glottis, creating a drop in pressure across the larynx."

"They said you'd been traumatized," she interrupted. "That . . . you were unable to communicate."

Eddie nodded. "I became very frightened when the agents pointed their guns at me. I did not like when they did that."

"I didn't like when they did that, either. I was very scared, too."

"I heard the doctor say I was unconsciously trying to protect myself. I didn't know that's what I was doing. But everyone was leaving me alone and I liked that so I decided to keep doing it." His voice remained emotionally depleted. It reminded Skylar of how she must have sounded right after learning of Jacob's death.

"Do you know what time it was when you first started being able to hear the doctor?"

"It was 3:17 in the morning. I know because there's a clock on the wall." He pointed weakly to the clock.

Skylar still couldn't process what she was hearing. "So what have you been doing since then?"

"I have been lying here, thinking."

"Thinking about what?"

"Birds. Lots and lots of birds. I thought about belted kingfishers. And green-winged teals. And common terns. And hermit thrushes. And swallow-tailed kites. And blue-winged warblers. I remembered how beautiful they sound. And how much better they make me feel. Birds don't use expressions. They never expect me to interpret what they mean, so I never feel confused or embarrassed around them. I could hear them so clearly in my mind it was like I was actually hearing them. Do you ever do that, imagine something so clearly that it almost seems like it's real?"

"Yes, I do." She thought of Jacob. Then tried very hard not to. Skylar took a moment to consider that for the last seventeen hours, Eddie had managed to remain perfectly still while imagining birdcalls and nothing else. Zen Buddhists spent a lifetime in pursuit of such focus. "Incredible."

Eddie smiled ever so slightly. "You were right, you know."

Skylar didn't follow. "About what?"

"That if I spent enough time outside Harmony House, I would lie, because everyone lies sometimes. Even you."

She was astonished. "What did you lie about?"

"I let the doctors think I couldn't answer them when I could have. It was a lie of omission."

"I don't know that I'd say you were lying. I'd say that you were acting, like the policeman who pretended to have a heart attack to help us."

"He was still lying." Eddie glanced around them, looking more like his old self. "I don't like this room, Skylar. I don't like the way it sounds. There are too many hard surfaces. I like my room in Harmony House much better. And I really don't like the needle in my arm, or the adhesive stuck to my skin. It's itchy and uncomfortable."

All at once, she couldn't stop the tears from streaming down her face again. "I'm so glad you're okay."

He studied her. "You're crying."

She nodded. "Happy tears."

"I don't know how to cry happy tears. Do you think you can teach me?"

"I'll do my best." Skylar did not actually intend to hold his hand at that particular moment. It just happened. She reached out and gently placed her hand in his. It would have been a completely natural gesture, were Eddie anyone else. But he was not anyone else. He was more special than anyone she'd ever known. Skylar was just about to apologize when she realized Eddie had not withdrawn his hand from hers. In fact, he had not flinched at all. He was letting her hold his hand. "Wow."

He didn't know what she was referring to. "Why did you say that?"

She was staring at their hands. "We're holding hands."

"I've never held hands with anyone before."

"That's why I said wow." This was the most physical contact Eddie had ever voluntarily had in his life. It was powerful. And utterly pure. It was something she had always hoped would happen with her little brother, Christopher, but it never did. Skylar could not stop staring at their clasped hands. Which she soon regretted, because Eddie pulled his back.

He seemed lost in his own world. "I did not let them have the echo box, Skylar."

She took a deep breath before she answered. "I saw them take it from you. There was nothing you could do to stop them."

He looked at her with absolute sincerity. "You are wrong, Skylar. There was something I could do."

He said it with such conviction that she almost gave him the benefit of the doubt. "What?"

His eyes darted around the room for a moment, as he hesitated. "This is just another one of those things that you're going to have to trust me on."

She couldn't help but smile at his imitation of her. "I can do that." There was a light knock on the door. Skylar quickly leaned down to

Eddie. "I don't want you to talk to anyone else. Do you think you can keep acting for a little while longer?"

"I can do that." He said it just like she had. He smiled briefly, then turned his blank gaze toward the ceiling, just as the door opened.

Ziggler poked his head in. "Dr. Drummond, pardon the interruption, but there's someone who would like to speak with you."

Skylar stepped out of Eddie's room to come face-to-face with a man she recognized from watching the news. His name was Senator Corbin Davis. As the shorter agent made introductions, she struggled to connect the dots. *What the hell is he doing here?*

The senator turned to the agent. "I would like to speak to Ms. Drummond—excuse me, Dr. Drummond—privately." The agent led them into the patient room adjacent to Eddie's, which was vacant. The agent left them alone.

Davis studied her admiringly, just as most men did upon first meeting Skylar. "You've had quite a couple days."

"Yes, I have."

He paused meaningfully. "I'm sorry about what happened to Jacob Hendrix."

"So am I."

He nodded. "The man Homeland Security believes to be responsible for his murder was found dead early this morning."

She bluntly asked, "How?"

"An explosion. It appears to have been an accident."

"That's what they said about Jacob."

He nodded again, sounding almost apologetic. "We get it right eventually."

"Nothing will ever make this right." She paused, increasingly curious as to why the senator was there. "What's going to happen to Fenton?"

"New York City Police have opened an investigation into his involvement in the crime, but it's unlikely anything will come of it."

He did not take his eyes away from hers, but she didn't flinch. "The echo box. It doesn't work. But you knew that, didn't you?"

No, as a matter of fact, she'd had no idea. It was working just fine last time she heard it, but she was not about to let the senator know that.

"It was quite clever making Fenton believe the technology was functional."

She nodded almost imperceptibly. *Why do they think it doesn't work? Is this what Eddie was referring to? What did he do?* "Am I still under arrest?"

"No, you are not. You're free to go."

Skylar now believed she understood why the man was here. Damage control. They were concerned about what she was going to do. Which meant there was an opportunity. "What about Eddie?"

"He will be returned to Harmony House."

"Not if I have anything to say about it."

"You don't."

"Then why are we talking, Senator?"

"Because you could." He proceeded to outline a scenario that had been carefully scripted for him. The plan put more than a slight smile across her face.

CHAPTER 110

Harmony House, Woodbury, New Jersey, May 29, 8:31 a.m.

The senior and most respected doctor on the grounds of Harmony House, Dr. Marcus Fenton, glanced out his office window the next morning. After spending much of the previous day at what was left of Michael Barnes's residence, answering a repetitive litany of questions from a battery of Homeland Security agents and a pesky New York City detective, Fenton had decided to arrive in the office bright and early. Harmony House was his home. His sanctuary.

At least for the moment.

He watched as a limousine pulled up to the security gate at the facility's main entrance, which was now being manned by one of several temporary security personnel employed by a third party with the proper government clearance. The firm, Oak Ridge Security, was the smallest of several competitors, but had been given a particularly strong endorsement from Senator Corbin Davis, whom Fenton had wanted to appease. He had assumed Davis had personal knowledge of the firm. That assumption could not have been further from the truth, but Fenton would never know. Due to the death of Michael Barnes and the still-unexplained disappearance of the rest of his security staff, Oak

Ridge had been hired on an emergency basis twenty-four hours ago to provide the security needs for Harmony House until a more permanent solution could be worked out.

Fenton wasn't expecting anyone that morning, so he pressed the intercom on his desk. "Stephen, are we expecting anyone?"

His assistant had no idea of the weekend's goings-on. "No, sir, not until eleven thirty."

Fenton glanced at his desk clock. It was only 8:47. "Then find out who the hell just pulled through our front gate."

Before his assistant could get a response from the new gate guard, Fenton watched the limousine proceed to the building's entrance. The driver got out and opened a rear passenger's door. Senator Corbin Davis stepped out. Fenton knew this couldn't be good. He stood up to greet the senator without waiting to see if anyone else got out of the limo.

Stephen Millard was on the phone with the front security gate as Fenton left his office and walked right by him. Millard quickly cupped the phone. "Sir, it's Senator Davis and—"

"I know who it is," Fenton interrupted tersely, heading into the front lobby toward his approaching guest. Fenton assumed Davis had come out to check on their temporary security arrangements. "Senator, what brings you all the way out here to Woodbury?"

It was only now that Fenton saw Skylar Drummond walking behind Davis, which stopped the older doctor dead in his tracks.

The senator's response was cold and direct. "Let's talk in your office."

Fenton didn't take his eyes off Skylar. "I thought she was in federal custody."

The senator answered matter-of-factly. "I ordered her release."

Fenton's hands started to shake. "What the hell is going on?"

"The same thing that happens when a major drug bust turns out to be a truckload of baking soda. Changes are made so that it never happens again."

"You're being oblique, Senator," the doctor sniped.

"Not for long. Like I said, your office."

((•))

Fenton closed his office door and sat down behind his desk as if this was going to be a meeting like any other. He glanced with suspicion at Skylar, then turned to Davis. "Does she need to be here?"

The senator nodded. "She does."

"You do know that whatever claims she's made are lies."

"She hasn't made any claims." Davis glanced at Skylar. "I have."

Skylar sat directly across from Fenton in the uncomfortable folding metal chair, just as she had done during her job interview, which now seemed so very long ago.

Davis chose a more comfortable armchair as he addressed Fenton. "I'll get right to the point. Pack up your things, Marcus. You're fired."

Fenton hung his head, but didn't say a word.

The senator continued. "Dr. Drummond is here because I have asked her to be your temporary replacement until we can find a permanent one. She has graciously accepted, which means that as of this moment, she has operational control of this facility."

Fenton shook his head in disbelief. "This is ludicrous." He glanced up to the ceiling to see if his world was literally caving in.

Skylar stared across the desk at Marcus. She spoke with all the restraint she could muster. "You have thirty minutes to clear out your belongings."

Fenton slowly raised his head to look at her. "You can't do this to me."

Skylar remained stone-faced. "Oh, but I can."

Corbin Davis smiled ever so slightly. "With my full support."

She stood up slowly, obviously relishing the moment, then looked him directly in the eyes. "If you are not off the premises by the time I return, I will have you escorted out by security personnel." Skylar exited without another word.

Weakly, Fenton asked the senator, "Why?"

The senator got up and moved slowly around the office, glancing at the framed photographs of Fenton with various presidents and other notables. "You have wasted a lot of people's valuable time, energy, and resources for years with this nonsense. This weekend was the last straw. You led us on a wild-goose chase over nothing. And you nearly ruined that young lady's life."

"What exactly do you mean, 'over nothing'?"

"The goddamn technology doesn't work. The echo box. It never has, and it probably never will."

Fenton sputtered. His world was spinning. "What the hell are you talking about? It does work. That's why she fled. Look, whatever she told you—"

Davis cut him off. "She didn't tell me a damn thing, Marcus. I told her." The senator moved to the door, where he paused to glance out the windows at several Homeland Security vehicles arriving at the facility. Fenton was about to speak, but Davis had no intention of listening to another word. "Homeland is arriving to take possession of all your computer records, both here and in your residence, so I wouldn't plan on taking any with you. What you should consider is hiring the best lawyer you can find. Because if you or Michael Barnes were dumb enough to leave any kind of a trail, you're going to need all the help you can get."

Corbin Davis glanced at the security guard manning the front gate as his limousine exited Harmony House grounds. The senator took out his encrypted phone and dialed Bob Stenson to report that Marcus Fenton had been relieved of his duties.

((•))

Skylar had been suspicious from the moment Senator Davis had offered her Fenton's job. *Anything that sounds too good to be true always is.* But how could she have said no? She would be getting revenge on the man who'd ordered her lover's death, and would have unlimited access to Eddie, at least for the time being. Just over twenty-four hours ago, she'd been informed by an overly zealous Homeland Security agent that she would never see her patient again and was losing her rights as an American citizen. Now she had her dream job, which should have taken her another twenty years to achieve. Skylar guessed that the government was desperate to keep the situation contained. The last thing they wanted was her going public with her story and suing Homeland Security for false imprisonment. If they kept her happy, she'd remain quiet. That was the deal. In fact, she'd signed a confidentiality agreement to that effect.

Skylar was certain there was more to the story, but realized she would most likely never know it. What she did know was that people changed their minds all the time. There was no guarantee how long she'd have free rein within Harmony House, so she was not about to waste time. She had to act while she had the opportunity.

The moment she stepped inside her office, she went right to the stack of storage boxes labeled *Parks, Edward*. She opened the first box, which contained his earliest records, and pulled out the first couple inches of folders. She riffled through them, looking for something specific. A phone number. Which she found in short order. And dialed.

CHAPTER 111

Dr. Marcus Fenton's House, Pine Hill, New Jersey,
May 29, 9:19 a.m.

Federal agents had already been searching Marcus Fenton's home for over thirty minutes by the time he pulled into his driveway. He parked directly behind their vehicles and got out, carrying with him the few keepsakes he had taken from Harmony House. These included several framed photographs of his deceased wife, Ruthie.

To no one in particular, Fenton said he was going to hire the best lawyer he knew, who would readily put a stop to all this. He went inside to his home office, where he sat down behind his desk. His computer and all his technology had been removed. *How dare they?* Fenton placed the photographs on his empty desktop, then opened a drawer, which was not a drawer at all but the cover of a small safe with a combination lock. He turned the dial two rotations to the right, one to the left, and one to the right. He opened the safe and removed several notebooks. Behind them was a small jewelry box. Inside the box were two plain white pills. Each was 500 milligrams of a lethal, untraceable compound known only as KT-186. It was going to look like Marcus Fenton had a heart attack, which would be completely believable given the circumstances.

Michael Barnes had had his escape plan. Marcus Fenton had his.

He poured himself a glass of water and swallowed the pills. Both went down smoothly. Nothing happened immediately. He didn't expect it to. He calmly closed the small jewelry box and placed it and the notebooks back inside the safe, which he then locked. He closed the small drawer, concealing the safe, and looked at one of the photographs of his wife. "See you soon."

Fenton's heart stopped beating twenty seconds later. Agents would find him on the floor behind his desk several minutes afterward, in a puddle of his own bodily fluids. Paramedics arrived eleven minutes later. They would reach Jefferson Hospital in Stratford twenty-seven minutes after that. The once senior and most respected doctor on the grounds of Harmony House was pronounced dead at 10:07 a.m.

CHAPTER 112

Harmony House, Woodbury, New Jersey, May 29, 12:22 p.m.

Skylar wouldn't learn of Fenton's death until later that night, by which time she wouldn't be able to give the news the attention it deserved. She was too focused on Eddie's return to Harmony House to give much focus to anything else. She was joined by Nurse Gloria in front of the facility's main entrance as they waited for his arrival. Gloria was still suffering the effects of too much alcohol over the weekend. "Doctor, is it true?"

Skylar played dumb. "Is what true?"

The nurse appreciated the young doctor's humility. "That you got Fenton's job?"

She nodded modestly. "It's only temporary until they can find a more suitable replacement."

"Well, congratulations, anyway. It's still a hell of a thing." Gloria was already trying to figure out how to condense all this information into a brief text to her other employer later that day.

The ambulance arrived with little fanfare. Lying on the gurney, Eddie remained comatose as the paramedics wheeled him back to his room. He stared blankly upward at nothing in particular. Concern was evident in Nurse Gloria's face. She had never seen him like this. "How long has he been this way?"

"Roughly thirty-six hours."

"Do you know what happened?"

"I do," was all Skylar replied.

What bothered Gloria most was that the doctor now in charge of Harmony House showed such little concern for Eddie. Apparently now that she had the big job, the young doctor didn't care about her patients like she used to. At least Fenton had pretended to care.

When they got to Eddie's room, Gloria was surprised to see that the echo box was already there. Which meant that it had arrived separately from Eddie. In the entire time she had known this very special patient, he had been separated from it on only a handful of occasions. "That's strange."

Skylar asked innocently, "What?"

"He took his box with him. I wonder how it got back here before him?"

Skylar shrugged. "Homeland Security must have delivered it."

"Homeland Security? What were they doing with it?"

"I don't know. You'll have to ask them." She eyeballed the nurse for a moment, and then asked, "Would you mind excusing us? I'd like some privacy with him."

The nurse nodded and left the room, realizing that she might have to break her other employer's rules and send two messages that day. Gloria just didn't see any way she was going to fit all this new information into one brief message.

Inside Eddie's room, Skylar sat on the edge of Eddie's bed as he continued staring vacantly at the ceiling. "You can stop acting now."

He continued staring at the ceiling. His eyes didn't move.

"Eddie?" A hint of concern crept into her voice just as his gaze turned slowly toward the echo box, which was positioned exactly where it had been the last time it was in his room.

"I am becoming a good actor, don't you think?"

She smiled. "Yes, Eddie, I do. A very good one."

He closed his eyes. "Doesn't it sound wonderful?" He was referring to the silence.

"What's wonderful is seeing you smile again."

He opened his eyes and looked around his room, feeling more comfortable than he had in days. He SIGHED with relief. "I'm glad to be back in my room."

"I'm glad you are, too."

"I don't like the outside world."

"I can understand why."

Eddie sat up, staring at the echo box. He was wondering the same thing Nurse Gloria had. He got up and moved toward it, gently running his hands around the device and then the laptop supercomputer. He noticed the scratches where he had dropped them. "Somebody scratched them."

Skylar said, "You did."

"When did I scratch them?"

"You dropped them outside your childhood home in Philadelphia when the agents pointed their guns at us."

Eddie kept looking around his room, anywhere but at Skylar. "I don't remember dropping them."

"You were going into shock."

He thought for a moment, trying to remember. "I did not like going into shock."

She motioned to the two machines. "Were they damaged when they were dropped?"

"I will check." He popped open the laptop's chassis and carefully inspected each component, as well as those in the echo box. Both devices appeared fine, and both started right up. He ran a brief series of diagnostics, which revealed all machine functions were operating normally. "They were not damaged, which is good because it means I won't have to perform any repairs."

She paused a moment and carefully asked, "Eddie, do you know if the echo box is still working properly?" She knew it wasn't, but was curious how he'd answer.

"Yes, I do know." He looked out the windows, wondering which of his bird friends would visit him first.

She rephrased her question. "Is the echo box working properly?"

He shook his head. "No."

She pretended to be confused. "But you just said neither device was damaged."

"That is correct. Neither device was damaged."

"Then why aren't they working properly?"

Eddie looked down at the floor as if he had done something wrong. "Because I made them not work properly."

She had already come to this conclusion on her own, but was still amazed to hear him confirm it. "Is that what you were doing on the train to Philadelphia?"

He nodded.

"Why did you do that?"

"I did not want anyone taking the echo box away from me."

"But what about hearing your mother's voice? What if we had gotten to your old address and your house was still there?"

"The echo box is in here." He pointed to his own forehead. "If my old house was still there, and the people who lived there had let us inside, I would have made the echo box work again."

"Just like that?"

Eddie nodded. "Just like what?"

"How long would it have taken you to make the echo box work again?"

"Approximately as long as it took me on the train to Philadelphia when you fell asleep. Seventy-three minutes." He looked at her briefly before turning back toward the windows, hoping to hear a chickadee or a bluebird or a grebe or even a starling. He was desperate to sing with the birds. And rate his next meal. And fill another notebook with questions and observations. "If I cannot hear my mother's voice, I have no reason to make the echo box work again."

She inched closer to him because she wanted to whisper what she had to say next. It was a secret. A great big secret. And she wanted it to have all the impact this secret deserved. "There is still a way you can hear your mother's voice."

Eddie perked up immediately. All of his sadness and melancholy suddenly seemed to disappear. He could barely contain himself. "How?" Skylar smiled in a very particular way. By now, he knew exactly what this expression meant. It was an easy one to memorize. "You're going to ask me to trust you on this one, aren't you?"

$$((\cdot))$$

Eddie sat in the wheelchair with utterly no expression on his face, just as Skylar had instructed, while she wheeled him briskly toward the Harmony House main entrance. The echo box and laptop supercomputer were both in his lap. They were ten feet from the door when a uniformed man in his late forties intercepted them. He spoke with a slow Tennessee drawl. "Excuse me, Dr. Drummond, may I be of some assistance?"

"It would be great if you could hold the door open for us, thanks."

The guard did so, asking ever so politely, "May I ask where you're going?"

"I'm taking the patient off campus for some location therapy."

He stepped in front of Eddie's wheelchair. "Not without being escorted by my men, you're not."

Skylar stiffened. "Excuse me?"

"Perhaps the rules have not been explained to you."

"Who the hell are you?" She studied him angrily.

"Yancy Packard, new head of security."

"Well, Yancy, why don't you enlighten me?" She was indignant.

"Please forgive my being blunt, Dr. Drummond, but in matters pertaining to security, this facility is mine, not yours." His tone was not in the slightest bit arrogant. In fact, he continued to sound very eager to please. "My only objective is to maintain the safety and security of you and all your patients. I will be happy to arrange a car that will take you anywhere you'd like."

"I don't want a driver. I prefer to drive myself."

"I would prefer that one of my men drive you."

"Nobody rides in the car with us." She said it with finality. The young doctor was only going to be pushed so far.

"Then I will arrange for an escort vehicle to lead you on your way. Would that be acceptable?"

She paused, pretending to think it through. Of course she knew they wouldn't be allowed to leave the facility without armed guards. But her objective had been achieved. She and Eddie would be alone in her car, which had been towed back to Harmony House the day before. The drive would give him the time he needed to work his wonders on his device without prying eyes. The echo box would be fully functional by the time they reached their destination, which was just over two hours away.

CHAPTER 113

Route 323, Saylan Hills, Pennsylvania, May 29, 2:53 p.m.

Saylan Hills, Pennsylvania, was 117 miles from Woodbury, New Jersey. It took exactly two hours and nineteen minutes for Skylar and Eddie and their escort vehicle to reach the city limits. Or, more specifically, to reach the lone traffic light that marked the town's eastern border. It was a small farming community surrounded by rugged mountains full of coal and other greenhouse-gas-producing minerals.

Eddie sat in the back seat with his devices beside him as he took in the scenery outside his window. "It looks like I remember from the last time I was here. Most of the buildings are the same, except that barn. It used to be red." He pointed to a faded yellow barn in the distance. "That field wasn't planted with corn. It had rows of string beans. My grandparents said the people who owned the field wouldn't mind if I picked some to take home with me."

"Did you?"

Eddie shook his head. "My father wouldn't stop the car. He said we didn't have time."

"How old were you the last time you were here?"

"I was seven years, three months, and nineteen days old. My father had asked Nana and Papa if I could live with them, but they said no.

Their house used to be right over there." He pointed to a large field now planted with corn. There wasn't a structure anywhere near where Eddie was pointing. "It's quiet here. I think I would have liked living with my nana and papa."

"If you had lived here, you most likely would have never gone to Harmony House, and we might never have met."

"Then I am glad I never moved here." He stared at an old church in the distance ahead of them. "Is that where we are going?"

"I believe it is." She followed the Harmony House security vehicle as it turned into the church parking lot, passing a sign that read: "St. Christopher's Episcopalian Church, Founded 1907."

"Where was the church before 1907?"

Skylar smiled. "It hadn't been built yet. *Founded* is another way of saying when it was built."

"Then that's what the sign should say."

She studied the church, which was a small wooden building with a slightly sagging roof. Dilapidated, but charming. "This church is over a hundred years old. There must be a lot of echoes inside it. Will that make it more difficult for you to reconstruct the ones you want to hear?"

"As long as I know the date and time the echoes I am trying to reconstruct were first heard, it should not be more difficult than in any other building."

Skylar parked beside the security vehicle. She turned toward Eddie as the Harmony House guards approached their car. "Remember, keep acting until I tell you it's okay to stop."

Eddie nodded. "I will remember." He put on a glazed, vacant expression.

Skylar got out of the car and opened the trunk, where she had stored the wheelchair Eddie supposedly needed. The guards asked if she would like a hand, but she declined. Skylar positioned the chair outside Eddie's door and helped him into it, putting the devices on his lap. He clutched them like security blankets.

As she wheeled him toward the church, the guards remained with them. One in front, one behind. They were clearly well trained and took their jobs seriously. Which was why they reacted strongly when Skylar informed them, "You will not be coming inside the church."

"Doctor, our instructions are to remain with you wherever you and the patient go."

"The patient's name is Eddie. His grandparents are waiting for us inside this church. It's the first time he will have seen them in almost twenty years. The whole point of coming here is for Eddie to feel as comfortable and safe as possible. Your presence is working against everything I am trying to achieve."

The guards looked to each other, and then surveyed the surrounding environment. There were no trees within a hundred feet of the church. There was no way to enter or exit the building without being seen. "We'll wait for you by the exits. How long will you need?"

"As long as it takes." Skylar wheeled Eddie inside the church as the Harmony House guards took up positions at opposite corners of the building. Inside the church, an elderly couple was sitting in the first pew as Skylar and Eddie entered. The couple stood up immediately and turned to face them. The man's face was weathered from decades of farmwork, but he still looked warm and kind. So did the woman, particularly her eyes, which lit up the moment she saw Eddie.

"Is that my grandson?"

Eddie did not respond. He stared vacantly until Skylar leaned down and whispered to him that it was okay for him to stop acting. "Yes, it is. Is that my nana?"

"Your one and only." She moved to him, but her husband grabbed her arm, a reminder that their grandson was not comfortable with physical contact and that she shouldn't try to get too close.

Skylar stepped toward them.

Eddie's grandfather extended his hand. "I'm Bert, and this here is my wife, Charlene. You must be the doctor we spoke with on the phone."

Skylar shook hands with him firmly. "I am. Skylar Drummond. Thank you so much for seeing us."

Charlene replied, "No, thank you. It's been so long since we've been able to see our grandson. We've honestly had no idea how to get in touch with him, or even how to find him."

"His father never told you where he's been living?"

Bert answered, "We haven't spoken with Victor since the last time he was here with Eddie, when he was just a boy. That visit didn't go so well."

Eddie chimed in. "That was the time when he asked if I could live with you, and you said no. He also told me I couldn't pick any string beans because we didn't have time."

Regret was evident in Charlene's face. "At the time, I just didn't think we could have handled the extra responsibility. You understand . . ."

Skylar sympathized. "I do. I honestly think you made the right decision. He's been living in a facility that is uniquely suited for his needs."

Eddie added, "Harmony House is a special place for special people."

His grandfather didn't like the way that sounded. "Is it some kind of, you know, one of them institutions?"

Skylar nodded. "It is. But Eddie's right. It really is a special place."

His grandparents clearly weren't buying it. "Why is he in a wheelchair?"

Skylar answered, "It's merely a precaution."

Eddie stood up, clutching the laptop and the echo box. "I'm acting."

His grandparents looked both relieved and confused. Skylar interjected quickly. "So, you said this was the last place you remember Eddie's mother singing?"

Bert nodded. "Michelle sang here with the choir most every Sunday from the time she was twelve."

Eddie looked around the church's interior walls, imagining the many, many ECHOES bouncing around the building's surfaces. He placed the devices on the floor and turned on the laptop. "She sounded like an angel, didn't she?"

His grandmother smiled. "A lot of people thought she did."

Bert looked suspiciously at Eddie and his devices. "What's he doing?"

"It's a little hard to explain. But like I said on the phone, it would be really helpful if you could recall a specific date and time when she sang here."

Charlene handed a weathered photo album to Skylar. "It might seem a little silly to you, but I was so proud of my daughter that I kept every program that included Michelle's name."

"That doesn't seem silly at all." Skylar flipped through the pages of paper programs. Most were from the church, but others were from high-school performances and community functions.

Bert turned to watch the echo box as the device sprang open and the eight satellite microphones started their synchronized dance. "What's that thing?"

"It's an echo box." Eddie kept his eyes on the progress bar on his screen as the device acoustically mapped the room. *Seventeen percent . . . twenty-two percent . . . twenty-nine percent . . .*

"It's a what?"

Skylar jumped in. "It will be much easier if he shows you. Eddie, is it working?"

He nodded, still watching the screen. "Forty-three percent. Forty-nine percent."

Skylar turned toward Bert and Charlene. "Did Michelle have an unusually strong sense of hearing?"

Charlene answered, "You mean like Eddie's? No, not that we were ever aware of."

"She did have perfect pitch, though," added Bert. "For as long as she lived in Saylan Hills, nobody's piano was ever out of tune."

Skylar flipped to the last church program, which was in the middle of the photo album. The pages of the last half of the book were all empty—a reminder of the young life that was cut short.

Eddie looked up from the laptop. "I'm ready for a date and time."

Skylar studied him. "Are you sure you're ready?" He nodded slowly. She read the date of the last program. "July 26, 1987. It was a Sunday. The concert started at two p.m."

Eddie entered the date and time, looking to study the particular waves. The only problem was there weren't any. The three-dimensional representation of the room on-screen was empty. He immediately panicked. "There aren't any waves!"

She moved toward him, preparing to hold him if necessary, when she noticed something on the screen. She pointed to it. "That's because you put in the wrong year, Eddie." He had accidentally typed *1897*.

He quickly typed in the correct year. On the computer screen, the three-dimensional representation of the room immediately filled with all varieties of sound waves. Eddie hit "Play."

The congregation was heard murmuring as they settled into their seats. Then a pastor welcomed friends and family members to their annual summer concert. His voice had very little distortion, thanks to the acoustic nature of the room.

Charlene was taken aback. "That's Pastor Maxwell's voice. But he died several years ago."

Bert asked, "So how can we be hearing him like he's standing right here in front of us?"

Eddie began his lecture. "The science of acoustic archeology has been around for quite a while."

Skylar cut him off. "Think of the echo box like a special kind of tape recorder. Instead of being able to play back sounds that were recorded, the echo box can re-create sounds from the original sound waves still bouncing around, even though they never were recorded."

Bert listened to the pastor addressing the congregation. "This is for real?"

Skylar nodded. "Eddie has spent his life developing the echo box so he could hear his mother's voice."

Charlene turned toward Eddie. "Well, for goodness' sake, fast-forward the thing about thirty minutes ahead, then. Our pastor had a tendency to ramble on a bit."

Eddie did so until a single sound wave appeared on the three-dimensional rendering. He took a deep breath and hit "Play."

The next sound he heard was the single most beautiful thing he would ever hear. It was the voice he'd been waiting to hear his entire life, and it came through loud and clear:

> *Amazing Grace, how sweet the sound,*
> *That saved a wretch like me.*
> *I once was lost, but now am found,*
> *Was blind, but now I see.*

Bert and Charlene both had to sit down immediately. Their legs practically buckled. Bert searched his pockets for a handkerchief as tears rolled down his face and clearly weren't going to stop anytime soon.

Skylar's chin trembled as she watched and continued to listen. Eddie's mother did indeed sound like an angel. It was no exaggeration. She had never heard a voice like it. Those who had heard her in person had not lied.

Eddie stared at the pulpit from which his mother had sung. It was as if he could see her there now, standing before him. Singing with all her heart. As if she had never left. As if she was singing to her one and only child. Her beautiful and unique baby boy.

It was clear that Eddie wasn't only *hearing* her voice. He was feeling it. As he turned to Skylar, a single tear rolled down his cheek. And then another. And then the floodgates opened. He touched his wet cheek with his finger and examined his fingertip. With great pride, he said, "Happy tears."

Skylar nodded, also crying tears of joy as they listened to the angel's voice. Eddie's angel. Whatever was to come, whatever would happen, Skylar had done something good. She had not failed him. She had not broken him. She had helped Eddie achieve his lifelong dream. He had heard his mother's voice like she'd promised he would. His joy was her joy, and it was pure. The hole in Skylar's heart, the one that she had carried around since the death of her little brother, now seemed just a little bit smaller. And it felt absolutely wonderful.

Through many dangers, toils, and snares
I have already come;
'Tis Grace that brought me safe thus far
And Grace will lead me home.

CHAPTER 114

Harmony House, Woodbury, New Jersey, June 1, 10:12 a.m.

Several days later, the last of the morning dew had evaporated from the rolling lawns surrounding Harmony House as Eddie and Skylar took their morning walk to nowhere. It was already part of their daily routine. They moved slowly, enjoying the crisp morning air. At least, Skylar was. Eddie was busy rotating his head from side to side. "The birds are happy this morning."

"How can you tell?"

"They're singing."

She closed her eyes, listening intently. "I wish I could hear them, too."

He continued listening to the birds. "Why do you think I can hear so much more than everyone else, Skylar?"

"That's a good question."

"Why is it a good question?"

"Because it's something I want to know the answer to as well."

"Well, you know what they say, 'Great minds think alike.'"

Skylar paused, dumbfounded. "Eddie, you do realize that's an expression."

"Yes, I know." A devilish look came over his face.

"I thought you didn't like expressions."

"I don't." He paused, waiting to see if she would understand his intent. "It was a joke, Skylar."

She shook her head, marveling. "Will wonders never cease."

"I hope not." They kept walking.

(((•)))

Later that morning, Eddie waited in the cafeteria lunch line with the rest of the Harmony House patients, along with the nurse's aides who selected the food for those not capable of choosing for themselves. Binder #138 was tucked under his arm, and there was tissue paper sticking out of his ears, just like there always was. It was Thursday, and that meant lunch consisted of chicken tenders, french fries, canned corn, and several different Jell-O options for dessert. Today's choices included yellow, green, and red. Eddie was thankful that the Kraft food company did not make purple Jell-O, or if they did, that Harmony House never served it.

Jerome smiled at Eddie from behind the counter. "What's up, Eddie?"

"Fluorescent lighting." He looked up to the ceiling. "It makes an annoying buzzing sound, which is why I always have tissue paper in my ears during mealtime." He pointed to the tissue, which was not difficult to spot. Eddie made no effort to conceal it.

"I was getting worried about you, man. Didn't see you around here for a couple days. You doing okay?"

"I'm doing much better than okay, Jerome. I am doing great. Can you guess why?"

"Because we're serving your favorite dessert, yellow Jell-O?"

"I got to hear my mother sing. She really did have the voice of an angel, just like people said." He was beaming.

Jerome glanced over to his boss, Ida, who did not seem pleased to see him chatting up this particular patient. Jerome backed away, clearly moving on to other business. "I'm happy for you, man. Let me know what you think of the Jell-O."

"It will be my pleasure," Eddie replied, and then carried his tray to a table. He placed the binder next to his tray and methodically moved the food items onto the table. He spaced each plate evenly distant from the others, then sampled the food items, recording the score of each in his binder. The chicken tenders got a four; the french fries a three; the canned corn a two, which was why he spit it back out onto the plate; and the Jell-O a five. He savored every last bite of the dessert, and looked back to the counter to see if there was any more. Had there been, Eddie would have certainly gone back for seconds.

He carried his tray to the "Dirty Dishes Here" sign, then counted the 113 steps back to his room. He was surprised to find the door slightly ajar. Eddie was sure that he had closed it when he had left. It was not unusual for nurses or other Harmony House personnel to enter his room when he was not present, but they had never left his door open before.

Eddie knocked on the door. "Hello, is anybody in there?" There was no answer. He pushed the door open carefully, only to find the room was vacant. He entered, surveying his various possessions. Everything was in its proper place: the echo box, his special laptop, his binders, his pencils, the sharpener, even his Batman pillowcase was just as he'd left it. But then he saw it. He raced out of his room, running right into Nurse Gloria.

"Eddie, what's wrong? I was just coming to see you."

"Nurse Gloria, somebody put something in my room!"

She responded calmly, just like she always did. "What? Who did? What is it?"

"It shouldn't be there! It doesn't belong in my room! Don't you see it?" He pointed inside his room.

"See what?" She had no idea what he was talking about.

Eddie continued past her, racing down the hallway to Skylar's new office, which until recently had been Dr. Fenton's. She hadn't yet had time to hire her own assistant, which explained why Stephen Millard still had his job. He looked up as Eddie rushed in. "Dr. Drummond isn't in. Is there something I can help you with?"

Eddie didn't respond as he continued directly into Skylar's office. All signs of Fenton had been removed, but there was still little that identified the space as Skylar's. Stephen poked his head in the door. "I told you, Eddie, the doctor isn't here."

"Where is she?" His panic was growing.

"All I know is she had an outside appointment."

"I don't know what an outside appointment is. Outside what?"

"Outside Harmony House."

"Well, this is an emergency. She needs to come back."

Nurse Gloria entered, having heard the last bit of conversation. "Eddie, until Dr. Drummond gets back, can you tell me what the emergency is?"

"I want it out of my room!"

"I will be more than happy to help you. But, first, I need you to calm down. Can you do that for me?" Her voice was soothing as ever.

Eddie took a deep breath and nodded.

"Will you show me what we're talking about?"

He nodded again and led Nurse Gloria out of the office.

((•))

After they departed, Stephen waited a moment before removing a phone from his pocket. It was the same model Senator Davis now carried with him. Stephen pressed the speed-dial button for the only number he was ever to contact with it. "You said I should call if anything unusual happened."

ACKNOWLEDGMENTS

This novel exists because I was fortunate enough to receive the help, support, and expertise of a great many people. I would like to mention a few: Jessica Tribble and the entire team at Thomas & Mercer and Amazon Publishing and Kevin Smith, for their incredible collaboration; Paul Lucas and everyone at Janklow & Nesbit, for taking a chance; Adam Levine, Karl Austen, and Tom Strickler, for never wavering; Steve Silberman, for his exhaustive research on the history of autism; Elizabeth Bingham, Steve Bernt, Susanne Bernt, Karin Colquitt, Josh Goldstein, Patti Goldstein, Sister Judith Costello, and my other early readers for their invaluable critical feedback; David Moore, for his continuing guidance; and, last but not least, the two teachers who convinced me I could write: Mark Parish at James Madison Memorial High School and Reginald Gibbons at Northwestern University. You two changed my life.

ABOUT THE AUTHOR

Photo © 2017 Conner Martin

Eric Bernt was born in Marion, Ohio, and raised in Gladwyne, Pennsylvania, and Madison, Wisconsin. He attended Northwestern University, where he learned that journalism was not for him—but storytelling was. Upon graduation, he moved to Hollywood, where he wrote seven feature films including *Virtuosity* (starring Denzel Washington and Russell Crowe) and *Surviving the Game* (starring Rutger Hauer, Gary Busey, and F. Murray Abraham). He has also written for television (*Z Nation*). Eric lives in Agoura Hills, California, with his wife and three children.